The Scales of Justice

D1528651

The Scales of Justice

by JB Heart

Library of Congress Control Number: 2012903548
ISBN: Hardcover   978-1-4691-7297-2
                   Softcover   978-1-4691-7296-5
                   Ebook   978-1-4691-7298-9

To order additional copies of this book, contact:
Xlibris Corporation
1-888-795-4274
www.Xlibris.com
Orders@Xlibris.com
84672

Contents

Dedication

Once again, I dedicate this book to Bruce Riddle. His love and compassion for his nephew Sammy inspired me first to write *Silent Fear* and, now from the heavens, *The Scales of Justice*.

The love and compassion Bruce portrayed still flow through my pages. Bruce passed October 2, 2009, two days after reading my first manuscript. It took me exactly one year to the day to finish the second of my trilogy.

I especially dedicate this book to Bruce's sister, Lori Fain, without her love and support, *The Scales of Justice* would never have come to fruition. I thank my Texas family for their contributions to my novel. My heart, love, and immense gratitude go out to them for allowing me to still be a part of their beautiful family.

Although I use an adaptive speech program called Jaws, which is a screen reader to write my novels as I am blind, I truly thank my son Ricky, Ma Marble, Mason Parker, Rick Parker, and especially Kimberly Finnegan, for spending countless hours editing *The Scales of Justice*. Special thanks go to my friends on Out-Of-Site.net for being my beta listeners and believing in me.

My dedication would not be complete without thanking my gracious friends, Joe and Robin Marble, who not only helped me behind the scenes but became wonderful characters to write about.

Acknowledgement

The characters depicted in this book are fictional and in no way represent Florida, Orlando, or any of its officials.

Chapter One

Harris

There Is a New Florida Hurricane, and We Are Not Talking About the Weather

ORLANDO, Fl.—Harris Robertson, son of Mark Robertson, the former Orange County prosecutor originally nicknamed the "Florida Hurricane," is following in his father's footsteps. The article went on to reveal, Robertson won his first major trial today, suave and debonair like his father, he paraded in front of the jurors taking them by storm and obtaining a conviction. At just 28, he is the youngest person to become an assistant district attorney in the state of Florida. Justice runs in his family; his grandfather, Judge Ronald Harris, now sits on Florida's Supreme Court. Let's hope this new Florida Hurricane doesn't burn out like his father did.

The article referred to his father, Mark Robertson, who burned to death in a cabin on the outskirts of town twenty years before. The irony surrounding the fire was a hurricane lamp. Orange County Sheriff's Department determined it was the sole cause of the fire—a hurricane destroying a hurricane. There were many speculations concerning the suspicious and untimely death of Robertson—he was in the middle of a questionable trial.

Harris left the courtroom followed by a slew of reporters asking questions about his past, but he limited his comments to the trial he had just won. He had befriended the DA's lead investigator Joe Marble, and together they had uncovered a major marijuana ring with the police, making over forty arrests. Along with the arrests, the authorities retrieved a large amount of guns along with $250,000 in cash.

He was surprised that Hugh Gallagher, the longtime district attorney in Orlando, entrusted him with a case of this magnitude since his promotion to assistant DA took place six months ago. Gallagher was a large man, standing six foot three with salt-and-pepper hair that gave him a distinguished look. His broad shoulders and patronizing manner made him an imposing public figure. That same imposing figure was now pushing through the throng of reporters, heading straight toward Harris.

"You are just like your father," boomed Gallagher as he clapped Harris on the back. "The law comes natural to you, I knew you could get an easy conviction on this one."

Harris had wanted to prove to Gallagher he was worthy of his confidence and could win cases just as fast as a hurricane could blow through the state. He was amazed at how easy it was for Joe and his team to obtain the necessary evidence and how quickly he, Harris, had been able to convince the ringleader to squeal on the witness stand. He knew the press called him the New Hurricane, but to him, the win felt more like a soft breeze than the eye of a storm! Harris had inherited the same drive and confidence his father possessed in the courtroom; however, he was still young and often oblivious to the possibility of someone higher in the ranks of the judicial system manipulating him. As Hugh Gallagher continued to steer his new assistant DA away from the reporters, Harris's phone rang.

"Excuse me, Hugh," Harris said as he reached in his pocket for his phone, pausing at the bottom of the courthouse steps. A familiar voice spoke on the line.

"Nice win, son, it is on the news even here in Tallahassee!" The voice rushed on without giving Harris a moment to respond. "You're making headlines everywhere! I always believed you would become a better attorney than your father."

"Grandfather, how are you?" Harris finally managed to say.

"I'm fine, son, but enough about me. How do you feel after your first major win?"

"I feel exhilarated, sir," Harris replied. "Thank you for your support, it means a lot to me."

"Harris, my boy, you don't need my support, you're a natural."

"Thank you again, Grandfather. How is Grandmother?" Harris quickly changed the subject.

"Good, son, good. She is recovering from some minor surgery on her face, but other than that, she's fine. She's right here with me and sends you her best."

"Are you sure she is OK? What happened?" Harris asked, a look of concern crossing his face. "Yes, Harris, I am quite sure," his grandfather replied dismissively. "How are your mother and Joshua? It's been a while since I've spoken to them. Work is quite consuming, as you well know."

"They're fine, thank you, Grandfather. I'm going over to their place for dinner on Sunday."

"Good lad, I'm proud of you. Please give them my best and tell your mother I will call her soon."

"Yes, sir, will do."

"Take care, son, we love you."

"I love you too, bye." Harris shared a great respect for his grandfather, although he spoke few words, he always made his point. Harris expressed to his grandparents how much he loved them whenever possible because his own father could never say those three words to his son. Harris reflected on his famous father's inability to share any emotion. Although his mother told him the reason behind not saying those three words was because of an abusive childhood, Harris never accepted her excuses. He'd heard stories of the beatings throughout his father's upbringing, but it was his uncle Joshua who endured the countless blows. His father never suffered the physical abuse; he just watched it and was thankful to God it wasn't him. Still, his uncle made sure to say those three words to him every chance he could. Joshua Robertson was the best uncle a boy could ever have had. Harris loved him far more than he did his own father. After Mark Robertson's death, Uncle Joshua helped Harris's mother, Mary Ellen, pick up the pieces of her life, and a few years later, they married.

Growing up, Joshua always spoke with fondness of his brother, trying to make sure Harris's memories of Mark were good ones. Harris listened to his uncle, not wanting to hurt his feelings, but he resented his father for the loss of his hearing and the silent fear he lived in. He never shared with his uncle the nightmares he woke up from, nightmares caused by the arguments and all-out fights he heard between his parents, which they had whenever his father got drunk.

Harris remembered countless hours working with his mother to learn sign language. His father hated the time it took away from him and Mary Ellen; he said she was wasting her time. Once his cochlear implants were in place, his uncle Joshua took years teaching him to speak with eloquence. He still spoke with a slight speech impediment, he has a slight slur in his voice, but his uncle had spent every waking moment throughout his childhood helping Harris to pronounce each word with perfection.

There were times when the boy would get so frustrated and tired, but he was determined. He shared his father's trait in respect to not quitting; they both fought with grace and determination like white Bengal tigers. Different from his father though, Harris exuded both charm and an innocent sweetness about him. It made him hard to resist. Harris was afraid the courtroom pressure would lead to alcohol abuse and would bring out the dark side in him like it did his father. When Mark's alcoholism grew worse, it turned him into an abusive father and husband. Harris never touched a drink and swore he never would.

Wit came easy to Harris; it was something else he learned from his uncle J. The two of them were insufferable at times, but their laughter was infectious to everyone around them, something his father never indulged in. Joshua told some of the oldest and worst jokes, more often than people wanted to hear, still laughing every time he told them. His favorite one was about a duck.

The fondest memories Harris recalled were of his uncle, including fishing trips, his first basketball game, and his favorite memory of his high school graduation. Harris had received his diploma, torn off his tassel from his cap, walked over to his uncle J, and handed it to him with tears in his eyes. His uncle was so proud of him; there was not a dry eye between them.

Every Sunday until he left to pursue his jurist doctor degree, the two of them went to lunch. It was their special time together to talk over any issues he may have encountered or to see if any of his courses needed changing. Although Mark left behind a rather large insurance policy, Joshua paid for all his schooling and put Mark's money aside. Harris never understood why his uncle micromanaged his finances and career, until later in life when he purchased his first condominium with cash. It was then he realized his uncle's disdain for his grandfather when he would not allow him to contribute toward Harris's education or any other expenses.

Thinking about his grandfather led Harris to think about his plans for the future. His goal was always to become a judge, like his grandfather. Uncle Joshua supported, guided, and helped him whenever he could, even though he was not pleased that a judgeship was the path Harris chose to follow. There were still secrets about Mark, which Joshua had not divulged, and he hoped and prayed he would never have to.

As Harris pulled into his parking space, the phone rang again.

"Howdy," said the voice on the line.

"Uncle J!" Harris said, a grin spreading across his face. "Grandfather called to inform me my conviction was on the news in Tallahassee, can you believe it?" Harris talked fast due to his excitement.

Joshua was proud to hear about his nephew's win, but not so excited about the call from his grandfather. He had been relieved when the judge moved to Tallahassee; he hoped he would leave the boy alone and never have the chance to suck him into his corrupt world.

"What did your grandfather have to say?" Joshua asked inquisitively.

"Oh nothing much, except to tell me I made the news in Tallahassee. He was proud I won my first major trial. It should score me some big points in the

DA's office too, don't you think, Uncle J?" Flashing his innocent smile at no one in particular, Harris was always looking for his uncle's approval.

"He said Grandmother was well," Harris continued. "And he told me to tell Mom he would call her soon."

"OK, son, well, I guess you can tell her when you come to supper on Sunday, right?" Joshua was fishing, making sure he was still coming; he loved his nephew's visits and made it a point to confirm with him each week.

"Of course, I'll be there, Uncle J! You know I love my Sundays with you and Mom. It's the one day a week I get a home-cooked meal," Harris laughed.

"Make sure you bring a dessert and none of the healthy stuff, son. Good old rocky road ice cream sounds brilliant."

"I know it's your favorite. You ask for the same kind every week," Harris chuckled. It always made Joshua shake his head because his nephew's laugh was so contagious.

"Make sure you don't forget the rocky road," Joshua reminded him again, still smiling. "Speaking of rocky roads, do I need to draw you a map, or do you have one of those newfangled GPS systems in your new fancy car?"

"You're hilarious. Tell Mom I love her, and I'll see her Sunday. Love you too, Uncle J."

"Love you too, Harris." Hanging up the phone, Joshua sat back in the Queen Anne leather chair that had once belonged to his brother, placed close to the fireplace in the study. *The first deaf person to become an assistant district attorney in the state of Florida*, he reflected back on Harris's cochlear implant surgery and how Judge Harris managed to make all the arrangements secret and then provided him with the necessary fake documents he would need. He remembered when the doctor first turned on the implants.

There had been so much anticipation in the room. The doctor instructed Joshua to turn his back toward Harris and say something to him in a normal voice. Joshua told Harris he loved him, and silence filled the room. He felt his heart stop beating, his hands started to tremble, and his knees weakened. When he turned around and looked at Harris, waiting for what seemed a lifetime to hear his response, there was none. Joshua remembered falling to his knees, tears streaming, his thoughts racing wildly as he prayed to God begging him to let Harris hear. His efforts seemed pointless. He knew he needed to face reality; the surgery hadn't worked.

Just as he was about to give up hope, Harris stuttered what sounded like, "I love you too."

Joshua's stomach felt a sickness, and his throat was so dry it was hard for him to breathe. The smile which came to Harris's face was the most priceless and precious moment of his life since the day his nephew was born and placed into his arms for the first time. A tear trickled, dropping onto his cheek.

"Joshua, what is that tear about?" Mary Ellen asked as she entered the study.

"I am sorry, darling," Joshua replied, shaking his head as he came back to the present. "I was reminiscing about the past."

"Oh, yes, what about it?"

"Nothing of any relevance." He quickly changed the subject. "I called Harris today to make sure he was coming on Sunday, it was good hearing his voice."

"It's always a blessing hearing him speak, isn't it?" Mary Ellen responded, reaching out to take her husband's hand.

"Yes, darling, it is truly a gift from God." Joshua smiled, giving his wife's hand a squeeze.

"Was he excited about his first major conviction?" she asked.

"He was tickled pink. I'm sure he will no doubt tell you all about it on Sunday. By the way, Ronald called to congratulate him." Mary Ellen always heard a change in his voice when he spoke about her father, but he would never tell her why.

"Did Harris say how Mommy and Daddy were?"

"I guess they are fine. Your father will call you soon. I'm sure Harris will tell you the whole conversation when he's here." Joshua stood up, pulled Mary Ellen into his arms, and held her tight. Her head fit perfect on his shoulder, and he held it there lovingly with one hand.

Joshua had never thought he would find true love. After all, who could love him with the years of emotional issues he had endured? He was a plain man with next to nothing to offer anyone, but he possessed the greatest gift of all: love.

"I do love you, my darling," he said tenderly.

"I know you do, Josh, and I love you too with all my heart," Mary Ellen murmured against his shoulder. She was concerned about his mood; he was never quite the same since his brother died. Joshua became more introverted the closer Harris progressed toward his judgeship; it seemed as if he were afraid Harris would die the same way his brother did once he reached his goal. Mary Ellen understood his loss since she experienced it; in addition, a death so sudden and unexpected can rip out a person's heart and mangle it until it is unrecognizable.

Thank goodness, it's Friday, thought Harris the next morning as he walked into the courthouse. He placed his briefcase on the conveyor belt, took out his cell phone and keys, and walked through the metal detector.

"Good morning Mr. Robertson, nice conviction yesterday," John, the morning security guard, greeted him. "You're going to be just like your father. I noticed the newspaper headlines called you the new Florida Hurricane. Judge Robertson would have been proud."

"Thank you, John, it felt good," Harris replied. It sounded strange hearing the security guard refer to his father as Judge Robertson, given the fact that his father died the day he received his judgeship. He shook his head as he picked up his things and walked toward his office, thinking how unimaginable it would be to reach his goal just to die.

Opening the heavy oak door to his office, the first thing he noticed were the congratulation signs. His associates all shook his hand while he strode back toward his own office. As he reached his door, Harris stopped . . . looked over to his right . . . and there sat the most beautiful girl he had ever seen in his life.

Taken aback by her presence, he found it difficult to breathe. He tried desperately to say hello, but the words would not form on his tongue. She looked straight at him, and his legs weakened as he nearly passed out. Her radiant, dancing dark brown eyes looked right back at him. Her long brown wavy hair lay on her shoulders and glistened with cinnamon-red highlights. His first semicoherent thought was that she bore a striking resemblance to his mother. Her high cheekbones blushed with shyness, and hers were the most kissable lips he had ever set eyes on. Blushing himself now, he tried to regain his composure.

"Hello, Mr. Robertson, and congratulations," the vision greeted him. Harris's first reaction was, *She actually spoke to me.* Her voice was even sexier and more angelic than her looks.

"Is everything OK, sir?" She looked at him, puzzled, probably wondering why he was staring at her so strangely. All he managed to do was nod his head.

Rushing into his office, he focused on his chair and lunged into it before his jellied legs gave way. He inhaled deeply, her stunning beauty leaving him in a daze.

"Wow" was all he could muster. Paging through to his secretary, he asked, "Tara, who is the new girl sitting outside my office?" He tried to sound nonchalant.

"Oh, you mean Markita," Tara replied. "She is our intern for the next six months."

"Is she mine?" his mouth said while his brain was thinking something else.

"What on earth do you mean, sir?" giggled Tara.

"I meant, is she *our* intern?" This time he tried to sound more authoritative.

"Yes, sir. I did say for the next six months," replied Tara, surprised, yet amused at his reaction. Harris hung up the phone and sat back in his chair, almost drooling, holding his hand over his rapidly beating heart and thinking about calling a bug exterminator to extinguish the butterflies occupying his stomach. He wondered, *Is this what love at first sight feels like?*

"Markita," he spoke her name out loud. "What a perfect name for the sexiest woman in America." His body felt quite warm inside his business suit, and his head was giddy with thoughts of her. Although he had acted rather foolish in front of her, one thing was for sure: he was definitely going to get to know her better.

Sunday morning came around, and Harris awoke feeling lazy. His alarm tried multiple times to wake him, but the snooze button thwarted its attempts. His dreams were about him with the new intern; he could not shake his feelings for her.

It was not too long, however, before he crawled out of bed and took a shower. He threw on a maroon polo shirt, his favorite Lee jeans, and sneakers. Weekends allowed him to dress casually; it was a nice relief from the stuffy suits he wore to work all week. Harris looked at himself in the mirror, combed his brown hair to the side, and made sure his light mustache was perfect.

Harris had grown to only to five foot seven and a half, but the half was important to him. He had round baby face and pinchable cheeks, which some would call "cute"; along with his mischievous smile, it was what charmed everyone who met him. His nose was small and eyelashes so long, he made many women jealous. His earlobes were larger than most, and he wore his hair a little long to cover the cochlear implants. Two things bothered him about himself: one was his two left feet, which could not dance a lick. The other was the fact he had no butt. However, he was a handsome-looking young man, favoring his uncle Joshua's features more so than his father's which pleased him.

Harris lived in a modest condo in downtown Orlando, but it was large enough to suit his needs. He had paid for it out of the money Joshua saved from his father's life insurance policy. He did not want for anything as he was a plain person with simple ideals. Apart from the condo, he owned only two other expensive items: one was his car, and the other his elaborate sound system, due to his love for music. The ceilings in the condo were high, which made the music echo and sound great upstairs. His kitchen was plain but tastefully decorated by his mother, even though he hardly ever cooked there. Usually he either he grabbed fast food or went to Uncle J's and his mother's to eat.

Harris named his new gold Jaguar Purdy. It was his pride and joy. The license plate number read *PURR-D-2*; his father's plates had read *PURR-D-1*. He remembered as a small child when his father bought him a little red pedal car. Mark put Harris's photo on the back of it with the license plate number, making it look like a real car. It seemed as if it were the only good memory of his father that he had.

Pushing aside these memories, Harris ran downstairs and grabbed his keys, heading for his Jag. Inserting his favorite CD, he drove to his mother's house.

Upon arrival, he got out, pointed the remote to lock his car, opened the front door, and walked inside.

"Harris, my boy," said Joshua from the kitchen, beaming with pride.

"Harris, my darling, how are you?" gushed Mary Ellen as she swooped in to give him a kiss.

"I'm fine, guys," Harris laughed. "Here is dessert, Mom," he said, lifting up a bag containing rocky road ice cream. "Shall I put it in the freezer for you?"

"Oh no, baby. Give it to me, and I will take care of it. Our steaks are marinating in the refrigerator. Your uncle J will grill them for us later."

Harris walked over and kissed his mother on the cheek. She put her arms around her son, holding him tight. After letting him go, she took the ice cream into the kitchen.

His uncle J walked over to him, and the two of them high-fived, then low fived, and hugged while slapping each other's backs. Once the formalities were over, they began with their usual playful banter.

"So, Uncle J, no psycho movies to write about yet?"

"No, not yet, at least my students don't squeal like your psycho witness did, little one," retaliated Joshua. They continued ribbing each other until Joshua motioned to the kitchen; it was time to grill the steaks.

"Let me help you, Uncle J," Harris offered, reaching for the steaks.

"Right, last time I let you help me grill, we ate burned offerings for supper," Joshua muttered.

"You are so not cool, Uncle J," Harris said with a playful pout.

"When we have Thanksgiving dinner, and I burn it, you can comment, but until then, you be quiet, you young whimppersnapper." Joshua snatched the steaks from his nephew.

"Uncle J, I keep telling you it's 'whippersnapper,' and that saying is older than you are. Can you not come up with some new material?"

"What do you need new material for? Are you planning on making the duck a jacket?" Uncle J grinned.

"Please, Uncle J, not the duck joke, I beg you, please!"

"OK, I agree, no duck joke," interjected Mary Ellen. "Let's get supper cooking. You two could go on forever, and we will never eat."

"Not us, Mother, we're just joshing." Harris goofed on his uncle again.

"Oh! I know, let me tell you a joke about a duck who was looking for lip balm, young man." Joshua could not resist telling the joke anyway.

"Yes, please do, old man," Harris said with a heavy sigh. He thought by agreeing to the joke, his uncle would not tell it. No such luck.

"The duck went into the pharmacy and could not find cherry lip balm, and so he asked the clerk to help him find it. 'It is here,' said the clerk, pointing it out. 'Thank you,' said the duck. 'How would you like to pay for this, cash or charge?' 'Just put it on my bill!'" Joshua had laughed a thousand times at this joke and now laughed once more. He laughed until his stomach cramped and tears formed in his eyes. He may have told the joke numerous times, but it was still the funniest one he ever heard. Joshua went outside and fired up the grill, still chuckling to himself, Harris following behind him.

"How does it feel sitting behind your father's desk?" asked Josh, his tone turning serious.

"It feels a little strange sometimes," Harris admitted. "I didn't like or respect him, but he was a good DA."

"Yes, he was, son. He could smell a rat bastard from a mile away."

"Hmm, then why did he not smell Bellamy?" Harris sounded a little sullen now, knowing his father's instincts should have screamed out at him when it came to this man.

"We have discussed this situation before, son. Bellamy was a pro when it came to deception."

"Dad should have realized he was a child molester, don't you think?"

"At the time, there was a lot going on in your father's life, and like I said, Bellamy was a pro," Josh patiently explained, trying to dispel the anger and frustration his nephew felt for his father. He could not help himself from defending Mark. After all, he was his brother, no matter what else he had done.

"I have often wondered what my grandfather's involvement was with the Bellamy case," Harris mused, watching Joshua adjust the flames.

"Why do you ask about your grandfather's involvement now?" Joshua was a little unsettled at the question.

"I remember as a child staying in the cabin with you and Charlie, the day after my hearing was restored, and my grandfather was the first person you wanted me to call. Once Dad died, you wouldn't talk about him anymore, and I have always wondered . . . why?"

"Your grandfather is a very powerful person. For your safety, I felt it necessary to keep him at a distance."

"What do you mean, Uncle J? You are always so vague when it comes to him."

"I don't mean to be vague, son. I would prefer you advance in this world by your own merit and not by using your grandfather's resources. Sometimes they come with a hefty price." Joshua continued to mess with the dials on the grill, not looking at Harris.

"There you go again. Uncle J, being vague." This was the longest discussion between the two of them concerning his father's death; Mary Ellen interrupted the conversation when she opened the sliding glass doors with one hand and carrying the steaks in the other.

"Hey, guys, it's time to put the meat on. I have prepared the salad, and everything is ready except the steaks."

"As usual, Mom, we are waiting for Uncle J to get his game on."

"Let's see you cook the steaks, takeout king," said Josh, trying to lighten the mood.

"OK, OK, you have me there. I'm not a cook," Harris confessed.

The family enjoyed their steaks and the infamous rocky road ice cream. When they were done, Mary Ellen cleared the table, and Joshua and Harris shot some hoops for a while. Afterward they relaxed on the patio swing, striking up a conversation about the past, present, and future.

When it came to the future, Harris happened to mention that Hugh had hired a new intern to work with Tara. Joshua and Mary Ellen were attentive to what Harris was saying, asking all kinds of questions. Harris blushed, trying to avoid any further interrogation, but they were on him like the hurricane he was in the courtroom.

"Are you going to bring her next Sunday?" asked Josh.

"No, I am not. I saw her for the first time on Friday, and we have not even talked, except for 'Congratulations, Mr. Robertson.'"

"Congratulations could mean a lot," said Mary Ellen with a sly grin.

"No, it doesn't, Mother, it just means congratulations."

"Oh, yes, it does, son. It means 'I like you very much.'"

"You guys are nuts and making far too much of this. I think it is time I leave. I have to get up for work in the morning."

Joshua continued to tease his nephew. "What's the matter, can't take the stick, son?"

"Oh, I can take it, I'm waiting for you to give it."

"I can tell there are sparks already. Your face is a dead giveaway. This girl has gotten to you."

"You're crazy, Uncle J, I only said hello."

"Sometimes, son, 'hello' is all it takes," said Mary Ellen, thinking about her and Josh. "When you are ready, Harris, please invite her to Sunday supper."

"Mom, it's not happening. I have to concentrate on becoming a judge, and I have no room in my life for romance."

"Your thinking is wrong, son. Life will be lonely without someone special to share it with, and you would be blessed like we are if you have children like yourself."

"Uncle J, there you go again. You love kids."

"Yes, I do, and you are the reason why. Your mother and I want you to have at least five of your own for us to spoil."

Harris picked up his keys and started for the door laughing. "Mom, I will call you through the week and, Uncle J, you know I love you, even if you are crazier than a loon. If I have five kids, when would I ever have time to become a judge?"

"You'll have plenty of time to have kids and become a judge. You are handsome, intelligent, suave, and debonair, you make good money." Joshua paused, considering. "Hmm . . . sounds more like me than you," he finished with a mischievous grin.

"I hear you," Harris said. "And if you don't call me by Wednesday, I will call you."

"Love you," said his mother.

"Love you too, guys." Harris left with a big smile on his face. He loved spending time with his mother and Uncle J. Getting back into the car, he popped in his favorite Journey CD.

As he drove home, his mind started to wander back to the new intern. Her long hair was flowing in the wind as he took her into his arms. They danced together on the beach. The moon was shining, and the sand was warm beneath their feet. He held her so close, trembling with every turn, wondering how he was floating on air when there was no music and he could not dance. He realized it was his thoughts of Markita making him feel wild and free. His heart started to pound hard in his chest. In his mind's eye, her skin was soft and her smile so sweet. One day, she would share in everything with him. She was the one; she had to be.

He had progressed through high school and college not dating. Instead, he concentrated on excelling academically in order to overcome the delay his deafness, because of his father, had caused him. He was grateful to his uncle J for teaching him how to speak with elegance and for getting the surgery done. No one but Harris knew Joshua was the one who kidnapped him as a boy to get him away from his father, nor did anyone know he took care of the surgery. Harris swore to keep it a secret forever.

Markita drifted back into his thoughts, and he realized how much she was affecting him. Conscious now that he was smiling, he looked in the rearview mirror, seeing his bright red face. *This girl is one in a million*, he thought. *I have to figure out a way to get her attention and make her a part of my life.* His belly experienced the fluttering of the butterflies again. He felt the need to pinch himself; these feelings were all new to him.

Thank goodness, he was home. Opening the garage door, he drove the car inside, sitting there for a few moments looking in the mirror. He wondered if she would ever consider someone so plain being in her life. *The question is*, he thought to himself, *how am I going to find out more about her?* He wasn't sure how he would approach the situation or how he was going to overcome his insecurities. After his first encounter with her, it was obvious he needed to stay calm and collected around her. To make things even more difficult, Hugh Gallagher did not approve of office romances; in fact, Harris heard him on more than one occasion condemn them.

The CD finished playing, and Harris returned to reality. He shook his head, grinning while he walked into his condo. From inside the fridge, he grabbed a green tea and caught himself smiling and thinking about Markita again.

Harris was big on vitamins, herbal supplements, green tea, and anything else healthy. He worked out at the gym three days a week lifting 225 pounds in four rotations. His body felt exhilarated after a good workout. Recently, he reduced his visits to the gym to one day a week in order to prepare for his upcoming trial. He looked at his watch; it was about time for him to go to bed. *Of course, I could listen to some music for a while, the music sounded good,* he thought to himself. Putting the radio on, he turned to some slow, easy listening tunes and sat back relaxing in his favorite oversized plush tan swivel rocker, which he called his fat boy chair.

Markita entered his mind yet again. He tried concentrating on what drew him to her, and he concluded it was everything. The DJ announced a song, *Could I Have This Dance for the Rest of My Life.* Harris had heard this song many times; his grandmother had often played it on her harp. His mother told him she played it at his parents' wedding. It was such a pretty song, maybe he would dance to it at his own wedding with Markita.

His attention turned to his living room for a moment. First, he looked at his couch, thinking how he never had any reason to sit on it. *Couches are for couples,* he told himself. Then he looked over to where his full wall of law books inherited from his father were located. A large throw rug covered most of the tiled floor. His fat boy chair sat in front of a TV cabinet, which also housed the stereo equipment. Displayed on the fireplace mantel, located in the corner of the room, were his family photos, but none of them contained his father.

"This place needs a woman's touch." He smiled. There was no point in decorating until he laid eyes on Markita. Unhappy memories of his parents and his father's abusive treatment toward his mother left him shying away from relationships, wondering if his father's violence ran through his veins. He remembered bruises his mother tried to hide, and he would never forget the hurt, which used to fill her eyes when he looked into them.

His goal had always been to finish all schooling necessary and become a judge, then he could concentrate on meeting a special person. Markita could certainly change his planned-out life. Harris smiled while saying her name. He drifted in and out of sleep in his chair for a little while having beautiful dreams. He awoke looking over at the clock and realizing it was time to take himself upstairs to bed. It was back to work tomorrow after a long weekend. *At least I will see my pretty Markita,* he thought, smiling yet again.

Morning came before he knew it, but Harris felt well rested. He showered and shaved, making sure not to touch his mustache. Venturing into his wardrobe, he would usually pull out the next suit to wear, but today he pondered and thought about which one made him look the best. He finally chose a pale blue suit, selecting a navy blue shirt and a white silk tie to go with it.

"I look very sharp, if I may say so," he chuckled, looking at himself in the mirror. Slipping on his leather shoes, and then grabbing his briefcase, he headed downstairs. His coffee had already brewed, coffee being his one bad habit, but he limited himself to one cup a day. He loved its aroma first thing in the morning, and it always helped him to wake up and feel refreshed. Once finished, he placed his cup in the sink, turned off the coffeepot, and headed out toward the garage. He fired up the Jag, slipped in a new CD, and thought about how happy he was returning to work today.

Arriving at the courthouse less than minutes later, Harris opened the heavy oak doors and started down the hallway toward his office, his face already beaming. He looked expectantly over to Markita's desk.

She was not there.

His heart sank. Where could she be? Why was she not at her desk? He gave a quick glance around the large room, his eyes searching out every inch of the place but no Markita. It was like someone had sucker punched him and knocked the wind out of him.

Tara looked over at him with an odd look on her face. "Good morning, Mr. Robertson. Is everything OK? You look a little pale."

"I am fine, thank you, Tara," Harris snapped at her, which was out of character for him. His sharpness surprised Tara and made her feel a little hurt. He had never chirped at her before.

"Would you like your messages, sir?" she asked stiffly.

"Yes, please, Tara. I am sorry I snapped at you," Harris replied, feeling foolish and guilty at the same time.

"It's all right, Mr. Robertson," said Tara, thankful for his apology, although still a little surprised at his sharpness.

On the way to his door, Harris asked, "Tara, by any chance, is Hugh in yet?"

"No, sir, I have not seen him this morning."

"When you do, would you please let me know? I would appreciate it." He tried to recover from his rudeness.

"Of course, Mr. Robertson."

"Thank you, Tara." He opened up his door, walked in, and slumped down in his large leather chair. He was so disappointed Markita was not at her desk, but he did not want to bring attention to himself by asking Tara questions concerning her whereabouts.

He was sifting through his messages when Tara rang through on the intercom.

"Yes, Tara?"

"Mr. Gallagher is in now, sir."

"OK, can you see if he has a moment to spare for me?"

"Sure, Mr. Robertson, right away."

He took his letter opener and slid it through an interesting piece of mail. The return address belonged to a Mr. Edward Johnson. Inside was an old newspaper article. It read,

> *The execution of Jake Johnson took place today for the hanging of a young black man. The circumstances surrounding his guilty plea were highly suspicious. There was no evidence to put Johnson at the scene of the crime. His defense attorney, Ronald Harris, had not tried many cases and had never defended a murder suspect.*

Harris sat back in amazement. This was the second blow to his stomach today. What on earth . . . ? This was his grandfather they were talking about. What did they mean "suspicious"? *My grandfather is one of the most respected citizens in the state of Florida, he sits on Florida's Supreme Court for God's sake,* Harris thought. He was frustrated and angry at how anyone could write such garbage about his grandfather. *Why would someone send me an article like this? How cruel.*

Tara paged through to him. "Mr. Gallagher is free now," she stated. The page startled him as he was deep in thought. Harris gathered up the article and envelope and then hurried down to Hugh's office. Gallagher's secretary instructed him to go in as the DA was expecting him.

"Harris, young man, nice to see you," Gallagher announced, reaching out to shake his hand.

"Nice to see you too, sir," Harris replied.

"Did you have a nice weekend?"

"Yes, sir, I went to my mother's house for dinner, and I always enjoy my visits there."

"Good job, son," Gallagher said approvingly. "Family is so important in this world. Don't you agree?"

"Yes, sir." Harris thought his question was odd given the strange letter, which had just crossed his desk. Harris handed him the envelope and the article.

"What do you think about this?" Harris asked. "I don't understand. My grandfather is one of the most respected people in Florida."

"First of all, Harris," said Gallagher while he looked at the mail, "It is addressed to me, but that's beside the point. I can only imagine how you feel. I will take care of this, do not worry. This was years ago, and someone is probably out to hurt you because they see how good you are. You know how jealousy and that sort of thing goes. Don't you worry yourself about it."

"OK," Harris said, at least feeling better about the situation. *Gallagher is right,* he reasoned. *People are cruel sometimes when someone starts to gain success. Why did I not come to the same conclusion? I am worrying over nothing. I learned growing up with a hearing disability not to let other people's meanness affect me.*

Hugh took the newspaper clipping and envelope and filed it in a folder. "Harris, I have a new case I need you to work on," he said, turning Harris's attention back to where he was. "Do you think you are up to it after your last win?"

"Of course I am, sir. I am always ready to take the justice system by storm, especially now that I have inherited the Florida Hurricane's title." He smiled.

"Well, son, let me tell you about your next case." Harris sat down across from Gallagher, eager to listen.

Hugh sighed with relief, observing that the young man had apparently shrugged off the article, even though Hugh knew it meant trouble for Harris.

Chapter Two

The Executioner

Hugh handed Harris a large manila folder as thick as *War and Peace.* "You need to keep this file under lock and key," Hugh said somberly. Take it out only when you are working on it. There are many dangers that come with this file. You guard this with your life."

The secrecy intrigued Harris; what kind of case could come with such a warning? Looking at the front of the folder, he noted the subject: "The Executioner a.k.a. P. Smith." A cold shudder rippled down the back of his spine. Harris knew this name, as well as the reputation that went with it.

"I see you know of him." Hugh had noted the look of shock on Harris's face. "This guy went underground for a long time," Hugh went on, warming to his task, "but it seems he has resurfaced. We have tried to convict him many times, but he always manages to elude conviction. I have faith in you, Harris," he continued, leaning back in his Italian leather chair. "I know you can put this scumbag away. I am also concerned for you though. The Executioner is one of the most dangerous criminals on our streets. His crimes stretch throughout the States. We have linked him to at least five here in Orlando—two recently. If you are not up for this task, you need to let me know now." Hugh leaned forward again, looking Harris squarely in the eye. "I have to concentrate on the Barnes case, which is going to require my utmost attention. It will be coming up on the dock any time now. So I need to know now if you are in or out. I can't do this with you." Hugh was lying, covering his real intentions.

"You know you can count on me, sir," Harris said, his previous chills already forgotten. "I was born to win convictions." Hugh smirked inwardly at the young man's enthusiasm, showing nothing but fatherlike concern on the outside. But the concern he portrayed for Harris was phony.

"Great! Why don't you take this folder back to your office and read every word until you memorize everything about him. Understand him, think like him, and always make sure you are one step ahead of him, or he will kill you without a second thought. But"—Hugh held up a warning finger—"lock the file away in your safe until you are ready to look at it again."

"Yes, sir. I appreciate your confidence in me," Harris replied, thoroughly intrigued.

"I will be honest with you, it is possible I just handed you your death sentence, so please, son, don't thank me yet." Hugh was doing his best to sensationalize the situation in order to manipulate the young and overly zealous Harris. "You need to know there are no public records concerning anything to do with Smith or the allegations against him. Everything you read in this file is what I have compiled and recorded." What he did not tell him was that the file contents comprised only what he wanted Harris to know. "This character is so slick," he continued, "and seems to keep beating the system. I have watched you for a long time, Harris, and I'm confident you are the one to take this bastard down for us." Hugh reiterated his confidence in the boy.

The same chills ran back down Harris's spine, but this time, not from fear but from the anticipation of a challenge. Quickly recovering, he rose to go, eager to read the file and find out who the Executioner was and what made him tick. He tried not to show his excitement or his pride while Hugh praised him, knowing those traits were the ones which led to his father's conceit and arrogance, which in turn led to his father's demise. He needed to keep those traits in check. Harris left his office exhilarated that Hugh would again entrust him with such an enormous responsibility.

As soon as Harris closed the door behind him, Hugh got straight on the phone with Harris's grandfather. Old Ronald Harris himself picked up the line.

"How are you, Ronald, old man?"

"Not so much of the 'old,' Hugh," Judge Harris rumbled his deep belly laugh. "I'm still in my prime, just like you." With the formalities over with, the judge got straight to business. "So to what do I owe the pleasure of this call? I am sure it has something to do with my terrific grandson. He showed excellence in the courtroom last week," Judge Harris positively gushed. "I told you he was going to be another Florida Hurricane and sweep crime off the map here in our sunny state."

"It is not good news, Ronald." Hugh cut to the chase. "Harris received a newspaper clipping today. The article contained your name. It referenced the execution of Jake Johnson, whom you represented. The boy was horrified to read about Johnson's execution for the death of an African American. To make things worse, across the article it had written in red, *Ronald Harris hanged Jake Johnson.*" Here he paused, and when the judge said nothing, he continued. "It is odd the Executioner has resurfaced. I am hoping the two have no correlation, but I smell trouble."

The judge could hear the trembling in Hugh's voice, and he was not impressed at hearing this information. The fear coming from Hugh's voice, however, covered the secret plan constructed in order to take over the Practice and its escrow, knowing what would happen to him if Judge Harris ever found out scared him to no end.

"I'm sure you were sensible enough to tell the boy it was a nasty hoax," the judge finally replied. "Because he won his first big case or something else along those lines, correct?"

"Of course I did, Ronald."

"Keep me apprised, Hugh, and make this situation disappear. I don't care how you do it, just make sure my grandson does not find out anything. Do you understand?"

"Of course I do, Ronald. I am working on it as we speak."

"I want the Executioner released and back underground. Make it happen today. I don't have to remind you of the consequences of him spending time confined."

"I am on it, Ronald, I can assure you."

"What about the article Harris received?" the judge asked, his voice crisp and businesslike, without a trace of fear. "Do you have any idea who might have sent it? I sure would like to know who mailed it to my grandson." The businesslike tone had been replaced with true menace.

"Of course not, Ronald. If I knew the answer to that question, I would have told you already," said Hugh, all the while lying through his teeth, knowing it was he himself who sent it to Harris.

"You are going to find out and let me know, right?"

Before Hugh could answer, the judge hung up.

Judge Ronald Harris was furious. Hugh was sweating when he sat back in his chair, taking extra breaths to calm his nerves. He wondered if his planned takeover of the Practice was worth his health. The fleeting thought of all the money soon to be coming his way replaced any negative thoughts with his greed. For many years, he had been planning to take over the Practice. Harris joining the DA's office only made his plan sweeter. He watched the boy try case after case, winning every one of them on his own merit. He tested Harris, manipulating his first big trial; he wanted to know if the boy noticed any discrepancies. Hugh suspected Harris was like his father: so eager to win, he noticed nothing, except the triumph.

Hugh already knew the exact location and time the Executioner would arrive at the predetermined location. He knew if Judge Harris caught wind of his plan and found out he was setting Harris up to convict the Executioner, he would become a target himself. Once Harris incarcerated him, this would provide Hugh with a clear path to take over the Practice, leaving Hugh alive. The task was not to get Harris killed before he served his purpose. If Judge Harris suspected any kind of a takeover, things could get messy. Hating the fact he had to appease the judge for now, he hoped it would not last for much longer. One, he did not like Ronald Harris, and two, he could not wait to get his hands on the money. Hugh threatened Harris with his silence; he was on a need-to-know basis, which was important to everyone's health, especially his own.

Rushing back to his office, the thick pack of documents clutched tightly in his hands, Harris asked Tara to hold all his calls, barely even glancing Markita's way; he needed to put her out of his mind while he read his assignment. Throwing himself down behind his desk, he pulled out the case history and began to read.

He could not put it down. Harris read page after page, sometimes sweating and feeling sick at the contents inside. Did this sort of thing still take place in America? Its contents shadowed the mafia; one crime seemed to connect to the next. He anticipated the need to finish the file for it to make sense, because so far, nothing did. Realizing the process would take time, all he could do was pray God would protect him. After reading the folder for several hours, Harris began to wonder if, in fact, he was ready for this deep of an assignment. He was beginning to experience extreme fear of the Executioner. According to his file, this convict did not do well in confined spaces, but it was time to go see him. The visit was not one he was looking forward to at all. Continuing to read through the documents, he noticed the defense attorney on record was one from his grandfather's old firm, the Practice.

Knowing his family first owned that law firm made him proud, but over time, its reputation had become tarnished. His great-grandfather inherited it from a stranger back in 1962 when he died in 1968, it was willed to Ronald Harris. Then his partners swindled it away from him, and Harris's father then regained it back for the family. An anonymous investor purchased the firm from Mark and brought back Stewart Pope as a partner. He heard there were second—and third-generation families running it now. The other rumor was a power struggle: some outsider was trying to move in and take over.

Harris made a call through to the jail, setting up an appointment within the hour to interview the Executioner. This was the first time he was nervous about meeting with a convict. Feeling his legs buckling under him, sweating profusely, he waited in the small interview room for the guard to bring the Executioner in. The space seemed especially cramped, and the thought of being that close to this man accused of such horrible crimes made him more than a little nervous.

The prisoner entered the room in shackles and handcuffs, which, after reading this perpetrator's file did not make him feel any more secure. The guard directed the prisoner to his chair at the table opposite Harris. The young lawyer watched while he sat down, trying to avoid his eyes, looking away while putting his briefcase on the table. Harris knew it was the wrong thing to do even as he did it; this man could sense fear and would exploit it to his full advantage. Feeling the Executioner's eyes piercing through him, Harris gained the courage to look back at him straight into his eyes; all he could see were the eyes of death. There was no soul behind them, nothing there except for the coldest blank, dark stare he had ever witnessed.

Harris suddenly felt he could not stand being in the room with this man another second. Again knowing it was the wrong move, he picked up his briefcase, which he had not even bothered to open, and headed for the door without saying a word. He nodded curtly to the guard, waited for him, a heavily armed man, to move to unlock the door and let him out. As he waited, a voice, just as dead as the eyes, drifted across the table behind him.

"Scared, are we, Mr. Dead Prosecutor?" the man sneered at him in a hoarse whisper. Harris spun around to look at him one last time and heard words coming from his own mouth, not knowing how he managed to speak them.

"Of you? Not a chance in hell!" The guard opened the door, and Harris exited, taking what felt like an asthmatic breath once he reached the relative safety of the jail's main corridor.

Harris was not proud of his behavior, but once he looked into death's eyes, he knew there was no point in interviewing this animal. It would have been pointless asking him any questions; he would never have received a straight answer from that man. He knew he was better off leaving the Executioner wondering about him than giving away too much sitting there with the man for too long.

Once outside the interview room, Harris felt some of his composure return, but not his confidence; he was having doubts about getting a conviction on this person, assuming he could get as far as a trial. The Executioner had racked up forty-three arrests, but he never once stood trial. Despite his fears, Harris was determined to find out why.

Walking down the long corridor to the exit, he started to wonder why Hugh would put him on such a dangerous case; was Hugh's confidence in him so strong, or was he being played? It made him think back to the newspaper article addressed to Hugh about his grandfather and wondered if the Executioner was connected.

It was getting late; Harris wanted to find a drive-through and pick up something to eat, then relax in his fat boy chair at home. Once home, however, he only ate half his meal before calling it a night, but sleep did not come easy. Thinking about the day's events left him with a sleepless night. He tossed and turned, unable to get rid of all the questions, which were floating around in his head.

As he drifted into sleep at last, he dreamed about a fight his parents got into years before. He remembered his mother telling his father, "You would be nothing or no one if it wasn't for my father." From his hiding place, a young

Harris overheard his mother say her father helped with their mortgage as his job barely paid his student loans. In addition, her father helped jump-start his career by getting him a junior partner position at the Practice. The dream had been so vivid—why is this memory resurfacing now? Harris sometimes wanted to ask his grandfather for advice with his studies, but his uncle discouraged him every time. "You need to make it on your own merit, son," his uncle would harp. He wanted to understand why his uncle disliked his grandfather. Now awake, he lay staring at the ceiling, not looking forward to the day ahead.

Morning arrived sooner than he wanted it to, and he was tired from the lack of sleep. Harris took time showering, picked out his suit, then headed downstairs for his coffee. His thoughts turned to Markita, wondering if she would be in the office today, and a smile returned to his face.

As he did every day, he opened the large oak doors and walked toward his office, saying good morning to everyone, but knowing his interest was in seeing one person. Recovered from his case of nerves at the jail the day before, he was feeling a different type of nervousness as he approached his office door, his heart beginning to pound a little harder in his chest. There she was . . . His face lit up, and his smile broadened, almost reaching his ears. He could not believe he started to tremble or how the saliva in his mouth was starting to dry up at the sight of Markita. She was so beautiful he sighed to himself.

"Good morning, Mr. Robertson," Markita said in her sexy Southern voice. He looked at her like a puppy dog who just received a treat. Sighing like a lovesick schoolboy, he thought how sexy she said his name. All he could do was stand there and stare at her. Tara let out a giggle, and it brought him back to reality. He coughed, then cleared his throat.

"Good morning, miss." He looked starry-eyed at Markita.

"And good morning to you, Tara," he said a little more informally.

"Here are your messages, Mr. Robertson," Tara said, handing them to him. Harris tried asking Markita where she was yesterday, but it all came out wrong. He felt like such a fool.

"Where there you were yesterday, miss?"

"I'm sorry, sir, what is it you asked?" Markita cocked her head to one side, waiting for clarification.

"There were you yesterday," Harris said. It still did not come out right! His tongue felt all twisted, and he turned candy apple red. Tara smirked behind her hand, trying her best not to laugh aloud at him. He cleared his throat again, taking one last stab at regaining his dignity in front of her.

"Ahem, I was wondering where you were yesterday, miss."

"Oh, I was at the courthouse taking notes, sir. Was I supposed to let you know? Mr. Gallagher said he would clear it with you."

"It's OK, but he must have forgotten. I did not know." Harris could feel the burning sensation leaving his face now. He was beginning to regain control.

"I would appreciate it if you could please let me know yourself if you are going to be absent from the office," he continued more formally now. "I like to know where my staff is. I also like to make sure they are OK." He hoped he did not sound arrogant or possessive, but he wanted her to know the welfare of his employees was important to him.

"Yes, Mr. Robertson, I will tell you in the future." She again said his name so angelically, he could have stood there and looked and listened to her all day, but thought he should get to his office before he made an even bigger fool out of himself. Closing the door behind him, Harris sat down in his large leather chair and paged Tara.

"Please bring me the charges on Mr. P. Smith." Tara knocked on his heavy oak doors and entered into his office, handing him the file he asked for. "Mr. Robertson, is there anything else I can get for you?"

"No thanks, Tara, this will do for now." She left his office. He began reading the events of the Executioner's most recent arrest. There was no doubt he expected denial of the bail based on this report. The arresting officer recognized Smith and called it in to dispatch. The lead officer instructed him to apprehend the suspect based on the outstanding murder warrant. The officer called for backup. During his preliminary search, he found a woman's head on the backseat of his car covered by a sheet. The Executioner was going to have a difficult time explaining this one to the judge. Once he got bail denied, he could keep this creep off the streets until he could study him some more. *This could be an excellent training opportunity for Markita*, he thought to himself and paged her to come into his office. He cleared his throat first, determined this time to sound coherent. He put on his best intellectual voice.

"Markita, could you please come in here for a moment?" At least he sounded competent after the morning's fiasco of trying to talk to her. Markita knocked on the door with a light tap and then proceeded to enter his office. This is the first time he has seen her standing, and he was in awe of her beauty. Sitting back in his chair taking an extra breath, he grinned at his thoughts.

"What can I do for you, Mr. Robertson?"

"Here is your chance to get your feet wet, Markita. I need you to call over to the courthouse and see if there has been a bail hearing set for a P. Smith, then verify Nigel Pope, his defense attorney. If a time has been set, please put it on my calendar and page me if the attorney is still Nigel Pope or if there has been a change, will you?"

"I will get right on this, Mr. Robertson," she said in the sweetest voice. Harris watched her leave his office, and once she closed the door behind her, he sat back and held his heart. *How am I ever going to muster up the courage to ask her out? What if she says no?* On a whim, he found himself dialing information for a florist's number, then ordering a dozen red roses with one single white rose in the middle. He addressed the flowers to the office and arranged to have them delivered to her for tomorrow, with no note. Pleased with himself, he sat back in his chair and smiled.

He was getting ready to leave the office for the day when Markita paged through to him to let him know she had obtained the information on the bail hearing he wanted.

"Please come into my office, Markita," he said, excited at saying her name. This gave him a chance to talk to her before leaving the office. Markita knocked on the door and entered. She walked over to him. He motioned for her to sit down.

"The bail hearing is set for two p.m. tomorrow in Judge Poe's courtroom and a Nigel Pope from the Practice is still defending Mr. Smith."

"Go figure," said Harris.

"What do you mean, Mr. Robertson?"

"It's a long story, Markita, but my great-grandfather first owned the Practice, then it was handed down to my grandfather who lost it in a land deal. He helped my father regain it for the family. It carried a good reputation back then, however, there is now talk of corruption. They always seem to represent perpetrators like Smith."

"Your family was all attorneys?" Markita asked. She seemed comfortable talking to him, and Harris was beginning to feel more comfortable talking to her.

"And judges," Harris replied. "My grandfather is the chief justice and sits on Florida's Supreme Court."

"Whoa, Judge Harris is your grandfather?" Markita sounded impressed.

"Yes, he is," said Harris, proud of the fact. "My father was once the district attorney in this office until he died. It was ironic, but he died on the day he became a judge."

"Oh my gosh, how devastating," she said with such compassion and empathy that Harris wished he could take her in his arms to comfort her. Instead, he gave her what was fast becoming a his trademark bumbling reply.

"Not at all, Markita, my father and I were not close." *Great,* he thought, *now she is going to think I am a jerk for not being close to him. Why did I have to put my foot in my mouth yet again?* However, Markita continued on not paying any mind to the fact he was close to his father; she did not even know who hers was.

"But still, to die the day you become a judge is terrible. It is so hard to get appointed a judgeship. You know, it's something I would like for myself one day."

"It is?" Harris asked in surprise.

She giggled when she answered. "It's why I am interning here, Mr. Robertson."

"Markita, when we are alone in here, would you mind calling me Harris? Mr. Robertson is so formal."

"It is not appropriate, but I will honor your wishes, if it is what you want," Markita said, smiling with approval.

"Thank you, Markita." He loved saying her name. The letters seemed to roll off his tongue.

"Well, good night, Mr. Robertson . . . I mean, Harris," she said, giggling again, getting up to leave. He wanted to ask her out, but knew it was too soon. And he knew there would be talk in the office.

"Good night, Markita, I will see you bright and early in the morning." The large oak door echoed as she closed it. He slumped back in his chair for a moment, thinking about her, trying to catch his breath. He began daydreaming about them dressed up in Halloween costumes: he was a pirate; she, a cat. They were riding on the back of a tractor on a hayride. Markita was laughing, and he noticed she looked so cute with pink ears and her nose colored black with whiskers drawn on her face. Her lips looked even more kissable with ruby-red lipstick on them, and she wore little white mittens. His arm was wrapped firmly around her as they bounced up and down along the country road. His thoughts progressed into them getting naked, and he jerked himself back into reality. Phew! He wondered why he daydreamed about Halloween as he never dressed up for the holiday before. It brought a smile to his face as he closed his briefcase to leave.

Picking up a hamburger on the way home, he sat it next to his computer while he ate and started to research the Executioner's attorney, Nigel Pope. It was customary for him to learn everything he could about the opposing counsel. Interestingly enough, Nigel was the son of Stewart Pope, who defended a man named Bellamy, opposite his father. The gist of the news articles stated that Pope had defended Bellamy in a poor manner; council astonished the court reporter, Nancy Marble, at the deliberate lack of representation. He found several other articles by Nancy Marble slamming and discrediting his father; it was obvious she despised him. He knew his father was a cold, uncaring rat bastard. The coldness directed at Harris was because he did not want children. Still he did not believe his father was corrupt as Marble implied. Joshua told him his father was a brilliant attorney and would have served as a great judge. Upholding the law and putting the criminals away was what drove his father as well as himself. Why would this woman slander him in the papers? Harris was getting perturbed and decided to call it a night. He lay in bed for the longest time dreaming of him and Markita before falling into a deep sleep.

He was not looking forward to dealing with Smith tomorrow. There was nothing good about this man. His body shuddered thinking about being in the same room with him, remembering his last visit. Once he arrived at work, he looked over for Markita; again, she was not there. He continued walking toward his office, feeling his heart sink.

"No intern today, Tara?" he asked in a casual manner.

"Yes, she's here. She walked a case file down to Mr. Gallagher's office."

"Oh, OK. Hmm . . . nice flowers."

"Yes, they came for her this morning with no card."

"No card? How unusual," he remarked.

"Maybe she has a secret admirer in the office," snickered Tara.

"Was she surprised when they arrived?" He now felt his face starting to burn, wishing he had not pursued his line of questioning. *It is the attorney in me*, he thought.

"I wasn't paying any attention to her." Tara was starting to assume they came from Harris; she could not control herself from giggling.

"What is so funny? Is my tie not on straight, Tara?" he said, trying to divert her thoughts.

"No, sir, your tie looks fine." He walked off toward his office feeling foolish. *I have to stop acting this way when I am around Markita or when I talk about her.* He waited a few minutes then paged Tara, trying to sound nonchalant, but again, he made things worse.

"Tara, whenever what's-her-name returns from Hugh's office, can you send her in here?"

"You mean Markita, right, sir?" said Tara, snickering. She worked for him from the first day he became the assistant district attorney, and she had never seen him act so flustered. Harris did not like the impression he was giving, but every time it concerned Markita, he acted like a lovesick rock band groupie. There was a gentle knock on the door.

"Come in," he said, regaining composure.

"Good morning, Mr. Robertson, Tara said you were looking for me."

"Harris, please," he said.

"Good morning, Harris," she repeated.

"Markita, would you like to accompany me to a bail hearing this afternoon? It should not take long to get bail denied for this assailant. I think it provides good training for you."

"I would love to, Mr.—I'm sorry, Harris," she said all excited.

"Great, then we'll drive over in my car, if it's OK with you."

"I would love to, sir, thank you for the opportunity to see the Florida Hurricane in action." Her statement took him by surprise. *Mercy, what if I screw up in front of her? I will look like a total moron, talk about pressure.* This time he tried remaining cool, calm, and collected.

"It's my pleasure, Markita. It's always nice to see young people interested in pursuing a career in the law." As usual, nothing came out right when he spoke to her. He sounded more as if he was talking to a teenager, and she was not much younger than himself. *I wish I did not get so nerdish around her. It will tarnish my image*, he thought, grinning.

"Is there anything else, sir?" she said in a shy voice.

"Yes, yes, thank you, I will see you later."

Markita sat down at her desk and turned to Tara

"Is he always like that?" she asked.

"Like what?" Tara said, smiling.

"I don't know, strange."

"What makes you say strange?" Tara asked, again smiling.

"Well, one minute he's all . . ." She stopped and paused for a second then continued on, "he's sweet, then he turns all . . . official and strange—like." Tara was having a hard time not laughing; she did not want Markita to feel uncomfortable.

"He's just shy and gets nervous sometimes," Tara said, covering for him.

"How can you say he gets nervous? People call him the Hurricane and say he is so swift in the courtroom, criminals do not stand a chance against him."

"He is different in the courtroom, it's his comfort zone. But flirting is new for him." Tara could not hold back any longer.

"Flirting? I don't think Mr. Robertson would flirt with me." Markita sounded a little offended so Tara thought she better leave her well enough alone.

"I'm sure he is just preoccupied with the bail hearing this afternoon," she said.

"Yes, I'm sure you're right."

Harris pulled Smith's arrest file out of the safe, leaving the Executioner's folder in there. He sat down, opened up the file, and then started to read. How can a person with so many arrests never have a conviction? Someone in the judicial system is aiding this perp. He started to read over the latest arrest.

Smith was leaving a local bank when an officer recognized him. The officer called in his suspicion, and he was informed there was an outstanding warrant for his arrest on a murder charge. The officer called for backup then proceeded toward the car. The suspect had the car door open with one leg inside. The officer asked him to step out of the vehicle. Smith sat down and reached under the car seat looking for his gun. The officer grabbed the suspect, throwing him to the ground facedown. The officer had his knee in Smith's back while grabbing one arm and then the other pulling them tight behind his back. Three patrol cars arrived on the scene. The officers assisted in the apprehension of the suspect. They read Smith his Miranda rights. The officers handcuffed Smith and then proceeded to take him down town.

Harris thought, *Everything seemed in order, including the proper procedures for booking the suspect.* I should be able to obtain a denial for bail without a problem. He should not even have to mention the gruesome head they retrieved from the backseat of the car. Harris set Smith's file aside then pulled out the Executioner's folder from the safe. Digging further into his life, he read until he came across an outstanding warrant. Smith was a suspect in a murder of an Officer Parker, who was in the process of suing the Practice. The firm was representing Parker's son on a drug charge. The officer's son was a straight A student and had never done drugs in his life. The attorney's representation at the Practice was questionable right from the beginning. The officer was taking the firm to the Florida Bar. Officer Parker's son died under suspicious circumstances in his jail cell, and Parker turned up dead in his home the next day. There was an eyewitness linking Smith to the death of the officer and no mention of the person's name in the folder.

Harris shook his head, wondering whatever happened to his grandfather's firm. He paged through to Tara and asked her to get hold of Joe, his lead investigator, and instruct him to assemble an investigative team expediting the situation for him. He then locked the Executioner's folder back in the safe and placed the arresting case file into his briefcase while walking outside to pick up Markita to take her to the courthouse with him. They made small talk, all the while learning little things about each other. Harris's butterflies kept getting stronger. It was not long before the bailiff announced the case number and introduced Judge Poe.

"Good morning, Your Honor, in the case of the *State versus P. Smith*, we would request for bail to be denied," said Harris.

"Mr. Pope, proceed," said the judge, looking over at Nigel Pope.

"Your Honor, the defense will establish our client has been wrongly arrested. The State will claim they can identify our client, as the person who murdered an officer of the law, except the eyewitness is now deceased. Why the district attorney's office did not know the warrant was recalled is beyond me, Your Honor. Therefore, we strike for the case to be thrown out as there was no cause for my client's arrest. It is incompetence on the district attorney's office, Your Honor," said Nigel with a smug look on his face. He knew he was pushing buttons, but he wanted the Florida Hurricane to know he was not afraid of him. Hugh already apprised Judge Poe of the circumstances surrounding this case. Unbeknownst to Harris, Hugh deliberately kept information from him.

"Watch yourself, Mr. Pope," said Judge Poe.

"Yes, Your Honor, I beg the court's forgiveness," he said in a sarcastic tone. Of course, Judge Poe knew who P. Smith was. He was also aware there was no paper trail leading to him. He knew caution was the upmost of importance whenever dealing with any case which could have implications on him. Poe was in fear of exposure as the corrupt, perverted, and arrogant bastard he was, so he participated in Hugh's harebrained schemes. Sometimes he enjoyed his part in the conspiracies; life became boring after the death of his wife. He has been a judge for over twenty years in the Orlando court system. There was nothing or no one who snuck passed him.

Harris could have crawled under the desk. He could not believe what he was hearing. There was no way this was happening.

"Your Honor, there is still the question of the head on the backseat of Mr. Smith's car," said Harris in desperation.

"Again, Your Honor, there was no probable cause for the arrest to begin with," Pope smirked, looking over at Harris.

"Well, Mr. Robertson, file the appropriate motions, and I will set an arraignment hearing for two weeks from today. Are both sides in acceptance?" Judge Poe knew Hugh did not want the Executioner released as he had other plans for him. They both answered the judge with a yes.

"Bail is denied," said the judge as he banged his gavel down and called for the next case. Harris shuffled his papers and threw them in his briefcase in anger. He slammed it shut and motioned for Markita to follow him out. On the ride back to the office, he did not utter a word, and Markita felt she should not say anything either. She knew he was already angry and did not want to add to his frustration. He slammed the large oak door behind him entering his office.

He paged Tara, "Get me Gallagher on the phone, Tara." She did not even have a chance to reply before he hung up with her.

"Phew, what happened at the courthouse?" Tara asked.

"It wasn't good, the eyewitness to the murder was found dead, and the warrant was recalled," replied Markita.

"How could Mr. Robertson miss something so crucial? He is always so thorough."

"At least the man's bail was denied so he has plenty of time to find out." Harris came out of his office; he caught the last part of what the girls were saying.

"Markita, when and if you ever become an attorney, the first thing you will need to learn is never go in front of a judge unprepared or uninformed." Markita turned a dozen shades of red.

"Tara, did you get hold of Joe? If so, he has not gotten back in touch with me. Can you tell him it's imperative he calls me now please?"

"Right away, Mr. Robertson, he should have called you." Tara thought a bit of support for him now would go a long way.

"Markita, put the date for the pretrial hearing on my calendar, please," he spoke to her in a different tone, acting as if he had not scolded her. He went back into his office and shut the door hard, almost a slam but not quite. Tara looked over at Markita's tear-filled eyes.

"It's OK, Markita, he is not mad at you, I can tell he is angrier at himself. Mr. Robertson is like his father, neither of them likes to lose in the courtroom. When it comes to the law and corruption, it seems both men have the same passion to uphold and fight it." Markita felt a lot better, but now she was feeling empathy for Harris. She smiled to herself as she said his name under her breath.

"Would you like me to call Joe for you while you finish the motion you were filing?" she asked Tara.

"Yes, thank you, I would appreciate it as I am already running behind today." Markita walked over to the large Rolodex on Tara's desk and asked, "How is Joe's number listed?"

"Joe Marble, he is our lead investigator. He worked with Mr. Robertson on his first big case. Joe is five foot eleven with brown hair and a cute mustache. You will like him, he is extremely Southern, and a funny guy, plus he likes to tease Mr. Robertson. He is a handsome man," Tara said, smiling as she had a secret crush on him.

"Thanks." Markita dialed the number.

"Joe Marble, how can I help you."

"Yes, sir, this is Markita with the district attorney's office. Mr. Robertson would like to meet with you as soon as possible."

"Yes, I know I got Tara's message earlier but was working on something for Hugh. Tell Harris I will be there in an hour, if it's OK with him."

"If it is not, I will call you back, OK?"

"Yes, my dear, it will be fine." Markita hung up the phone thinking what a nice man he seemed. She paged through to Harris.

"Mr. Robertson, Mr. Marble said he would be here in an hour if it is OK with you."

"It's fine, Markita. I appreciate you taking the initiative in making the appointment for me. It is important to see him today in light of what happened this afternoon."

"Yes, sir," she answered so softly. *There she goes again with her sexy voice, phew. Now look I have goose bumps.* He grinned.

Joe Marble was punctual. Tara let the assistant district attorney know Joe had arrived, and Harris instructed her to escort him into his office.

"Harris, young man, how are you? It has been what? Two weeks, since I saw you last?" He chuckled as he started to sit down.

"Would you like some water or a soda?" asked Tara.

"No, thank you, but it was nice of you to ask." Joe smiled at her as she left Harris's office.

"My, my, my, Harris, you have two beautiful girls working for you. Hmm . . . must be nice! It's obvious you impressed Hugh winning your big case."

"The new one is Markita, she is interning here for six months," he tried, explaining without turning all kinds of red.

"Must be a pretty good intern, if your face is any indication," Joe chuckled.

"It is hot in here, don't you think?" Harris said, fanning himself.

"No, it is quite comfortable," said Joe, amused. Harris tried changing the subject.

"Joe, something strange happened this afternoon, a suspect named Smith was arrested because of an outstanding murder warrant. I was in court today along with the new intern, getting bail denied, and Nigel Pope from the Practice informed Judge Poe the warrant was recalled, due to the fact the eyewitness, which could put Smith at the scene of the crime, was deceased."

"Whoa! The judge denied bail, right?"

"Right, but I saw the warrant myself, and it was still outstanding. I called to double-check this time, and the clerk informed me there was a warrant issued. Judge Poe did not even consider this fact. The arresting officer did everything by the book. I can tell you I was not thrilled standing in front of Judge Poe with my britches down."

"What a sight for the new intern," Marble chuckled louder this time. Harris's face began to turn the color of a freshly ripened tomato.

"You know what I mean, Joe. Pope stood in front of the judge informing him the warrant was recalled. Now the clerk tells me there never was one issued. It doesn't make sense."

"You're right there, Sherlock, something stinks like a rat."

"I even mentioned to the judge that there was a decapitated head found on the backseat."

"The what?" Joe exclaimed.

"Yeah, it's another reason I called you in. I am curious to know the story behind this one." Even though Harris knew it was the work of the Executioner, he could not tell Joe decapitation was one of his MOs. He still needed to know who she was and what the story behind her death was.

"Today's bail hearing is on the public record. I can understand your frustration. What do you want me to do?"

"I want you to investigate this for me. Try not to ruffle any feathers though, it is obvious this is bigger than you and I. Proceed with caution and report only to me. I would appreciate it if, for now, you would not even confide in Hugh. I can tell you this much, there was an Officer Parker and his kid who was arrested for drugs, something went wrong, and the boy was convicted. From what I read, he got a pretty harsh sentence. Officer Parker was taking the Practice in front of the board and suing them for negligence. They discovered the kid dead in his cell and the officer suffocated at home the next day. There was an eyewitness who put Smith at the crime scene."

"I remember Parker, he was a good detective, and there was no way his kid was involved in drugs. I transferred to Chicago about then for six months thinking I would like the cold weather, it did not take me long to change my mind. I never followed up on the case, now I am curious. I am not as good as the Florida Hurricane, but I can sniff something foul here myself." He chuckled again.

"I don't think you have to be a good detective to sense something is quite wrong with this picture, even an amateur could figure this one out," he said in a playful manner, mocking Joe.

"Are you challenging me, Mr. Robertson? Because I'm telling you, if you are, then I challenge you to ask out the pretty lil' intern of yours."

"Joe, you are being childish and immature." Harris bit back a grin, trying to keep a straight face.

"Oh-ho-ho-ho, childish and immature, am I? Well, I'll bet you $100 you're too chickenshit to ask your intern out." Joe was ribbing him so hard Harris could feel his face flaming. Harris cleared his throat then spoke with his voice cracking.

"Ahem, although she is a beautiful woman, I will not ask her out. Even if it was an option, I would not place a bet on her."

"It's a good job, you uphold the law, man, and don't have to be put on the witness stand because your face is a dead giveaway for the truth." Joe Marble was having a bit too much fun at his expense.

"She is a sweet girl, I'm sure she has a boyfriend, and Hugh would not appreciate me flirting in the office." He tried to sound professional, but his face was still giving him away.

"So you haven't asked her out yet? I knew it! For a hurricane, you blow pretty slow." Joe let out a huge laugh as he rhymed his words. Harris was even more embarrassed but managed to laugh with Joe.

"Hmm . . . good one, Joe, you know what they say, you are a poet, and you didn't know it, and in my opinion, you're a pretty bad one." There was a little dig in Harris's voice.

"You are going to need a better defense if you are going to deny you like the pretty little thing."

"OK, Joe, enough, she is a sweet girl, and it is obvious she is attractive, but I am working on a judgeship and do not have time for fraternizing."

"Right, or you're, like I said, too chickenshit to ask her out." He was laughing harder now but decided it was time to give Harris a break.

"I will start an investigation for you first thing in the morning, and I will get a report to you as soon as possible."

"The judge gave me two weeks before the arraignment, this time when I go in front of him, I would like to have my ducks in a row."

"I understand," said Joe.

"By the way, talking of ducks, have you heard the one about the duck who can't find lip balm at the pharmacy?"

"Harris, if you tell the stupid duck joke, I swear I will come across your desk and bust you."

"The pharmacist found it for the duck and asked how he was going to pay for, it cash or charge? The duck said, 'Put it on my bill.' Harris cracked up, laughing, getting in his humor to annoy Joe for giving him a hard time. *If I have to endure the joke whenever I see my Uncle J, then why shouldn't Joe?* He knew it got under his skin as much as it did his own.

"I am warning you, the duck joke is getting as old as me."

"Yes, and that's pretty old, huh, Joe?"

"I think I am out of here, Harris. It is always a pleasure, man, it will be cool working with you again. I will get on this right away. Tell your uncle Joshua to come up with some new material which is at least funny."

"That's funny, Joe, I told him he needed new material, he wanted me to use the material to sew a new jacket for the duck, and he broke into his famous joke."

"Wow, what a quack-up, it's time I get quacking on this. I'm leaving before I go quackers," Joe could not contain himself.

"Thanks, Joe, you're the funniest, now leave."

"And don't you forget it. I will see if the intern will go on a date with you on my way out."

"Don't you dare, Joe Marble! I will have you arrested for harassment!"

"Later," said Joe.

"By the way, before you leave, I was going over some old newspaper clippings involving a few of my father's cases. There was a court reporter who did not care for him. Her last name was Marble, I was wondering if she was any relation to you?"

"Ah, I wondered when this would come up, she is my mother, I hope you won't let her dislike for your father hinder our relationship? It was the nature of the business she was in, and of course, you don't have to worry about her, she is retired now."

"Fair enough, Joe, we will leave it there. Let me know whose head it was on the backseat of Smith's car, freaking gruesome."

"Think about the poor schmuck of an officer who found it, I bet he upchucked his lunch. What is with this Smith guy? Any clue?"

"All I can tell you, Joe, is there is no soul inside his body. He looks like the grim reaper and has the coldest damn eyes I have ever seen."

"I will let you know what I find out as soon as I can. Have a great evening, Harris, and let's shoot some hoops soon."

"You got it!"

"I need an extra paycheck this week. Of course, if you ask the hot mama for a date, you owe me one hundred bucks," Joe said, getting the last word in as he left the office.

Chapter Three

Vanished

Joe awoke early the next morning wanting to follow up on Harris's request from the previous day. The background check he ran on Officer Parker came back squeaky clean; his work history and ethics were impeccable. Joe next headed down to the precinct and asked a couple of beat cops if they knew of any inside dirt on Parker, but they all praised his outstanding service to the community. By midafternoon, there was no doubt in Joe's mind that Parker was a clean cop with no skeletons in his closet.

His investigation of Parker's son yielded similar results. The boy had had a great reputation with his teachers and excelled academically; his attendance was perfect, and his friends all vouched for him, informing Joe they never saw him doing or selling drugs. In short, there was nothing to indicate Parker's son was anything but a good, honest kid. As with the father, Joe had a firm belief on the boy's innocence of any wrongdoing.

Joe called a friend of his who worked in the records department at the courthouse and left her a message asking her if she could get him a copy of the transcripts from the Parker boy's trial, along with a copy of the transcripts pertaining to Smith's bail hearing yesterday. He wanted to see who at the Practice represented Officer Parker's son, as well as which officer searched the boy at the crime scene, ultimately finding the drugs that led to the boy's arrest.

Since he needed to wait on her return call, Joe thought he would pay a visit to the car impound lot and request to see Smith's car. Although he was sure the department had already done so, he wanted to see if he could retrieve some hair follicles and blood samples from the head found on the backseat, in order to do some discovery of his own. He was not happy with his findings. When he arrived at the impound, he discovered that someone had stripped the car and taken out the entire backseat. "What happened here?" Joe asked the security guard on duty, indicating the stripped car.

"Your guess is as good as mine," he replied, shrugging his shoulders. "When I arrived this morning, I saw the rear passenger door torn off and the backseat missing. I checked the rest of the lot, but this was the sole car tampered with. When I headed back to my desk to call this in, I stumbled over the body of the night guard. I called for an ambulance straight away, and from what the paramedics said, it seemed as though he died of suffocation. I certainly didn't see any outside signs of trauma." The guard glanced around nervously and continued. "I called all this in to my superiors hours ago, but no one except you has come to investigate," he finished, a trace of anger starting to creep into his voice.

"You can't be serious!" Joe cried in shock. "What about the surveillance cameras?" he asked, his heart racing at this violent, and unexpected, twist to his investigation.

The guard, looking haggard, shrugged again in frustration. "It appears the camera wires were cut along with the alarm system. Nothing has been recorded from just before the paramedics think the guard was killed through now. I haven't touched anything—just been waiting for someone, anyone, to come down here and investigate. Any chance you're the guy who's going to start that investigation?"

"Not officially, pal, but I'll see what I can do," Joe said, slapping the worried guard on the shoulder. "I'll see what I can do," he repeated, then turned and headed back to his car, his brain working to unravel this new mystery. *Hmmm . . .* he mused. *Suffocation, huh? My conclusion is Smith was somehow trying to cover his tracks. But how could it be Smith?* he asked himself. *He was locked away last night . . . unless of course he has an accomplice?*

"Damn, there's nothing more I can do here, I may as well go pay a visit to Smith," Joe muttered to himself as he climbed back into his car. Reaching for his cell, he called the jail to arrange the visit. He could not believe what he heard on the other end of the line.

"Smith was released late last night," said the deputy at the jail.

"Are you kidding me? There was a woman's severed head on the backseat of his freaking car!" Joe nearly screamed in exasperation.

"You're talking to the wrong person, man. If you've got a problem, call the sheriff." Joe hung up and immediately called Harris. "Hey, man, I hope you're sitting down," he said through clenched teeth the moment Harris picked up the phone.

"I am, what is it?" Harris replied, sensing something bad was coming.

"Smith was released from jail last night."

"What? Joe, please, please tell me you're joking!" Harris was aware he was hoping for a miracle, but he needed to hope for something good concerning this disastrous situation.

"I know it's bizarre, and I wish I was wrong. But there's more, and it's just as bad. I just came from the impound lot, and Smith's car was stripped last night. The backseat's gone, along with the rear door. And the guard on duty was murdered—apparently suffocated. No surveillance cameras—the lines were cut. And"—he took a deep breath—"according to the current guard on duty, no one but me has been down there today to investigate this."

Harris sat stunned for a moment or two, shocked and lost in thought. "It's definitely Smith's MO," Harris muttered, slipping up. He had momentarily forgotten Joe was still on the other line.

"What do you mean it's his MO?" asked Joe, getting testy. "What is it you're not telling me?"

"It's not something I can divulge at this point," Harris replied, trying to recover from his blunder. "You are going to have to trust me for now, Joe."

"I don't like working in the dark, Harris. It's how cops get killed."

"I promise you, I won't let anything happen to you, but it does seems like you're on the right track, so be on your guard," Harris warned, trying not to say any more.

"I will tell you this much, there's a definite problem with this picture. I'm going to get to the bottom of it, don't you worry," Joe affirmed, his voice laced with conviction.

"I need to make a few phone calls," he continued. "Got to try to find out who gave the order to release Smith and what judge signed off on it. I want to know what the circumstances were for the release, although I am beginning to think I am going to come up with another dead end. Get it, Harris, another dead . . . end?" Joe chuckled at his pathetic attempt at humor.

"Not funny, Marble," Harris replied nervously. "You do some more digging, Joe, then call me later with whatever it is you find."

"Sure thing," said Joe.

"Be careful, my friend. I don't like this."

"I'm not thrilled with the idea of someone like Smith being on the streets either," Joe reassured him. "Nor the constant roadblocks I am running into, so no worries, right, friend?"

Harris hung up with Joe, feeling guilty at not being able to reveal any information concerning Smith. Harris knew exactly how dangerous this man was. Joe, on the other hand, did not, but being intuitive, he knew Harris was not giving him a full deck of cards to play with.

Harris paged through to Tara, "Is Hugh in yet?"

"No, sir, he isn't, but I expect him soon."

"OK, let me know when he gets in please, it's getting late, and I can't believe I haven't heard from him. It's not like Hugh not to keep in touch." He hung up and sat back in his chair, confused and annoyed. Staring up at the ceiling, Harris tried to piece things together in his head.

Who would let Smith go with all the evidence against him? Even with the warrant recalled, there was the woman's head found on the backseat of the car.

No judge in his right mind would have released him. If there was no warrant, however, and no arrest and no seat in the back of the car . . . His train of thought was interrupted as his private line rang. It was Joe.

"This is getting more out of control as we speak, man," Joe said without waiting for a proper greeting.

"What is it now?" asked Harris, now seriously worried for his friend and the case.

"I just came from forensics, and there is no chain of evidence logged in and no sign of the head. It's like the arrest never happened! I'm on my way to meet with yesterday's arresting officer. Maybe he can shed some light on what the hell is going on around here."

"I damn well hope so because this cover-up is way too obvious. It smells of corruption, Joe, and I don't like it one bit," Harris said in anger.

"I know what you mean. It stinks worse than a three-day-old fish. Smith must have an accomplice. It wouldn't surprise me if he knew someone on the inside."

Harris, worried for his friend, knew he was digging into a can of worms which might get him killed in a heartbeat. Where the hell was Hugh? "Let me know what you find out from the officer."

"Later," Joe said and hung up.

Joe had arranged to meet Smith's arresting officer in Langford Park. It was a spacious park with many benches shaded by huge oak trees. The park had a long nature trail with old wooden bridges and rope handrails. The bridges crossed over several streams, loaded with fish. Joe knew the park would be crowded at lunchtime, so he presumed it was safe for them to meet there.

Joe Marble was a brilliant detective, one of the best, so as he listened to the officer tell his story, it did not take Joe long to realize the officer was lying; he seemed to be trying to backtrack and recreate the arrest with lots of fabricated information.

"I knew the warrant was recalled, but I chose to ignore it," the officer was saying. "But I arrested him anyway. It was obvious it was Smith. I just figured we could get something to stick," he finished.

Joe cocked his head and stared hard at the young officer. "You are so full of bull," he said calmly. "Who put you up to this? You may as well fess up because when I get to the truth, I'll hunt you down like the dog that you are."

"I am telling you exactly what happened." The officer glanced around nervously as sweat started pouring from his brow.

"I know it gets hot here in Florida, Officer, but you're starting to sweat like a rat bastard. Why don't you start again, and this time, remember the oath you promised to keep. Who is behind all this shit?"

"Please, Joe, I have a family. Being here with you is putting me in jeopardy. Just let it go. I've told you everything I can. It's time to back off before you get one of us hurt."

"I guess we are going to spend some quality time together, Officer. I have all day and have no intention of—" Joe stopped suddenly as the young officer leaned over and fell into Joe's lap. "Shit," said Joe aloud. "What the—"

He looked around, but of course saw no one. In the distance, he heard a car speed away, its tires screeching. His blood pressure went sky-high for a moment before he was able to tell himself to stay calm. *I need to get the hell out of here and find some cover*, he thought. His mind raced, going into defense mode. His shirt was now wet with the officer's blood. *I was lucky he fell on me*, Joe thought, *or the shooter might have used me for target practice next.* His second thought was more disturbing: maybe he *was* the intended target! Either way, he felt more and more uneasy about this whole situation—and that was putting it mildly.

Joe knew he needed to make the call to the cops although he was unsure of how he would explain his circumstances without sounding crazy. After gingerly moving the limp corpse off his lap, he made the call and waited for the circus to begin.

The cops arrived in a moment, almost too quickly, he thought, and they interrogated him back at the station for hours; trying to explain he was an investigator for the district attorney's office was getting him nowhere, and telling them he was questioning the officer in reference to an arrest they made concerning Smith the previous day did not faze them at all. Although the cops tried to check their records in order to verify yesterday's arrest, they were, of course, told there was no record of any such arrest. At that point, they cuffed Joe and carted him off to a cell. His one phone call was to Harris

"Hey, man, things are not looking good for me," he said the second Harris picked up the line. "The officer who arrested Smith yesterday is dead, and I am the number one suspect in his death." Harris was too shocked to even respond, so Joe quickly continued to recount the afternoon's events. "The shot came from close range and a frontal angle, and I was sitting to the left of him, so it's virtually impossible that I could have shot him, but these morons don't believe a word I'm saying because when they called in to confirm yesterday's arrest, it wasn't on record, which is another damn twist to this sordid affair." He paused for a breath, then finished quickly, again before Harris could interrupt. "You need to get me out quick, Harris, 'cause I have a feeling I won't last long in here. I'm actually surprised they let me make a call." Joe wiped his brow with the back of his hand as he waited for Harris to digest the information.

On the other end of the line, Harris took a shaky breath. "Joe, I am so sorry for getting you wrapped up in this mess. I'll work as fast as I can to get you released. Just stay calm and don't answer anymore questions." After reading the Executioner's file, Harris felt he should have known better. He hated himself for allowing his friend to do any investigating concerning this man. It seemed as though the Executioner was untouchable, even for the great Joe Marble. "I'll do what I can," he reassured his friend.

"Please hurry." Joe's voice portrayed an urgency and fear Harris was unfamiliar with.

"I will," he said and hung up with Joe. Harris immediately paged Markita, asking her to find him a judge, any judge, who could hear Joe's arraignment and get him a bail hearing in the next few hours following formal charges, if there were any.

Markita was thrilled he entrusted her to do this for him, after all, she was just an intern. It was exciting to her, and she loved the adrenaline rush. After a few minutes of calling around, Markita paged back through to Harris with good news and bad news.

"Yes, Markita, what did you find?"

"Mr. Robertson, we received word Joe was formally charged, and so I have a bail hearing for you with Judge Poe in one hour."

"Thanks, Markita, you're a sweetheart." He could not believe he was so forward with her at work, but he was just so ecstatic she got him a hearing so soon he didn't even try to be as formal.

Markita blushed, knowing he was pleased with her efficiency.

It was late, so Harris told Markita to go home since he would likely be in court the rest of the day, but she pleaded with him to let her go to the hearing with him. Elated, he consented and asked if she wanted to ride over with him. He asked the question, hoping for a certain answer, and was not disappointed.

"I would love too, thanks," she replied in her soft, sexy flirtatious Southern voice.

Mercy, how am I supposed to concentrate on driving? he thought to himself. After meeting in the lobby, they strode quickly to the parking garage in relative silence and headed out to rescue Joe. When they arrived at the courthouse, they met with Joe and proceeded to appear in front of Judge Poe.

"Mr. Robertson," Poe began. "I do not appreciate being summoned this late in the afternoon. I was about to undertake a round of golf." He gazed sternly at Harris. "You better have a good argument for me to grant bail for this man."

"Your Honor," Harris began, staring right back at the judge. "Joe Marble has been a private investigator with the DA's office for ten years now and is an impeccable citizen. He was questioning the officer who was killed today in regard to a case he was working on for the DA's office."

"I am aware of who Mr. Marble is," Judge Poe responded curtly.

"Your Honor, if I may," said Harris. "Mr. Marble is innocent of this killing. I will, however, take Mr. Marble off this case. We will pursue other avenues concerning our investigation."

"Wise decision, Mr. Robertson, but let me ask Mr. Marble one question." He turned his head to regard Joe. "Of what, if anything, did the officer inform you?"

Harris could not believe the question had been asked, and judging from the look on Joe's face, he was just as shocked. The investigator was good at thinking on his feet, however, and after recent events, he felt he knew how to play the game.

"Your Honor," Joe replied as respectfully as he could. "The officer in question, the deceased, admitted to nothing more than making a big mistake in an arrest I was investigating."

"Were you satisfied with his answer, Mr. Marble?"

"Of course, Your Honor. He is, was, an officer of the law sworn to tell the truth."

Seemingly satisfied, Judge Poe returned his gaze to Harris. "Mr. Robertson, bail is set at one hundred thousand dollars. Do both of you understand the terms and conditions? If so, is the amount acceptable to you?"

Even though Harris thought this was ludicrous, he didn't push his luck. "Yes," he answered. "Your Honor, it is most acceptable." *As opposed to Joe spending the night in jail for a crime he didn't commit,* Harris thought to himself.

The judge slammed down his gavel, but stopped Harris as he turned to reach for Markita's arm to guide her out of the courtroom. "Mr. Robertson, one thing before you go." Harris turned, and Markita stopped and looked up at the judge. "I have great respect for your grandfather," he began, "but you, on the other hand, are trying my patience. Do you understand?"

"Yes, Your Honor. I beg Your Honor's pardon."

"Good night, gentlemen." The judge rose from the bench and left.

"What the hell did we just experience?" asked Joe ask they walked briskly from the now-empty courtroom.

"Your guess is as good as mine, but it certainly does leave us with some more unanswered questions, huh?"

"You bet your ass it does. I don't like this stinking mess at all," said Joe, his face growing red as he finally allowed himself to show his anger at the day's events.

Both men stopped at the entrance to the courthouse and held the doors open for Markita. Harris continued to discuss their next move as the three walked down the steps toward the street. "I haven't seen Hugh in two days," Harris admitted, "but when I do, I'll have him give us some guidance here."

"What are we going to do about my bail?" Joe asked, now sounding a bit worried. "A hundred thousand dollars is a bit out of my price range.

"I'm going to post it, don't worry, Joe," Harris replied with a wink.

"I'm not worried. You got me into this freakin' mess, and you are rich enough to throw money away. I am not a proud man, so go post it so I can get the hell out of here," he said, finally grinning.

The two old friends shared a halfhearted laugh that stopped abruptly as Markita spoke up at last. "Mr. Robertson, you were brilliant," she said, her heart pounding with exhilaration. Harris had nearly forgotten that Markita was with them, until he heard her angelic, sexy voice.

Joe looked down at the young intern, as if he too were aware of her for the first time that afternoon. "Yes, Harris, brilliant," he mocked, laughing.

Recovering, Harris found his own voice. "Don't mind him, Markita, he's a moron. Would you like to go for a drink and maybe catch a bite to eat before returning to the office to pick up your car?"

"Smooth," said Joe, laughing while holding his hand over his heart and rolling his eyes.

"I am rather famished," she replied shyly. Markita had not realized how hungry she was, and this opportunity would also give her more time to spend with Harris. Something she thought she'd like to do very much.

"There is a great place called the Bistro around the corner," Harris offered. "My father used to eat there all the time. It is a lovely place."

"Yes, just lovely," said Joe, mocking again.

"You better hush, Joe Marble, or I won't post your bail, now let's get out of here." He turned to Markita, elated she agreed to go with him, and guided her toward the bail office where they stopped and posted bail for Joe, then they headed for the Bistro.

Back on the sidewalk, Joe looked up and down the street, then at the two young people in front of him. "Well, thanks, Harris. Can't say it's been fun, but thanks just the same. I'll be in touch with you tomorrow, and we can plan our next move."

"Sounds good," Harris replied, his mind only half on what he and Joe would do next. "Lie low tonight, and I'll talk to you in the morning."

"It was a pleasure meeting you, Markita," Joe said as he shook Markita's hand. "You two have fun." He winked at Harris and set off down the street to catch a cab back to his car.

Harris watched his friend head down the sidewalk, then offered Markita his arm. "I hope you like this place," he said as they moved toward the corner in the opposite direction.

"I am sure I will, Harris."

"I have always liked the quaint English flair that it offers," he told her. "There is a dark oak horseshoe bar with brass footrails, and the booths are in red leather. They even have authentic British dartboards," he continued, almost wistfully. "The walls are covered in old historic pictures of places such as Buckingham Palace and the likes of Winston Churchill."

"Wow, Harris, you make me want to visit England."

"But that will take eight hours on a plane to get there and we are here now," he responded with a grin, once again holding the door open for her as they entered the Bistro. They were greeted almost immediately by an English barmaid named Brenda.

"How are ya, young Mr. Robertson, and oohh . . . look at this beautiful bird ya have with ya tonight," she greeted them in an authentic, and heavy, Cockney accent. Markita blushed, lowering her head a little in shyness while Harris beamed with pride. The barmaid was likely old enough to be Harris's grandmother, but she bubbled with youthful energy and enthusiasm. She had always told Harris stories about how his father loved the food at the Bistro.

"Handsome fellow was your father, young Mr. Robertson," she said with a roguish grin as she led the pair to an empty table near the back. "Here's a nice booth. Why don't you and your lady friend sit here, it's nice and quiet." The two of them sat down across from each other, Brenda eyeing them sagely. "What can I get ya lovebirds to drink?"

"I'll just have a glass of lemon water, please," said Markita.

"And I will have the same, please," Harris said.

"You can have something stronger if you like, Mr. Robertson—oops," Markita stopped to correct herself. "I mean Harris. It's OK with me, I won't tell anyone." Again, the shy smile.

"It's OK," Harris responded with a smile of his own. "I don't touch the stuff, it's evil."

"Oh," she sounded surprised, yet relieved, as she did not drink either. Her own father's alcoholism was the reason her mother never married him.

"What a day this one was." He let out a heavy sigh. He was glad the evening was winding down, and he was now with the most beautiful, angelic, and sexy girl in America "Well, this evening was interesting, to say the least, don't you think, Markita?" Her name rolled off his tongue like a chocolate-covered strawberry topped with whipped cream.

"I can only hope to be half the attorney you are," Markita replied admiringly.

"It was bizarre, wasn't it, Markita?" he said her name again. She noticed and giggled. *Oh my,* he thought trying to stay focused. "With my help, you will make a good attorney. With my guidance, you will make a brilliant one someday." *Man,* he said to himself, *there I go sounding arrogant and conceited just like my father.*

"From what I have seen so far, I'm training under the best there is," she said.

He liked the admiration she showed for him but remembered his uncle J telling him it was better to be humble than to be a pompous ass. It was hard for him to contain the emotions he felt for her; no one ever gave him butterflies in his stomach, nor flustered him the way she did. He wanted to leap out of his seat, take her in his arms and hold her tight, and tell her he never wanted her to leave him.

The barmaid brought him back to reality. "So what would ya two pretties like to order?" she asked.

"I will take a ham and pepper jack cheese sandwich please," said Markita.

"I will take the same, please," Harris answered again.

Brenda eyed the two critically, then pronounced, "I could tell ya two lovies were made for each over. You even like the same sandwiches!" The barmaid walked away chuckling to herself, leaving Harris and Markita both blushing.

"So, young lady, what do you think of Orlando? Do you like it here?" Harris asked, trying to smooth over the awkward moment.

"Yes, it is a beautiful city, but I miss Tallahassee. It is an older city and seems more personable than Orlando. Here, no one is from 'here.'"

"I am," Harris said with pride.

"Yes, my point exactly," said Markita.

"What do you mean?"

"Well, you seem different from most everyone else I've met. You don't seem to have many friends, and from what I can tell, you lack a girlfriend as well."

He wondered if she was fishing and smiled to let her know it pleased him. "No, no, I don't, but I choose to be alone. I want to be a judge someday like my father. I know between work and studying it takes a lot of my time, and few women can tolerate such commitment. They need a lot of attention, and when I find the right lady, I want to give her all of mine," he was starting to get flustered again.

"You are so sweet, Harris," Markita replied; it was hard to tell if she was joking with him or not.

"What about you, Markita, do you have a boyfriend?"

"No, not at all," she answered, taking a sip of her drink. "Guys are intimidated by my desire to become a judge. It scares them away."

"Good, then I stand a chance," he said, his face turned flaming red. He smiled, trying to hide his embarrassment, not believing what he'd just said aloud.

"If you don't mind me asking," Markita said, changing the subject. "Something seems wrong with this guy Smith and his arrest. Isn't it strange the cops arrested your friend Joe? The evidence is so weak."

He thought for a moment before answering her. "There are some things I cannot discuss with you, and I'm sorry, but Smith is one of them. Please don't get offended, but I would prefer you not think about Smith. Put today aside and don't dwell on what happened."

"You can't tell a curious woman not to dwell on today's peculiar events and not expect her to ask questions, Harris. I'm bursting to know what is going on."

"Nothing you need to worry your pretty little head about."

"Don't patronize me," Markita said impatiently, raising her chin with pride. "I am a worthy ally for you, not just some dumb intern."

"Oh, Markita, I didn't mean to offend you. I just want to keep you safe."

"What do you mean? Is this case dangerous?"

"I hope not, but there's nothing for you to worry about, Markita, I promise. It's just this particular case is frustrating me."

"Harris, I am not stupid by any means. If you need an ally or friend, please confide in me. I would love to help. I know I am a woman in a man's world, and the law is not always just. I know there is corruption in our judicial system. It is one reason why I chose this career path. I want to fight for the cause . . . the cause of justice." She was beginning to get mad at herself for sounding like a college protester.

"You are admirable to a tee, Markita. I have the same passion and enthusiasm you do. I can appreciate where you are coming from, but the fact is, there is still your safety to consider. Some things need to be handled with extreme confidentiality."

Markita was getting a little perturbed at Harris thinking she was some wallflower who could not compete in a man's world. Her mother brought her up to learn her place, yet strived to attain what she wanted in life. Her mother taught her to trust what she believed in. Markita was not afraid of Harris's world. She was accustomed to the secret phone calls and mysterious meetings her mother disappeared to for hours at a time when she was growing up. It was what initially drove her to come to embrace this world and lifestyle.

"I never knew my father," Markita told Harris. "But my mother always told me he was strong and a fighter, yet charming and passionate. He was a good man, caught in a trap, she said. The system manipulated him from the beginning of his career. My mother protected him while she could, but in the end, the corruption sucked her in too. It's the reason why she uprooted and escaped to Tallahassee. So please don't shut me out because you think I am shy and timid. Beneath this exterior is a hungry cat waiting to get her claws into a juicy case."

Harris smiled, excited that Markita seemed to embrace the law with the same passion as he felt. He thought about his uncle J for a second and how he would have made some quick-witted comment about Markita's last comment, something like: with as much catlike enthusiasm as Markita has, she should be sponsored by Meow Mix. He choked on his water laughing.

"Are you all right?" she asked.

"Oh, yes, sorry, just a silly thought."

"Care to share?" asked Markita.

"Oh no, it's nothing," Harris said smiling, knowing if he shared his thought with her, she would throw her water over him. Her feistiness surprised him. It was most attractive. She was beautiful, angelic, sexy, and a spitfire to boot. Imagining her driving around in a burgundy 1966 classic Mustang, he grinned, telling himself he would purchase one for her one day.

His brief daydream was interrupted when Miss Brenda brought their food; they chatted and laughed together while they ate.

"Do you dance?" Markita asked him suddenly.

"No, I have two left feet."

"Then I'll teach you. Dancing is another passion of mine. I am sure if you give it a whirl, you could do it." She smiled, seeing him out of his comfort zone.

"I'll try anything once," he said warily, "but I warn you, I'm bound to hurt your toes."

"It's OK, I'm a good teacher. If you are willing to partake in the challenge, I would love to show you how."

The butterflies began fluttering in his stomach. He felt so lucky accompanying such a beautiful woman, but he couldn't help wondering why she did not know more about her own father; he decided not to press her about him in case it was painful for her.

"What does your mother do, if you don't mind me asking?" he asked instead.

"No, it's OK. She was a legal secretary here in Orlando for many years, and then she got offered a position at the governor's office. She moved to Tallahassee and then retired a few years ago."

"Wow, the governor's office," Harris responded admiringly. "No wonder you are such a smart lady—you must take after your mother."

"Why thank you, Harris. She would love to hear you compliment her."

"I would love to meet her sometime," he said, being polite.

"I'm sure you will one day. What about your mother? You said your father died, so is she alone?"

"No, she married my father's brother, Joshua, but I call him uncle J. He is a fantastic guy, and I could not have asked for a better father figure. My mother is happy with him."

"I would like to meet them sometime," she said, smiling and being polite, returning his respect.

He could not stop the words from leaving his tongue as he heard himself ask, "How about Sunday?"

"Sunday what?" she replied.

He could not believe he was going to repeat the question, but clearing his throat, he tried again. "This Sunday, would you like to meet them? I eat there every Sunday."

"I would love to," she answered with real enthusiasm.

"Whoa, wait a minute before you get all excited. My uncle J is a ham, and he will interrogate you worse than a hurricane prosecutor. He also tells the oldest and worst jokes you have ever heard."

"Great, I'm up for the challenge," Markita replied with a grin.

"How about I pick you up at noon?" Markita took a pen from her purse and wrote her address and phone number on a napkin and handed it to him. He wrote his cell phone number on a napkin for her. "I hope you don't take this the wrong way," Harris said after they exchanged numbers, "but it's better if we keep this under our hats. Hugh does not like the staff mingling."

"It's fine. I don't mind being discreet. Tara already stares at me and laughs from time to time."

"Oh, what about?" he asked as casually as possible.

"Hmm, someone sent me twelve beautiful roses with one white one in the middle and no card attached. My suspicion is she thinks it was you," Markita replied slyly. Harris nearly choked on his water again.

Brenda returned to collect their plates and leave the check.

"Your father would be proud of you, young Mr. Robertson," she said, sizing up the two of them again. "You picked a lovely lady. In fact, she's a beauty like 'is secretary that he used to come in here with." The barmaid's comment about his father's secretary went straight over Harris's head; he was too busy recovering from Markita's comments about the mysterious flowers and was simply grateful the barmaid returned when she did. Again his face was burning with embarrassment.

"Thank you," he responded somewhat numbly. "Markita is an intern at my office, we're just . . ." he paused for a second. He wanted to say they were friends, but he wasn't sure how she would respond. Maybe she would think he was too forward.

"Friends," Markita said for him.

"I know these things, dearies, and I can tell ya both. Ya gonna be more than friends, mark me words." She walked away chuckling.

Harris left the cash on the table with a larger tip than normal; he liked what Brenda had said about them being more than friends. He did not want the evening to end, but knew it was time to take her back to the office to pick up her car. He walked with her and made sure she got in her car safely.

"Good night, Harris. Thank you for a wonderful evening. I will see you in the morning."

"No, thank you, Markita. I cannot remember a time when I enjoyed myself this much. Drive safely." Wanting to kiss her, but not daring to try, he simply waved as he backed away from her car. He watched her drive away, then made his way to his own car, turning his radio to his favorite soft-rock station. He drove home, smiling all the way.

He did not sleep well that night, his thoughts racing from the bail hearing to poor Joe's arrest, then back to his earlier encounter with Smith. "What a day," his restless mind told him. Trying to clear his head, he decided to think about Markita so he could sleep, but at first, it was not happening. His mind saw her eyes open wide and wanting him, her sweet smile enticing him, and her kissable lips teasing him. Drifting off at last, his lingering thought was of them naked and making love.

The alarm woke him up an a few hours later; Harris dragged himself out of bed, showering and getting ready as slow as a snail. Most days he limited himself to one cup of coffee, but he drank two cups this morning in an effort to wake up, knowing he was going to have another rough day. "I need to get moving," he said out loud. He was putting his cup in the sink when his phone rang.

"Hello," Harris said answering the call.

"Howdy, Harris, it's Friday, and your mother and I have not heard from you all week. You were supposed to call us by Wednesday. You are coming on Sunday, right, son?"

"Of course, Uncle J, and before you ask, I will bring the rocky road."

"Now, did I say anything about ice cream?"

"You don't have to, Uncle J. You ask me the same thing every week."

"Are you bringing anyone with you?" Joshua asked him, certain his answer would be no.

"See, you always ask me the same questions, but for once, I have a different answer for you. Yes, in fact, I am bringing a friend with me. How do you feel about that, Uncle J?"

He could almost hear his uncle's jaw drop to the floor. After a moment's pause, he replied, "I know your mother will be over the moon. Of course, I knew you had it in you, son."

"I didn't say it was a female friend," Harris teased, working to straighten his tie as he balanced the phone on one shoulder.

"Darnik," said Joshua, disappointed.

"I don't know anyone else in this world who says darnik, Uncle J. You are just too funny. Oh, by the way . . . gotcha! Not only is she female, but she is the most beautiful girl in the whole world. Her name is Markita."

"You wait, you rascal! I'll get you back for teasing me! I bet you haven't taken her out on a date yet though, have you?"

"As a matter of fact, we went out to eat last night, thank you very much."

"Great, then we will see you both on Sunday," Joshua said, excited for his nephew.

"I hope you both behave, especially you, Uncle J."

"What do you mean? I always behave."

"Well, I'm not sure if she is, or ever will be, ready for the duck joke."

"Now, Harris, would I tell her about the duck on her first visit?"

"You bet your ass you would!"

"Hey, hey, enough of that language, you young whippersnapper."

"Mercy, Uncle J, when will you ever update your material to the new century? I swear you think you're still in the sixties!" Harris and his uncle started laughing.

"I hate to cut you short, but I need to get going. I'm already behind for the day."

"You can't cut me any shorter, I am only five seven and a half, as it is."

"Now see, you got me below the belt."

"It would be if you cut me short."

"I can't take any more," Harris said, continuing to chuckle at his uncle's awful humor. "I'll see you Sunday. Give my love to Mom, and I love you too, Uncle J." He meant every word.

"I love you too, Harris. Take care and see you Sunday with . . . what's her name again?"

"It's Markita. I would appreciate you remembering it."

"We will see you and Marcia Brady on Sunday."

"You are not funny, Uncle J!"

"Oops, a minor slip of the tongue."

"Make sure you don't slip on Sunday, funny guy."

"Who me, son? Never. I promise I won't slip on Sunday, I'll wait until Monday." They hung up, both laughing at each other, just like they always did.

Harris was running late now and rushed out of the house. He could not wait to see Markita's beautiful face at work. He had a bounce in his step as he walked toward his office, but once again, she was not at her desk. His heart sank with disappointment.

"Good morning, Tara," he greeted his secretary without enthusiasm.

"Good morning, Mr. Robertson," she replied, that knowing smile again on her face. "I just got a call from Markita. Her car wouldn't start this morning, something about the battery, so she's running late. But she did say she would be here," she added finally.

"Thanks for letting me know, Tara," Harris responded, feeling a bit better now. "I have some phone calls to make this morning, but I would like to know when Hugh gets in, or is he here already?"

"No, he actually called this morning to say he will not return until Monday. He was handling something urgent for the governor."

"Three days in a row without a word from him is unacceptable!" Harris nearly shouted in exasperation. "I need to talk to him right away. Did he leave you a number where we can at least contact him?"

"Yes, he did, but just for emergencies he said. I can give it to you once you are in your office, if you'd like."

"Thanks, Tara." Harris entered his office, and Tara paged through the number to him. But before he could put a call in to Hugh, his private line rang.

"Good morning, Harris."

"Hey, Joe, how are you this morning? Recovered from your little adventure, have you?"

"I don't think you ever recover from those kinds of trips. It was a short stay, but it was one I could have done without. It was long enough to know I do not ever want to go back. How was your date last night? Did you get lucky?"

"That is so inappropriate, Joe. But I had a great time, and it was not a date. We were both hungry."

"You are a chickenshit, Robertson. I bet you didn't even get her number, did you?"

"As a matter of fact, I did."

"Maybe you're not such a chickenshit after all," Joe mused. "So anyway, I went to the morgue this morning. I thought I would come and check if the medical examiner was going to do an autopsy on the officer who died on me yesterday. I wanted to know what caliber the bullet was, but like everything else to do with this case, the body never arrived, it's like it vanished."

"What do you mean? It is not there?" Harris's voice started to rise with annoyance.

"It's evident, at least based on the lack of evidence, that there was no shooting yesterday, thus no dead body," Joe said, his voice full of sarcasm.

"It gets more interesting by the minute, doesn't it?" Harris retorted.

"I sure would like to know who is behind all this," said Joe.

"It's OK. We'll get to the bottom of this or die trying."

"Hey, I'm too young to die and far too damn handsome," said Joe, trying to lighten Harris's mood.

"It is weird," Harris said, voicing a concern that had been growing over the past few days. "Hugh has been gone for three days now without any word, it is unlike him. I am beginning to have concerns about him too."

"You think he is involved?" Joe asked.

"I'm worried he might have met with foul play."

"Well, if and when you find something out, let me know."

"Will do." Harris tried to respond with a confidence he wasn't sure he felt. "I'm going to do a bit more digging into the arresting officer's background on my own, this morning. I also need to stop by the courthouse and pick up some transcripts from Officer Parker's son's trial along with your bail hearing. I'll get back with you later."

"Just be careful, Harris," Joe reminded him. Then he added, "Hey, if you're any kind of man, ask the chick out on a date. Don't let us men down," he said in his deepest "tough guy" voice.

"Later," said Harris with a grin as he hung up the phone. He then dialed the number Tara gave him for Hugh.

"Hey, Harris, how are you?" Hugh greeted him on the second ring.

"I'm fine, sir, but there are a lot of unbelievable occurrences happening around here, and I need to make you aware of them."

"Like what?" Hugh asked, uneasy about what might be coming.

"Well first, there was the bail hearing for Smith. The warrant was recalled, which is odd in itself as I personally saw it, but something even more extraordinary happened when I had Joe Marble follow up on the warrant. He was informed there was never a warrant issued. He went to the impound lot to check out the car, but it was stripped, the backseat was missing, and the security guard on duty was found suffocated. And then there's the troubling fact that Smith was released from jail, and strangely enough, no one knows who released him."

"How the hell did he get out?" said Hugh, sounding frantic. This information blew his whole plan of having Harris convict Smith and get him put away so he could remain safe once his takeover of the Practice was complete. Now he would have to start making inquiries of his own, taking up more of his precious time.

"Your guess is as good as mine, Hugh. It gets more bizarre though. Joe went to meet with the arresting officer, and during the meeting, the officer was shot by an unknown gunman before Joe could get any information out of him. The police then arrested Joe for the murder, which was ludicrous. I got a quick bail hearing for Joe yesterday afternoon, but Judge Poe asked Joe some peculiar questions before setting bail for $100,000. I paid his bail in order for the judge to release him. And finally, as if all this weren't enough, Joe went to the morgue this morning to investigate the shooting and now there's no record of the body ever arriving." Harris paused, barely believing himself all the bizarre occurrences of the past few days. Hugh appeared to feel the same way.

"Jesus, Harris, what the hell is going on there?"

"That's the million-dollar question of the day," Harris responded, a bit defensively. "I'm doing everything I can to find out, but the door closes on me at every turn. I was hoping you could shed some light on a few things."

"Not right now, Harris. I'm in the middle of a crisis myself. I'm hoping to return to the office on Monday. Do you think you can hold the fort until then?"

"Of course, Hugh. If I come up with anything else I'll let you know."

"I hate to say this, Harris, but I am already behind schedule taking the time to talk to you now, so if it could wait until Monday, I would appreciate it."

"Sure, no worries, Hugh," Harris said with a confidence he did not fully feel. "I'll save it all for you when you return."

"Thanks, Harris. You're a good man. See you Monday morning." Hugh hung up.

"OK," said Harris to the empty phone line. He sat back in his chair bewildered. He felt as if he received no guidance from Hugh whatsoever, just more questions. *How could all these inconsistencies be possible?* he asked himself.

If it was one big conspiracy, it had to involve several people. It was time to call his grandfather.

He paged Tara. "Judge Harris, please."

"One second, sir, I will put you through."

Seconds later, he heard his grandfather's gruff "Hello."

"Grandfather, it's Harris, how are you, sir?"

"How are you, son? What a wonderful surprise. Is everything all right?"

"Yes, Grandfather, I'm fine."

"Your mother, she's fine too, right?"

"Yes, Grandfather," he repeated. "Everyone is OK."

"Thank goodness, I was worried there for a moment."

Harris found this somewhat odd, but he had questions he needed answered, so he pushed forward. "Grandfather, I need some advice and maybe even some help, if you can spare me some time."

"Of course, Harris. Anything for you. Is it a lady?" he asked. Harris could almost hear the grin on his grandfather's face. He wished it were something that simple.

"No, sir, I wish it was. It seems there is a huge cover-up going on here. I am not sure how to proceed."

"Well, Harris, I don't know how I can help you, but fire away. Maybe telling me might help you to sort things out."

"Thank you, sir. I have a suspicion the Practice might be heavily involved, along with some judges. I have noticed certain criminals are getting off scot-free, not just the little cases, but also some of Hugh's bigger ones. It seems whenever he goes up against one of the Practice's defense attorneys, he loses, and I know he's a better prosecutor."

"What do you think the cover-up is, Harris? Are you insinuating Hugh is corrupt?" the judge asked, trying to sound concerned.

"Well, Grandfather, it all started with this guy named P. Smith, a.k.a. the Executioner." The judge listened intently, shocked to hear Harris even knew Smith's name. As Harris recounted the same events he had just outlined for Hugh, the old judge's agitation grew. By the time Harris told him about the judge's warning at Joe's bail hearing, Judge Harris was seething. As Harris wrapped up his story, the judge rose from his seat and began pacing back and forth, trying to remain calm. Once he regained his composure, he proceeded with the conversation, trying to sound unbiased, while inside he was ready to have someone killed.

"Who was the judge, son?" Judge Harris asked through clenched teeth.

"Judge Poe," Harris replied. "I know he is known as a fair judge, but he was acting inappropriately. I don't know what the hell is going on, but I can tell you, Grandfather, I don't like it."

"You're a good man, Harris, just like your father used to be. It sounds like a lot is going on there. I will call Hugh and get his take on all these discrepancies. You know Hugh and I are good friends."

"Yes, Grandfather, I would appreciate it, except he's been unavailable for three days and has no clue regarding the situation. I filled him in this morning, just a few minutes ago as a matter of fact, but he won't return back to the office until Monday, so I'm afraid he can't help you."

"Well, Harris, leave things with me. I will call Judge Poe and the medical examiner. I still have a lot of pull down there in Orlando, you know. I'll make a few inquiries at the Practice. The place has never been the same since your father sold it." No one knew that Mark Robertson had secretly sold the firm back to Judge Harris, using Stewart Pope as the front man to make the purchase. This was something he planned on keeping a secret from his grandson.

"I know, Grandfather. It is really starting to gain a bad reputation around here."

"Let me see what I can do, and I will get back with you. Please do me a favor in the meantime, Harris. Stay away from Smith. He does not sound like a character that you need to mess with. Do you understand me?" The warning here was genuine.

"OK, and thanks for listening to me, Grandfather. I feel better after consulting with you, like something might actually get done."

"You're a good man, Harris," his grandfather said again. "You know you can come to me anytime with anything. And don't worry, these things have a way of sorting themselves out. I will get on it right away for you and call you back as soon as I know something. Don't forget to stay away from Smith," the judge reiterated sternly.

"Yes, sir." Harris scrunched up his face in puzzlement as he hung up the phone; it almost sounded like his grandfather actually knew this Smith character. Of course, he may have run across him in his courtroom from time to time, given Smith's numerous arrests. Just never a conviction, it seemed.

Chapter Four

The Johnsons

Late one Monday afternoon, Mr. and Mrs. Edward Johnson received a letter from the Charterhouse Nursing Facility in Orlando. It was from a Stewart Pope, Esquire. It asked them to make arrangements to visit him at their earliest convenience. Intrigued, the Johnsons discussed what this man's intentions might be, wondering what he could want with them, an elderly couple in their eighties, living the quiet life of retirement. Mr. Johnson knew "Esquire" meant he might be an attorney, maybe some relative they did not know about. Pondering over the letter, he smiled, thinking maybe someone died and left them some money. Either way, Mr. Johnson was curious to find out what this was all about. Calling the nursing facility, he set an appointment to visit the mysterious Mr. Pope for the following Monday morning.

Upon arrival on the appointed day, the curious couple checked in at the front desk. They noticed on their way how modern and upscale the facility looked. It was located on fifteen acres of land and was filled with beautiful tall oak and maple trees, all surrounding a shallow, crystal-clear lake. Spread out in the shade were several wooden benches conveniently placed for the residents to partake in their favorite activity of the day: feeding the ducks. Each room of the main building enjoyed a large picture window, allowing for plenty of sunlight. Both the building and the grounds were immaculate, making it easy for the Johnsons to observe how expensive the nursing home must be.

As they waited at the front desk, a rather plump nurse with a bubbly personality greeted them. "How may I help you?" she asked cheerfully.

"We are here to see Stewart Pope?" Mr. Johnson stated tentatively. "We have an appointment."

"Oh wonderful!" the nurse exclaimed. "Mr. Pope has been with us for a few years now, but he has never had any visitors. This is so exciting. Are you relatives?" she asked, her curiosity aroused.

"No, ma'am. We received a letter from Mr. Pope asking us to come here."

"Well great," she said with enthusiasm, motioning for them to follow her, taking them to Stewart Pope's room. The nurse knocked loudly on a door far down the hall on the left and called out Mr. Pope's name. After waiting a moment, she turned the knob and entered the room with the Johnsons following behind.

"Good morning, Mr. Pope! You have visitors, isn't that nice?" she said, her words loud and running together as if talking to a child.

Stewart Pope was sitting in a big chair with two pillows behind his back, staring out of his own picture window across the expansive lawns. The nurse walked over to him, leaning over to fluff his pillows. She patted his hand, smiling. "I'll check on you in a while, Mr. Pope. You enjoy your visit." The nurse then left, and the Johnsons sat in two nearby chairs, facing Stewart Pope.

"How are you, Mr. Pope?" Edward asked nervously, glancing over at his wife as he did so. This man was around their age, yet they were not quite sure how to proceed.

"Fine, thank you, who are you?" Stewart answered gruffly, although he sounded competent enough.

"We are Mr. and Mrs. Edward Johnson? You wrote to us, asking if we would pay you a visit? I must say your letter intrigued us. Your name didn't ring a bell with us, but then again, we are not as young as we once were," Edward explained, taking a stab at some light humor.

"Well, that makes two of us. I don't know you either," Stewart replied, returning his gaze to the window.

Edward looked over at his wife, opening his eyes wide as if to say, *Help me here.* His wife merely shook her head in confusion, saying nothing, so he carried on. "You signed the letter Stewart Pope, Esquire. Are you, or were you, an attorney?" Edward was hoping the question would jog his memory.

"Why, do you need one?" Stewart asked them, turning back to the couple with one eyebrow cocked higher than the other, looking confused.

"Oh, no, sir, not at all, we thought maybe a relative might have left us something in a will we didn't know about."

"Then I am baffled as to why you nice folks are here, because I haven't practiced law for years, and I don't remember writing to you. How long ago did you say you got this letter?"

"We received your letter last week." Edward Johnson could tell the man was a little uncomfortable with them being there, but now he was becoming frustrated.

The room was silent for a few moments. Stewart scratched his head. "Johnson. Johnson," he mused. Why does the name ring a bell?" He strained to remember. Stewart's eyes looked empty at times; at other times, it seemed like a glimmer of light returned when he would remember something.

"The only time my wife and I had anything to do with lawyers is when our son Jake was convicted of a crime he did not commit and was executed for it," Edward Johnson said bitterly. His voice saddened as he explained about his son.

"Ah . . . now I know who you fine folks are," Stewart said, proud of himself for finally remembering. He continued, "Jake Johnson, your son, he was accused of hanging an African American on a tree, right?"

"Yes, he was!" said Edward defensively.

"Terrible thing," Stewart mused. "You know Jake didn't do it though, right?"

"Well, we have spent our entire retirement and most of our lives trying to clear our son's name to no avail though," said Edward, still on the defensive.

"You must not give up. Jake was innocent—at least of the hanging."

"What do you mean?" asked Edward, confused.

"He was busy raping a woman at the time of the hanging."

"How do you know?" Edward whispered, slumping back in his chair and hating what he was hearing about his son, not knowing if anything Pope said was true.

"I was in the room when he came to the law firm. It was called H & H Law Firm back then. Old man Harris and his son were partners. You would know it as the Practice now. I heard your son tell his attorney that at the time of the hanging, he was on the other side of town attacking a young woman. He told us that during the rape, the woman, of course, was fighting him off. When he went to put his hand over her mouth, he scratched her right cheekbone by her ear. He explained to his attorney that the wound was bad enough to have left a decent-sized scar."

The old man continued. "Jake told the attorney if he would call her, she could easily identify him. He seemed willing enough to tell them about that crime. I recall him telling the attorney the reason he went after her was that he was disgusted by her having had sex with a black man. His intentions were to rape her then kill her, but he was disturbed before he could carry out his act, and so instead he settled for scarring her face and he ran."

Edward and his wife sat in horrified disbelief as they listened to their son being called a rapist and a racist. Edward's heart broke at the bittersweet news, but at least now he could get Jake's name cleared of the murder charges. Knowing they could not bring their son back devastated him, but clearing his name was still something of extreme importance to him and his wife, as was wanting the real murderer found and brought to justice.

"Do you remember the woman's name?" asked Edward after a few moments of stunned silence. He was now sitting on the edge of his seat in anticipation.

"No," Stewart shook his head. "I can't say that I do. I'm terrible when it comes to names and dates. But"—he raised a finger as a thought had come to him—"I do remember Jake knew her though. I wish for you, nice folks, I could recall more. My memory is not what it used to be, you know." Stewart stopped abruptly. The empty stare returned to his eyes as he asked them, "Who are you, people, and why are you in my room?"

A frustrated Edward answered, "We're Jake Johnson's parents, remember? You were telling us the truth about what happened to our son." Stewart sat in silence, staring out the window again. "Please try to remember, Mr. Pope," Edward begged. "It is so important to Jake's mother and me," Edward tried again, now desperate.

The sound of Edward's voice seemed to startle the old man; scratching his head for a moment, Stewart's fleeting memories began to return, and he began speaking somewhat coherently again.

"Oh. Oh yes, I'm sorry, it's coming back to me now. I do remember Ronald, his lawyer, being agitated with Jake. He left him in his office while he went outside to calm down. Ronald was an angry young man in those days."

"Why was the rape never brought up when Jake went in front of the judge to enter his plea?" Edward asked quickly, afraid of Pope's memory slipping again.

"I don't think your son was well educated, if I remember correctly," Stewart replied. "I'm not sure Jake knew *what* he was pleading guilty to. Ronald was a master at manipulation and intimidation. The judge and district attorney may very well have orchestrated both the plea and the verdict, giving the judge free rein when it came to the sentencing."

"But," Edward interrupted, confused. "You knew the truth. You could have stopped our son from being executed for something he clearly did not do. Why didn't you say something?" he stated angrily.

"I was asked to leave the room before that information was shared," Stewart explained simply. "It was several hours later before your son left the law office. I did not know back then what had transpired between your son and Ronald, and I still don't."

"I cannot imagine why my son would plead guilty to murder when he had a solid alibi," Edward said again, bewildered. He looked over at his wife and, seeing tears in her eyes, reached over to clasp her trembling hand, trying to comfort her.

"Something more must have transpired in that room when I was sent out. It's all I can tell you about that. I don't quite know how to answer your questions about your son," Stewart continued. "But this I do know: the Harrises back then were into some very bad practices. They had ties to the Klan. They also had a small ring of officials who helped them prevail in many of their trials." Stewart paused a moment to collect his thoughts, then went on.

"After your son was sentenced, Judge Zielinski, the man who presided at your son's trial, unexpectedly retired, and Jake's lawyer was sent away by H & H to an office in Oakmont, Pennsylvania, until the case was out of the news and long forgotten. Ronald's return to the H & H Law Firm is when things drastically started to change. After his father died and he inherited what is now the Practice, he talked me and two other partners into joining what he called the Order. We were promised that our clients, for the most part, would be set free. Most of all, by following orders, we would be filthy rich, both of which he accomplished for all of us. You need to understand that back then, at least for us, it was all about winning cases and making money. Justice had no part in what we did. Over the years, the Order brought more law enforcement officers, even other city officials, onto its growing payroll. It was quite a booming business. And we were all very rich."

"How come none of you were ever caught?" Edward asked, half in curiosity, half in anger that such a corrupt system could have existed for so long.

"We were well protected by the Order. We had little to fear when so many were on our payroll. And we paid them well."

Stewart rubbed a gnarled and arthritic hand across his face, seeming to sink lower into his easy chair. "I can't speak for anyone else," he continued, his voice showing the guilt he now felt. "But in the end, my conscience caught up with me, so I left. When Ronald's son-in-law, Mark Robertson, left the Practice to serve as the district attorney, the old man sought me out and forced me to come back. I was reluctant to return, obviously, but Ronald had too much dirt on me. At first, I was to be a silent business partner, but they blackmailed me into throwing the Bellamy case. It was a high-profile televised trial back in the day." Stewart stopped and shook his head almost admiringly. "Ronald Harris is a brilliant man. Even today he controls what happens in this city."

Edward had been sitting in silent fury at the thought of corruption in the judicial system, and even more so at the knowledge that this corruption had cost his son his life; it pained him to no end. His son's execution, however, was now starting to make some kind of sense for the first time since their ordeal began so many years ago. At the mention of the name Ronald Harris, however, Edward was jolted from his silent thoughts.

"Ronald Harris?" he repeated. "You mean *Judge* Harris, the one who sits on our Florida Supreme Court?" he asked abruptly. "Is he the same Ronald Harris who represented our son all those years ago? Is he the Ronald Harris you are referring too? I don't believe it!" Edward was beside himself, his blood pressure rising by the minute. His voice started to rise in anger. "You mean to tell me you knew a young man was innocent, and you let him be executed for a crime he did not commit?" He was nearly screaming now. "And now, the man who was supposed to defend him, who also knew the truth, sits in a position of power while my son rots in his grave?"

Suddenly, the bubbly nurse came back into the room, but she was no longer bubbly. "I am afraid you will have to leave now," she said sternly, glaring at Edward. "We can hear you all the way in the nurses' station! Mr. Pope is a sick man—you should be ashamed."

"Mr. Pope can rot in hell for all I care."

Both the nurse's and Edward's heads swung sharply in the direction of Mrs. Johnson. She sat stiffly in her seat, her knuckles white from where she was gripping her husband's hand.

"He can rot in hell," she repeated, tears now flooding from her eyes.

Mr. Johnson spoke up, echoing his wife's words. "You're right, nurse, he *is* a sick man. And I hope he rots in hell too." Rising angrily from his chair, Edward pulled at his wife's hand, motioning at her to leave with him.

"Who were those people, nurse?" Stewart whined. "Why was he getting angry with me?" The old man was now agitated, banging his fist down on the arm of his chair.

"Calm down, Mr. Pope," the nurse said soothingly. "Those people are leaving now. You'll be just fine. Here, let me fluff up your pillows again for you." Stewart calmed down, drifting back into his familiar world of hazy memories and half-remembered faces.

After rushing home, Edward Johnson went straight to the closet in the guest room, Jake's old room, and pulled out his old scrapbooks. He went through all the newspaper clippings, every article pertaining to his son's trial, finally taking out the one that reported on the execution date and wrote across it in red pen: "Ronald Harris hanged the African American. Justice will be served."

Edward fought back the tears as he wrote the words, his heart heavy, aching for his son. He could not remember a time in his eighty-nine years of life ever being this full of hatred, except for the day of his son's execution. Shaking his head, he reflected on the morning's visit, not wanting to believe anything he heard since Pope's mind was not exactly clear. At least he knew his son had not murdered anyone. It saddened Edward Johnson, however, to learn his son was a both a rapist and a racist.

Edward knew Stewart Pope had just provided them with the ammunition they needed to pursue a lawsuit that could clear their son's name. The first obstacle Edward could foresee was finding an attorney in this city who was not corrupt, and second, one who would be brave enough to go up against the chief justice on Florida's Supreme Court. *We will have to put a second mortgage on our house,* thought Edward. *But I will get this done if it is the last thing I do—or I will die trying.*

Brilliant, it's Sunday morning, thought Harris. Yesterday had been one of the slowest days he could ever remember. Jumping out of bed, he rushed to get his shower. Normally, he would use his everyday soap and deodorant, but today was going to be special, one of many he hoped, where he would be picking up the sexiest girl in the world.

For this occasion, he would use the expensive-smelling stuff his uncle J and mom bought for him every Christmas. "Hmm . . . Not bad," he said, smelling his favorite cologne and making sure not to put too much on. He didn't want to appear too obvious. Looking in the mirror, he grinned at himself. "Mmm . . . Mmm . . . ! I do smell good! Even if I say so myself!" He grinned again and brushed his light mustache into place with his finger. Pulling on his favorite jeans and newest maroon polo shirt, he flashed a mischievous grin as he looked in the full-length mirror on his wardrobe door. "Hmm . . ." he repeated. "Not bad."

Pacing through his condo, he tried keeping himself occupied until it was time to go pick up Markita. The closer the time got to noon, the more nervous he became. At eleven thirty, he left his condo to go get her. Before starting the Jag, he browsed through all his CDs looking for the perfect one to play, finally deciding on Journey's *Greatest Hits*; it was his favorite group. He wanted to make sure the song "Open Arms" was playing when she got in the car with him, hoping she would get the hint. *I hope she likes it,* he thought. It only took him twenty minutes to get to her apartment, and so he was early.

Knocking on her door, his body trembled slightly; he hoped when she saw him, she wouldn't hear his knees knocking together. He was about to knock again when she opened the door.

"Oh my gosh, Markita, you are . . ." He paused, stunned, amazed, and flabbergasted.

"Oh no, what's wrong? Is this dress not appropriate?"

He could not stop himself from letting her know his approval. "Oh no, ma'am," he grinned, trying to relax. "You're the sexiest woman I have ever seen." He felt his heart double beat; the butterflies were going crazy inside his stomach. Markita blushed, her cheeks red as an English tea rose. "Thanks. You are so sweet," she managed to say. "Would you like to come in for a while?" she asked, recovering somewhat.

"Thank you," replied Harris and entered her apartment. They talked for over an hour before Harris finally stood up and walked over to her. "May I?" Harris held out his hand hoping she would accept. "Thank you," she said, taking hold of his extended hand. The two of them walked out to his car where, of course, he opened her door for her like a gentleman. Once in the driver's seat, he popped in the Journey CD, The song he purposely chose began to play.

"Oh, I love this song. It's one of my favorites," Markita said, smiling at him.

"Great! We love the same kind of music," Harris said, smiling back. "I somehow knew we would." Confidence showed in him now. Driving to his parents' house, they were quiet, both enjoying the music. As soon as they arrived, Harris jumped out of the car, rushing to open her door for her.

"Thank you, Harris. You are a gentleman."

Opening the door to the house, they walked right in. "Hey," he called. "We're here! Where is everyone?" His uncle Josh flew out from the kitchen.

"Hey, Uncle J, how are things?"

"How, wow, wow dee there!" His uncle screeched in amazement.

"Now, now, Uncle J, don't start."

"Come on in, sweetheart, make yourself at home," Josh said, gesturing Markita toward the living room. As she walked past him, he raised his eyebrows up and down at Harris. "You sure are a sweet purdy lil' thang," Josh said in his best Southern accent.

"Uncle J, stop now. What did I tell you? Behave, please." He rolled his eyes and turned to Markita. "Don't mind him, Markita, he is being an arse."

"I haven't been called one of those in at least a week." Josh grinned.

"It's OK," Markita said pleasantly. "How are you, sir? It's so nice to meet you."

"Oh, my dear, I am fine, fine, and phew, just fine."

"I am warning you, Uncle J, you are pushing me," Harris said, smiling at him.

"Did you bring the rocky road?" Josh asked suddenly, looking Harris up and down. "I don't see any in your hands. What's the matter? That fancy GPS system of yours not up to looking for any rocky road?"

"Oh mercy, I forgot," Harris answered, genuinely surprised at himself for forgetting such an important item. I am so sorry. I navigated right past the store. It's what happens when you drive a real car, Uncle J," he said in quick retaliation, although he still felt bad for not remembering the ice cream.

"It's OK, son, I'm sure you had other things more important on your mind. Hubba bubba."

"Uncle J, you are embarrassing me . . . again," Harris said through the side of his mouth.

"Then I'm doing my job, young whippersnapper," Josh hissed back at him.

"Oh no, please, Uncle J. Behave. Please not yet. Markita hasn't even made it to the living room yet."

"Master Harris would like us to retire to the living room," Josh said, turning to Markita. "Please follow me, lovely lady. Markita, right?"

"Yes, sir," she replied. She took an immediate liking to Harris's uncle, thinking how alike he and Harris were. The special connection between them was obvious.

Leading the way, Joshua took them past the stairs and around the corner to the right where the living room was located. Offering Markita Mary Ellen's chair, Harris sat in what used to be his father's chair, a chair that his uncle now claimed as his own. It had never bothered him that Josh now called it his; he felt Uncle J deserved it more than his father ever did.

Joshua walked over to the nearby couch and sat, just about to tell Markita the duck joke, when Mary Ellen entered the room from the kitchen with a glass of water in her hand.

"Hey, Mom," Harris called over to his mother, a smile on his face. "I would like you to meet my friend, Markita."

Mary Ellen walked over to greet the girl, but the closer she got to her, the more the hair on the back of her neck stood up. Mary Ellen fixed her eyes on Markita and then gasped, dropping her glass. It shattered into tiny pieces, the water spilling everywhere. Everyone jumped, and Joshua was immediately at his wife's side.

"Are you OK, darling?" he asked, concerned.

"Yes, yes, I'm just clumsy," she replied, although she had turned pale, acting as if she were looking at a ghost.

Joshua disappeared into the kitchen, bringing back a broom and a towel. While he swept all the glass into a pile, Harris wiped up the water from the floor, after insisting that Markita stay where she was. Joshua went back into the kitchen and returned with a dustpan. He scooped the glass into it, and then he and Harris mopped the floor until it was dry. No one spoke a word until Josh returned from putting everything back in the kitchen.

"There we go, no good crying over spilt water. Call me Mr. Clean," he said, trying to lighten things up a little.

"First, you have too much hair to be Mr. Clean," Harris chimed in. "Second, you are a terrible actor. Third, it's crying over spilt milk."

"Your mother did not spill milk, son. Can you not tell the difference between milk and water?"

"Are you OK, Mom?" Harris asked, going over to his mother and ignoring his uncle's latest humor.

"I am fine, son," she snapped at him.

Harris stepped back at her sharp tone, but then leaned in and took her by the hand, leading her to Joshua's easy chair, wondering what on earth could have gotten into his mother. She sat down staring at Markita, not taking her eyes off the girl. Markita was now beginning to feel a little uncomfortable and wondered what she could have done to get this kind of reaction from a woman she had never met.

Joshua sensed an elephant in the room, so he decided it was time for the duck joke.

"Markita, I bet you haven't heard this one. A duck walks into the pharmacy to buy some cherry lip balm but can't find it. The pharmacist goes over to help the duck, pointing it out to him.

"'Thank you,' said the duck.

"'How would you like to pay for it? Cash or charge?' asks the pharmacist. "But the duck says, 'No, just put it on my bill please!'"

Markita laughed good-naturedly, and Harris was never sure if she really thought the joke was funny or if she was just trying to be polite.

"It's about time someone appreciated my humor," Josh said, a trace of pride in his voice.

Harris was never happier to hear the joke; it broke some of the tension in the room. "You may be laughing now, Chiquita," Harris warned her. "But wait until you have heard the joke a hundred times. It's Uncle J's favorite."

"Aha, whippersnapper. You stole the pet name I gave your mother when I met her."

"I hope you don't mind me stealing it from you. I've always loved it, Uncle J."

"It's fine son. It is a compliment."

"So, Markita, how did you meet my terrific son?" Mary Ellen suddenly asked.

Before she could answer, Harris spoke up, "Markita is interning at my office for six months, Mother."

"How nice. So are you still in school then?" Mary Ellen asked almost sarcastically, as if Markita was a young schoolgirl playing grown-up.

"I'm down here from Tallahassee for the internship, and then I will be finishing my last year at Florida State College of Law," Markita replied.

"How nice," Mary Ellen echoed again. The room went quiet for quite some time before she asked another question. "Have you always lived in Tallahassee?"

"Yes, ma'am, I have." This answer seemed to make Mary Ellen a little more comfortable.

"What does your mother do?"

"Oh, she is retired." Markita gave a quick and short answer now; Mary Ellen's questions felt more like an interrogation rather than polite "getting to know you" questions, and she wasn't sure how to take this behavior.

"What does your father do?" This time Mary Ellen sounded more like she was on the attack.

Harris came to the rescue. "Mom, enough with the questions, please. Isn't supper ready?"

"I was just being polite, son, trying to get to know Mark—" she stopped in her tracks, not able to get the rest of the girl's name out. Mary Ellen was staring at her again.

This time Joshua stepped in and lightened up the room. "It's Marcia Brady," chimed Joshua, winking at Markita.

"Yes, and our son is Greg, right?" Mary Ellen said rudely. Harris's embarrassment started to show on his face along with his annoyance at his mother's behavior.

"Uncle J, why don't you take Mom in the kitchen to check on supper?" he suggested, not looking at his mother. "I'm going to take Markita outside to see the pool." He offered Markita his hand, and they headed quickly toward the back door.

"Good idea, son." Relieved at Harris's suggestion, this would give Joshua a chance to deal with his wife's issue with their guest, whatever it was. He had never known her to be this rude, especially in front of someone who was so obviously special to her only son.

"Darling, is something wrong?" Joshua asked once they were alone in the kitchen.

"You don't see it?" Mary Ellen snapped at him, not understanding how she was the only one who saw the resemblance.

"See what? I see she is a beautiful woman with whom Harris seems quite smitten. Is that it, darling? Do you feel threatened?"

"Don't patronize me, Joshua Robertson. I want Harris to find someone special as much as you do."

"Then why not lighten up on the poor girl? Give her a chance. This is her first visit, and we have not exactly made her feel welcome."

"You really don't see it, do you, Joshua?"

"I guess not, darling," he said, getting exasperated at her mysterious behavior. "I don't *see* anything but a nice girl and your bewildered son."

Before Mary Ellen could say another word, Harris and Markita reentered from outside.

"Hey, Mom, is supper ready yet? Whatever it is, it sure smells good," Harris said, trying to put his mother in a better mood. Joshua leaned over to Mary Ellen and squeezed her hand. As Harris led Markita into the kitchen, she tried talking in a more pleasant tone, addressing Harris.

"It's one of your favorites, son."

"Hmm . . . it must be . . . spaghetti," he said, smelling the delicious aromas of tomato sauce, garlic, and warm, fresh bread.

"Yeppers, with salad and garlic bread," chimed in Uncle J. "You know, darling, I think we have some Neapolitan ice cream in the freezer, which would go great with the wonderful supper you have prepared for us. Let me go check, seeing 'brains' here forgot the rocky road." Again, Joshua needled his nephew, but Harris understood he was trying to get the heavy tension out of the air. He headed to the fridge while Mary Ellen turned to Harris.

"Why don't you and . . . Markita . . . go to the dining room and have a seat? I will bring in supper." The girl's name had stuck in her throat yet again.

What is going on with my mother? thought Harris; he was beginning to worry about her. Maybe something was wrong with her that he didn't know about. Still wondering what might be going on, he took Markita's hand and led her toward the formal dining room.

It was an expansive room, and necessarily so, as many years ago, his parents would host elaborate parties for his father's associates, as well as for other important dignitaries. The room had one large half-moon window adorned with slated mahogany blinds. There was a fireplace with a matching mahogany mantel. Along one wall were two china cabinets full of expensive china and crystal pieces, things his mother loved to collect. The focal point of the room, however, was a huge polished mahogany dining table, which seated twelve people. One end was laid out with a red-and-white checkered tablecloth, set for four. In the middle of the arrangement was a beautiful tall centerpiece filled with various red-and-white flowers; there was even a replica of the leaning tower of Pisa. Mary Ellen had brought out a set of her Waterford crystal goblets for the occasion.

Each place had a nametag in the shape of the Italian boot. Markita remarked at how creative Mary Ellen was. "It looks so authentic in here," she said, trying to be as pleasant a guest as possible.

"I guess you are sitting here next to me," Harris said, noting the names on the place cards and pulling out a chair for her.

"Thank you, Harris. Again, you are a true gentleman."

He blushed as his uncle J walked in, rolling his eyes again. "Did you guys hear the one about—" he started.

Harris cut him off. "Not now, Uncle J, we are about to eat, and Mother will get upset at you if you allow her delicious food to get cold." He grinned knowing he had stopped another very bad and old joke.

Mary Ellen brought out the spaghetti in a large ceramic bowl, along with the salad and bread, all on a large silver tray. Joshua brought in the bowl of fresh tomato sauce, a silver-handled ladle poking out over the rim. He went back to the kitchen and returned with an expensive-looking crystal jug full of ice water. After they were all seated, Joshua said grace, and then began to serve Markita, filling her plate with spaghetti and sauce. He placed a small amount of salad in her bowl and picked up a piece of garlic bread with the tongs, putting it on her side plate.

"OK, enough hosting for me. The rest of you can dig in and serve yourselves," Joshua said laughing and looking over at Harris.

"You mean I can serve myself, right? Because you always take care of Mom, and I know you'll end up serving yourself the largest bowl, seeing you for the porker you are," Harris joked.

"Good, googa mooga boy," growled his uncle in mock disapproval.

"Now, now children," Mary Ellen admonished them, seeming to be in a better mood. "Let's not act childish and immature at the dinner table please. We have a guest."

Joshua finished serving Mary Ellen and himself. Harris then took a moderate amount of spaghetti; although it was his favorite, he did not want Markita to think he was a glutton. They all dug into a wonderful meal, managing to make conversation without sending Mary Ellen off into another incomprehensible snit.

"Great job on the spaghetti, Mom, it was delicious," Harris commented as he leaned back in the chair, an empty place before him.

"Yes, ma'am, it was wonderful," Markita chimed in.

"*Mary Ellen* will do fine, Markita," Mary Ellen responded coolly. "*Ma'am* is for old people."

"Well, dear," Joshua tried again to lighten things up with his humor. "You are getting older every day . . ." he began. Harris saw his opportunity to score points with his mother and hoped she would soon chill out.

"Yes, Uncle J, but she gets more beautiful with every minute, don't you think?"

"Holy guacamole! The boy scores a touchdown," Josh laughed.

His mother looked over at him with a big smile of approval, "Thank you, son. You are so sweet."

"Yes, Harris, so sweet," Josh mocked.

Everyone had cleaned his or her plate, even Markita, who was quite full halfway through her meal, but did not dare to leave any food untouched, not with the way Harris's mother was treating her.

"Anyone for ice cream?" Joshua asked. "Oh wait, that's right. 'Brains' here didn't bring any." Joshua could not resist one more stab at his nephew.

"It's just as well I didn't bring any as I'm quite full. I have to compliment you though, Mother, everything was fantastic."

"No dessert for me, either, thank you," Markita said, grateful to Harris for saying no thanks, but waiting for another cold comment from Mary Ellen.

"Me neither, darling," Mary Ellen said to her husband. "I am quite full myself."

"Well then, I will go in the kitchen, take out a spoon, and dig into the Neapolitan bucket myself, which I bought out just in case the whippersnapper failed on the rocky road—which he did. No, never mind—it just leaves more for me."

"May I help with the dishes?" asked Markita.

"No, thank you, dear, we can get them." Mary Ellen replied, somewhat more softly than she had spoken to Markita all evening. "Why don't you and Harris go back to the living room and have a seat?"

"Well, Mom, I hate to eat and run, but I have to get up bright and early in the morning. Hugh hasn't been in the office for three days, so I have plenty I need to go over with him."

"Anything I should know about, son?" Joshua asked.

"No, Uncle J, it's routine stuff." He felt bad inside lying to his uncle as they had always shared everything. He had made a promise to Hugh though that he would tell no one what he was working on, and he always kept his promises. He tried not to think about involving his grandfather in this.

Harris walked over to Markita's chair, pulling it out for her, and waited for her to stand. She was never so relieved to escape from such an awkward situation, "Thank you, Harris."

"Why aren't you pulling out my seat for me?" Josh wailed, mocking Harris again, wanting them to leave on a silly note.

"Uncle J, I don't know what I am going to do with you. You are too much."

"Yes, but I love you, son," Joshua replied, employing his standby retort.

"I love you too, Uncle J—and you too, Mom," Harris said, walking over to his mother and kissing her on the cheek.

"It was great meeting you, young lady," said Joshua, reaching out to shake Markita's hand." I hope you will visit with us again," he added hopefully.

"Thank you, sir. It was so nice meeting you and . . . Mary Ellen." She almost gritted her teeth as she said her name. Mary Ellen said nothing; she just kept stacking the dishes and taking them into the kitchen.

"Don't forget, whippersnapper, next week rocky road! Got it?"

"Yes, sir, I got it." Joshua gave Harris a big hug then took Markita's hand and kissed it affectionately.

"Uncle J, behave now," Harris warned him playfully.

Joshua led them to the door and waved as they left the driveway. When they were out of sight, he strode back to the kitchen, determined to get to the bottom of his wife's uncharacteristic behavior.

"What on earth was wrong with you, darling?" he asked. "I have never seen you act the way you did in front of anyone, let alone the first girl our son brings home."

"I don't want to talk about it. I need to get these dishes washed," she replied, attacking a serving bowl with a soapy sponge.

"Darling, the dishes can wait. It is obvious you are upset with something about this young lady, but what?"

"Joshua Robertson, I said I don't want to talk about it!" Mary Ellen grabbed another bowl and forced it under the soapy water, not looking at her husband.

Well aware of the significance of calling him by his full name, Joshua knew it was time to back off until she was ready to talk. He helped her finish cleaning up in silence before they both retired to the living room where they sat in continued silence together for the rest of the evening.

———

"I don't think your mother likes me very much, Harris." Markita was the first to break the silence between them as they pulled out of the Robertsons' driveway.

"I have never known my mother to dislike anyone, but I'll admit I have never seen her behave quite the way she did today," Harris answered still puzzled and embarrassed over his mother's actions that evening.

"Staring at me the way she did freaked me out," Markita admitted. "It was as if she had seen a ghost."

"I can't argue with you," Harris admitted. "She was weirding me out at times too." He was still trying to figure out what could have upset his mother so much for her to be so rude to his girlfriend, when suddenly he stepped on the brakes, almost running a red light. *Girlfriend,* he thought. *I sound as conceited as my father. How could I be so presumptuous? Why would someone as young and attractive as Markita want to date someone as boring and plain as me?* "I do apologize for my mother's behavior tonight," he said aloud, waiting for the light to turn green. "I hope it won't deter you from us having a friendship."

"Of course not!" Markita replied reassuringly. "We work together after all, so we will always be courteous to each other."

He knew it! She wanted a business relationship and nothing more. How could he blame her, after the way his mother treated her today?

Moments later, they arrived at her apartment, and his heart saddened as he worried about this being the last time they would spend this kind of personal time together. However, it did not stop him from running around the car to open her door for her, this time afraid of taking her hand.

Walking her to the door, Harris's heart pounded so loudly he watched her closely, wondering if she could hear it beating. They stopped on the small front porch of her garden apartment, both looking into each other's eyes. Harris so wanted to ask her out again, but was afraid of her answer.

Markita stood in the moonlight, waiting for a kiss she wasn't sure would come, flipping her hair back off her shoulder, exposing her beautiful cheek; Harris stroked it with the back of his hand before lightly kissing it. Markita took hold of his hand giving it a gentle squeeze.

"I had a lovely time, Harris," she said softly. "The food was great, and your mom is an excellent cook. And I like the special bond you have with your uncle J." Her words came out in a rush. "He's a funny man, just like you. I can see why you love him. I wish I could have experienced the same kind of relationship with my father, but I never got to spend much time with him," she said wistfully. It was the first time she had mentioned her father with any kind of affection.

"I had a wonderful time too, Markita. I don't suppose you would like to go out with me again . . ." He let the question hang in the air.

She could not contain her excitement. "Oh yes, yes, I would love to," she responded breathlessly.

Harris could hardly believe his ears. "You would? Are you sure?" he said, sounding as surprised as a child who just received the one gift for Christmas that he wanted most of all but was sure he wouldn't get.

"Yes, I think you are a very . . ." she paused, trying to think of the correct words to say. After all, he was her boss in a sense, at least for the next six months.

"Boring? Plain?" Harris tried to finish for her.

"No, no, Harris," Markita said, looking up at him, flustered. "I was trying to search for the right words to tell you what a wonderful man I think you are. I love your humor and quick wit. It is attractive . . . just like you," she added and blushed at telling him how she felt.

"Thank you," Harris responded awkwardly. Things were beginning to get a little awkward; between the two of them, neither one knew what to say next. "I guess I should say good night, sexy lady," Harris tried finally.

"Good night," she replied simply, now looking down at her hands, but still standing close to him.

"May I call you sometime?"

"Please do, I would love that."

"Right then, I will see you tomorrow," Harris said, looking once more at her kissable lips. On impulse, he took his index finger, kissed it, and touched his finger to her lips.

Markita's heart skipped a beat, quivering as he touched her. "Until tomorrow," she sighed, leaning back on her front door.

Harris smiled gently at her and then walked back to his car, turning once to wave at her as she let herself into her apartment. Once settled in the front seat, he sat for a moment, reflecting on the evening. How could he have gotten lucky enough to take out such a beautiful woman? Starting up the Jag, he realized the butterflies had returned—had they ever really left? Pushing in the CD, he pressed the Search button once again to Journey's "Open Arms," sat back, and let the car drive him home, thinking about Markita the whole way.

He had just opened the garage door when it hit him: the evening was over, and he had returned home alone. Walking inside, he grabbed a green tea bottle from the fridge, then rushed upstairs and grabbed the phone by his bed, dialing Markita's number like a schoolboy with a crush, hoping she would not be upset with him for calling so late.

"Hi, this is Markita," she answered in her sexy voice.

He was in awe hearing her voice again so soon; hearing her say her own name was music to his ears. "Ahem, howdy there," he said, wondering if his voice sounded as strange as it felt right now. "I was calling to let you know I made it home safely," he told her, hoping she would take it as the joke it was.

"You are too cute." She gave a little giggle.

Harris breathed a sigh of relief. She hadn't hung up on him. "You think I'm crazy, right?" he asked.

"No, I think it's really sweet of you to let me know you made it home safely."

"You are too nice, but I'm sure you think I am a nut, right? The truth is, I just wanted an excuse to say good night again."

"I do *not* think you are a nut," Markita said firmly. "I think you are a gentleman, and I am glad you called. It gives me chance to say good night and to wish you sweet dreams . . . of me," she added mischievously.

He laughed as his heart skipped a beat when she told him to have sweet dreams of her. The butterflies were back.

"Good night, pretty lady," he whispered and then hung up the phone, breathing a heavy pleasurable sigh. He fell asleep right there in his clothes, dreaming sweet dreams of her as she requested.

———————

Joshua and Mary Ellen retired for the evening. As he did every night, Josh placed his wife's head on his shoulder as they lay next to each other in bed, caressing her hair and holding her close to him.

"Chiquita," he began tentatively. These were the first words he'd spoke to her since she'd snapped at him in the kitchen hours earlier. "I don't know why Harris's friend upset you today, but whatever it was, you can tell me. You know you can share anything with me, don't you?"

"Yes, Josh, I know, darling." She turned her head a little to look over at him. "Didn't you think . . . didn't you think that girl looked like your brother?"

"What!" he said in amazement. "Sweetie, there's no way! What on earth did you see in her that would have you thinking she looked anything like Mark?"

"Joshua, the color of her eyes, the color of her hair, her cheekbones, her smile, and my god, Josh, her name. Don't you see it?"

"To begin with, brown hair and brown eyes are pretty common, darling, and I don't think she looks anything like Mark. As far as I know, my brother bore no other children. He hated kids, remember?"

"You really don't think she looked anything like him?" she asked, seeming to soften. Joshua's reassurances that there was no resemblance had started to make her feel a whole lot better.

"No, my darling, not at all. I think her name is coincidental, and it threw you for a loop. I am so glad her looks are the only thing that concerned you. You worried me there for a minute. I thought there was something medically wrong with you, and I missed it." He let out a sigh of relief along with a little laugh, then turned to her, kissing her passionately, holding her close, and caressing her warm body, just as he did night after night. Their two hearts beat as one, and when the two of them came together in synchronized harmony, he thought what a lucky man he was to have his Mary Ellen. "I love you," were the last words he spoke to her before falling into a deep sleep.

Chapter Five

The Takeover

Hugh returned to his office Monday morning, sitting back in his chair reflecting on the last week's activities. He had gone to great lengths to ensure his takeover of the Practice would be a smooth one. Harris's call informing him of Smith's early release from jail, however, was a definite game changer. It indicated to him that someone might be trying to undermine his plans. Hugh himself had arranged Smith's arrest; his plan was to then have Harris prosecute him. Judge Fredrick Poe would guarantee a conviction, thus leaving a clear path for Hugh's scheme to work. Now he would need to devise a completely new strategy.

Originally, Orange County Sheriff Hank Jackson, a.k.a. Hank the Tank, was to have arranged for an "accident" to happen to Smith during his incarceration. Jackson, a big, burly, muscular man who gained his reputation because he loved rousting drunks, was a key player in the Order. Although loyal to Judge Harris, Jackson, like everyone else in the Order, was in fear of the Executioner, so Hugh's plan to eliminate him made perfect sense. With Smith a.k.a. the Executioner, out of his way, Judge Harris would be unable to have Hugh killed if he somehow discovered Hugh's betrayal. His next move would be to arrange for the Practice's Nigel Pope, his accomplice in the takeover, to also meet with his demise. This would leave Hugh as sole owner of the Practice and, best of all, in full control of the shares and the $150,000,000 escrow. He had spent the last twenty years as the district attorney, and his loyalty to Judge Harris had been unwavering up until the last three years. During those three years, he did not feel that he was receiving a big-enough piece of the pie, so he felt it was time to take what he was owed.

It would take Judge Harris years to find and train another animal like the Executioner to come after him. By that time, he would be long gone with the money. Money Hugh didn't want to go to anyone else but himself. Judge

Harris, while currently in good health, was now in his eighties. If something were to happen to him before Hugh's plan went into effect, the judge's grandson, Harris, would inherit all the money, as well as the Practice. Hugh was not going to let this situation happen on his watch. Harris didn't have a corrupt bone in his body, so who knew what he would do with the money once he inherited it? Let alone when he found out it was dirty?

How could this all have gone so wrong? Hugh wondered. It had taken him years of planning to put his takeover together. Spending the last three days of the previous week cleaning up after Smith's mess, he concluded Smith was getting too old for the game and was becoming sloppy.

Hugh assumed that Judge Harris had moved more quickly than he had anticipated in getting Hank Jackson to let Smith out right away. Hugh didn't hold that against Hank; his disobedience to the judge would have resulted in his own head on a chopping block. Smith really was getting sloppy; however, he should have destroyed all the evidence, including the car, not just taken the head and seat. He left the car full of fingerprints and questions, which dog-sniffing investigators like Joe Marble could have uncovered. In broad daylight, he shot the arresting officer, leaving even more evidence. Hank shook his head, considering all the other strings he needed to pull to get rid of everything the Executioner had left undone.

Hugh needed to pay off the medical examiner in order for him to dispose of the officer's body; he then set fire to the car himself without anyone detecting him. In addition to everything else, he asked a huge favor of Judge Poe in the matter with Joe Marble. This could have extreme ramifications if it exposed Judge Poe's ties to his takeover plans; Poe's warning to Harris and Marble to back away from the case might have tipped his hand.

His intentions for the week had been to meet with Nigel Pope, but everything else had taken precedence. It wasn't until late Friday night that he was able to meet with the attorney, the sole senior partner at the Practice. The meeting was supposed to finalize their plans, tying up any loose ends and dealing with any last minute details before the takeover. Nigel thought he and Hugh would continue to be partners, sharing the $150 million dollars and shares; but Nigel was unaware that Hugh's greed dictated a different outcome for him; in Hugh's private plan, things did not meet with a pleasant ending for Nigel.

Hugh had his own reasons for wanting to go the rest of the plan alone. He was a desperate man with huge gambling debts and no intentions of sharing the money with anyone. Trying to figure out who might have sent him that newspaper article from the past, Hugh had questioned Nigel on Friday, asking him if he had recently visited his father at his nursing home. Nigel told him that although he felt somewhat guilty, he had not seen his father since the day he entered the facility, explaining that Stewart had not recognized his son since the time, three years ago, when the Alzheimer's first took control of him. Which still left Hugh with the question of who could have sent the newspaper article to him? Although he felt himself clever to have thought of placing the article in Harris's mail, anticipating his reaction in order to manipulate him, Hugh needed to know who the original sender was. The fact that someone was out there apparently trying to either blackmail him or scare him, or both, meant there must be a leak in the Order somewhere; this was an elite organization which Ronald Harris entrusted Hugh to run when the judge started his appointment to the Supreme Court in Tallahassee. He needed to find out who could be betraying him before there was more trouble. Hugh continued to mull over his options, unaware that Judge Ronald Harris was always one step ahead of him. Unbeknownst to Hugh, Harris was unwittingly keeping his grandfather apprised of his betrayer's movements.

Hugh's deep concentration broke when his secretary paged him, letting him know Harris was anxious to meet with him. He was not looking forward to all the detailed updates Harris was getting ready to dump on him or the fabrications he would have to create in order to divert the young man's suspicions.

"Send him in please, thanks," he responded, trying to put on a positive face. Harris entered Hugh's office, hurrying to sit down. Straight away, he began explaining the events that had taken place during the previous week, making sure not to leave out any important information; Hugh tried his best to look as if he was listening intently.

"I could not believe Judge Poe gave me a warning to back off from my investigation," Harris exclaimed indignantly at one point. "There is definite sabotage concerning this case, I can assure you, Hugh." Harris continued, making every effort to relay to Hugh even the smallest of details.

"The cover-up is so obvious, Hugh. If people weren't being killed, it would be laughable. It was like having one of those nightmares where you wished you could wake up before you fall over the cliff."

"I can tell how distraught you are over this entire situation, Harris," Hugh responded calmly. "But this is the reason I asked if you were ready for a case of this magnitude," Hugh said, obviously patronizing him.

Although those words stung, Harris continued, completely unaware of the bomb he was about to drop on his boss. "Hugh, I know you swore me to secrecy about this whole situation, but I was desperate to sort things out, and when I couldn't get any help or guidance from you, I sought advice from my grandfather."

Hugh about fell out of his chair. He could not believe what Harris was saying. He nearly gasped for breath.

"I told you, Harris, not to tell a soul," he finally got out, almost choking on his words as he tried not to let his anger show, all the while wanting to strangle Harris until his last breath left his body.

"Hugh, I'm sorry, but corruption is becoming evident in our city. My grandfather is a brilliant chief justice. He can cut through a lot of red tape for us and maybe get to the bottom of whoever is behind all of this." Harris continued to plead his case. "You have to agree, after the information I have relayed to you, there is more than one person enabling Smith. Grandfather told me Judge Poe is a friend of his, and he will make some inquiries."

Hugh started to feel short of breath again; he could feel his body temperature rising, as well as his heart rate and blood pressure. He needed to get Harris out of his office before he suffered a major heart attack, or before he leapt across the desk and strangled Harris with his bare hands.

"Harris, you need to leave all this to me. I will call Ronald, and together he and I will sort all this mess out. But for God's sake, man, do as I ask from now on and keep your big mouth shut concerning this case! I know you are respectful of Ronald and the position he holds, but what goes on here needs to stay in this office. I told you how dangerous the Executioner is. Now you could have put your grandfather at risk, as well as yourself. It is my duty to keep my people safe. You have jeopardized our case. You gave me your word you could keep silent, and I trusted you." Hugh shook his head, hoping he had made his point without arousing any further suspicions in Harris. "Now, if you don't mind, I need to make some calls and see if I can salvage any of this mess."

Harris knew he was being dismissed, so he left Hugh's office, not liking the disappointment in Hugh's voice, and certainly not expecting his infuriated reaction. He understood Hugh being angry with him for breaking his silence, but what he could not understand was why Hugh could not trust his grandfather. Harris still felt his grandfather's position as the supreme law in Florida could be of great assistance to them. It left Harris with more suspicions and many unanswered questions. Walking down the long hallway back to his own office, the first thing he decided to do was call Joe.

"Hey, man, what's going on?" Joe greeted him on the second ring.

"Joe, we need to meet somewhere, preferably not in my office."

"How about meeting at the coffee shop over on Orange Avenue?" Joe suggested, wondering what all the new secrecy might mean.

"You mean Mama's?" Harris asked.

"Yes, that's the one—say an hour?"

"Yep, I'll meet you there." Harris hung up.

Before he left for the coffee shop, he e-mailed Markita thanking her for joining him yesterday and again apologizing for his mother's bad behavior. He also offered his assistance if she needed help with her car. He deleted the message from his Sent box, not wanting to leave any trace of their budding relationship. Markita e-mailed him back right away, telling him not to worry about his mother. "I had a wonderful time," she wrote. "We will have to do it again soon . . . but maybe not at your parent's house, smile." She ended the e-mail: *Always, Markita*. Harris hoped she too remembered what he had told her about Hugh not liking fraternizing in the office and deleted her message from her own Sent box. Despite his worry, Harris's butterflies from the previous night returned the moment he received her e-mail; he read it, smiled, deleted it, and then left for the coffee shop to meet Joe. He wished she could have accompanied him, but he needed to keep her safe.

Harris arrived at the coffee shop just few minutes later, Joe already waiting for him in a secluded booth in the back.

"Hey, man, what's up with not wanting to meet in the office?" asked Joe, curious.

"I briefed Hugh this morning on the events of last week," Harris told him as he slid into the booth. "Let's just say I did not expect the reaction I received from him, and his responses confused me. I think it's best if you and I keep this investigation to ourselves until we find out who all the players are. I don't know who we can trust right now."

"Ooh . . . ooh . . . intriguing, my friend," Joe responded, rubbing his hands together. "You know I'm always up for a good challenge," Joe said, his blood pumping with anticipation.

"Right, I wouldn't have won my first big case without your brilliant detective work, Inspector Gadget," Harris said, taking a stab at his friend, knowing that first part of his statement was true—he thought.

"I don't want to discredit you in any way, Joe," he went on, voicing a suspicion that had been growing in the back of his mind, "but I am now beginning to wonder if my first big win was manipulated. Thinking back, it seems all too convenient how it all just fell into place." He ticked off his main points on his fingers. "The clues you found surfaced too easily. Then there was our suspect who just admitted the dope was in his house, and we just so happened to come across the money and firearms. It all seems a little too open and shut, don't you agree?"

"Well, now that you put it that way, yeah. I would hate to think any of this is true, Harris, but anything is possible." Joe was not thrilled when he realized someone could have played him, played them both. "Do you have a plan?"

"I got to thinking about Smith's arrest, or should I say the one that mysteriously never took place," Harris began. "Whoever stole the car's backseat and head made a grave mistake by not taking the whole car. It can prove there was an arrest. The car will have Smith's prints and maybe DNA all over it."

"Good observation, Batman," Joe stabbed back, annoyed that he hadn't brought up this obvious fact himself.

"Well, Robin," Harris continued with a grin at his friend, "it's not much, but it's at least a place to start, although do be careful. I don't know if your junky old Batmobile will aid you in a quick getaway."

"Funny guy," Joe shot back. "Don't you dare make fun of my car. It's a fine piece of machinery, and I bet it lasts longer than that foreign thing you drive."

Harris grinned again, and then his voice sobered as he returned the serious discussion at hand.

"Joe, I want you to be careful when dealing with this Smith character. I can't say anymore, but he is not going to like us poking around in his business."

"Got it, man, don't you worry about me. I can handle myself. I am the great Inspector Gadget, remember?"

Joe could tell Harris was still keeping something from him, but was smart enough to know he was not ready to share whatever it was. Knowing Harris was an honest man, he would place his trust in him . . . for now.

"You might want to do some investigating into the Practice," Harris continued. I have noticed Hugh losing a lot of cases to them in the last six months, ones he should have slam dunked. It's just a hunch that I have about him, but we should check it out."

"Okeydoke." Joe made some notes to help keep him straight and then changed the subject for a moment.

"So, lover boy, how are you getting along with the pretty little chick-a-dee in the office?"

"I am not discussing her with you, you moron."

"Thou dost protest a little too much," Joe chuckled, enjoying pulling Harris's chain. "What's new?"

"Nothing is new, and even if there was, I would not tell you."

"Aw, come on, chickenshit, spill the beans. I can see it written all over your face. You took her out. Yes, you did—I can see by your reaction."

"OK, OK," Harris said, his telltale blush giving him away. "I did not take her out as such. I did, however, take her to my parents for supper last night."

"I knew it, I knew it. Found you a hot mama? I owe you one hundred bucks, bubba."

"Would you please stop?" Harris pleaded, blushing even further. "You do not owe me anything. I told you I was not going to bet with you. Markita is too much of a lady," Harris said, embarrassed.

"So how did the old parents take it, huh? I bet they were all over her like a marriage made in heaven."

"Not exactly. My mother's reaction was rather odd. I have never known my mother to be rude to anyone, but she sure was on the verge of it all afternoon with Markita."

"Aha, that explains everything. You're such a mommy's boy, she's threatened that there is a new woman in your life. All mothers hate letting go. It's a harsh reality for them realizing they have to untie the apron strings."

Even though Joe called him a mommy's boy, he was cool with Joe's analogy. It made perfect sense, and he would have to relay Joe's theory to Markita, hoping it would help her understand where his mother was coming from.

"Well, Joe, it's been a trip as usual with you, but it's time I got back to the office. Some of us have to work, you know."

"Right, and some of us can't wait to be in the company of a hot mama," Joe hinted, finishing his coffee.

"I'm warning you again, Joe Marble, don't push me," Harris warned, only half-jokingly.

"Who me? Never! Catch you later, man." He got up to leave.

"Hey, Joe, it's OK. I'll get the check," said a mildly annoyed Harris.

"So you should, my friend, so you should. You're the one who makes the big bucks." Joe left, smiling.

Hugh was still in his office trying to figure out his next move, when his secretary paged him.

"Mr. Gallagher, Judge Harris is on the phone for you. Should I put him through, sir?"

"Yes, please," he told his secretary, knowing this call was inevitable; he was already having a bad day after his meeting with Harris, so he decided to get Ronald's call over with.

"Good afternoon, Ronald," he greeted the old judge warmly, not giving him a chance to speak. "I have been expecting your call." He tried to be pleasant given the circumstances.

"I'm sure you have," Judge Harris responded gruffly. "What in the hell are you thinking, Hugh? You'd better have a damn good explanation as to why my grandson knows anything about our friend Smith and why Joe Marble and my grandson are investigating him. There should be no paper trails leading to Smith or the fact he is called the Executioner, so tell me how Harris knows of him?" Judge Harris shouted furiously.

"Hold on a minute, Ronald," Hugh said, trying to hold back his own irritation. "Let me explain, before you go getting all irate."

"I'm already irate, and I am waiting," said the judge.

"Let me first point out that I am not the one who got arrested. Smith is responsible for his incarceration. He should have been more aware of his surroundings. I was working on getting him released, per your request, when someone had already let him go. I am, however, the one who gets to clean up his garbage. Next, I come to find out he does a sloppy job of disposing of evidence. Yes, he took the backseat and head from the car, but he left the damn car itself! I spent all morning sneaking into the impound lot and setting fire to the freaking thing without being caught. I then paid off the medical examiner to dispose of the arresting officer's body, and then Smith decided to have target practice in broad daylight, killing another police officer right in front of Joe

Marble, Harris's close friend and a private investigator. Another smart move, right?" Hugh's voice was rising, but Judge Harris made no move to stop him. "To make matters worse, Marble, who is a like a bloodhound with a scent, got too close to the truth, which is why your Executioner struck again, and hence Marble ended up in jail." Hugh paused for breath and continued before Judge Harris could interrupt. "In addition to everything else going on, I put Judge Poe's reputation on the line having him warn Harris and Marble to back off, so my life has not exactly been a bed of roses here, Ronald. You might want to have a few words with your aging Executioner." Hugh let out a sigh of relief and exasperation, glad this part was over.

"You may think you're in the clear here, Gallagher, but tell me how my grandson knows about Smith."

"That one I can't answer, Ronald," Hugh lied. "Like I said, I was out of the office for three days last week playing cleaning maid, so I have not had chance to question Harris yet."

"I am sure I'm going to receive a phone call from you when you have all your facts together," said Judge Harris coolly. "But in the meantime, I will be watching you, understood?"

"Yes, Ronald," Hugh responded calmly. Glad his interrogation was over, he believed, he hoped, his answers satisfied the judge, at least for now. If nothing else, it would give him the time and opportunity to devise a new plan to get rid of the Executioner before the judge turned the Executioner loose on him.

"We have another dilemma, Hugh," the judge was saying now. "I received a call this morning from Sue Lee, the bumbling idiot over at the nursing facility. She informed me Stewart Pope invited visitors there last Monday, an old couple in their late eighties."

"Who were they?" Hugh asked, curious.

"If I knew the answer, Hugh, I would not be calling you for it, now would I?" the judge said in a sarcastic tone.

"Did they sign the visitor's book?"

"Hugh, I know you are under some duress there, but I told you she did not know who they were. She was so busy being excited that Pope received visitors for the first time in three years, that she forgot to pay attention to her orders, somewhat like you." Hugh did not appreciate the snide remark or its tone.

"I'll investigate the matter myself," Hugh responded. "I'm beginning to think if you want things done right around here, you have to do the job yourself," he said, snapping back at the judge.

"Fill me in sooner rather than later," Judge Harris replied, seemingly unaffected by Hugh's rising temper. "And make sure you keep my grandson away from Smith, or you might receive a visit from him yourself, get my drift?" He slammed down the phone to emphasize his point.

The conversation put Hugh in an awful mood, and he took it out on everyone around him for the rest of the day. Planning and scheming all afternoon, wondering how to regain his advantage back over Judge Harris, he concluded that he needed to devise a new plan of action, thus regaining control. After racking his brain for hours, a brilliant but dangerous idea popped into his head. After thinking it over for a few more minutes, he picked up the phone and made a call.

"Hugh Gallagher for Judge Fredrick Poe, please," he asked and then waited on hold for what seemed like an eternity.

"Judge Poe, how can I help you?" His abrupt tone matched his egotistical personality. Hugh knew him well and was aware how people were often deceived by his handsome and distinguished looks. His Southern charm, square jaw, and thick salt-and-pepper hair could put easily a witness at ease, but once you heard the cold conceit and arrogance in his voice, the kindly gentleman persona was quickly erased.

"Fredrick, it's Hugh," he greeted him jovially. "How does your schedule look for tomorrow?"

"It's pretty clear after two p.m., why?" Poe sounded suspicious.

"Thought you like to play a round of golf followed by a few cocktails, my treat of course?"

"Well, old man, a game and cocktails sounds inviting, how can I refuse?"

Hugh did not fail to notice how the judge's tone changed from abrupt to one of interest now; his favorite pastime away from the pressures of the courtroom was to partake in a relaxing game of golf.

"Why don't we make it for around three p.m. to be on the safe side? I will call Bay Hill country club now and reserve a tee time for us, and then see you tomorrow."

"How about we make the game a little sweeter?" Poe suggested. "Say, a wager of five big ones?"

"You're on," Hugh responded with feigned enthusiasm. "Five big ones it is."

Hanging up, he pondered his new plan, satisfied it would resolve quite a few issues: it would keep Harris occupied with something other than Smith's arrest, and if all went well, maybe he could get Judge Harris's shares of the Practice without having to actually run the damn law firm, which was an extra headache he did not need. He would entice Nigel Pope into his scheme by promising him full control of the Practice. *Hmm . . . Life is good again.* He smirked, leaving the office for the day.

Hugh and Fredrick met at the country club the following day.

"Cocktail before we start?" he asked the judge, knowing Fredrick liked to knock back a few; besides, he could always use an advantage.

"No thanks, Hugh. I'll need to keep a clear head. You are a worthy opponent, and five thou will give me a nice weekend away . . . on you."

"Not so fast there, sir. I intend on winning this game myself," Hugh challenged the older man. Clapping Poe on the shoulder, the two men walked to their carts where their caddies awaited them.

It was not until the fifth tee, when Hugh instructed the caddies to take one cart, while he and the judge took the other one to the green, that Hugh had the chance to run his plan by Fredrick. Hugh drove at a slow pace while he revealed his newest idea.

"It is going to be necessary for you to rough up one of Miss Dixie's girls," Hugh explained. Knowing what Hugh knew about his friend, he did not think Fredrick would object to the task.

"I do not quite understand your purpose for this," Poe said, slightly uncomfortable with Hugh's suggestion. "It sounds a tad drastic, if you ask me." He wondered if there were rumors circulating about his perverted behavior. Maybe Hugh had caught wind of one and was about to blackmail him with his perversion. If this was the case, there wasn't much he could do about it; this was the way their secret organization operated.

"Smith has bungled any chance of a smooth takeover of the Practice, so I have devised a new plan which will work out in everyone's best interest," Hugh assured him.

Judge Poe breathed a sigh of relief and was now intrigued with hearing more of Hugh's new plan.

"If you could rough up one of Miss Dixie's girls," Hugh explained further, "it would piss off Smith."

"Your purpose for this is what, may I ask?" Poe interrupted, concerned at the thought of having anything to do with Smith.

"I have no doubt in my mind Miss Dixie would have Smith come after you, but we would be prepared for him, you would be in no danger," Hugh rushed to calm Poe's concerns.

"Are you out of your mind?" Poe exclaimed. "I would be a sitting duck for that psychopathic killer."

"I will have bodyguards protecting you at all times, and my team will be ready to move in as soon as he is spotted."

"You've started now, so you may as well finish explaining your ludicrous idea," Fredrick said, starting to feel queasy at just the thought of Smith coming after him.

"At the same time that you are keeping the Executioner busy, I will take down Miss Dixie's operation, thus arresting her and throwing her to Hank. He will take care of things for us from there."

"I still do not see your reasoning behind this elaborate scheme of yours. It seems a trifle extreme, given Hank's loyalty to Ronald. You are taking an enormous risk trusting him."

"Fredrick, we need to gain back our leverage over Judge Harris. He's not happy with the recent events here. We don't need him watching us like a hawk."

"I don't see why you have to close Miss Dixie's down. Her escort agency provides our organization a great service."

"Yes, Fredrick, we will all suffer a loss," Hugh said dryly, "but only for a short while. I will have Sassy Jo take over until we can call a mistrial, if that makes you feel any better. It will be for the good of the Order, and in the long run, even better for our pockets."

"Let me absorb this for a bit. Meanwhile, let's move on, man, I have a golf game to win." Poe desperately wanted to change the subject, hoping Gallagher would give up on this crazy idea.

Driving the golf cart a little faster now, Hugh continued trying to convince Fredrick his plan would work out.

"I will have young Harris Robertson prosecute the madam, making sure she reveals no names. Pope will be ticked, but he has to lose a trial once in a while. This is for a good cause. It will also keep my nosey assistant DA and his blood-sniffing hound Marble occupied. I will convince Smith to scare Harris for now but not hurt him . . . yet this in turn will give us negotiating power with Ronald."

"So you want me to let young Robertson win this one, huh?" Poe asked, warming to the idea, not that he figured he had much choice.

"Correct, Fredrick, but you will call a mistrial and as long as no harm comes to Dixie, Smith will not execute any of us. We all have to do our part to get what we want."

"Very well, Hugh," Poe sighed, knowing he really didn't have any other option all along. "I'll go along with this, but I am telling you I will be throwing your ass in jail if that maniac gets anywhere near me, understood?"

Exiting the golf cart, the two men met their caddies at the tee. "Understood," Hugh said with a smug grin on his face, knowing he again had the upper hand. "Now give it your best shot," he said as Poe readied for his next shot. "Because I'm going to get a birdie," Hugh said with confidence.

"That's what you think," Poe responded. "Watch this."

Judge Poe made his own birdie, Hugh managed par, and the two continued with their game until the final hole.

"Hey, Hugh, my friend, would you like to double our bet? We're even at this point, so it would be down to this last putt," Fredrick said, his ego larger than his pockets.

"You're on, Fredrick, let's go for it." Hugh putted first and missed; Poe was elated as he drained the putt and won the game.

"Sorry, Hugh, but I must say it was an exhilarating game!" Poe crowed triumphantly as they took to their carts and headed back to the clubhouse. "Cocktails are now in order, and I recall you saying they are on you."

Hugh led the way to the clubhouse in yet another bad mood; he hated to lose, even at golf, and especially when he had to do so on purpose. He was beginning to wonder if he would ever get a break. At least Poe had agreed to go along with his plan.

The following day, Judge Poe called Miss Dixie to arrange an appointment with one of her girls; he would need an escort in two weeks, on Saturday night, from eight until midnight, he told her, hoping that would give him enough time for Hugh to put his plan into action.

"I have the perfect lady for you, Judge," Miss Dixie drawled. "She's a little on the young side, but a real beauty. I think you will be pleased."

"I expect to be, Miss Dixie. Make sure she is punctual."

"Of course I will, sir, and thank you, as always, for your business," Dixie said, trying to hide the apprehension in her voice. The last escort he took out said he got a little rough with her. Miss Dixie was willing to give him the benefit of the doubt and give him one more chance since he was one of her higher-paying customers.

Poe called Hugh to let him know the time and date, also warning him once again that nothing better go wrong with his plan. He was not at all comfortable serving as bait for Smith.

Hugh would have to work swiftly in order to put everything together, sending two of his best men on their payroll from the SWAT team over to the judge's house a few days before their liaison, making sure they familiarized themselves with their surroundings and Judge Poe's habits in order for them to protect the possible target. Hugh informed the team that Judge Poe was receiving death threats from an ex-con that he had previously put away and who was now seeking revenge. In the briefing, Hugh instructed them to shoot, but not kill, if the judge were to be attacked.

At the appointed time, Judge Poe picked up his escort from Miss Dixie's boardinghouse, taking her to dinner at the country club. Miss Dixie was not kidding when she said his escort was a little on the young side; she could not have been more than twenty or twenty-one. She was slim and pretty with long, wavy blond hair; her eyes were the color of the blue Caribbean Sea, and her smile was sweet and innocent, just like a child's. He ordered the filet mignon, and she ordered fish. Guessing she could not have weighed much over one hundred pounds, this did not surprise him in the slightest. *Her type always worries about their figure,* he smirked to himself.

"Are you from Orlando?" Poe asked, trying for some small talk.

"Yes," was all she responded. After trying several times to get her to talk, asking about her education, her hobbies, and other trivial subjects, Poe was getting bored with having no stimulating conversation whatsoever, so he was glad when the dinner was over. She may have been beautiful to look at, but her head was empty. *No wonder girls like this turn into tramps,* he told himself. Her constant use of the words "whatever" and "like" also annoyed him, so he was thankful that they drove back to his place in silence.

Upon arriving at his house, Poe took the girl straight upstairs to his bedroom. Not hesitating for even a moment, he began shedding his clothes, his adrenaline already pumping. The girl put her purse on the nightstand without a word and then walked to the end of the bed, slipping off her shoes.

"Do you have any music you like to listen to," she asked quietly; this always helped her keep from thinking about the act in which she was about to engage.

Ignoring her question, Poe walked over to her, at first running his hands somewhat affectionately over her body, gently turning her around and unzipping her dress, which slipped off her shoulders and fell to the floor, exposing a pink lacy bra and matching panties. Gently placing all her hair to one side, he passionately kissed her neck, running his hands up and down her body, caressing her firm breasts, and then turning the girl back around to face him. She reached out her hands to touch his chest, but he slapped them away, hard, telling her not to touch him.

Her heartbeat began to rise, in fear, not passion, as he pulled her into him and reached behind her to undo her bra; it fell to the ground along with her dress. He began groping her harder. Her hands still stinging from the slap, the girl did not like what was beginning to happen. He was starting to hurt her. She tried to keep her body from trembling, knowing she was there to perform a job, but he was so very rough!

Not even bothering with her panties, Poe abruptly grabbed the back of her head, clenching a handful of it and pulling her down with it until she was on her knees, forcing her face into his groin. He pushed and pulled her head back and forth with the handful of hair he held tightly in his hand, inserting himself inside of her and forcing her to relieve his throbbing body. Once he satisfied himself, he slapped her face hard and then pulled her back up by her hair. Trying to be strong, but wincing from the stinging slaps, the girl could not control the flow of tears running down her face. His roughness was getting more painful, and so she made the mistake of asking if he could please be a little gentler.

In response, Poe screamed and roared profanities at her, screaming at her to shut her mouth, then slapping her again across both sides of her face. She had heard many stories about tricks like him, but always prayed she would never encounter one. It appeared her luck had run out.

The young escort stood there, nearly naked, not daring to make a move when suddenly he began kissing her neck and running his hands up and down her body again, pushing himself against her, squeezing her roughly again, working himself up once more. He threw her onto his bed facedown, roughly ripping off her panties, and then paddling her backside until it was red and raw. The girl sobbed uncontrollably, praying her ordeal would hurry up and be over, begging God not to let him beat her any more severely than this. She didn't bother to plead with her abuser; she knew it would only enrage him further, so she suffered as silently as she could.

Adrenaline raced through Poe's body, so ready to satisfy himself now; he mounted her from behind, throbbing as he penetrated inside of her. Gritting his teeth and yelling out as he roughly finished, he ignored her muffled cries of pain, not caring about her at all. His interest was all about satisfying his own needs of perverted pleasure. When he was finished with her, he rolled over onto his back.

"Get your clothes on, you filthy bitch, and get the hell out of here," he ordered her. Without a word, the poor girl slid her sore and trembling body to the side of the bed, still crying. Slowly pulling herself up on her feet, she didn't even take the time to find her panties or to put her bra back on; she just zipped up her dress, shoved on her shoes, grabbed her purse, and left this man's house as quickly as she could.

Once outside, she took out her cell phone and called Miss Dixie to come get her, telling her briefly what had happened between her sobs of humiliation and pain. When the madam arrived, she was beyond furious with Judge Poe, vowing he would never touch another one of her girls. As the poor girl climbed gingerly into the back of Miss Dixie's limo, the older woman reached out and held her, softly stroking the back of her head until her hysterical sobs turned to quiet tears. As they headed back to the boardinghouse, Miss Dixie told the girl not to worry; she knew someone who would be more than happy to return the judge's cruelty. It did not help the girl feel any better about her, but it would have to do.

———

Smith was lying low in a shabby motel room when he received a call from his special friend.

"Hey, Smitty," the voice echoed.

"Hey yourself, Dixie doll. It's been a while. How are things with you? Business good, I hope?"

"I can't complain, sweetie, how about you? Are you keeping out of trouble?"

"Right, doll, me keeping out of trouble? Not a chance. It's my middle name, remember?"

"I hear you got yourself arrested."

"Now, how would a beautiful lady like you know of such things?"

"Oh, I keep my ear to the ground, you know how it is. The clientele who frequent my establishment like to wag their tongues. There is not a secret in this city that I don't know about. I like to be knowledgeable and stay up with everything that goes on around here, staying apprised of everyone's business. In my line of work, it's essential, especially if I want to stay on top of the game."

"Talking of work, everything OK concerning the problem you were having?" Smith asked, a note of menace in his voice.

"Funny, you should ask," Miss Dixie replied. "It's the reason I called. That bastard, Judge Frederick Poe, smacked around another one of my girls the other night. Slapped her around pretty bad. She was a mess when I picked her up."

"You're kidding me," he rumbled, no emotion in his voice. "Scum like him don't need to live."

"Whoa, whoa, amigo, not so fast," Miss Dixie interrupted. "I just want you to teach him a lesson. I don't need you offing anyone else for me."

"Doll, I would do anything for you. Listen, you can't let these tricks or bitches get the better of you. Just like the last tramp who stole those expensive earrings from you. It's not something you can let someone get away with. You have to teach them a lesson or they'll all try to run over you."

"I know you care, Smitty. You're a good man," Miss Dixie said soothingly. "But did you have to slice her head off?"

Ignoring her question, he instead warned her about himself. "Huh. You're the only one who thinks I'm a good man. Everyone else has the sense to be afraid of me. I've told you numerous times you need to stay away from me. I am one mean son of a bitch."

"I know you better than anyone else, Smitty. There is a good side to you. I can see it, but you hide it well. It's there though. You may have buried it long ago, my friend, but it is still there, and I can relate, know what I mean?"

"Yeah, doll, I know what you mean. Don't take the way I feel about you to heart though, because if I am instructed to off you, I will. It's nothing personal. It's just the bastard I am." He paused, letting that reminder sink in. He did what he was paid to do—it was just business. "I will take care of your little problem," he went on. "You leave things to me. He won't be smacking any more girls around, I can assure you."

"I don't wanna know there, big guy, but you watch your back."

"OK, doll. You take care and stay in touch, woman."

"Hey, hey, not so much of the woman . . . I'm a lady you know."

"Right, doll, later," he said as he softly hung up the phone.

Smith was calm, telling himself he would only cut off the judge's hands, which would surely stop him from slapping anyone else. Maybe he'd even mail them back to him in a nice package as a gift.

The Executioner immediately headed out to the local camping store to prepare for his new assignment. It would be a lot less crowded than a department store, and they would have a good selection of hunting knives. Looking for a lightweight knife, it needed to be sharp enough to sever off a hand with one swipe. He looked around searching for the perfect one trying to find it before someone came to assist him. After a few minutes, he found what he was looking for then took it to the cash register. There a very chatty store clerk tested his patience.

"Did you find everything you were looking for, sir?" she asked cheerfully, ringing up his single purchase.

"Yes," he responded dully, not wishing to start any sort of discussion.

"This is one of our top-of-the-line hunting knives, you know. Are you going to use it for deer or rabbit?" she asked, trying to be helpful.

"Deer," he responded, again with one word, hoping his short answers and his tone would let her know he was not interested in conversation.

"Then this knife will be perfect for you," she went on, not taking the hint. She took his money, gave him his receipt and change, and then placed the knife in a bag. She was about to ask him if there was anything else she could get for him as she handed him his purchase, when she happened to look into his eyes. A chill ran down her spine. She couldn't help but see the complete emptiness in those eyes.

"You have a good day, sir," she said abruptly, hoping he would hurry up and leave. When he finally did, she hugged herself to quell the shivers, glad he was gone.

Smith knew he would have to take some time planning his revenge for Miss Dixie's girl. It would take him a couple of weeks of casing the house every day, noting when the judge left and returned, needing to check for any staff, pool, or lawn maintenance people. Smith knew that the schedule of a judge was often variable as his routines usually depended on the number and types of court cases on his docket. He also needed to check whether or not the man was single and if he was taking escorts to his house or somewhere else. He needed to be sure that if there was a wife, that she wasn't on a world cruise with the girls or some other crazy explanation that would allow her to come home unexpectedly to interrupt his work. Rich perverts like Poe pretty much did what they wanted, Smith had observed, so he could afford a trip somewhere for a wife when his sick fetish reared its ugly head. Not wanting to leave anything to chance, he planned to check everything twice so he could simply swoop in to sever the bastard's hands and leave with a clean getaway.

Lasting for as long as he had in his line of work was due to his skillful planning of quick entries and even quicker exits. He trained for many of his later years at the target range, after someone paid for him to get away from the orphanage where he spent most of his childhood and escape to the small, isolated cabin located in the thick of the woods far outside Orlando's borders. He was clueless as to who provided everything for him, but he obeyed whatever the Voice on the phone instructed him to do, grateful to be out of the hated institution and living on his own. A boy needed to become tough, living in such an environment as that orphanage, or he would end up bullied every day for the rest of life or worse. This toughness allowed Smith to actually thrive in the isolation of his new cabin home.

Having little else to do in the cabin as he awaited instructions from his mysterious benefactor, Smith had taken advantage of the weapons and ammunition stocked throughout the cabin. He would shoot at cans for hours, using them for target practice; he eventually moved to hunting live game and learned to pick off a moving target at several hundred yards.

He met Miss Dixie when he still lived in the woods. She was a young prostitute in those days, working the corner next to the combination motel and country store near town where he would go to restock his food stores every few weeks. They chatted on occasion and slowly got to know each other. He used to call her China Doll back in the day; she hated the name Dixie. Never understanding why someone so sweet and fragile worked on the streets, he respected her enough not to ask, but always wondered. Watching out for her, he made sure no John ever hurt her. If one did, he would have killed him in a heartbeat.

Miss Dixie would sometimes give him some of her earnings so he could go get a motel room and clean up. Apart from the money she gave him, she saved every dollar she made, swearing to herself one day she would get out of this scary life. Smith watched as she climbed to the top of her profession, emotionally keeping his distance, but remaining friends.

After many years, with his help from time to time, he showed her how to defend herself. And instead of getting out of the game, she took control of her life and became a madam. She purchased a boardinghouse a few years back when the housing market crashed. It wasn't in too bad of a condition when she bought it, but with business picking up all the time, she was able to renovate it periodically, making it look more like the classy mansion it once was. Her clientele soon became judges, senators, and other high-ranking officials, some of which offered their protection of her and her girls in exchange for the madam's discretion. Miss Dixie clearly understood the business of hiring young girls and turning them into high-quality escorts; her establishment was profitable and always busy. And she was always grateful to Smith for watching her back and protecting her girls from bad tricks.

Dixie treated Smith to her personal expertise from time to time although he never had intimacy with any other woman. He felt sex was a weakness; he also did not feel worthy of a good woman, so it made him shy away. Even Miss Dixie could not get him to loosen up enough to have the total experience, but she made sure he felt pleasure. She often wondered if his lack of intimacy was what made him so twisted. Even though she cared for him, she was also scared to death of him. She knew he could turn on her as quick as a breath, snapping her neck before she knew what had happened.

Chapter Six

Revenge

For the past few weeks, Harris's schedule had been a hectic one, spent mostly at the courthouse. During this time, he had officially taken Markita under his wing, so she often accompanied him to the courthouse. In addition to knowing how much this courtroom experience would help her during her internship, it also made him feel good to have her by his side; she made an impression when judges, lawyers, bailiffs, and even the public, asked who the beautiful woman was helping him with his caseload. Without realizing it, they made a great-looking couple.

Today was an office day, so it was time for Harris to catch up on paperwork, which was a task he dreaded as he was a little unorganized. Tara would try desperately to keep up with his files, but with his caseload, it sometimes became a tedious and difficult chore. Markita was aware of his distaste for paperwork after spending many hours of her own time going through and organizing his files.

As Harris opened the first file to make his notes, he could see that her attention to detail had certainly paid off: Markita had already done the notes for him—a good job too. Smiling, he moved on to the next file needing his attention. He noticed the notes were already typed and organized here too. Placing this file on top of the previous one, he picked up a third. To his surprise, the third folder was also completed.

Sitting back in his chair with a huge smile on his face, he turned to open his e-mail. The butterflies started fluttering. *How should I start this?* he thought, wanting his note to Markita to be cute. Thinking first about how Joe called her a "hot mama," he immediately discarded that idea. *No way, too forward. Next!* He thought about addressing her as little girl or cutie, but thought, perhaps wisely, that she might be offended. Chiquita rhymed with Markita, but it was his uncle J's pet name for his mother, and Markita was prettier.

He settled with a simple greeting and wrote to thank her for her help.

Hi, Markita, he typed. *Thank you for taking the initiative to straighten out my files. Because of your efficiency, I have enough time to take a lunch break today. You were so kind, making my notes so neat and organized, I was wondering if you'd like to accompany me to lunch? Signed, Harris*

Sitting at her desk, Markita's attention was diverted from her work as her computer announced that she had mail. A smile spread across her face as she read Harris's note, thrilled that he had noticed her efforts; she accepted his invitation with pleasure.

Paging through to Tara, Harris asked her to hold his calls while he took Markita to lunch. "She's saved me so much work organizing my court files," he said by way of explanation. "She deserves a break."

Tara was a bit miffed as he had never once taken her to lunch. Appearing from his office, Harris stopped by Markita's desk to collect her for their outing.

"So much for no fraternizing," said Tara under her breath.

Out in the parking garage, Harris opened the passenger door for Markita, smiling all the way back around to his side.

"How about the Bistro, is that OK with you?"

"It would be superb, thank you, *sir*," she responded flirtatiously. He noticed and liked it.

The British barmaid saw them the moment they stepped into the restaurant and came around from behind the bar to bustle them over to greet them.

"Looky here!" she greeted them happily. "It's me own little lovies. How are ya?" she said with a cocked smile and an approving grin.

"Just fine, thanks, Miss Brenda, but we are a little hungry."

"Then ya lovies have come to the right place. Come on over 'ere with me," Miss Brenda said, leading them to a secluded corner booth. "Lovies, I do say you're a 'andsome-looking couple," she commented, smiling approvingly. "I knows ya are both wanting lemon water, right? Will ya both be 'aving your usual ham and pepper jack cheese sandwich?"

"You are amazing, Miss Brenda. Thanks for taking such good care of us," Harris said, smiling at Markita.

"You are as kind as ya ole man was . . . and as good lookin'," she said, giving him a wink.

"Thank you," Harris responded, blushing just a little. "I'm sure my father would have appreciated your admiration for him. And you're right. I will have the ham and pepper jack cheese sandwich please."

"How about ya, lovie?" she grinned while asking Markita.

"I'll take the same please."

The barmaid left to get their order.

"She is such a hoot, isn't she *me lovie*," Harris said with a grin.

"Oh *ya lovie*, and you're so *handsome*," Markita joked back.

"I love her accent," Harris said, raising an eyebrow.

"Oh boy, I suppose mine is chopped liver," Markita quipped.

"Yours is angelic and sexy, little girl." There he said it. He hoped she did not jump all over him for calling her a little girl.

"Well, little boy, you're not bad yourself," she retorted.

Lunch was turning out to be a great idea, and he could not be more pleased; maybe now would be a good time to ask her for another date. He stopped himself, though, as their food arrived.

"Darnik," he said aloud.

Markita let out a laugh. "What's darnik?" she asked as another waitress placed their plates on the table. "Oh, it's a word my uncle J uses instead of 'damn.'"

"I like it. It's adorable—just like you." Markita flirted with him yet again. This time he smiled *and* blushed.

Finishing their sandwiches, Harris at last plucked up enough courage to ask her out again. Clearing his throat nervously, he asked as casually as he could: "Would you going out consider again?"

As soon as the mangled words were out of his mouth, he sunk down in his chair, feeling foolish yet again. *I cannot believe I screwed that up. Why do I get so flustered around her?*

"Run that by me again, will you please?" Markita asked innocently. She knew precisely what he meant to say, but enjoyed watching him squirm.

Clearing his throat for the second time, he tried again. "I think it would be great if we could go out somewhere special together." He sighed, relieved to have finally ask her coherently.

"Thank you, yes. I would love too," she replied.

"Where would you like to go?" he asked, his nerves about shot now.

"You're the one taking me on a date, so you decide. Surprise me." She looked over at him, her eyes opening as wide; it was as if they were talking to him, asking him to pursue her. Her smile teased him, her lips saying *kiss me*. His heart began beating faster, and his body quivered. His throat started to dry up; grabbing for his water, he tried to stay calm. She was the most beautiful woman he had ever laid eyes on. How could he be this lucky? His mind began to race like a car in the Daytona 500. *Where am I going to take someone this beautiful? What if she hates where I pick? Mercy, what am I going to do?* Becoming more nervous by the second, he realized the butterflies were back. His mind still a blank, he decided to ask his uncle J for suggestions at the first opportunity. Harris considered him the perfect romantic, so he would know just where to take her. He felt his uncle J was good at everything.

Seeing him calm now, Markita asked if he was OK.

"You look rather pale," she said, teasing him yet again.

"I'm fine thanks. Would you like dessert?" he asked with more confidence.

"No thanks, the sandwich was rather filling."

"Yes, I agree." He waved at the barmaid for the check.

"Everything OK, me lovies?" Miss Brenda asked as she approached their table.

"Everything was great, thanks." Harris took out his wallet to pay, making sure he overtipped Miss Brenda.

"Thank ya, laddie. Ya are always good to me. You kiddies have a lovely day."

"We will, thanks," Harris said smiling and holding out his hand to help Markita up out of her seat.

As they drove back to the office, Harris thought the whole way about where he could take her, but could not come up with anywhere special enough; he wanted everything to be perfect. After dropping Markita back at her desk and thanking her for a wonderful afternoon, he headed straight for his office and picked up his phone.

"Hey, Uncle J, how are you?"

"Who is this?" his uncle replied sternly.

"Uncle J, don't start with me."

"I'm sorry. I don't know who you are." Harris was laughing at his uncle. He always played with him like this when Harris missed a Sunday dinner, and since he hadn't made it out last Sunday due to his workload, he was about to pay for missing it.

"I'm sorry, I'm sorry, I'm sorry. Pretty please, forgive me," he begged his uncle, still laughing.

"How can I forgive someone I don't know?" came the reply.

"You are really starting to irritate me, Uncle J," Harris said, still laughing. "I have a serious question to ask."

"You are going to ask me a serious question, son? What are you, nuts?"

"You're an expert at charm and wit, so I know I'm calling the right man for the job."

"Flattery will get you everywhere, son," his uncle chuckled. "Now, what is this dilemma I need to help you out with?"

"I don't want any of your goofy answers this time. I need you to tell me where I could take Markita on a date."

"Oh, you think you can ask me an awkward question, and then tell me I can't tease the piss out of you? I don't think so, son."

"Uncle J, you are too much."

"I know. It's why you love me."

"Yes, it is, so do you have any fantastic ideas?" Harris repeated.

"As long as your date does not fall on a Sunday, I might have an idea or two up my sleeve." He paused, as if considering his options. "You could always take her on a picnic. I did it for your mother one day, and she was tickled pink, telling me I was all romantic-like and she fell in love with me all over again. I think she was impressed with me, don't you? But then who wouldn't be?"

"It's a brilliant idea! I love it, and you uncle J. I have to go, but I'll see you and Mom on Sunday, OK? I promise."

"OK, Harris, I love you too. Take care. Oh, by the way," he added. "Don't forget the rocky road and remember to take ant spray on that picnic." They both hung up laughing at each other; Harris did not know what he would ever do without that man.

Joshua Robertson had brought so much happiness into his and his mother's lives. He remembered how miserable his mother used to be when she was with his father, especially with all the drinking. He started thinking about the time he found his mother on the bathroom floor, all bruised and her lip cut; she told him she fell, but he knew better. It was a memory that often haunted him, along with many others of the abuses they both suffered at the hands of his father. He hated letting such memories come into his mind. Getting a little sad now, he sunk his attention into his case files, not giving his father another second to rent space in his head.

Hugh worked diligently trying to get everything ready for the take down of Miss Dixie's. The special agents had been in position at Judge Poe's for nearly two weeks prior to the incident with the escort, but there seemed to be no movement from the Executioner. It was all a wait-and-see game at this point. Everyone was set to go on a moment's notice. Hugh was not so worried about the takedown of the brothel; he was confident Miss Dixie would not give up any names. He was worried about Judge Poe though. If anything happened to him, the plan would fall apart, and he would lose everything, although other than that, losing Poe wouldn't be such a bad thing. Even before his initiation into the order, Judge Poe was corrupt. He quickly became a valuable asset, earning extreme bonuses from the Order in exchange for his predetermined rulings. He was as corrupt as they come, and just as perverted, but he was also someone who received great respect from his peers, gaining a reputation in the legal community as the judge who "put 'em away." No criminal wanted him to preside over his trial. The only chance a defendant stood with him was if his defense attorney was from the Practice, but one needed to be rich to afford one of those. Poe was also a close friend of Judge Harris. If anything was to go wrong, and Judge Poe lived through it, he would turn on Hugh in a heartbeat. One call from Poe to his friend Judge Harris could lead to a decapitation by the Executioner; it was the hit man's favorite MO, and the thought of it sent chills down his spine. *Nothing will go wrong*, he told himself.

It was pretty close to quitting time, so he thought he would leave a little early, maybe stop somewhere for a bite to eat along with a cocktail or two before heading home to spend a quiet night reading in his study. He loved legal thrillers, and his current book, *The Silent Fear,* had him totally hooked. On his way out, he stopped at Harris's office.

"Harris, my man," he greeted his assistant DA. "I'm heading out for a bite to eat and then heading home. Before I leave, I wanted to let you know the Barnes case is on the docket for Monday. Get up to speed on it over the weekend and report to Judge Hall's courtroom at nine o'clock. You should take the new intern with you. Let her see how the Hurricane storms in here in Orlando and gets a quick guilty verdict." Teasing him, acting as if he liked him, he handed Harris the case file. Harris took it almost gratefully, not realizing that there was always a motive for any action where Hugh was concerned.

Harris opened the thick file and skimmed its contents, reciting the general details as he already knew them. "This is the case where Barnes sent out his girls to look for men with expensive cars with orders to entice them to a secluded area so Barnes could then beat the men to death and strip the cars of their VINs. His crew then repainted and sold the cars, if I am not mistaken, for quite a hefty profit," Harris said with confidence, having heard Hugh discuss the case several times.

"You've got it," Hugh replied. "I worked a long time putting this case together, but I have some other trying things to attend to at the moment, so I need you to win this one for me. Make me look good," he added, clapping Harris on the shoulder. "You'll need to get with Joe Marble. He's the one who persuaded one of the girls to nark on Barnes."

Suspicious, Harris wondered why Hugh would be throwing him into his big case at the last minute.

"What about the other case I'm working on?" Harris asked, referring to the Executioner's case.

"Leave that one for the moment. I'm still working on some details with your grandfather, but there is no rush at the moment."

"OK, sir, you have a nice evening," Harris replied as his boss turned to leave. He still felt uneasy about this latest development, but he kept his thoughts to himself.

Hugh left happy with himself; this would keep Harris and Marble from snooping into the Executioner's screwup, at least for now, while he was waiting for his new plan to go into action. He left the office, satisfied that things were going his way.

Meanwhile, Harris paged through to Tara. "Please get Marble on the phone and put him straight through when you get a hold of him."

"Yes, sir," she said, not happy to do this task as it was getting close to five o'clock and she wanted to get out of there on time. She had a hot date. Markita could see she was bothered and offered to make the call for her. Besides, she liked Joe; he was one of the good guys. Tara gratefully thanked her and headed out the door.

Joe answered the phone on the first ring: "Joe Marble here."

"Hi, it's Markita, from the district attorney's office."

"Hi there, young lady. How are you?"

"I am fine, thank you. Harris needs to discuss a case. Are you available to talk to him?"

"Oh what a shame. I thought you were calling to talk to me."

Markita smiled. "Oh, Joe, you're always the prankster."

"Yep, pretty lady, that's me. What does the Hurricane want?"

"I don't know, but I could put you through to his phone, and you could find out for yourself."

"Whoa, put me in my place, why don't you?" Joe laughed while she put him through to Harris.

"What's up there, big guy?"

"Can we meet at Mama's in about thirty?"

"Sure can."

"I have four days to prepare for the Barnes case, and I'm going to need your help to get up to speed."

"What are you doing on the Barnes case? Wasn't that Hugh's baby?"

"Let's talk about it over java," Harris said. "I'm paying, of course, because you are but a poor investigator."

"Sounds good to me, see you in thirty." Joe's curiosity was now piqued. He was bursting at the seams to find out what was up Hugh's sleeve.

"See you then," Harris said. As they hung up, Markita knocked on Harris's door.

"Is everything OK?" she asked.

"Yes, fine. Monday morning, Hugh wants you to accompany me to Judge Hall's courtroom to assist me with a case of his. He thinks you will enjoy this one."

"Sounds great, I can't wait," she said, excited. "Is Joe a part of the case?" she asked.

"He will be testifying at the trial and helping with the investigation, yes. Why do you ask?"

"Oh, he just seems like a nice guy."

"Yes, he is," Harris answered slowly, feeling a twinge of jealousy about her admiration for Joe. He wondered if she liked him in a more intimate way, and this thought did not make him at all comfortable.

"I have to go meet Joe now to catch up on the facts of the case, so I will see you tomorrow," he spoke to her in a sharp tone.

"OK, tomorrow then," she responded, sensing his jealousy and not sure how she felt about it. She left quietly, leaving Harris to his thoughts.

Harris placed the Barnes case file in his briefcase and left in a bad mood. Joe was already eating a slice of pizza and drinking a soda when Harris got to Mama's.

"Hey, want something to eat? You're paying so you might as well," Joe said through a mouthful of cheese.

"No thanks, I'm not hungry," Harris said a little shortly, still thinking about Markita's remarks about Joe.

"Whoa! What's up with the attitude? Have a little tiff with hot mama, did we?" This did not help Harris's mood.

"We did not, and I would appreciate it if we could stick to this trial. It's going to be a long-enough night as it is. You know I like to prepare thoroughly for cases I prosecute," Harris said in a stuffy, all-business voice.

"It is obvious you are upset, man. Did the little lady turn you down?" Joe asked, still trying to tease Harris back into a better mood. His tactics weren't working.

"I said let's stick to business," Harris snapped back at Joe.

"Fine by me." Joe could tell Harris was in no way in the mood to be teased tonight, so he decided to stick to a business tone himself. The two men spent four tedious hours going over Joe's investigation and his testimony. Once they finished, Harris asked if Joe could spare him any time in his schedule tomorrow. He wanted to go over the suspect's interviews as well as the collected evidence. They agreed to meet at the same time same place.

Joe left the meeting confused at Harris's mood; they always got along, and this behavior wasn't like him at all. Joe liked and respected Harris; he could not say that about many people in his line of work. He hoped whatever it was that was bothering him resolved itself soon.

———

It was 11:00 p.m. when Hugh received a call from Officer Baso, head of the security team protecting Judge Poe.

"It's going down," he barked. "We need backup now!" The voice was calm but conveyed a sense of urgency. Hugh, on the other hand, began to sweat immediately. His hands shook as he tried to make phone calls to alert everyone on the backup team into position, and he found himself praying nothing would go wrong.

———

The Executioner entered the premises and went upstairs; Judge Poe was already in bed. Smith leaned over his body and poked him, wanting the judge to see him so he could taunt him before doling out his punishment. As the judge's eyes snapped open, Smith grabbed a pillow and started to smother the judge. At first, the older man struggled, trying to fight back, but Smith was too strong for him. The harder he fought, the more he gasped for breath. In desperation, he tried to inhale, heaving his chest up off the bed. He felt his heart trying to explode out of his chest, and again he tried to take a breath, but it was in vain. He saw nothing but darkness and felt an eerie silence surrounding him, except for the occasional beat of his heart, until there was nothing but calm. Trying to take one last short gasp of breath, he felt himself fading . . . But what did he hear in the distance? He thought he heard what sounded like gunshots. He tried to count them; were there two or three? Sounds seemed to fade in and out although he thought he heard the distorted wailing of sirens. Was that possible? *Are those heavenly bells I hear?* He felt an amazing calmness come over him, and he fell into what seemed like a deep sleep. A light seemed to appear in front of him; it was as bright as everyone describes. *I must be gone,* he thought without fear.

Noises broke into the silence that now enveloped him. He heard unfamiliar voices: "STAT!"

What did that mean? he wondered idly.

Ouch! He felt a sudden jolt of pain. *I didn't think you were supposed to feel pain in heaven.* His left arm got tight—a blood pressure cuff? He felt a sharp needle going into his arm. He was so confused; how was he feeling pain when he was dead? Is this what happens on your way to heaven? And if this was heaven, where was his wife? Why was she not waiting to take him into the light? She promised him on her deathbed that she would be there to guide him, and they would spend eternity together. It must be his sins that had changed things. He had been so angry at losing his wife to cancer that he ended up taking his aggressions and frustrations out on "wasteless" women as he called them, like Miss Dixie's girls. *Oh god, no, it can't be!* he thought, frightened at the thought of the alternative to a heavenly end. This must be why he could feel pain. He didn't think he was in heaven at all.

"Dilated," he heard a faraway voice say as he saw a bright light for the second time. *There is the light, thank you, God, for having mercy on my soul.*

"Judge Poe, Judge Poe, can you hear me?" the same voice asked, louder now.

"Yes, God, I can hear you," he tried to say, not sure if the words were sound or mere thought in his mind. The judge felt his heart start to beat faintly as he felt a hard jolt to his body; he responded with a gasp of breath. Now panic-stricken, the fear inside him returned. Gasping again, he opened his eyes; the first thing he remembered seeing were about five or six men leaning over him. *What was going on?* he thought. *Why are all these people looking at me?* He faded out again.

"He's flatlining, stand back." There was another jolt to his body, and he felt himself arch upward on the bed. This time, things were clearer. He saw a light shine in his eye and heard someone's voice.

"You are going to be OK, sir, just relax," said a paramedic. Judge Poe tried to speak, but could not. He tried to remember what happened, but couldn't do that either.

"Get him on the stretcher," said another voice.

"What about the bodies?" he heard someone else say.

"Apparently the big guns are coming out for this one. They said to leave the bodies. They'll bag them after the investigation."

"Someone is going to have a long night dealing with this," he heard the first voice say. Judge Poe tried to understand what was happening around him. He felt like someone had punched in his chest, and everything was blurry; he could not get his eyes to focus. He felt the shift of his limp body from something soft to something hard—a stretcher, he hoped. Then his mind went blank once again.

———

Harris got a call at eleven thirty to go to Judge Poe's house. There was a break-in, two men were dead, and Judge Poe was on his way to the hospital in critical condition. Harris threw on some jeans and a polo shirt and raced to the scene, calling Joe from the car.

"From the report I got, there are two men down, the judge is on his way to the emergency room, and no one has a clue as to what happened. I'll meet you there." Before Joe could respond, Harris hung up. Joe wondered if his friend was still harboring his strange animosity, remembering the coffee shop earlier in the day. He could not, for the life of him, understand what he could have said or done to upset him.

They arrived at the judge's house within minutes of each other. By this time the ambulance was leaving with the judge in it, and there were patrol cars, fire trucks, media, as well as a slew of other people surrounding the home. Joe's first instinct was to find out who was in command and to see if he could assist with eliminating people who did not need to be on the scene. It would also give him a chance to take some notes of his own. He headed off to find the officer in charge.

After flashing his credentials at an officer on the perimeter, Harris lifted the yellow tape surrounding the crime scene and rushed upstairs as another officer gave him a report on the situation in the judge's bedroom.

"Nasty mess, sir," the officer admitted as they entered the master bedroom.

The first thing Harris noticed was that the two bodies on the floor both took gunshots to the forehead at point-blank range. One body was quite close to the bed, but the other was just inside the door. Harris surmised the first victim may have surprised the killer, but it looked like he was ready for the second one. The crime scene unit would be there for hours collecting evidence and taking photographs of everything they found, logging each item into evidence. Harris observed two bullet casings on the judge's bed and a bullet hole in the ceiling above the bed. As he watched, one of the crime scene investigators bagged a pillow.

"What's with the pillow?" Harris asked, curious.

"We think the judge was nearly suffocated with it," the investigator replied.

Harris turned to survey the rest of the room and noticed a set of bloody footprints leading from the bed over to a set of open french doors, which led out onto a deck overlooking over the pool. There were more bloodstains on the long white drapery. Judging from this trail of blood, he guessed that the attacker had been wounded and raced down the outside stairs from the second-floor balcony to escape. He made as many notes as he could, checking everything he could as thoroughly as possible. After several grueling hours, he decided he had what he needed and got ready to leave.

On his way out, an investigator stopped him. "I thought you might like to know the two victims have been identified already. They were SWAT team sharpshooters."

This sent Harris's mind racing. *Why would two guys from SWAT be in the judge's bedroom?* Even more puzzling, no matter why they were there, he knew these men would have been trained experts in firearms. How could someone get the jump on them, unless the attacker was even faster and better with a gun than they were? Instead of heading home for some much needed rest, he spent another two hours looking around downstairs, but there did not seem to be anything out of the ordinary to note. As he headed outside once more, he noticed the crime scene unit taking photographs of the trail of blood from the bottom of the door where the killer had escaped. Maybe it would lead them to the killer, but somehow Harris knew the guy was too smart to leave evidence. If, in fact, he was wounded, Harris suspected the killer would stop the trail of blood way before he went into hiding.

He made his way outside to talk to Joe, but before he could find him, there was a bright light shining in his eyes, along with a camera and a microphone. It was Amber Andrews with Channel Nine News; she was a sharp reporter who loved to uncover a good story.

"I'm here with Assistant DA Harris, a.k.a. "the Hurricane," Robertson, live at the scene of tonight's brutal attack on an Orlando judge. Mr. Harris, can you tell us why there were two SWAT team members found dead in Judge Poe's home?" She shoved the microphone in his face.

He could not believe she knew this information already as he just found out himself. "No comment," he replied, trying to move forward. Amber Andrews blocked his path.

"Do you know the identity of the killer and if the judge was indeed suffocated?"

"No comment," he repeated. It was amazing how quickly the press could find out about the facts of a case.

"Do you think it has anything to do with Judge Poe being a frequent customer at the infamous 'Miss Dixie's' brothel house?"

Whoa, thought Harris, *that question came out of nowhere!* Although he tried not to show it in front of the glaring camera lights, he was surprised and knew he needed to take a serious look into this allegation. He'd heard rumors about Miss Dixie's but never anything connecting Judge Poe to the establishment.

"No comment," he replied again. Joe suddenly came to Harris's rescue, pulling him quickly away from the reporter and her crew. The two of them escaped to their cars, and Harris called Joe on his cell phone.

"Meet me in Mama's coffee house, and we can catch each other up on what we've found," Harris said.

"OK, man, see you there."

Twenty minutes later, the men met in the coffee shop. Harris never drank coffee this late at night, but after the grueling evening he'd endured, he made an exception.

"Does anyone know if the judge made it?" asked Joe.

"No, not yet, I am going to the hospital when I leave here."

"Did you find out anything interesting?" asked Joe.

"Well, ordinarily I would say it was like any other crime scene, but in light of recent events, I am convinced there is more to this one than meets the eye."

"You intrigue me, Mr. Robertson." Joe smiled at his friend. "Tell me more."

"My first question was, what were two SWAT team sharpshooters doing at the judge's house? This was undoubtedly a special assignment. I would have thought Hugh would have told me if something was going on with one of our most respected judges. Then there is a question of a pillow possibly used to suffocate the judge, which led me back to the two SWAT team people shot execution style right between the eyes. We both know whose MO this brings to mind."

"You think Hugh has something to do with this?" asked Joe surprised.

"I'm not so sure he doesn't. Amber Andrews from Channel Nine News asked me if there was a connection between this incident and Miss Dixie's brothel house. Allegedly, Judge Poe likes to frequent there. I would like you to look into her allegation further for me, please, Joe."

"No problem."

"Whoever killed the SWAT guys may be wounded. There were bloody footprints leading to the french doors in the bedroom, and the blood continued onto the deck area which overlooked the pool. They also continued down the outside stairway. The crime scene unit was collecting blood samples from the grass in front of the stairs when I left. I don't know how far the trail went because Andrews stuck her microphone in my face."

"If I am not mistaken, my mom trained her," said Joe somewhat sheepishly. Harris wanted to make a comment but restrained himself. He was not fond of reporters because of how they had hounded his father, especially Nancy Marble, and she went after his father like a shark out for blood. Even though he had no sympathy for his father, he always believed when it came to the law, his father was not corrupt.

"If, in fact, my suspicions are correct," he went on, "I don't think the blood trail will go too far. This guy is too good at what he does to lead us to him. You need to go back to the crime scene and see if you can get us a swab of blood so we can run it ourselves." Harris was on his second cup of coffee after having a long day and an even longer night. Joe munched his third piece of pizza.

"How on earth can you eat so much pizza this early in the morning?" asked Harris, incredulous.

"It's good stuff! Builds character," Joe laughed through yet another mouthful of cheese. "I don't know how you can drink coffee this late, or should I say this early," he finished.

"I am so wired," Harris responded. "And I still need to go to the hospital to check on Judge Poe. Hugh is going to want a full report in the morning." This time Joe offered to pay the check.

"No, no, it's OK, Mr. Marble, I'll get the check, and it's on Hugh anyway," Harris smiled.

"So, man, are we OK? You were a little off earlier. I have to admit, it threw me there." Harris was about to answer him when his cell phone rang; it was Markita. His heart began to race, and his eyes lit up like a Christmas tree.

"Harris, are you OK?" she asked him in a worried voice.

"Yes, I am fine, why do you ask?"

"I saw the early morning news and Amber Andrews's interview with you."

"Mercy, it's all over the news already?"

"Yes, Harris. What happened? You didn't get hurt, did you?" Harris was wearing a huge smile now; he was elated to hear the concern in her voice for him.

"I'm fine, Markita. But it was sweet of you to call."

"I was so worried, Harris. It looks like something big went down with a judge."

"Joe and I have endured a long evening, but we're both fine. I'm going to visit Judge Poe now to see what happened, and I will be in the office later this morning."

"Please come by and let me see you when you get in," she said. "I just want to make sure you are OK." Harris was happy she did not ask if Joe was OK and that she was more concerned with his well-being.

"I'm so glad you called, Markita. See you soon."

"Please take care, Harris—and be careful."

"I will, little girl." He was now beaming; he could not hide his excitement. Joe noticed him glowing and could not resist a comment.

"Hmmm, little hot mama worried about you?" Harris did not even care to hide his pleasure.

"Sure was," he said, holding his head high with pride.

"Good job, man, you go for it." Harris smiled wildly again. His cell phone rang once more; this time it was Hugh.

"Hey, Harris, how did it go at the crime scene?" Hugh fished for information.

"I will have a full report for you first thing this morning after I visit with Judge Poe."

"Don't worry about the report, Harris. I am on my way to the hospital as we speak. Why don't you go home and get some sleep, and we can meet in my office around noon? I will even spring for lunch if you're hungry."

"I appreciate the offer, Hugh. I am a little tired. Guess I could do with some sleep before coming into the office."

"I will let you know how the judge is later."

"Hugh, I have to ask, sir, did you know anything in advance about tonight's incident?"

Hugh turned evasive. "I will explain everything to you when you get in later, so don't concern yourself about anything now. There's a reasonable explanation for everything." Harris did not know how to take his boss's calmness or whether to even believe him. The young assistant DA wanted answers to many questions, so he hoped Hugh would come up with some good ones, or he would be conferring with his grandfather again.

"Well, Joe," he said as he hung up the phone. "Thanks for all your help tonight. Let's get together tomorrow night, and we can go over our notes."

"Sure, Killer," he responded, happy his friend seemed to be back. Joe could tell his demeanor was quite different after a certain young lady's call.

Chapter Seven

The Takedown

It was eleven o'clock in the morning when Harris opened his eyes; he had tried to go back to sleep several times, but nothing was working. His mind would not shut down. Like most of the time now, his thoughts turned to Markita and about how concerned she sounded last night, or should he say, earlier this morning. *Ugh*, he sighed. It was too early in the day for him to be thinking about what went down in the last twenty-four hours. There were many questions that needed answers. He was wide awake now, though, so he figured it would be a good time to get up, take his shower, and head on into the office.

Packing a duffel bag, he threw in a pair of jeans, a polo shirt, and his sneakers to change into for his meeting with Joe later this evening. He wanted to be comfortable after being in a suit all day. Taking one last look at himself in the mirror, making sure he looked good, he gave himself a quick wink. A grin appeared on his face as he wondered if Markita would also think he looked good. With that happy thought in his mind, he headed off to the office.

He had barely sat down in his chair when Markita came bursting into the room.

"Harris, are you OK?" she said, rushing toward him with a panicked look on her face.

"Yes, little girl, I'm fine," Harris assured her. "I'm not sure what all the fuss is about, but your concern for my well-being is sincerely appreciated. Not only is it appreciated, it is awfully sweet of you," he added in a near whisper. She made him feel all warm and fuzzy inside. Calling her "little girl" came more naturally to him this time, and he hoped she was OK with it.

"The news anchor and Amber Andrews reported there were two SWAT team members down at Judge Poe's, and the judge was taken to the hospital in critical condition," Markita reported breathlessly. "They said he flatlined on the scene, but the paramedics revived him. Isn't he the judge we encountered when we dealt with Joe's incident?"

"Yes, Chiquita, he is one and the same. I can't put my finger on it yet, but something smells all wrong with this picture," Harris said.

"Is it because of the SWAT guys being there, Harris?" Markita asked, more intrigued than frightened; she would love to work on a case like this with him.

"There are several things going on around here which are not adding up, but don't you worry yourself, little girl. I'll get to the bottom of it, trust me."

"Are you referring to the other news story that Amber Andrew's reported on?"

"What other story?"

"It was about the cop that got shot when Joe got arrested. They think they have found his body under the I-4 bridge, but the body is barely recognizable," she said. "The worst part is that where the bullet was, there was a hole cut out, and the bullet had been removed."

"Oh my god, Markita!" Harris replied, shocked at the news. "That is horrendous. The officer's family must be beside themselves."

"Amber Andrews seems to think the medical examiner is in on the cover-up."

"Really, little girl, that is most interesting. Thanks for the heads-up. I'll need to inform Joe." Harris made a few notes. "Going back to the other issue, have you heard from Hugh this morning as to whether Judge Poe is OK? He was supposed to go see him last night," asked Harris.

"No, he didn't say when he came in this morning. The only thing I heard him tell Tara was that she was to tell you to go straight to his office when you got in." Her eyes grew wide. "Oops! Sorry I forgot to mention that to you," she said guiltily, as she knew she should have told him that information first. It was just that she had been so concerned about him that everything else got pushed to the side.

"It's OK, but I guess I better get my butt moving then, don't you think?" he said grinning, starting to stand up.

"Well, Harris, I am glad you are all right," Markita responded, almost backing out the door. "I was worried about you."

"I could tell, little girl. You really are so sweet. And again, I appreciate your concern," he said beaming, but trying to stay cool in front of her.

"Can we catch up later so you can tell me everything?" she asked, wanting to know all the details. Maybe he would let her help him with the case.

"I have to go over the Barnes case with Joe again tonight. Would you like to come with me?" he asked, moving toward the door and his appointment with Hugh. "It's obvious you take great notes."

"I would love to, thanks," she replied, excited to be included once again.

"I would be happy for you to accompany Joe and me." He watched for her reaction as he mentioned Joe's name.

"OK, little boy, I am looking forward to it too . . . and to see you later." She turned to walk out of his office. *Did you see the way she just flirted with me*, he told himself. He was even more excited about her referring to him as "little boy." It made him feel young. *Life is good today,* he thought with a smile. Harris walked down to Hugh's office with a smile on his face, where Hugh's secretary showed him directly into the spacious office.

"Good morning there, Harris," Hugh acknowledged his assistant DA, not getting up from his desk. "Are you all rested up?"

"Yes, thank you, sir," Harris replied respectfully, watching his boss carefully. "It was a pretty long night, though, I must admit. Oh, excuse me, sir," Harris said putting his hand over his mouth while he attempted to stifle a yawn.

"Would you like to go grab a bite to eat?" asked Hugh, hoping they could talk about last night's events somewhere more private.

"Sure, some place where they serve breakfast would do fine . . ."

"Let's go over to Billy's Biscuit House. They do a fantastic breakfast. His biscuits are homemade and so fresh."

"Sounds good to me," said Harris."

"We can ride over in my car. It will give us a chance to catch up on things." It was fine with Harris; he wanted Hugh to brief him on his visit with Poe the previous evening.

"Did you go by and see the judge last night?" asked Harris.

"Yes, I did, but he wasn't lucid. They had given him a sedative to calm him down and informed me I should return later today," said Hugh.

"I can go for you if you would like," Harris offered as they headed out of Hugh's office. "It will give me chance to ask some unanswered questions I have."

"No, it's OK. You have plenty to do following up with last night's crime scene. Besides, Fredrick is a good friend, and I want to make sure he's OK. I can promise you he won't be in the greatest of moods either," said Hugh, trying to discourage Harris from visiting Poe.

Harris decided not to push, and they arrived at the restaurant just a few minutes later. Harris ordered his first coffee of the day, along with a blueberry muffin and oatmeal. Hugh ordered biscuits and gravy with a sausage patty.

"I would like to know why there were SWAT team guys staying at Judge Poe's house," Harris asked not pulling any punches with his questions.

"Years ago," Hugh explained, "Poe sent a guy named David Armstrong away for dealing drugs, typical slime bag. He was carrying a firearm at the time of the arrest. Poe gave him life. He served thirty years, and he recently received parole, for good behavior." Hugh shook his head, feigning disgust. "He is one nasty piece of work, and this is just his style, I am sure. When we catch him for what he did last night, Poe will make sure he doesn't get out this time. Armstrong had been sending the judge death threats, and he was also an expert when it came to firearms. Everyone on the streets knew to watch out for him. He would befriend a dealer then shoot him in the back. Fredrick Poe is a colleague and a friend, so I felt it was my duty to protect him, thus the SWAT team on duty at his house," Hugh finished, thinking this sounded like a reasonable explanation.

It was not flying with Harris. He made a mental note of the name David Armstrong. He thought life for dealing drugs was extreme. There had to be more to this arrest and sentence than met the eye. He would have Joe look into this slime bag Armstrong character.

"The two men were shot execution style, which is the same MO this Smith character you have me investigating likes to use," Harris pressed, trying to piece together some of the peculiar details Hugh was relaying to him.

"Like I told you, Harris, this ex-con Poe put away was an expert shot," Hugh reminded him.

"OK, maybe I could concur with this theory, but then there is the question of Poe's suffocation by a pillow, another familiar MO of Smith's. It seems just a little bit too coincidental for me."

"I suppose it does sound similar, but it may very well just be, like you said, a coincidence," Hugh said, trying to sound agreeable, and then shrugging off Harris's suspicions.

"Yes, it could be, I suppose," Harris said slowly, not quite believing him.

"After all, Harris," Hugh said, "Poe has nothing to do with Smith. Maybe I can get some more answers once I visit the judge later today." He hoped he had appeased Harris's curiosity.

"Yes, sir, I guess that's our best option right now," Harris said, full of sarcasm. He did not believe in coincidences. He continued with a change of subject.

"I have Joe checking out an accusation Amber Andrews from Channel Nine made last night."

"Interesting, why don't you run it by me?" Hugh's interest was piqued.

"She alleged Judge Poe likes to visit Dixie's brothel house, the one I have asked you about in the past." Harris heard there were many high-level parties held at the house, with Hollywood celebrities and Washington diplomats always on the invitation list. He had also heard several high-ranking officials in their own city visited there.

"We cannot go on rumors, Harris," Hugh cautioned. "We live by the facts."

"You're right there, sir, but I'll have Joe check on it anyway," Harris said, getting annoyed with his constant dodges.

Hugh could tell his assistant DA was not convinced with his explanations. *This boy is good,* he thought. *He is like his father—suspicious of everything and everyone.* Those suspicious instincts were one of the reasons he hired Harris at such a young age; the other reason was that old judge Harris had paid him to do so. He thought that after a while he would be able to manipulate Harris and maybe corrupt him. Hugh knew everyone had his price, even the pure ones. He just hadn't found Harris's price yet. Hugh did, however, feel rather uncomfortable knowing he could get Harris killed by setting him up to take a fall, but thinking about all the money he stood to gain soon relieved him of that guilt. Harris interrupted his thoughts by changing the subject back to Poe's house.

"If I am not mistaken," he was saying, "when Joe goes by forensics this afternoon, I would bet my last dollar they will have found the dead SWAT team boys both fired a single shot. I found two casings on the judge's bed. I am assuming they were from the killer's gun and there was a bullet hole in the ceiling above the bed. My guess is one came from one of our guys. Again I am assuming, but I think one of them was startled. I am positive the killer suffered a wound considering the amount of blood I saw around the judge's window. I would imagine the bullet is still lodged in him. Like I said, I will know more when Joe goes by and talks to the lab guys."

Hugh was not thrilled to hear Smith might be hurt. If Ronald got wind of this one, he would receive another ass chewing. *I have suffered one too many of those lately.*

It was about that time that their meals came. The two lawyers ate with little conversation, finished quickly, and returned to the office after Hugh paid the check.

Hugh left after dropping Harris back at the office and proceeded to the hospital to check on Judge Poe. After nodding to the guards outside Poe's door and walking into his private hospital room, Hugh saw the judge sitting up and not looking too friendly.

"You . . . son of a bitch!" hissed the judge between clenched teeth when he saw Hugh. "You assured me nothing would go wrong, that I would be safe. I could have died, you incompetent shitbag! The bastard nearly suffocated me!" Poe's eyes were nearly bulging out of his head as Hugh tried to calm him down.

"You are fine," he soothed. "I know it got a little out of control, but my men were right there. In fact, more arrived within minutes of the call," Hugh said, defending the plan and himself.

"Minutes you say? You asshole! Minutes, huh? One more 'minute,' and I could have been as dead as those two poor SWAT team schmucks. I have never been so close to God as I was last night. I was actually praying for my sins, you son of a bitch."

"Now, now you need to calm yourself," Hugh tried again. "You are OK, and that's what matters."

"Oh, you might think so, but it is *not* OK with me." Hugh needed to do some damage control and quick. Poe was becoming enraged. He began to feel that coming here might not have been a good idea.

"Fredrick, we accomplished our mission, and you are safe, and you are what matters here. From what Harris Robertson tells me, he thinks Smith is wounded."

"Let me tell you right now, Gallagher, I want the monster killed. I also want the whorehouse brought down. I am going to send her away for a long time. Do you understand me, Gallagher? I want one of our cops to set her up. Make sure they are wearing a wire. I want an ironclad case. Have her throw one of those high-society parties she enjoys. Make sure none of our guys are there. I want her for sex trafficking, and I want the charges to stick. Do you understand me?"

"Yes, loud and clear." Hugh was glad Poe was still in on the plan.

"Good because if I don't get what I want, I will make a call to Ronald, and you will be Smith's next victim. I promise, where he failed with me, he will succeed with you."

"Don't worry, Fredrick. I will take care of everything. Our plan is working." Judge Poe settled down for a moment, moving on to his next gripe.

"I saw on the news this morning where the two SWAT team boys went down," he said, looking out the window. "They showed my house on the television." He turned angry eyes back to Hugh. "You better get someone out there to clean up the bloody mess before I get home." Poe was more concerned about his house being a mess than the two "poor schmucks," who lost their lives. Hugh looked at him with wonder. *What a cold bastard.*

"Amber Andrews is going to be all over my case wanting answers to this fiasco. You better take care of her too, Gallagher. The last thing I need is another Nancy Marble circus in my courtroom. God, I hate freaking women. They are such nosy bitches. I am telling you one last time. Take care of all this shit." He turned back to the window, muttering. "I should never have let you talk me into your absurd scheme. Now get the hell out of here and let me be."

Hugh was all too glad to leave the judge. He was not exactly happy at the ass chewing he'd received, which left him in a real pissy mood. Now, in addition to his work, he needed to set up a sting operation to take down Dixie's, making sure none of his own guys were there. *Does the headache ever end?* he asked himself as he stalked out of Poe's hospital room.

Judge Poe received another visitor shortly after Hugh left; it was Joe Marble.

"How are you doing today, sir?" asked Joe, sounding concerned.

"Why are you here, Marble? I thought I warned you to keep your nose clean."

"Oh . . . I am, sir," Joe said through a faint smile. "It's why I am here. I came by to check on you and to make sure you were not too badly hurt last night."

"If I wasn't hurt, I wouldn't be in here now, would I, moron?" Judge Poe barked at the private investigator. Joe was not thrilled at the moron comment, but continued on in a professional manner.

"Nasty business last night, sir, are you OK?" Joe was trying to sound sincere.

"I just told you I wasn't fine, shithead," he replied irritably. "How many times are you going to ask me the same question, Marble?"

Joe happily obliged the cranky judge and changed subject. "Can you tell me what happened last night, sir?"

"I don't remember," Poe said abruptly.

"Well, did you hear or see anything?" Joe tried again.

"No, moron, there was a pillow over my face. I was being suffocated."

"I thought you said you didn't know what happened."

The judge turned his head, refusing to look Joe in the eye. His voice trembled, and he was getting defensive; Joe knew in an instant that Poe was about to lie.

The judge was certainly getting more agitated every moment. *First, Gallagher, and now, Marble. I am going to crucify them all,* he said to himself.

"Like I said, Marble, I have no idea what happened, but I am not too old to know there was a pillow over my face and I could not breathe, you moron." It was the third time Poe had called Joe a moron; it took every ounce of his energy to remain professional with the judge.

"Well, sir, I understand two SWAT team guys went down. Apparently they were staying at your house for quite some time." Joe was not going to let up; he did not like the judge's name-calling, but stayed calm and reserved hoping he could trick the judge into a clue.

"Yes, I received death threats from a bastard named David Armstrong, a shitbag I put away years ago. He recently was released, so Gallagher suggested I get protection."

"But the members of the SWAT are city employees, Judge. Why did you not hire regular bodyguards, sir?" Joe said, still trying to get something out of him.

"Look, Marble. I don't have the time or patience for your questions. Why don't you go ask Gallagher if you need more answers? His ass is not sitting in a hospital bed needing rest like mine." Joe could tell he was not going to get anything more out of the judge, but after questioning him, Joe was convinced there was more to the story. His experience taught him to recognize a 'rat bastard,' as Harris called them, when he smelled one.

"Well, sir, you rest up and get well soon. Our great city needs you to protect us," Joe said, being facetious now.

"Get out of here, Marble, and do your job."

"It is what I am trying to do, sir," Joe said respectfully. "By the way, just one more question: do you know why this David Armstrong was sending you the death threats?"

"David Armstrong is one of the slimiest, two-faced, double-crossing, drug dealing bastards whom I have ever encountered. You're supposed to be this exceptional detective, you tell me what makes shitbags like him tick."

"If you want my opinion, Judge, which I'm sure you don't, but two-faced, backstabbing, rat bastards like him deserve a lifetime in jail. Well, sir, thank you for your help, you rest up and get well soon," Joe said smirking, but trying to stay on his good side. The way this case was going, who knows when he would run into Poe on the bench again. The thought of this made Joe cringe. Once he left Poe's room, he called Harris.

"Hey, man, you're right, Mr. Assistant DA. There is more to Judge Poe's story than meets the eye."

"What makes you say that, Joe?" Harris asked, curious.

"Oh . . . it's a hunch right now. My visit with Judge Poe was most interesting. He sure doesn't like to say much, but his face gives him away. Hmm . . . Like someone else I know who keeps tight-lipped about the little lady," said Joe, teasing Harris. "Do not fear. I can assure you we'll get to the bottom of all this. It is going to take some time, but I *am* making progress."

"I ate breakfast with Hugh this morning," Harris said. "He tells me Poe was receiving death threats, and that's why Hugh assigned a SWAT team to cover him."

"I got the same story, man," Joe replied. "I'm heading back over to Poe's house right now to check out a few things. I'll call and check in later."

"Let's meet at Mama's around seven, OK with you, Joe?"

"Sure thing," Joe said, getting ready to hang up.

"Wait just a minute, Joe. There is one more thing. I want you to check out a David Armstrong for me. Hugh informed me that Poe put him away for life, just for dealing drugs. There is something wrong with the picture, but that's another case for another day. Apparently, they just paroled him. He was supposedly sending Poe death threats. It's why our boys were protecting the judge."

"Poe gave me the same name and details," Joe said. "My question is why our SWAT boys were at his house. Why not regular bodyguards?"

"Hmm, this gets more suspicious by the minute if you ask me," said Harris.

"You're right there, my friend. Later," said Joe.

"See you," Harris replied, hanging up.

Harris sat back in his chair to take a quick break, turning on his e-mail. He started to type. *Dear little girl,* he began. *Would you kindly join me on Saturday at two o'clock for a picnic in the park? I would gladly bring a basket containing ham and pepper jack cheese sandwiches. I will bring sweet tea, and we can pretend it is strawberry wine, which reminds me of the color of your lips.* He attached a song called "Strawberry Wine," then continued. *I will not allow rain.* He attached another song, "Like the Rain." He was on a roll. *We will lay our blanket out, along with our picnic basket, and eat amongst the beautiful flowers. I will take one red rose to break off the stem and place it behind your ear, running my hand through your gorgeous, long, wavy hair.* He attached a song called "Like Red on a Rose." Still typing, he added, *If the weather does get bad, I know of a little cave we can retreat to where there is a bed in case it rains for too long. I will keep you safe and warm wrapped in my arms. God made my shoulder for one special person, and I know when your head lays on it, you are the one.* He attached the song, "Open Arms," as he knew it was one of her favorite songs. Feeling frisky now, he started to finish up. *I don't want to sound too forward, but I want to tell you I wake up thinking about you and fall asleep with you on my mind.* He added the song, "Always on My Mind." *I think you are one in a million.* He attached the song by Ty Herndon, "Her Heart Is only Human." *I know I probably sound crazy, but from the first time I spoke to you, I knew I wanted to be with you.* He ended the e-mail with one more song,.38 Special's "Caught Up in You," then signed off with, *Truly, your little boy . . . smile.* He must have read the e-mail twenty times before he hit the Send button, hoping she would think he just took her on the perfect virtual date.

Working at her desk, Markita heard the telltale chime alerting her to a new e-mail. She opened her account and read Harris's invitation. She felt the fluttering of the same butterflies that often inhabited Harris's stomach. A big smile came across her face, and a small tear of happiness appeared in the corner of her eye. *Gosh, he is sweet,* she thought. *And so romantic.* She hit Reply and typed: *Little Boy, I would love to go on a picnic with you. There is nothing I would rather do on Saturday afternoon.* Mimicking his style of attaching music to his e-mails, she attached a song called "Saturday in the Park." *It will be so nice spending time with you. If you are good,* she added, *"I might let you kiss me.* She attached a song called, "Kiss the Girl." *I love the sound of the rose behind my ear; it reminds me of a Tanya Tucker song. Do you like her?* She attached a song called, "Delta Dawn." *Let us hope the weather stays nice for a while, but I hope at the end of it, we encounter rain, although I don't think there are any beds in caves around here. It sounds like a great date.* She signed it, *Always, Markita, YLG (your little girl)*

Harris pounced on his e-mail as soon as it announced he had a reply. His face sprung a big smile; by the looks of her response, Markita possessed intelligence along with a sexy wit. He was so lucky. *This woman is incredible and beautiful, but what she sees in me is beyond me,* he thought to himself. Although he had only known her for a short time, he knew already that she was the one. This girl was the love of his life, his hot Florida mama, as Joe teased him. He knew in his heart that this was going to be the girl he would marry one day. He e-mailed her back one more time, telling her it was a date and if she wanted a bed in the cave, there would be one.

It was another long day already, and Harris still needed to meet with Joe to go over the Barnes case, which was about to start on Monday. He paged through to Markita and asked her if she wanted to go to Mama's a little early. They could grab a soda before Joe arrived. Markita was definitely ready to go. Harris changed clothes, picked up Markita, and the two drove to Mama's in separate cars. Once the hostess showed them to their table and the waiter brought them their drinks, Harris started the conversation.

"Is pizza OK with you? It's Joe's favorite, and I know it is what he will want," Harris said to Markita.

"It is fine with me," she replied.

"While we're waiting, is two o'clock OK for Saturday?" He sounded a bit overexcited, but at least he spoke coherently for a change.

"Oh yes, little boy, two o'clock would be fine," she replied, sounding like the Southern bell he felt she was.

"There is a beautiful park right on a lake with paddleboats," he told her. "We could eat and then work off our food by paddling. There is also a huge oak tree with a rope, which people love to swing on and then let go and jump into the water from it. You probably should bring a bathing suit." Harris turned bright red thinking about her in a bathing suit. She could tell what he was thinking.

"My, my, little boy, where is your mind going?" she drawled.

"Hey, guys, am I interrupting anything?" Joe said as he sat down laughing. He watched them looking at each other all starry-eyed.

"Hey, Joe, how is it going?" Harris answered, clearing his throat and breaking eye contact with Markita. Joe looked at Harris's red face, wondering if he should take a jab while he could, but thought maybe he would give the assistant district attorney a break for a change.

"Hello, pretty lady, how are you this evening?" he said to Markita instead.

"Fine, thank you, Joe," she responded politely.

"We were waiting on you before ordering as I knew you would want pizza, big guy," Harris informed him.

"Well, you thought right. Let's order and get started. I have a date tonight with a blond chick named Robin, and man, is she hot."

"Oh yeah, how did you meet this one, Joe?" asked Harris.

"She's a singer in the club I frequent. Man, does she have some tubes," Joe replied, shaking his head admiringly.

Harris was about to get one over on Joe when he piped up again after seeing the look on his friend's face.

"OK, Harris, get your mind out of the gutter, boy. I meant her vocal tubes, buddy." Harris and Markita both laughed.

"Let's get started, we don't want to keep Mr. Hot Pants a moment longer than we have to."

Markita took out her notepad and wrote as the two men went over the case. They finished their sodas and pizza and then wrapped up the evening.

"Well, you fine folks, I guess I will bid you good night," Joe said as he stood up to go.

"Tell Robin we said hi," Harris said, teasing him.

"I will, big guy," Joe said with a smile. "You take this little hot mama of yours home and don't be doing anything I wouldn't be doing," he said laughing and leaving them with a wink.

Harris paid the check and walked Markita out to her car; she stood close to him looking at him with soft, warm eyes, her lips calling out to him. *Go for it, coward,* he heard his conscience tell him. His heart skipped a beat as he took hold of the back of her head, gently bringing her closer. He prayed that his legs wouldn't give way under him as he was trembling like a teenager getting his first kiss. His lips finally touched hers, and he forgot all time. Markita took her finger, rubbed it along his bottom lip, and then kissed him back. The two of them could hear each other's heartbeat; they both felt the passion of young love. Harris did not want the kiss to end, but he also did not want to go overboard and make a fool out of himself.

Slowly, he pulled back, carefully stroking her hair off her face and said, "Good night, little girl. This kiss will have to last you until we meet again. Please call me when you get home to let me know you got there safely."

"I will, little boy," she replied in a whisper. She squeezed his hand gently as she stepped away, gazing into his eyes.

Harris sat in his car for a moment watching Markita drive away. He had never felt this way about anyone before. He actually felt a tear come to his eye. His heart was full of love, and he thought it would burst. His adrenaline was rushing so much he felt lightheaded. This must be what love feels like, he said to himself, and then smiled before firing up the Jag.

When he walked in the door of his apartment, he heard the phone ring. He almost fell over the coffee table trying to get it before it stopped ringing.

"Hi," is all he could managed to utter.

"Hi, I made it home, LB. Thank you for a wonderful evening." Markita's voice seemed to tickle his ear like butterfly wings.

"Same here, little girl. See you at work tomorrow."

There was a pause, then, "You're a fantastic kisser." She hung up as quickly as she could before Harris could think of a reply. As he slowly replaced the phone in its cradle, Harris repeated to himself *LB*; he loved her calling him by a pet name. *She thinks I am a great kisser.* He blushed at the thought. He went to bed with good thoughts, sleeping so well, and dreaming about her all night.

The following morning, Harris was up early. He drank his coffee, putting the mug in the sink before he left for work. *Thank goodness, it's Friday,* he thought to himself. It had already been a long week, and with the Barnes trial starting next week, his days and nights would be rough ones. It was always grueling for him when he was in court because he liked being more than fully prepared before, as well as during the trial. He was like his father in that respect;

he wanted no surprises. Some of his father's closing arguments were examples used in law schools; he was exceptional at painting a picture for the jury. It was one of the reasons Mark Robertson won so many cases and had earned the nickname the Florida Hurricane. Harris intended to be better than his father.

He wasn't at work too long before he got a call from Joe.

"Hey, man," Joe greeted him. "You're not going to believe this, but I'm in trouble again."

"What do you mean?" Harris asked, thinking to himself, *This cannot be good.*

"I've been arrested . . . again," Joe said dejectedly.

"What for this time?" asked Harris, concerned for his friend, but inwardly sighing from the knowledge that he would have to bail him out again.

"After my date with Robin, I headed over to Miss Dixie's place," Joe explained. "Apparently she was throwing a big party in another part of the house which I was unaware of at the time. There were all kinds of celebrity-types, starlets, producers, you name it, they were there. Looked like there were some key players in from Washington too. Even a couple of Japanese businessmen. I also saw what looked like undercover agents wearing wires. They must have called in the raid. I was there to follow up on Amber Andrews's allegation when our city boys took the place down."

"So how does that get you arrested?"

"Come on, Harris. Do you really need me to explain?"

"Oh, Joe, you weren't . . . were you?" Harris stumbled, hoping the answer to the question of Joe being with a prostitute was no.

"Of course not, man!" Joe answered him quickly. "But it still doesn't look good for me. I was in a room with a broad called Bambi, but I was fully dressed asking her questions."

"I'm just asking, Joe, so I can get my ducks in a row, but was Bambi dressed?" Harris almost chuckled, wanting to ask him so badly if this would be an appropriate time for the duck joke, but he thought better of it.

"This is not funny, arsehole," Joe snapped. "I can't afford to be arrested again! The court will pull my bail on the other arrest."

"Hold on there, big guy," Harris said, trying to calm his friend. "Before you get your britches in a twist, I'm pretty sure Hugh is in this morning, so I'll go down and have him take care of things for you. By the way, why am I just now hearing about this?"

"Man, they've had me holed up all night. I don't know where everyone else is because I am in a holding room by myself, and I wasn't allowed my one phone call." Joe sounded angry. "Enough of the chitchat, Harris. Get me out of this one, Robertson, and I'll pay for coffee next time we go to Mama's."

"Great, Joe, you're such a big spender. Hold tight and let me see what I can do, man."

"Hey, Harris, before you go." Joe was serious now. "You need to watch your back there. I'm beginning to unravel some crap, and it is not good, man. I can tell you this: something went terribly wrong with the raid. I heard some of our own bigwigs were there and got arrested. It is not going to fare well for whoever is behind this mess."

"OK, stay calm there, Joe. I'll have you out in no time." Harris hoped what he told Joe would tide him over until he found out what was going down at Miss Dixie's place from Hugh. Harris walked down to Hugh's office. Before he even got to his secretary, however, he could hear Hugh screaming at someone on the phone. Harris glanced over at Hugh's secretary who looked embarrassed to see him.

"Do you think I should come back later?" Harris inquired.

"I don't think it would be a good idea for me to page through to him at this point," the secretary said, her eyes wide. "You might want to come back later." Agreeing with her, Harris turned to walk away, but Hugh suddenly came flying out of his office.

"Harris, I'm glad you're here," he barked. Harris wasn't sure it was good to be here after hearing Hugh's loud and angry voice.

"Come into my office—now," he demanded.

"What's going on, Hugh?" Harris asked, concerned, as they strode quickly into Hugh's large corner office.

"It's the city guys. They raided Miss Dixie's place last night."

"The problem with that would be . . . ?" Harris asked.

"The damn medical examiner was there as well as the freaking mayor," Hugh nearly screamed at him.

"Hmm . . . not good I suppose," said Harris, wondering why he would be concerned. If the law was broken, it was the job of his office to prosecute people breaking the law, no matter who they were. He realized this was a bit naive of him to think this way, but it was how he saw his own duty to the office of the prosecutor.

"Not only was the damn mayor there," Hugh continued, sputtering and pacing behind his desk, "but Senator Johnson also got himself arrested! He will be livid." Harris did not understand where Hugh's fury was coming from.

"Well, sir, we have another dilemma. Joe Marble was there doing some investigations for Judge Poe's situation."

"Then the damn fool should have kept his pants on," Hugh said furiously.

"His pants were on, sir, and so were the woman's. We need to get him out and the charges dropped because of the other incident he incurred."

"Yes, yes, Harris, fine. Why don't you go over to processing at the jail, and I will continue making phone calls trying to find out what this whole freakin' mess is all about?"

Harris nodded, relieved that Hugh was taking his side on this. Hugh waved at him impatiently as he picked up his phone again, so Harris made his exit.

As the door closed on Harris Robertson, Hugh put the phone down and dropped down into his leather chair, rubbing his hands across his face. He couldn't believe how things were turning out. Hugh knew the raid was set to go at his command, but he had never given the go-ahead. Hugh was now scrambling as it was obvious someone had undermined his operation. How was he going to cover the arrests of the mayor, Senator Johnson, and the medical examiner, the last of which did him a big favor by disposing of certain evidence in the Smith debacle? His other concern was his friend, the chief of police. Someone in his department screwed up, unless it was James himself, vying for a takeover. Maybe someone working for him was a plant? *Things could not be worse,* he told himself. He picked up the phone again to start making some serious inquiries.

Meanwhile, Harris headed over to processing, but on his way out of the office, he picked up Markita. As always, she was happy to accompany him. By the time they got to the jail, the processing and release of the mayor, Senator Johnson, and the medical examiner was complete, as it was for all the girls arrested in the raid. Harris noted Amber Andrews was already trying to interview the medical examiner although it was off camera. He was happy to find out Miss Dixie was still detained; this would give him a chance to question her once he got Joe out. He looked everywhere for Joe and was finally directed to a small holding room where he found his friend ecstatic to see him and Markita.

"What is going on out there?" asked Joe, now more interested in the raid than his own skin.

"From what I gather, they've released most of the big names. Amber Andrews is trying to interview them," Harris said. "I saw one of my colleagues from the DA's office, as well as the fire marshal still in processing. The chief of police was out there getting booked, making all kinds of threats. When he saw me, he instructed me to get Hugh over here immediately, but then he clammed up. So this leaves you and Miss Dixie, and it looks like she's not going anywhere today except for a cell."

Joe leaned back in his rickety holding room chair and shook his head in wonder. "My god, man. You should have been there last night. The city cops were all over the place. They stormed into all the rooms arresting people without even asking any questions. I tried to flash my PI credentials, but they wanted no part of any explanations."

"Thank God, it was only your credentials you were flashing." Harris looked over at Markita and winked. Joe frowned, not amused. "Do you know what your status is?" Harris asked, changing the subject.

"No clue. They just threw me in here. You are the first person I've seen."

"Well, you and Markita stay here, and I'll go find out what is happening."

"Thanks, man, you know I can't have another arrest on my record."

Harris smiled as he turned to get the guard's attention. While he waited for him to unlock the holding cell, he turned to Joe. "By the way," he said. "Behave yourself with Markita. She's a lady." Then Harris left the room, giving Joe the perfect opportunity to go fishing for information on his friend.

"Man, does the assistant DA like you or what?" he asked boldly.

"I don't know," Markita replied. "But he is excellent at his job, so I think he will have you out in no time." She beamed with pride as she talked about Harris.

"Wow, he has you whipped already," joked Joe.

"I don't know what you could possibly mean, Joe, but if you are referring to the fact I like working with him, then I would have to agree with you."

"A little defensive, aren't we?" Joe teased again.

Markita shifted in her seat across the table from Joe. "Hmmm. I don't think you're in quite the position to piss me off," said Markita sternly.

Man, what a little spitfire, Joe thought to himself. *So defensive of the assistant DA, I think she's hooked.* He was happy for his friend. He'd been hearing for years that Harris wouldn't let anyone into his life until he became a judge, and that always made Joe feel sorry for him. What a boring life. His own date the night before with the blond Robin was fantastic; in fact, he'd asked her out a second time and was glad Harris seemed to be enjoying life a bit more too. Just then, Harris reentered the room.

"Wow, man, you were gone long enough. Did you find out anything?" Joe ribbed him.

"Yes, my impatient friend. They are processing your release as we speak."

"You are the best!" Joe leaped up and clapped Harris on the shoulder. "Do you know if this is going against my record?"

"No, apparently not," Harris told him, looking somewhat baffled. "It will be as if the arrest never happened." Even though Harris was happy for his friend, something about this stank as bad as a skunk. He'd been told that Joe would have to sign some pretty unorthodox paperwork in order to use his "get out of jail free" card.

"At least I found out some info from Bambi," Joe was saying eagerly. "But we need to wait until I get out of here before we discuss the matter."

"That's probably a good idea, Joe," said Harris, wondering what was taking so long for his release. A moment later, an officer entered the room with papers in his hand for Joe to sign. The private detective read over them carefully then began to sign as quickly as he could.

"What do the papers say?" asked Harris inquisitively. "Do you want me to read them over?"

"Nothing major," Joe said casually. "It basically has me agree that I cannot discuss the arrest or incident with anyone."

"It smells, does it not, Joe? Might put a damper on our conversation later tonight," Harris said.

"Yeppers, sure could," Joe replied. "Stinks to high heaven, but I'll say anything I have to in order to get out of here."

When Joe finished signing the papers and the officer told him he was free to go, Harris asked Joe a favor. "Can you take Markita back to the office for me? I want to go see if I can talk to the police chief as well as Miss Dixie. Who knows? Maybe I'll get lucky and someone will enlighten me about what went down here."

"Sure." Joe smiled. "I would love to take this pretty mama anywhere with me." He winked again at Markita, and she gave a small smile in response.

"Enough Joe. Please try to be respectful," Harris said, smiling at his friend.

Markita was not happy with the situation. She wanted to stay with Harris, but knew she had little chance of changing his mind.

"Once I drop the little lady off, I'll head over to the medical examiner's office," said Joe as they walked out of the cramped holding room. "Maybe he is pissed enough about his treatment at Miss Dixie's to talk to me now about the missing evidence."

"Good luck with that. Let's check back in later this afternoon." Harris looked at Markita. "I'll check in with you too, if that's all right with you," he said, looking right into her eyes. Markita gave him one of her special smiles and said, "Of course. I look forward to your call." Then she turned to followed Joe out, leaving Harris to go see about arranging interviews with the police chief and Miss Dixie. He decided to start with the madam first.

After making arrangements to have her brought to a room for questioning, he allowed time for her to wait for him, wondering what might be coming next. When he finally entered the room, he showed nothing but confidence.

"Harris Robertson," he greeted her. "Assistant to the district attorney's office, nice to meet you." He offered her his hand in greeting, but when she didn't take it, he moved to the small table between them and sat down. Miss Dixie said nothing, but she did look him in the eyes, trying to get a good reading on him, he supposed. She was likely quite skilled at first impressions in her line of work.

"How are you, ma'am?" Harris asked, trying to sound as if he was halfway concerned.

"Just peachy," she replied in a heavy Southern drawl. "I love being arrested." She leaned back and stared at Harris as if he was wasting her time.

If her attitude bothered Harris, he didn't show it. "I wanted to let you know that all your girls were released without incident." Harris thought this might soften her up, but although he could tell she was relieved, she still said nothing.

"I'll come straight to the point, ma'am," Harris tried again. "If you give me some names, I am sure I will be able to get you released this afternoon. How does that sound?" Miss Dixie again stayed silent.

"It's your choice, Miss Dixie," Harris sighed. "You can make this easy on yourself or tough, but in the end, the district attorney's office will win, we always do. I think sex trafficking will be the first of many charges which will stick." Harris let the silence stretch for several long moments, but Miss Dixie barely batted an eyelash She was tough, he'd give her that. Harris knew he was not going to get a thing out of her right now, but he would be back.

"OK, if this is the way you want this to play out"—he spread his hands in a helpless gesture—"I hope you enjoy your stay." He rose from his chair and turned to leave, then paused. "I will give you one more chance to give me names," he said. "I will be a lot easier to deal with here than in the courtroom. Otherwise, I'm out of here."

She didn't even pause before giving him her answer. "Good-bye, Mr. Assistant DA. It was nice meeting you," she said coolly. Harris shrugged and walked calmly out the door. She seemed tough on the outside, but he bet himself she was not so tough on the inside. *We'll see,* he thought as he proceeded to the detention room holding the chief of police.

The chief started talking the moment Harris stepped into the room.

"It's about time you got here," he barked. "Did you tell Hugh to get his ass over here like I told you?"

"Not yet," Harris replied, trying not to show his nerves. "I thought we could have a friendly chat first."

"I don't need any friends, thanks," the chief said gruffly. "I just want to get out of here, and I'll need Hugh's help, kid," Harris did not appreciate the kid reference.

"How is it Hugh can get you released, sir? You broke the law, did you not?" Harris pointed out.

"You know, I am really in no mood for your amateur theatrics, *kid.* You're no Mark Robertson, so don't even try acting like your father." Harris was getting annoyed with the chief, but stayed collected.

"Knew my father, did you, sir?"

"Yes, I did. He was a good man, and he knew the score. I would have been out by now if he was here."

"I'm sure my father would appreciate your sentiment. I heard he was an outstanding prosecutor, but I don't think he would have pulled strings to release someone from jail who broke the law," Harris retorted, going into full hurricane mode.

"Look, kid, I'm not trying to being rude here, but I know how straight you are, so why don't you run along and tell Gallagher to get his ass here on the double. Got it?"

"Not really, sir. I am still trying to figure out how Hugh will get you out." Harris was now playing a little game with him, trying to sound inexperienced.

"You don't think I know the score here, kid, but I'm not saying another word to you."

"It is OK, sir, you have said quite enough. Enjoy your stay," Harris said as he left the room with more unanswered questions concerning Hugh and the events at Miss Dixie's than he started with.

He called Joe on his cell phone as he made his way down the station steps. "Hey, man," he greeted his friend. "Have you been to see the medical examiner yet?"

"Yes, sir, I sure have, and I have quite a bit to tell you, my friend."

"Can't wait to hear what you've got. I just came from the police chief's cell, and I have a report to give to you too. Let's meet after work today, OK?"

"Sure thing, partner. Call me when you get a chance. Later."

"Later, man, stay safe, my friend," Harris said as they both hung up.

Chapter Eight

The Date

Smith made it back home, but the bleeding had worsened. He needed to get the bullet out of his shoulder before he passed out. Removing the cap of a whiskey bottle he'd grabbed from beside his bed, he first took a couple of large swigs, then pulled out the knife he had planned to cut the judge's hands off with, and poured some of the whiskey over it. As he steeled himself for what he had to do next, Smith thought back over that evening's events, more than pissed that his mission had been interrupted, and worse, that he hadn't gotten the chance to sever the judge's hands as planned. He took a few more swigs of the whiskey before digging the point of the hunting knife into his skin. Gritting his teeth hard, he tried not to scream out.

"Damn," he said aloud. "It's deeper than I thought." A pulse-like sensation started to throb in his throat, and he began to taste his own puke. He was sweating profusely now. The knifepoint searched and finally found the bullet. Trying to steady his hand, he pulled the knife back some and then tried to slide the knifepoint underneath the bullet, this time lifting it up and popping the bullet out. His pain was now so intense he could not hold back any longer; he managed to grab a pillow and screamed into it. Now feeling faint and queasy, all he wanted to do was lie down, but he knew he needed to dress his wound first or he could bleed to death. Once again, he opened the bottle of whisky, this time pouring it over the open wound in his shoulder. Quickly, he grabbed the pillowcase and tore it at the seam. Using the shreds of fabric as a makeshift bandage, he wrapped his shoulder as best he could before passing out.

Night had fallen again when he finally regained consciousness. He seemed to remember waking one or two other times, but relapsed back into a semicomatose state. Leaning over, he turned on a small night lamp, which sat on his bedside table. As he moved to sit up, his whole arm hurt like hell. Looking around blearily, he noticed the bloody knife he used to extract the bullet from his shoulder lying next to him on the bed. Dried blood covered his bedsheets and the clothes he was still wearing. There were also bloodstains on the floor, directly below the knife, where the blood had dripped. Smith slowly pulled himself up from the bed and walked over to the fireplace, which sat in the corner of the room. His place was arranged much like a studio apartment, where the bedroom and living room were connected. The only two separate rooms were the kitchen and bathroom. He was a man with few needs, and his furniture, including his bed, a small sunken couch, a beat-up dresser with a broken drawer, an old wooden end table, which he used solely to house the phone, and a television, which stood on a rotted crate, were all items retrieved over time from a nearby Dumpster.

There were some logs in a box by the fireplace. He staggered across the room and placed a few of them in the grate, along with a fire starter. Smith began ripping off his bloody clothes and threw them in with the logs. He limped back toward the small dresser next to his bed and put on a clean pair of boxers. Grabbing his bottle of whisky, he took a few more swigs, hoping to deaden his pain. He set the bottle down carefully next to the phone, then removed all the bed linen, placing all of it in the fireplace with his clothes. Finally, he grabbed a lighter from the mantel and set the whole pile ablaze.

Smith stood back and watched for a few moments as everything burned. Once he was sure everything would soon be ash, he proceeded into the bathroom, taking off his make-do bandage and boxers, placing them both in the sink. He took a long, cold shower making sure all his blood dripped down the drain. He waited until all the red water turned clear.

Thinking more astutely now, he grabbed a towel, dried himself off with it, and put his boxers back on before placing the bloody bandage in the towel, making sure not to leave any traces of blood. He walked back into the main room where he threw both items into the now-blazing fire. Smith grabbed the bottle of whiskey again, taking it with him back into the bathroom. Underneath the sink, he kept some large gauze pads for occasions such as this. Taking one out, he doused with whiskey. He then opened the medicine cabinet and took out a roll of bandages. Placing the gauze on his wound first, he wrapped his shoulder tightly with the bandage.

Once he finished redressing his wound, he reached back into the medicine cabinet, pulling out a bottle of pain medication. Normally he could tolerate large amounts of pain, but right now, this was too intense. He took three pills with more swigs of his whisky. "That should kill the pain," he said aloud. An old bottle of antibiotics sat on the shelf staring at him; he opened that bottle too and took four, hoping to fight off any infection. Next, he went into the kitchen, filled up a bowl with bleach and soapy water, and began to remove all the remaining bloodstains from the floors, sink, and tub, being careful not to miss any spots. Dressing in dark clothes, he threw his boxers on the fire, then changed out the bowl of water and took it outside to his car.

It took him several hours and at least a dozen trips back and forth to the kitchen, refilling the bowl with clean water each time, in order to eliminate all the bloodstains. Every time he returned to the house, he stopped for a few more swigs of whisky; the bottle was almost empty now, which made his job all the more difficult as the effects of the medicine, combined with the whiskey, made his movements seem slow and labored. He often found himself pausing midtask, staring off into space.

The work was finally done, however, and Smith was satisfied that he had removed all the incriminating evidence from the car and his house. He even got rid of the bullet by burying it outside. He closed the front door behind him and headed back to the kitchen to dump his last bowl of bloody water. The phone suddenly rang, jarring his already-edgy nerves. Turning, Smith noticed the message light was flashing, which meant someone must have tried to call him while he was unconscious. Perhaps they were calling back now.

"Yeah," he answered as he grabbed the phone off the hook.

"Hello, son, how are you?" asked the icy-cold voice on the line.

"Fine, sir," Smith answered respectfully.

"I have a job for you."

Smith waited for the information he knew would come, gritting his teeth in pain. His shoulder was throbbing again.

"I want Stewart Pope taken out as soon as possible."

"Yes, sir, consider it done."

"Are you sure you're OK, Philip? You don't sound so good."

"Fine, sir."

"How is the new car and house which I found for you?"

"Fine, sir." The voice on the other end of the phone knew Smith was a man of few words, but tonight, his voice seemed unusually quiet and pained.

"Let me know when it is done," the Voice said softly.

"Yes, sir." Smith hung up the phone.

"But it will have to wait until this wound heals," he said to himself. "I can't risk leaving my blood sample anywhere for those bastard cops to find, damn assholes."

He had no great regard for cops, or for that matter, anyone with authority. He did, however, respect the Voice who called him from time to time to give him an assignment. It was the only consistent contact he had with the outside world. The Voice had checked on him throughout his orphanage years, providing everything he needed; in addition, this person trained him to become as swift as an animal at killing. He justified his lifestyle by believing the Voice cared about him—thus he owed this man his life. The Voice would always call him *son*, but when he asked one day if he was Smith's real father, the reply was no. Smith decided he was just grateful this person was his caregiver and would leave it at that.

Smith tried to lie down and go back to sleep, but the room was spinning like a carousel, and his mind began to torture him, unaccustomed as it was to failing in a mission. And of late, he hadn't failed just once. His mind had plenty to torture him with. First, he got himself arrested while taking Eleanor Woodsworth's head as a gift to Miss Dixie, and now he'd failed to sever the judge's hands as he had planned. His mind retraced his steps, wondering what kind of evidence he could possibly have left behind, knowing there had to be drops of his blood there—maybe not so much in the judge's bedroom, but possibly out on the deck where he jumped onto the ground. He remembered parking his car at the end of the drive, potentially leaving blood from the judge's house to the end of the driveway.

Clueless as to what day it was or how long he had been out, he reached over to the night table and took a few more swigs of whiskey, emptying the bottle. He hoped it would stop the pain from returning and make some of his thoughts disappear as well. Smith picked up the phone to call his old friend Miss Dixie. She was always a source of comfort to him the few times he needed it. He was shocked to hear an unfamiliar female voice on the other end of the line. She always answered her own private line.

"Is Miss Dixie there?" he asked cautiously.

"Who is this?" asked the girl. She sounded sweet, but he was sure she just thought he was a regular customer.

"I'm a friend of the Doll's," he responded gruffly. He hoped his pet name for the madam would ring a bell. Luckily, the girl answering the phone had heard Dixie talk about a friend who called her "Doll," and her tone changed from charming to wary.

"She's in jail," the young girl snapped, her voice hushed. Smith's adrenaline began to pump. He was furious at himself for not being there for her.

"What happened?" he asked, desperate for information. How long *had* it been since his aborted attack on Poe?

"We were raided," she told him. She did not seem to want to say anymore, and Smith understood; there was no telling if the phones were bugged, and she wouldn't want to get herself into any more trouble. One visit to jail was likely enough for her. Before he could say anything else, he heard the phone disconnect. He stared blankly at the dead phone in his hand, then hung it up quietly. Smith then stood up, walked over to the fireplace, and punched a hole in the wall. His anger over took his senses. The killer gritted his teeth while he rapidly sucked air in and out of his lungs, making a low growling sound. Snot dripped from his nose as he punched the wall a second time, leaving a large cavity in it. Now, not only did his left arm hurt, but his right fist throbbed as well. He grabbed the bottle of whiskey, remembered it was empty, then threw it into the fireplace where it shattered. Angry and frustrated at himself, he began looking for another bottle. He wanted to go out and do *something*, but he knew he couldn't go anywhere until his wound healed some. Vowing to get the bastard who did this to his Doll, Smith picked up the phone again and called Hugh.

"What the freakin' hell are you doing letting the Doll go to jail?" Smith burst out before Hugh could even say hello.

"Calm yourself," Hugh said. He could hear the other man's heavy breathing and noticed he slurred his words. Drunk, he guessed. "It's all a mistake," he soothed, "and I am taking care of everything."

"You better get the Doll out tomorrow," Smith threatened. "Or I am coming after you. Trust me, you will not enjoy the slow and torturous ending which I will deliver."

"It's not that simple, Smith. I'm doing all I can, but things are complicated. My assistant DA is involved, and I have to go by the book on this one. Don't worry," he said again. "I've made her my priority and will get her out as soon as I can." Hugh had thrown Harris straight under the bus, but that was his plan all along. This time everything was falling into place. *It's about time I caught a break,* Hugh said to himself.

"Then you can kiss your assistant DA and his family good-bye," Smith was saying. He was quite drunk now, Hugh could tell. He quietly hung up and smiled to himself, leaving the Executioner once again staring at a dead phone.

It was Saturday morning; Harris awoke with a huge smile on his face, knowing he was venturing on a big date with Markita today. Although thoughts of her consumed his mind, he did feel guilty for not been able to get with Joe the previous afternoon to go over what the two of them each discovered. Things were hectic around the office yesterday afternoon, and Hugh had been in a foul mood. Harris discovered that someone from their own office, another lawyer, had gotten caught up in the bust at Miss Dixie's, and Hugh was understandably pissed that the young man had gotten himself arrested. Hugh had fired him, but that hadn't sat well with the young lawyer; he'd threatened Hugh with exposure, of what, Harris was not yet sure. Later that afternoon, Harris heard Hugh dealing with the mayor. He could not hear the whole conversation, but it sounded like Hugh was going to try to work out a deal with him. He was not sure if his boss had visited the police chief yesterday, but he confirmed this morning that the chief, along with Miss Dixie, were still incarcerated.

Interested to find out what Joe learned from the medical examiner, he reached over to the side of the bed and called Joe's number, but there was no answer. He left him a message asking him to call him as soon as he could. He would be gone from two until at least five this afternoon, he hoped anyway. *Shoot*, thought Harris, *I will have to try him again later, unless our date goes into the wee evening hours*, he said to himself, smiling hopefully.

Lying in bed for a bit longer, he went over today's date with the most beautiful little girl in the world in his head. Harris then sprang out of bed, showered, shaved, and put on his favorite jeans and a brand-new maroon polo shirt. Dousing himself in Kenneth Cole cologne, he took one last look at himself in the mirror before heading downstairs to prepare everything for the picnic.

He took the basket from the pantry, a recent purchase that he picked up after his uncle J suggested this great idea. He made sandwiches with deli meat and cheese. Grabbing four bottles of his favorite sweet tea, he placed them, along with the sandwiches, into the basket. Going over his checklist, he made sure there were two plates, two cups, two spoons, along with some napkins. He planned on picking up coleslaw on his way to Markita's apartment. He also packed his MP3 player filled with music picked just for this occasion. He thought it would work out great as it contained all slow love songs. Not being able to wait any longer, he called Markita and asked if he could pick her up a little early and was pleasantly surprised when she responded with a sweet "Yes, LB."

He smiled with pleasure. "Damn, I am a lucky man." He locked up the house, ready to leave, when it dawned on him he needed a blanket for them to sit on. He also realized he'd forgotten his swimming trunks and a towel. He ran back upstairs, grabbed what he needed, and headed back out, rushing now so as not to be late. All flustered, he hoped there was nothing else he had forgotten. *Darnik, these butterflies in my stomach really need exterminating.* He wondered if Markita felt them as well. He surely hoped so.

Once the car was packed and ready to go, he headed out to pick her up, stopping for the slaw along the way. Then he proceeded on to a florist's, where he purchased a dozen roses. Wanting to impress her, he asked for eleven red and one white, which the florist placed in the middle of the arrangement for him. His heart gave a double beat, excited at the thought of giving her the bouquet. So far, he had been clumsy and tongue-tied; today he was going to try to be cool. This was the first date he'd had in a very long time, and certainly this one meant more to him than any other. He wanted everything to be perfect.

Harris parked the Jag in front of Markita's building and ran up to ring her apartment bell. The moment he saw her, he handed her the roses.

"For you my, fair lady." He watched her reaction.

"Oh, Harris, they are simply divine! You are so thoughtful." She smiled up at him, then gave a cute little curtsy. "Thank you, kind sir." She motioned him inside. "Please, come in for a moment while I put these beautiful flowers in a vase."

"Oh . . . wait a minute," she paused on her way to the kitchen. "It was you."

"What was me?" Harris asked, baffled.

"It was you that sent me the roses at the office. These are exactly the same: eleven red and one white."

"Ahh . . . you caught me, little girl," Harris said, smiling sheepishly.

"The prosecution rests, and you're guilty," she replied, and they both laughed. "I would love to take them with us to show them off, but they may wilt in the sun." She turned back toward the kitchen.

Harris could not take his eyes off her; she was wearing a short white sundress, which showed off her evenly tanned body, along with a pair of white sandals that showed off her perfect red toenails. As Markita picked up the bag she'd packed to take with her, Harris went over to the vase, pulled out one of the red roses, and broke off most of the stem, leaving enough to place behind her right ear. It matched her lipstick as well as her toenails and would look just right in her hair.

"You are such a perfect picture, young lady," he said.

"And you are a perfect gentlemen," she replied with a smile. He took her hand as they walked out to his car.

The man-made lake was wonderful; the sun shone on the water, making it glisten. Harris found a quiet spot and laid out the blanket for them to sit on. He pulled out his MP3 player, selecting the playlist he had created especially for her.

"Oh my, LB!" she sighed after listening to the beginning of the first song. "Love songs! What could you possibly have on your mind?" Markita giggled, her flirtatious eyes widening.

Harris had never been happier in his life. They chatted for what seemed like forever, discussing everything from politics to religion. They began to realize just how much they had in common; finally, they got around to the subject of family.

"My mother is coming to visit me next weekend," she informed him.

"That's wonderful, little girl. You must be so excited."

"Yes, I am, and I would love for you to meet her," Markita said proudly.

"I would love to meet her too." Harris smiled at her. "What should I call her when I meet her?"

"Trudy."

Harris suddenly flashed back to a fight his mother and father had once. He remembered his mother accusing his father of having affairs with someone named Brandy as well as a Trudy. He shook his head, wondering why that particular memory came to mind. He shrugged it off, wanting to turn his thoughts back to Markita.

They ate their sandwiches still talking and laughing until their sides hurt. They took a ride on the paddleboats and then changed into their swimsuits as Markita wanted to take a swing on the long rope, which swung out into the lake. As she slipped down her dress, she revealed a black-and-white bathing suit, which showed no tan lines. Harris's eyes nearly popped out of their sockets. He thought he must be dreaming as he pinched himself.

Markita seemed to read his mind and said, "You're not so bad looking yourself, Mr. Assistant District Attorney." They walked over to the rope, and Harris watched as she gracefully swung out into the middle of the lake and splashed down into the sparkling water. She came up laughing.

It was now his turn, so he went over to the swing, beat on his chest, grabbed the rope, and then hollered like Tarzan and jumped. He could not believe he let himself act this way. Normally, he was so reserved.

Markita swam over to him as he floated in the cool water.

"I hope I didn't embarrass you just now," he said concerned at what her answer might be.

"Not at all, LB. I love the fact that you can be silly around me." He took her in his arms then, and she wrapped her legs around his waist. Holding her tightly, he twirled her around, and they played together, laughing like little children. Suddenly they stopped . . . and just stood in the water looking into each other's eyes; it was one of those awkward moments where time stands still. It is at that moment when two people first realize they are in love.

Harris gently ran his fingers through her wet hair, cupping her head, and then kissing her softly. Markita returned his affection; their kisses became more and more passionate.

"I think we should get out and dry off, little girl, before we get into trouble in here," Harris whispered into her warm neck.

"Why, LB, you're blushing," she teased, pulling back and looking at him.

"I'm always blushing around you, little girl."

They held hands as they got out of the water. He led them back with such pride and confidence, Markita knew she could put her trust in him. With Harris, she felt secure.

Once back at their blanket, they took out towels and dried themselves, then lay together in the sun. Markita rested with her head lying on Harris's shoulder looking up to the sky.

"God made this shoulder just for you," he told her, his eyes closed. Her head felt so comfortable and right, lying on him. She leaned over and playfully nibbled on his lip, touching his mustache with her finger. He turned his head toward her with a smile on his face, and one eye opened.

"What is it you want, little boy?" Markita whispered in his ear, then holding him tight. Every now and again, he kissed her tenderly, telling her how beautiful she was and how he could not believe he could be this lucky.

Her heart ached for him with each moment they spent in such peaceful togetherness.

They listened to more of the music he brought with him. Every now and again, they would ask each other a question about themselves, trying to get to know each other's likes and dislikes, favorite colors, songs, foods. She asked him questions about his family and listened to him intently. No one had ever wanted to know everything about him as she did. He told her everything from his childhood, about his protective love he felt for his mother and strong relationship with his uncle J.

"You know, every December 20 and Mother's Day," Harris told her, "my uncle J takes flowers and lets off balloons in his mother's memory. She had been so sick, but he sat by her side making her laugh and be as comfortable as he could until the end. I think that kind of love and compassion is hard to find these days. Most people just want to ship their family members off to a nursing home out of the way."

Markita's heart exploded with admiration for him.

Harris had insecurities about his hearing and his speech impediment, but the longer they were together, the more at ease she made him feel. He could tell nothing about him bothered her, and it made him love her more.

They continued to talk for several hours. As the sun began to set, they packed up their picnic items and returned to the car. Harris drove her back to her apartment.

"Would you like to come in for a while?" she asked him.

"I would love to."

"I'm going to take a shower," she told him as she headed toward the bathroom. "Why don't you make yourself comfortable, and then you can shower afterward, if you'd like."

"Thank you, little lady." It was all Harris could do not to run into the bathroom and jump in the shower with her; he pictured her naked slender body under the water and then shrugged himself back to reality. He was too much of a gentleman, as well as shy.

Markita returned shortly, hair hanging in wet waves around her shoulders. She'd changed into a pair of comfy shorts and a soft T-shirt. She took Harris's hand and showed him where everything was for him to take his shower. After pointing out where the towels were, she headed back to the living room to wait for him to join her. It was also all Markita could do not to rush in and jump in the shower with him, but she did not want him to think she was a loose woman. Suddenly, she heard his voice calling her name. She hurried toward the bathroom.

"Markita, I need a towel," Harris said, feeling awkward.

"Then get out and get one," she teased.

"I am naked, little girl," he said apprehensively.

"Hmmm . . . you seem to have a dilemma, little boy," she teased again.

"Are you going to be nice to me, little girl?"

"I told you where the towels were. Why did you not listen to me, Mr. Robertson?" She was now laughing at him.

"I swear to you, little girl, if you don't bring me a towel to dry off with, you'll be sorry."

"Oh really, little boy? You realize *you're* the naked one?"

Harris thought for a moment. "OK, little girl, you win. Pretty please?"

He was so adorable she could not tease him anymore. She took him a towel.

"Thank you, little girl," Harris said with relief.

"You're welcome, Mr. Robertson," she retorted playfully, then left him to get dressed in privacy. Once he dried off, he reappeared in his polo shirt and jeans. Markita had prepared hot dogs for them. She hoped he liked them because they were easy to make and one of her favorites.

"Great hot dogs, Chiquita. How did you know I like mustard and only a few onions on mine?" he asked, not remembering he had told her earlier.

"I know everything about you, little boy. I would have put chili and cheese on the dogs, but I'm afraid I didn't have any. Sorry. And I only gave you a few onions as you are about to kiss me," she giggled at him.

"Well, if you insist, missy, come over here," he said, putting down his plate. She sat down on the couch next to him and leaned in as he gave her a quick, but sweet, kiss. They laughed about the day's events every now and again, going over Harris's Tarzan act as well as some of the other highlights. Harris suggested they turn the television on and watch a movie together.

It was getting late, and Markita missed the end of the movie; she had fallen asleep on Harris's shoulder. As the credits rolled, he woke her, stroking her hair and then her cheek with the back of his hand. She stretched her tired, but sexy body, confessing to him that she always fell asleep through movies.

"I am so sorry, LB," she said sweetly.

"I have to go, little girl," Harris said, reluctant to go, "or I won't be able to control myself. You are a beautiful lady."

"Thank you, Harris, for a perfect afternoon. I hope we can do something together again real soon."

"You bet your bottom dollar, little girl."

"What if I don't want your bottom dollar? What if I want the top one?" she teased. Harris loved her sense of humor.

"Let me walk you to the door," she said, getting up from the couch and pulling him up by the hand behind her.

Before he left, he kissed her gently on the cheek, then pecked her on the nose; his lips touched hers, but no kiss. "If you want the kiss, you will have to go out with me again," he murmured, fishing for a response.

"Anytime, LB, anytime," she whispered in his ear.

"I have to go to supper at my mom's and uncle J's tomorrow," he told her. "But is it OK if I call you?"

"I would be mad at you if you didn't," she replied.

"Good night then, sweet lady."

"Good night, little boy. Call me when you get home please."

"You have a deal." This time he gave her the kiss he knew she wanted, telling her it would have to last her until they could be together again. Harris left and drove home happier than he had ever been in his life. The first thing he did when he got into his bed was to call her, letting her know he arrived home safely.

Sunday morning came around, and the sunlight woke Harris up, warm on his face. He was so happy about last night he had forgotten to draw the blinds before getting into bed. His date could not have been more perfect, unless, of course, they had made love together. He did not want to push her too soon, however, and to be honest, he was nervous when it came to thinking about the subject. It would be his first time.

Everything about her felt so right, he just knew it would be OK when it finally happened. The ringing phone interrupted his thoughts.

"Hello, LB," said the sweetest, sexiest voice he'd ever heard.

"Hello yourself, little girl," he greeted Markita, a smile spreading across his face.

"How are you feeling this morning?"

"Grrreat!" he said, rolling his *r*'s like a roaring lion. "I slept fantastic, dreaming about this gorgeous woman who tried luring me into her web."

"Is that so, LB? The question is, was she successful?" Markita asked seductively.

"If you are fishing, little girl, I am hook, line, and sinkered."

"You are funny, LB, but you can't say 'sinkered.' It's not a word."

"Hmm . . . I added it to my dictionary."

"You are too much," she said, giggling. "I just wanted to say good morning and thank you for a wonderful day yesterday. It was perfect." "

"I am honored you had such a good time. Would you like to try your luck again and come to my mom and uncle J's this afternoon?"

"I would love to, LB, but I need to get a few things done before my own mom's visit next week."

"Is she flying or driving?"

"Flying."

"We can pick her up from the airport together if you like." He kicked himself for sounding so presumptuous.

"Oh, LB, you are so thoughtful, thank you," she said excitedly.

"Are you sure? Because I would hate to intrude on your mommy time."

"No, no, it's perfect. I want you to meet her. She will love you, just like . . ." she did not finish her sentence.

"Like what, little girl?" he asked anxiously. It sounded as if she was going to say, "Like I love you," but then her line beeped.

"I have another call coming in, LB. It could be my mom. Will you call me when you get back from your uncle J's?"

"For you, little girl, anything. Love ya. Later, bye." He ended the call wondering if she caught the "love ya" he slipped in as she clicked over to the other line.

"Yes," he exclaimed. "Yes!" He felt so energized, he got up, showered, shaved, and changed in record time. He floated downstairs turning on his stereo and singing along. An old Bob Seger song came on. He could not believe it, but it was one of the songs he'd e-mailed Markita to ask her on a date. *What a coincidence,* he thought. *Hmm . . . maybe it was meant to be.* He smiled.

He was still smiling broadly as he once again began to replay yesterday's date in his mind when the phone rang once more.

Darnik, who could that be interrupting my Markita time? Oops, maybe it's her, he thought as he ran to catch the phone. He heard a familiar voice on the other end, but it wasn't Markita.

"Hey, son, don't forget to—"

Harris cut him off. "Yes, Uncle Josh, bring the rocky road ice cream, I know. Have I ever forgotten?"

"Hmm . . . let me think for a while."

"I was just leaving, heading your way."

"Really, then why do you sound so out of breath?"

"Was I?"

"Yeah, yeah, I know, you were thinking about the pretty little lady," his uncle J said, cutting him off and finishing his thought for him. If he only knew Harris had been prancing around the living room like a bopping teenager, he would have had a field day with him. Harris grinned. He hung up the phone, turned off the stereo, and left.

"I'm here," Harris yelled out as he entered his parents' house.

"We know, son," Uncle J said as he entered the room. "Even the neighbors heard you're here with the amount of noise you made."

"Don't start on me, Uncle J."

"Who me? Not on your nelly."

"OK, Uncle J, I'm going to bite. What's a nelly?"

"I am not going to tell you anything if you intend on biting me," he replied as Mary Ellen entered the room.

"Can you tell he's full of it today, son?" she said as she walked toward him with her arms out.

"Give your mom a big hug and kiss. I have missed you so much, son."

"Wow, Mom, I will have to miss a Sunday more often," said Harris, teasing her.

"Don't you dare, boy! I will have your guts for garters," his uncle chimed in.

"There you go again, Uncle J. What do you mean?" Harris was now curious with all the new material he was hearing.

"Don't mind him. He's been watching too much of the British channel. It cracks him up," his mother explained.

"It's because he is a chicken egg, Mother—all cracked up."

"Very funny, laddie," Uncle J said in an attempt to sound Scottish. "Talking of quacking up, did you hear the one about the duck who went into the pharmacy to buy some lip balm?"

Harris put his fingers in his ears. "No, no, not again! Please, please spare me!" His uncle J was laughing so hard, he had to hold his belly.

"You two are intolerable," his mother said primly although a smile played across her lips. "It amazes me how no matter what you say, the both of you always seem to be able to bring up the damn duck joke," she said, happy to see her two favorite men interacting so lovably together. Her only regret was Mark could not have loved his son the way his brother did. She turned toward the kitchen, leaving the guys to chat while she put the rocky road ice cream in the freezer.

After she'd gone, Joshua turned to his nephew.

"So, you dawg, how did the date go?" his uncle asked him.

"Maybe I haven't been on it yet," Harris said evasively, trying not to grin.

"Really? You wanna lie to your uncle Joshua?"

"Not at all. I am merely avoiding the subject."

"Don't worry, son, you had a great time, the picnic was the perfect date, and you and the pretty lady fell in love."

"Would you stop?" Harris begged, turning his usual shade of red.

"Oh, I don't need to ask you any questions, mister. You have no poker face. You may be a hurricane in the courtroom, but when it comes to Marcia Brady, you are a jellyfish."

"Her name is Markita," Harris said with a smile.

"Oops! Excuse me, correct me, why don't you? By the way, don't think you have worked your clever lawyer stuff on me. I still want to know how the picnic went." Just then Mary Ellen reentered the room.

"What picnic is Joshua referring to, son?" she asked, as if she were a reporter for the "Enquiring minds wanted to know" paper.

"See, what you've done, Uncle J? Now I am going to get the third degree."

"Then you might as well sit down and spill the beans," Joshua replied with a shrug.

"If I spill the beans all over mom's rug, she will run me out of here. Which could be a good idea. I could get out of here early. Do you have any beans, Mom?" he asked.

"No, but we are having your uncle Joshua's famous Rebel hamburgers out on the grill. I can open a can of beans for you if you like."

"It's OK, Mom, don't go to any trouble on my account." He loved how naive his mother could be sometimes.

"Would you like me to go start the grill for you, darling?" she asked Joshua.

"No, it's OK, honey. Me and the lover boy here will go get it started, and you can bring out the burgers, if you would please."

"OK, I'll be in a few minutes to cut up the salad real quick." Uncle J and Harris went outside, closing the sliding glass door behind them.

"You might as well tell me, or you won't be leaving here today," Joshua told Harris as they headed for the grill.

"OK, Uncle J, if you must know, it was everything you said it would be." Harris was the brightest shade of red Joshua had ever seen.

"By the look on your face, son, it was one hell of a date." Harris knew he was fishing for details.

"Not yet, Uncle J. I will admit it crossed my mind a time or two, but she is a lady."

"I must say, son, you look radiant in love. It suits you, but you look better in jeans." Joshua cracked himself up again.

"I do have a serious question to ask you, Uncle J."

"Enlighten me, why don't you?"

"Markita was talking about her mother yesterday. She is coming to visit next weekend." His uncle J cut him off with a chuckle.

"Are we going to meet the new in-law?"

"Listen, I am trying to be serious with you. Silly me, but that seems to be impossible where you're concerned."

"No, son, go on. I'm sorry," Joshua apologized. "It's obvious something is bothering you."

"OK. So her mom used to be a legal secretary here in Orlando. It's why she felt comfortable sending Markita to intern here. Her mother thought she could gain more experience in our office with the higher crime rate we have, as opposed to where she is from."

"Nothing wrong with that, son. Where does her mom live?"

"She was originally from Orlando, but she moved to Tallahassee to work for the governor."

"What's her mom's name?" Joshua asked this question nervously now, almost afraid of Harris's answer.

"It's Trudy."

Joshua felt a sharp pain in his heart. *No, it cannot be,* he told himself. *Impossible. It had to be a coincidence.* His body tightened up with uncertainty. Harris could see and sense his reaction.

"What is wrong, Uncle J?" Harris had urgency in his voice. "Uncle J, you have never lied to me, please don't start now. You know I love you. If you know something, you have to tell me, please." Harris's voice was desperate.

Trying not to involve his brother Mark, but trying not to lie to Harris, he answered, "I once knew a Trudy, and she was, in fact, a legal secretary here and moved to Tallahassee, but it could be a coincidence." He was crossing his fingers, praying his explanation was good enough for Harris, but no such luck.

"I remember a fight Mom and Dad had once," Harris pressed on. "Mom said not only was Dad having an affair with someone named Brandy, she knew he was having one with a girl named Trudy as well. Mom ended up getting beaten." Harris choked up a little. Joshua's heart broke for him.

"I know those times were painful for you, son." Joshua would have given his life to take away those memories Harris retained of his mother covered in bruises. He never understood what had happened to Mark, except that alcoholism was a hereditary disease. Thank God Harris hated the stuff. He also said a small prayer for himself; he felt blessed that the disease had never touched his life either. Joshua had always tried to justify his brother's actions, blaming it on the pressures of the judicial system and never revealing to Harris that his grandfather's manipulation factored into his abuse. It helped him ease his conscience of his brother's death.

"Don't be sad, Uncle J. I know his abuse is why you kidnapped me and took me away from my father."

"Harris," Joshua warned. "You know we never talk about those times, especially with your mother in the house."

"I know, Uncle J, I just want you to know it's OK. I understand the lengths you went to protect me."

"I would do it all over again if the circumstances were the same, son, but it does not make what I did right."

Harris had always believed his uncle had been the one who killed his father. He had no idea it was his grandfather who committed the act. Joshua never told Harris the whole story. He knew the boy was close with Mary Ellen's parents, and Joshua did not want to come between their relationships, even though he loathed the judge for killing his brother. Joshua was grateful to God he did not go through with the assignment, which the judge and he had conspired together. He would never have been able to live with himself if he, in fact, had shot his own brother, no matter what the reason.

Mary Ellen returned just then with the hamburgers, handing the platter to Joshua. She set the outside table with paper plates along with plastic cutlery and napkins. The tray she carried out held the buns, already toasted, along with all the necessary condiments: simple mustard and ketchup. It was the only way Joshua and Harris liked their Rebel burgers. Mary Ellen placed the bowl of salad in the middle of the table and then looked at her two men, wondering what they had been talking about that made them appear so serious.

"It's fix-it-yourself day today, guys, so take what you want and make up your own plates."

"When and if the burgers get done," Joshua told her, trying to smile.

"Let's hope the grill whiz here doesn't overcook them like he usually does," Harris shot back, trying to lighten the mood.

"You two are not still going at it, are you?" Mary Ellen smiled.

"Who us, nev . . . ver, ev . . . ver." They both chuckled together and prepared to chow down on their burgers. Once they all finished, Mary Ellen picked everything up off the table and placed it on the tray to take back to the kitchen.

"You guys behave while I am gone, please. I have a little cleaning up to do, but I won't be long."

"Thanks, Mom. Everything was great. I would love to have a chili cheese dog next week. You haven't cooked those in a while." Harris thought back to last night and the hot dog Markita made for him. It was the best hot dog he ever tasted, even without the chili and cheese.

"It is your birthday next weekend, son, so you may have whatever your heart desires," said Mary Ellen with an indulgent smile.

"Oh, and I suppose you want it done light on the onions with a thin whipped strawberry milkshake, right, son?"

"How did you guess, Uncle J? Do you need any help taking the tray in, Mom?"

"I am not too old yet, son. You stay and visit with Joshua. I will only be a moment. "She deftly picked up the tray and headed once again for the kitchen. Harris turned to his uncle the moment she was out of earshot.

"There is something else I would like to run by you, Uncle J. I cannot give you all the details, due to my position, but there are some things I am uncovering in relation to a case I'm working on, and I do not like what I'm finding one little bit. I would like your input though as you have never steered me wrong." Joshua loved Harris having such high confidence in him. He always felt comfortable discussing anything and everything with him.

Harris started at the beginning with the newspaper article addressed to Hugh and the claim accusing his grandfather of hanging an African American from a tree and then framing Jake Johnson for the crime. He explained the circumstances of Smith's arrest and the warrants that mysteriously disappeared and about appearing in front of Judge Poe—twice. He did not, however, mention the name on Smith's folder: "The Executioner." He told him about the missing evidence and the string of dead cops that seemed to be piling up.

"I'm sure you saw the news the other night about Judge Poe nearly being killed in a hit."

"Yes, I did see," his uncle said. "Amber Andrews was all over the story."

"Yes, and I'm sure we haven't heard the last from her about the incident."

Finally, Harris filled his uncle J in on the brothel raid and all the high-level officials who had been arrested—and those who had mysteriously made bail while others had not.

"I ran some of this by Grandfather, but so far, he has not gotten back with me. I have this nauseating feeling not all this is a coincidence, Uncle J, but I cannot piece the puzzle together. Joe said he finally got some clues, but I haven't had chance to get together with him yet to get his scoop. It appears every time he or I get too close, evidence disappears."

Joshua sat intently listening to every word Harris had spoken. He was not happy to hear the part about Harris running things by his grandfather; Joshua was aware of the connections Judge Ronald Harris had. He was also shocked to hear about the Johnson case accusation; he knew the judge could be ruthless, but even this incident sounded out of character even for him.

"Wow, son," Joshua whistled. "It's certainly a large puzzle you're trying to put together. Do you think you are confusing one thing with another, and maybe that's why nothing is adding up?"

"You could be right, but it's not what my gut is telling me."

Joshua understood this as his brother Mark experienced those same instincts; that is what made him a great attorney.

"Maybe when you meet with Joe, things will become a little clearer for you." He hesitated before he spoke again. Joshua did not want to sound like an overbearing parent, but he needed to ask the question.

"Are you in any danger, son?"

"No, no, Uncle J, it's all routine stuff which I can handle. You know how I hate corruption. It's the only thing I will ever have in common with my father. As a judge, I want to make sure the scales of justice in our judicial system are fair and balanced."

"I am so proud of you, Harris," Joshua said with a tear in his eye and pride in his heart.

After Harris left, Joshua sat in his Queen Anne chair in front of the fireplace. He quietly thought back to the affair his brother Mark had with his secretary, Trudy. The memories of those days were still very raw for him as he remembered the hurt and pain Mary Ellen endured, all due to his brother. Could this be the same Trudy? If so, the implications of Harris and Markita's relationship could once again fill this family with heartache. *Please, God, do not let it be her*, Joshua said to himself. He went upstairs and joined Mary Ellen in their bed, holding her tight all night long.

"I love you," he whispered in her ear.

Chapter Nine

Discoveries

Harris awoke early Monday and was ready by 5:00 a.m., rehearsing his opening arguments for the Barnes case, which was to start at nine. Clearing his throat, he stood in front of his bathroom mirror, ready to give his argument one more run-through.

"Good morning, ladies and gentlemen of the jury," he began, his voice clear and confident. "This is a pretty open-and-shut case. I will prove to you without any doubt that the defendant, Mr. Barnes, successfully and illegally trained young girls to lure wealthy men with expensive cars into the woods, promising them sexual favors. Once the men were in a compromising situation, Barnes would then appear, acting as an officer of the law. He would convince the victims to get out of their vehicles and would then proceed to handcuff and blindfold the victims, have them drop to their knees, and would then shoot them two or three times, leaving them to the natural elements to dispose of their bodies. He would return to his car and leave the scene, while his female accomplice would drive the victim's car to a secluded body shop were the cars would be stripped, repainted, and issued a new serial number. Mr. Barnes then resold the vehicles on his car lot in Kissimmee, Florida. We have a witness who will testify to the fact that it indeed was Barnes who not only orchestrated the thefts, but also committed the murders." Pleased with his progress so far, Harris allowed himself a small smile before he began the next part. Just as he was about to begin, the phone rang, interrupting his train of thought. *Who on earth could this be calling me so early?*

"Harris," said Hugh's voice, sounding rushed. "I'm really sorry to call you this early, but I wanted to let you know that I will be handling the Barnes case after all. I'll be sending Ashley over to the courthouse to see if she can get a continuance, but I want you to come into the office early so I can go over what I need you to do instead of trying this case."

Harris was shocked into near silence at this unexpected news. He had put a lot of hours into this case and knew it would be a slam-dunk conviction for him. Now all that time was apparently for nothing. Frustration clogged his throat. A stiff "Yes sir" was all he could manage to say.

"I'll explain everything when you get in. Don't be long." Hugh hung up the phone before Harris could even get out a second response.

"Damn you, Hugh," he said aloud through gritted teeth. Harris was starting to lose all kinds of respect for the district attorney and was starting to think about how he might earn the position for himself. Maybe it was time to meet with the governor and lay some subtle groundwork. He knew his age and inexperience would go against him, but hell, he could do a better job than Hugh was doing. He ended this train of thought with an angry tug on his tie, trying to straighten the knot, then headed out the door to meet with Hugh. As he started the Jag, he made a mental note that no matter what the day would bring, he was determined to meet with Joe and compare notes.

Once at work, against his better judgment, he e-mailed Markita inviting her to lunch with him and Joe; he wanted to be close to her again today. He was worried about getting her mixed up in all this mess, but he justified it by telling himself that she took great notes and so was an invaluable member of the team.

"Good morning, little girl," he typed. "Thank you for a wonderful afternoon Saturday. Sorry I didn't call you last night, but I got home quite late from my parents'. On a business note, if you could, I would like you to call Joe when you get in and arrange lunch for you, Joe, and me at Cracker Jacks. E-mail me with the details. Thanks. Yours, Harris." He ended as affectionately as he dared since this was really a work-related e-mail. Just as he hit Send, Hugh strode into his office.

"Good morning, Harris, young man," he boomed cheerfully. "Did you have a nice weekend?"

"Sure did, sir," Harris replied, less formally than he'd meant to, thinking about his date with Markita.

"I'm sure you are wondering why I have taken you off the Barnes case," Hugh went on briskly, not even hearing Harris's reply. "Especially since I know you have been putting in a lot of hours catching yourself up with all the facts, but it's necessary that I take it over myself."

"I understand, sir," Harris said, not understanding at all.

"Oh," Hugh continued casually. "I wanted to give you a heads-up on a case involving your grandfather before you hear it in the news. I'm sure he will tell you more about it soon, but . . ." he shrugged, then went on. "I received a courtesy call yesterday afternoon from the state's attorney, Edward Rydell. It appears the Johnson family has reopened their son's case with new evidence. They're alleging your grandfather was the one who hanged the African

American all those years ago, and that he framed their son, Jake Johnson, for the murder. Apparently, they have a full confession from Stewart Pope, who was an attorney at the Practice when all that nasty business went down and who just so happens to be Judge Pope's father." Hugh looked at Harris sympathetically. "If it's any consolation, son, I hear Pope has Alzheimer's, so it's a possibility he is confused with the situation."

Hugh worked at trying to make himself look concerned for Harris. "The media is going to have a field day with this one, so for your protection, I thought I would keep you close to the office for a few days until things calm down," Hugh said by way of explanation. "That's one of the reasons I'm taking you off the Barnes case."

"I am not concerned," Harris replied at once. "My grandfather would never do anything so heinous. Once the truth comes out, I'm sure the state's attorney's office will apologize to him for even implying such a thing." Harris did not like the sick, angry feeling he had in his stomach now; he willed himself to control it.

"I'm sure you are right, son," Hugh said soothingly, then moved on to the more pressing business at hand. "There is another issue we need to deal with, and it's the main reason I'm taking you off the Barnes case. I will need my best man for this as it concerns the bust at Miss Dixie's brothel. I want you to handle this case as it is going to be extremely high profile, especially since we have some powerful and prestigious people involved. This one is going to be all over Court TV, I can assure you." Hugh sat on the edge of the desk, looking directly at Harris. "I have a feeling Miss Dixie will not give you names, but in case she does, you will need to inform me immediately so I can help prepare you. I want you to go after her hard and fast. The sex trafficking charge alone will put her away for years. If that doesn't faze her," he continued to coach his assistant DA, "then threaten her with the feds and tax evasion. Either way, I want you to make sure she is locked away for a very long time. I'll see if I can pull some strings and get this one on the docket as soon as possible, but heads are going to roll with this mess, son." Hugh sighed hard, shaking his head in mock resignation, relishing the thought of his plans succeeding.

Harris was honored at Hugh's trust in his abilities, but remained suspicious of his motives. "I am waiting to see if my luncheon appointment can make it," he told Hugh, measuring his words. "As soon as that's confirmed, I'll go over to the jail again and press Miss Dixie. What about the police chief? Is he still over there?"

"Yes, but leave him to me. I have an appointment with him this morning."

"OK, sir. I'll get started right away."

"Let's communicate together later in the day, OK, son?" Hugh said, thumping Harris on the shoulder as he stood to leave.

"Yes, sir." Harris watched as his boss strode out the door just as boldly as he had entered. He decided he didn't really like Hugh calling him son, but he was too respectful to correct him.

Hugh left the building and headed straight over to the jail; he noticed the media already starting to set up the cameras outside the courthouse and thought this could only mean one thing. He called Harris from his cell phone.

"You might want to think about cancelling your luncheon. The vultures are already outside waiting to pounce on you."

"I told you, sir, it is OK. I have nothing to hide and certainly nothing to fear from these people."

"OK, son. Good luck," he offered, then hung up.

Hugh arrived at the jail, headed for another meeting he was not looking forward to. He knew the police chief was going to be steaming mad at Hugh for leaving him incarcerated all weekend.

"Finally decided to show your face around here, did you?" the chief asked sarcastically as Hugh sat down in the small interrogation room.

"It's not like that, James," said Hugh as always, trying to calm someone down.

"Oh, then why don't you fill me in? I'm sure I will be thrilled at your explanation." The chief sat back in his chair and crossed his arms, waiting expectantly.

"Look, you are the one who bungled this whole mess," Hugh told him. "It was your responsibility not to push the button while there were dignitaries there."

"Oh, I love this, Hugh," the chief snorted. "So now it's my fault. You actually have the audacity to think I would push the button while my own pants are down? You're a damn moron."

"I had to make it look real, James. I will get you out of this mess, don't worry."

The chief snorted again, then leaned toward Hugh menacingly. "'Don't worry' he says. 'I'll get you out,' he says. What the hell are you going to do about my *career*? I have twenty-four years in the force!" His voice rose in anger. "You think I am going to get my pension after this, or are you so self-absorbed you don't care about the rest of us schmucks who are part of your master plan?"

"I have everything under control," Hugh said, trying, once again, to calm him down. "I am waiting for Judge Poe to get out of the hospital and back on the bench. He will throw out your case, and then everything will be fine. It is going to take time, that's all," said Hugh, hoping this was going to fly.

"'That's all' you think, huh? Well, now, it's my turn, Mr. District Attorney." The chief leaned even farther forward and poked a beefy finger into Hugh's chest. "If I go down, I can assure you, I am taking your ass with me."

"You need to concern yourself more with who blew the whistle," Hugh responded, unfazed by the threat. The chief now started shouting.

"I can't very well do anything from inside here now, can I? You're a damn fool," he shouted, fuming.

Hugh finally realized he would be unable to reason with the man; he'd just have to wait and see how things worked out for him, then they could talk. He started to stand up to go, leaving the chief with a parting plea for patience.

"Look, James, give me a little more time to get this whole mess sorted out. I will get you released as soon as I can. I want the name of the person who caused this debacle too. Whoever did this will receive a visit from the Executioner, I can promise you that. Please be patient, and we will all come out of this one smelling like roses." Hugh knocked on the door to alert the guard he was ready to leave.

"Hey, Hugh buddy," the chief said softly from behind him. "Think about this one while you're doing whatever it is you're doing: If I don't get out of here soon, you won't be smelling roses, but you will be pushing them up from under the ground. Get my drift?"

"Loud and clear, James, loud and clear," Hugh said, trying to keep his voice low and steady. He could not wait to get as far away from the jail as he could today. He wondered how Judge Harris had kept everything together all these years. He'd never had the problems with people like the ones he was now experiencing.

"Imbeciles, all of them are imbeciles," he repeated to himself as he brushed past the guard who let him out of the interrogation room. Still muttering to himself, he stormed out the front doors of the station and headed back to the office.

It was 11:00 a.m. before Joe called Harris's office. Markita answered the phone.

"Assistant DA's office, how may I help you?"

"You can tell me if lover boy is going to meet with me some time today?" Joe said half-jokingly.

"Aha, you finally are returning my call," she shot back at him, sticking up for her man.

"We are being a little touchy again, aren't we, missy? Is he in?" Joe knew not to mess with the little spitfire when it came to Harris; she was very protective of him.

"Yes, but he is on the other line. He asked me to make arrangements with you to meet him at Cracker Jacks for lunch."

"Is noon too soon? I bet you didn't know I was a poet, did you, pretty lady?"

"Not at all, but I do know you are a character, Joe Marble," she said laughing.

"If he can't make noon, call me on my cell."

"OK, I'll tell him, and we'll meet you there."

Huh, bringing the little lady is he, thought Joe as he hung up.

Markita paged through to Harris's office immediately to let him know about this important meeting.

"Can you come in here for a moment, please?" he asked her when she'd finished.

She quickly walked across to his office and quietly opened the door.

"Please sit down, Markita," Harris said, his tone serious. "I have to tell you something."

Markita looked up at him, a little worried.

"There are a slew of reporters outside," he told her, "which are probably going to mob us when we leave. They want to know if I am aware that the state's attorney's office had to reopen a case, an old case involving my grandfather when our family owned the law firm known as the Practice."

"I remember you telling me something about it," Markita responded, listening to every word intently. He told her the details of the case and what had happened to Jake Johnson.

"Oh, how awful," exclaimed Markita.

"Actually, it gets even worse. The Johnsons are now accusing my grandfather of the crime and saying he framed their son."

"Oh, Harris! I'm so sorry. Your grandfather must be devastated."

"I am sure he is, but I haven't called him yet. Hugh suggested I distance myself because of the media frenzy this is going to attract. But," he added, "I will need to call my grandmother soon. I can only imagine what this is doing to her." He got up from behind his desk and moved toward her, wanting to be near her. "So this is why I called you in here," he said, looking down at the floor. "If you would prefer to stay here for lunch, I will quite understand." He quickly glanced back at her face, not sure of her reaction.

"No way, Harris," she replied firmly. "We have nothing to hide." She reached out and gave his hand a gentle squeeze.

Harris felt the butterflies fluttering again. He was so relieved that Markita was willing to stand by his side.

"Well, let's go fight the crowds, little girl." He guided her by the elbow as they left his office and made their way to the front of the courthouse. They reached the main doors, Harris took a deep breath, and plunged through, Markita by his side. As soon as they set foot on the front steps, the reporters were on them, shoving and jostling for position, shouting questions, all asking the same thing.

"Mr. Robertson! Is it true your grandfather hanged a black man and then framed an innocent young man for the crime?" yelled Amber Andrews, holding her ground at the front of the pack.

Harris had already made the decision not to avoid their questions. He kept thinking of Markita's words reminding him that they had nothing to hide.

"Of course not, Miss Andrews," Harris answered briskly. "My grandfather is a respectable chief justice who upholds the law. Always has."

"Am I correct in saying, Mr. Robertson," Amber Andrews persisted, "that Stewart Pope, from a law firm formerly known as the Practice, signed an affidavit stating these allegations against your grandfather are true?"

"Mr. Pope has Alzheimer's, from what I understand. I would doubt he could remember events clearly." Harris and Markita were nearly through the crowd. They moved quickly forward toward his Jag where Harris unlocked the door for Markita and ushered her into the passenger seat.

"Isn't it true your grandfather was the head of the local KKK here at one time?" Andrews tried again.

"Miss Andrews," Harris said with his last ounce of courtesy, "Of course not. You are grasping at straws. If you are going to continue your career as a reporter, you should know better than to make accusations without all the facts." Harris was now furious as he lunged into his car; he had no respect for reporters to begin with, but he especially disliked Amber Andrews.

"Are you OK, Harris?" Markita asked as he carefully threaded his way through the crowd. She could tell he was rattled.

"Yes, I'm fine," he replied, irritated that he let his anger show. "It just irks me that they could so easily go after my grandfather. He's in his eighties and has given his whole life to the judicial system, for crying out loud! He's the chief justice on Florida's Supreme Court, but I guess that counts for nothing. And was she serious? My grandfather head of the KKK? She's just spewing out preposterous lies." As he closed his mouth, he realized he had almost been shouting.

"It will be OK. Harris," Markita reassured him quietly, her hand resting on his arm. "I am sure he'll be exonerated of all charges."

"I have no doubt there, little girl," Harris agreed firmly. He gave her a tight grin.

"Hmm . . . much better, little boy," she said. "You are so handsome when you smile." She grinned as he flashed a big smile just for her.

When they walked into the restaurant a few minutes later, Joe was already sitting in a booth. "May we join you, Mr. Marble?" Harris asked, offering his friend a mock bow.

"Not so much of the 'mister,'" Joe said laughing. "I'm not old yet, youngster." Harris helped Markita slip into the booth first.

"It seems like forever since we last met up, Joe, old boy."

"Hey, hey, hey! I said not so much of the 'old.' I had one hell of a busy weekend. How about you, lover boy?"

"I had a nice weekend, thank you."

"And you, Markita? Did you have a 'nice' weekend?" Joe looked at her expectantly.

"Yes, I did, Joe, thank you," she answered him primly. Neither of them had confessed their date, but Joe but smiled at each of their responses.

"Well, I can see neither of you are willing to kiss and tell, but my curiosity has my mind wondering. Are either of you going to ask how my weekend went?"

"Pray do tell us," said Harris.

"Apart from the fact I visited Judge Poe's house, which I will get into in a minute, I took that hot chick Robin out on another date Saturday night."

"Wow, she actually went on a second date with you? What's wrong with her?" Harris asked teasingly.

"We went to dinner at this Greek restaurant. I must say the food was good. We talked about a lot of stuff, and it seems we have a lot of values which are the same."

"So are you going to see her a third time, Joe?" asked Markita, curious.

"As a matter of fact, I am going to pick her up on my Harley next week. We are going to ride around for a while before going to the club so I can hear her sing."

"Wow!" Harris said admiringly. "She's a brave woman going on a third date with you, and even braver to get on that crazy machine of yours."

"What kind of music does she sing?" asked Markita.

"Anything from country to classic rock, but my favorite song she sings is a rendition of "Blue Bayou," man, can she belt it out, phew." Joe stared past Harris wistfully, lost in thought about Robin's voice.

"She sounds too hot for you, Joe," laughed Harris.

"I don't know what you're talking about, I'm a great catch."

"Ahem, ahem," Harris cleared his throat.

"On to business," Joe said, taking the hint. "I caught up with the medical examiner Friday night, and boy, was he ready to talk. He would not give up names as to who is behind the cover-up, but he did tell me the head belonged to an Eleanor Woodsworth. He was instructed to destroy her remains, but he gave me these photographs of her, before she lost her head, obviously." He slid a manila envelope across the table to Harris, who reached in and glanced at the first few shots. His face reddened as he glanced at the pictures, shifting to prevent Markita from seeing them. Joe noticed his friend's reaction.

"The guy in the photos is one sick pervert, I can tell you. Some of the photos of him and her, I couldn't even look at, they made me so ill. I wouldn't dig much further into that stack if you have any hope of enjoying your lunch. But," Joe continued, "take a look at the earrings this chick is wearing. They're certainly not costume jewelry. Those diamonds look to be the real thing. I'm guessing she was having an affair with one of our power politicians and was getting ready to blackmail him."

"Who is the man? Do we know?" asked Harris, still shaken by the shocking images in front of him.

"Yes, it was former governor Mason," Joe told him. Markita suddenly seemed to swallow her water wrong and started to choke. Harris reached over and held up her arm while smacking her lightly on the back.

"Are you all right?"

"Yes, yes, I'm fine," she gasped, smiling weakly at him.

"What was that strange reaction about, little lady?" Joe asked, curious. "Do you know Governor Mason?"

"Actually I do, or did," she replied without hesitation. "My mother dated him a long time ago. He kept promising to leave his wife, but it never happened, obviously. I was around six or so when she walked away from him."

Joe did not make a comment, but definitely made a mental note.

"OK," he said after an awkward pause. "Moving on! The ME was also kind enough to give me the bullet which was used by Smith to kill the arresting officer who ended up dead in my lap."

"It's just a hunch, but my gut tells me it's going to match the bullets found in our SWAT team guys," said Harris excitedly.

Joe nodded in agreement, then continued, while Markita took detailed notes. "I also went back to the impound lot, but what remained of the car had been set on fire, so again I was shut out there. I went back to Judge Poe's and collected some blood and a hair follicle. If I get lucky, the DNA between the two will match and belong to the same person. There were two bullet casings on the bed, which in all probability means the killer fired two shots. One at each of the SWAT team guys, as each one of those men had a bullet lodged in exactly the same spot, right between the eyes. The shooter had to be one hell of a marksman to get the second shot in so quick. Especially, as I believe, the first SWAT team guy shot him in his left arm probably between the elbow and shoulder. I think it's possibly the bullet from the second SWAT team person entering the room that ended up in the ceiling. We have established both SWAT team people fired a bullet, but only one bullet was recovered, which was the one extracted from the ceiling, so my guess is the other bullet is in our killer. If we get lucky, it will be his blood and hair follicle," Joe repeated, then paused and took a drink of his soda.

"OK, so now let's talk about the bust at Miss Dixie's," Harris prodded. "What did you learn there?"

"As I was cozying up with Bambi at the brothel," Joe told him, "I was asking her if I was safe there, being a city employee and all. Her response was that we were well protected as the joint had plenty of security from the law. I could tell she was young and extremely nervous, so I asked her if she had ever encountered a bad trick. She started telling me about an incident that happened to her a while back, with Judge Poe of all people. Apparently, he smacked her around quite a bit. And it was right after that, that the raid went down. It's awfully coincidental Hugh decided to take down the brothel now, after all these years, don't you think? I have not finished my investigation concerning this incident, but I think I need to let the dust settle a bit before I go snooping some more."

Markita scribbled notes furiously; when she had caught up, he went on.

"When I went to visit Judge Poe in the hospital, I happened to notice Hugh had just come from his room, but he hadn't seen me. When I questioned Poe, he was extremely agitated because I called him out on the SWAT boys being there; he told me to refer my questions to Hugh. The ironic thing is, when I followed up on Judge Poe's explanation, that he was receiving death threats from Armstrong, I discovered that even though Armstrong did, in fact, get released two months ago, on the night of Poe's break-in, the guy was killed in a drug deal gone wrong on the other side of town." He let that news sink in, then continued.

"Finally, I went to visit our police chief this morning and saw Hugh leaving the jail."

Harris interrupted him. "Hugh told me he was going over to the jail this morning to see the police chief," he said. Joe nodded. "I didn't get much out of him, but the chief was not happy with our district attorney and informed me that if he was not out of there within twenty-four hours to revisit him, then he might have more info for me."

"I have one last thing to go over with you, Harris, but it is very close to you, man."

"Go ahead, Joe, I want to hear everything." Harris had the feeling Joe was about to bring up his grandfather.

"After leaving the jail this morning, I went to visit Stewart Pope at the nursing home. I was given a tip by the medical examiner, suggesting I visit him."

"OK, Joe, I know where you are going with this. Hugh briefed me this morning after receiving a courtesy call from the state's attorney's office. He basically decided that because of this new investigation involving my grandfather, that I should be pulled off the Barnes case and be kept to office duties until this mess was cleared up.

"Speaking of Barnes, I am due to testify in that case at three," said Joe, looking at his watch.

"Oh, I guess you haven't heard," Harris informed him. "Hugh sent Ashley over to the courthouse to get a continuance on the Barnes case, so check with her before showing up."

"Oh, great, nice of someone to let me know," complained Joe.

"I just did, bozo," Harris retorted.

"You're the only clown around here, Harris Robertson," Joe quipped.

"And in this case, it is becoming a three-ring circus," Harris added, and all three laughed. At that point, a server finally appeared and took their food orders. As they waited for their lunch, Harris was anxious to continue defending his grandfather.

"I am telling you, man, my grandfather would never do anything as heinous as the Johnsons are alleging. I know they have tried for years to clear their son's name, but now they are trying to accomplish their goal by placing the blame on someone else. It is just ludicrous. My grandfather did everything in his power to get Jake Johnson off on that murder charge." Harris was trying to get his point across to Joe quickly, not wanting his friend to doubt his grandfather.

"I'm actually going to visit Stewart Pope myself first thing Wednesday morning, but tomorrow I am taking Markita to the airport to pick up her mother, as she is flying in from Tallahassee to visit," said Harris.

"I understand where you are coming from, man. Judge Harris is a well-respected individual," Joe tried to reassure his friend.

"Yes, he is, Joe. I can assure you he will be exonerated."

Joe sounded less certain. "Pope was quite explicit and seemed lucid when he told me his version of what happened to Jake Johnson. The kid seemed to have a pretty good alibi."

"Then why would he confess to something he did not do?" said Harris angrily, not wanting to hear any of these accusations against his grandfather.

"Stewart Pope told me about a vital piece of information, Harris. He said Judge Harris still owns the Practice, that there is an escrow account worth one hundred and fifty mill. I couldn't find any paperwork anywhere backing up his statement, but apparently, you will be the sole heir if anything happens to Judge Harris. So I don't know, maybe he is confused about these things, but then again . . ." he shrugged, trying to make his friend feel better, even though personally he knew he was going to do some more digging.

"He must be mistaken, Joe," Harris insisted. "There is no way that's possible. My grandfather could not be on the Supreme Court if he had ownership of a law firm. It would be a major conflict of interest. Besides, if my grandparents had that kind of money, they would be living a far more lavish lifestyle than they do. I also know for a fact my grandfather would never leave me dirty money. He knows exactly how I feel about corruption." Harris's stomach was beginning to get a sick feeling again, his jaws tightening with anger and frustration.

"Like I said, Harris, you know I would not shit you, man, especially about your grandfather, but I wanted you to know everything Pope had to say."

"Fine, I want you to find out who Jake Johnson was allegedly raping. The case is still open, right?"

"As far as I know."

"Maybe there is a logbook from the hospital with a name of someone who was raped on the night in question. If you say there was a nasty open wound on her face, it probably would have left a scar of some sort. It is another angle you could work on."

"Sure thing," said Joe, conscious of Harris's feelings and trying to be accommodating, even though he didn't think he would find much of anything concerning the decades-old rape.

"It's OK, Harris, anyone who knows your grandfather will know he is not capable of such a thing. Joe will get to the bottom of this, don't you worry," said Markita, reaching out her hand and touching Harris's knee under the table in an effort to console him.

"Well," Joe said after an uncomfortable pause, "I had better get going and check in with Ashley. If I am not going to the Barnes trial to testify, I'll get back on the trail and get this mess solved."

Harris, not missing an opportunity, sang, "Happy trails to you, buddy."

Joe shook his finger at Harris and said, "Don't start, Trigger."

Amused, Harris said, "I wanted to let you know that Hugh now wants me on the Miss Dixie case, and he wants me to go after her 'hard and fast,' as he put it. I am going to the jail after leaving here to question her again. I'm supposed to put pressure on her to reveal names."

"Good luck there, bud. She has been protected for years by some pretty high officials, so I doubt if she is one to nark," Joe remarked as he stood up to go. He felt badly for his friend, so he generously picked up the tab. "I'll get this one, big guy," he said, grabbing the check.

"Wow, is it Christmas already? I know it is not my birthday," Harris lied, as it actually was his birthday today, but no one knew except for his mother and uncle J. They were having a get-together for him this weekend.

"I will see you lovebirds later," Joe said with a wave.

"Right, call me as soon as you find out any more, please, Joe," Harris said, annoyed that he sounded desperate for more information.

"You know I will. Take care of him, Markita—he's one of the good guys."

"Yes, he sure is," said Markita with a big smile on her face. Harris reached his hand back out toward hers, holding it gently.

Joe turned to go, leaving them alone.

"Thank you for the kind things you said about my grandfather," Harris said fondly. "I know you only knew of him by reputation."

"I also know if he is a part of you, little boy, he is all good."

"How did I get so lucky, little girl?" he said, looking into her eyes lovingly.

"I think I am the lucky one, LB. There are not too many good guys left in the world today." She leaned in toward him, her lips seeming to call out to him again. He let his lips lightly brush hers, then told her that would have to tide her over until later. He smiled back at her.

"I can drop you back at the office, and then I really have to go over to the jail to deal with Miss Dixie."

"Please let me come with you, Harris. I can learn so much from you," she pleaded, looking at him with her big brown eyes wide open.

"Oh, little girl, how unfair you are, looking at me with those eyes of yours. How can I deny those beautiful eyes?" Markita pecked him on the cheek and gave him a big smile.

When they arrived at the jail, they showed their IDs and signed in, asking to meet with Miss Dixie.

"She is in with her attorney," said the guard.

"Ah, interesting. Can you see if it's at all possible for us to join them?" Harris was anxious to know who the opposing attorney was, even though his hunch was it would be someone from the Practice.

The guard returned. "Follow me please." He led them down a long hallway, which had doors leading into interview rooms on each side. At the end of the hallway were the electric gates, which led to the cells.

"She is in this one, sir," said the guard, motioning to a door on their right guarded by two officers.

"Thanks," replied Harris. He and Markita waited for one of the officers to open the door, then entered the room.

"Look who's here! Pray tell, Mr. Assistant District Attorney, what would you be doing visiting my client without her attorney present?"

"Well, Nigel, if you are not her defense attorney, what would you be doing here?"

"Don't get smart with me, Robertson, you had no idea I would be here," said Nigel Pope irritably.

"Anyone with half a brain knew someone from the Practice was going to be here defending her," Harris said as he pulled out a chair for Markita.

"It's not what I said, Robertson, and you know it." Nigel was even more irritated now. Markita was smiling on the inside, feeling a rush from the power and strength which Harris portrayed.

"Would you mind if I had a couple of words with your client, Counselor?" he asked politely.

"I will give you five minutes, Robertson. You had better behave and stay within the rules." Harris wanted to balk—whenever did anyone from the Practice play by the rules?—but decided that five minutes was better than nothing.

"Miss Dixie," he started right away. "You are still under your Miranda rights, and you have your attorney present, is that correct?" He was trying to intimidate her.

"Of course she knows," Nigel snapped. "Proceed, Robertson. Your time is running out."

"Miss Dixie," he tried again, "if you give us names, we can get you out on bond, then Nigel and I can come to some kind of plea bargain. It will save all of us from going through a highly visible court case, which could destroy many lives, including your own. You wouldn't want that, would you?" Miss Dixie looked him straight in the eye but said nothing.

"I guess you got your answer, Robertson. Time for you to leave," Nigel said, a smug grin on his greasy face.

"Nigel, my man, you know as well as I do she is only harming herself. Hugh wants her incarcerated for a very long time, and I am the man to do it," Harris said, his tone matter-of-fact.

This was a side of Harris Markita had not seen before. *This is why they call him the Florida Hurricane,* she thought to herself. *He is so different when it comes to business.* She hoped she could be as good as he was one day.

"How can she go down when she is innocent, Mr. Assistant DA?"

"Funny, Nigel, since several officials were caught with their pants down, I'm sure one of them will want to talk, but we will see, won't we? When you have convinced your client to do the right thing, call me so we can come to an agreement, as the offer I will make will not be on the table long. Sex trafficking carries fifteen years in prison, get my drift?" Harris spoke with conviction in his voice.

"We will see you in court," Nigel retorted.

Harris stood up to leave, letting Markita go through the door first.

"You were brilliant, Harris, just brilliant," she breathed when they were out in the hall and clear of the guards. "How exhilarating. You were brilliant! So cool calm and collected." Her compliments made him swell with pride.

"Oh don't, little girl, you have no idea what you just did to me," he whispered in her ear.

"Why . . . whatever do you mean, Mr. Robertson?" she giggled flirtatiously at him.

Harris opened the car door for Markita, and once inside himself, he said. "I have an idea, little girl, let's not go back to the office. It's almost five o'clock. We can stop and pick up some Chinese then take it back to my place."

"I would love to. It will give me a chance to check out what kind of bachelor you are."

"Hmm . . . Scary as my place is rather plain, just like me."

"There is nothing plain about you, little boy." At that he reached over and tickled her side, making her laugh.

"Ah, little girl, you are ticklish."

"No, no, little boy, you can't tickle me, I am a black belter in karate, and I will have to hurt you if you don't stop." Harris burst out laughing himself.

"We will see about that, little girl." He started up the car, and they drove to a little Chinese restaurant not far from his condominium and chose one of the meals for two. While they were waiting for their order, Harris called Hugh on his cell.

"Harris," Hugh answered, "I'm glad you called. I spoke with Judge Poe today, and he's already back to work. He's going to get Miss Dixie's case heard as soon as possible, and he's going to make sure he presides over the trial himself." Harris thought this to be a rather ominous coincidence, but said nothing.

"I went to the jail to question Miss Dixie," he told Hugh. "Nigel Pope is her attorney. She is not giving up any names as of yet."

"I have complete faith in you, Harris. If anyone can change her mind, Mr. Florida Hurricane, it's you," Hugh said, trying to butter him up.

"Thanks, Hugh. If that's all, I'll talk to you later."

"Later," said Hugh.

Their meal was ready as Harris hung up, so the two of them headed off to his place. He was nervous about her seeing his condo, but excited as well.

When they got there, Markita looked around the kitchen while Harris pulled out plates and drinks for their dinner.

"It is very nice, little boy, and so clean," she said approvingly.

"Why don't you look around some more, and I will get the meal put on the table for us."

Markita went into the living room. The first thing she noticed was the enormous television unit with his stereo equipment. She went over to the fireplace mantel and looked at all the photos. There was one of Harris and his mother, another with Joshua, then the three of them together. She noticed the picture of his grandparents, but none of his father. In the middle of the mantel was a photograph of a beautiful black Lab. Harris appeared at the doorway and saw her looking at the picture.

"That's Charlie . . . No one knows this, but my uncle J gave him to me when I was a young boy. It's a long story, but please don't ever tell my mother," he said mysteriously. She noticed a tear welling up in his eye.

"I can tell you loved him, where is he?"

"He died a few years back and is buried in a pet cemetery not far from here. I could take you there and introduce you to him one day if you like."

"I would love that," she said quietly.

"Supper is on the table." He walked over to his stereo and put on some soft music, then followed her into the kitchen. He had put a candle in the middle of the table.

"You are such a romantic man, Mr. Robertson."

"Hmm . . . I prefer little boy, little girl," he said, pulling out her chair and smiling at her.

After they ate, they cleared the table together. Markita rinsed the dishes under the faucet then put the dishes in the dishwasher. He could picture them living together, washing dishes, and sharing chores for the rest of their lives. He grabbed her hand as they went back into the living room together.

"Oh, I love this song," said Markita as Lionel Richie's "Hello" began to play. She slipped into Harris's arms and softly started to sing. *I've been alone with you inside my mind, and in my dreams I've kissed your lips a thousand times.* He was awkward with her at first, but wanted to dance with her, knowing how much she loved it.

"I can't dance, little girl," he reminded her.

"There is no such word as 'can't,' little boy. With me, you can do anything. Move from one leg to the other . . . there, you have it . . . slowly now . . . feel the music." He prayed he did not fall into his television unit; he was so wobbly on his feet.

She started to sing again softly. *I can see it in your eyes; I can see it in your smile. Your all I've ever wanted; my arms are open wide. Because you know just what to say, and you know just what to do, and I want to tell you . . . I love you.* She kissed his lips slowly and lovingly. Harris remembered the old video to the song; it was about a blind woman and a man being in love with her from a distance. This was how it had been for both of them, but now everything was about to change.

He began to feel the song; he held her closer to him, then kissed her nose, wanting to tell her that he loved her too. He flipped back her hair behind her shoulders then rubbed her cheek with the back of his hand. Markita looked up at him, leaning close to nibble gently on his lips, kissing his light mustache.

He kissed her on her forehead . . . her eyelids . . . the tip of her nose . . . then briefly her lips. He playfully blew on her ear before kissing it, his lips sliding slowly down to her bare neck; he could tell his warm breath excited her. He was holding her tightly now, never wanting to let her go. He brushed the back of her head with his hand as she started to undo his shirt, revealing his chest, and bending her head slightly, kissing it sweetly in several places.

"Come with me, little girl," Harris whispered in her ear, his voice choked with emotion and desire.

He took her hand and led her upstairs; she followed willingly. He guided her to his bedroom where they lay down on the bed together, still fully dressed, their tender kisses turning passionate. His hands started to explore her body as hers did his.

"I love you, little girl," he whispered. Finally, he had told her what he had wanted to say for a long time.

"I love you too, little boy," she responded, kissing his top lip again. She nestled closer to him, her head on his chest.

"I have to tell you something," he said as they lay in each other's arms. She nodded silently into his shoulder.

"Today is June 10, and I try not to make a big deal out of this date, but it's my birthday, and you are the best present God could have ever sent me. You make me so happy, Markita."

She squeezed him tight, but let him continue without interrupting.

"I have hated this day my whole life. My father never wanted me, and I knew he dreaded this day every year because it reminded him how much he wished I'd never been born. You have now made it a special day, little girl, by telling me you love me."

"I do, Harris. I love you," Markita finally whispered. "I think I have from the first time I saw you."

"Oh, I knew you were an angel the first time I laid eyes on you," he told her, his lips curling into a smile as they kissed the top of her head. "Then you spoke to me in your sexy voice and you had me at hello."

They began slowly peeling each other's clothes off now, pressing their bodies together, harder, passionately. They were both trembling, their heartbeats exploding like fireworks on the Fourth of July. Harris felt like his heart was about to burst; he had never felt like this before in his life. They had nearly reached the point of no return, when the phone rang.

Let it ring, he told himself.

It rang and rang and rang.

"Darnik," he muttered, unwilling to give in to its strident demands.

"It's OK, Harris," Markita said gently. "You should answer it. It might be really important with everything that's going on."

Harris did not want to stop as he was about to make love to the most beautiful girl in the world, but he knew she was right. With a great sigh, he finally leaned across her shoulders and grabbed for the phone.

"Harris?" came the sound of his grandfather's voice. "I am so glad you're home. I guess by now you know what's been going on."

"Yes, Grandfather." Harris sat up straight, his automatic respect for his grandfather even overriding his passion for Markita.

"I want you to know, son, the things they are accusing me of are ridiculous, you know that, don't you?"

"Of course I do, Grandfather! It's ludicrous, and I am sure the state's attorney's office will exonerate you as well as offer you its apology."

"You're damn right they will, Harris. Your grandmother is frantic with worry and will not stop crying. This whole thing has got her so worried about me."

"Tell her she has nothing to worry about, Grandfather. I am sure you will have this whole mess cleared up in no time." Harris had now pulled on a pair of jeans while talking to the judge, and Markita had straightened up her clothes as well. Harris leaned down and gently kissed her on the cheek, as if to apologize for taking so much time with his grandfather.

"I am sorry if this affects you at work, son," his grandfather was saying.

"Don't worry yourself. I can handle anything anyone throws at me. I know you are innocent, sir."

On the other end of the line, Judge Harris had to hold back a slight sadness in his voice, knowing his grandson's loyalty was undeserved, and that once again, because of his sins, his family had to endure pain.

"Please tell your mother and uncle Joshua that I am sorry for the embarrassment to the family."

"Grandfather, you have nothing to be embarrassed or sorry about, now, please go tell Grandmother I love her, and maybe I'll be visiting Tallahassee soon with my girlfriend. That should cheer her up." He looked over at Markita and winked, and she winked back in approval.

"Girlfriend? Harris, when did this happen? I want to know all about her."

"Well, not now, Grandfather. She is here with me, and it is getting late. I need to take her home."

"You are a good boy, Harris, I am so proud of you. I'll call you as soon as this mess is over, and you can give me the details then." The judge was impressed Harris did not say she was spending the night.

"Good night, Grandfather, and love to Grandmother."

"Good night, son."

"Wow, you and your grandparents are really close, huh?" Markita asked as she snuggled down on Harris's pillows.

"Yes, I guess so," he said humbly.

"I don't have any family except for my mother," she said, sounding a bit sad.

"That is a shame as you are a beautiful lady and should be loved by many." She smiled at him adoringly.

"I love you, little girl," Harris told her again as he sat down next to her on the bed. "But I have to ask though. Are you upset we didn't make love?"

"No, of course not," she said with a smile. "It will happen when the time is right. I love you too." She looked at him with that adoring look again.

I still don't know how I got this lucky, thought Harris.

"Well, I guess I should take you home as your mother is coming tomorrow. We should leave your car at the office, seeing how I am coming with you to pick her up from the airport. We can pick up your car later, OK?"

"Sounds great," she replied, hopping up off the bed and following him back downstairs.

"Sounds like a wiener to me."

"A wiener?" she laughed.

"It's another Uncle J joke, don't worry." Harris smiled thinking about his uncle and wondering what he'd think about his newfound love with Markita.

Chapter Ten

The Breakup

It was a quarter after one when Smith awoke; it seemed his fever had finally broken. He was still in a lot of pain, but he was thinking more clearly. Hauling himself slowly out of bed, he shuffled into the bathroom, removed his make-do bandage, then showered, once again washing away the dried bloodstains. Glancing down at his healing wound, he thought his shoulder was looking a lot better. He poured more of the whiskey on some new gauze and redressed his wound.

A memory of getting a phone call from the Voice while he was delirious flashed through his mind. He checked the phone for messages, found he had just two, and pressed Play. As he listened to the first one, he realized from the date stamp that he'd been out for days. That fact, and the cold voice that now crackled on the machine, sent a chill down his spine.

"The job I asked you to do was not carried out," the Voice said. "Why is Stewart Pope still alive? Call me when your assignment is completed."

Damn, Smith thought. *I need to hurry up and get the job done before the Voice gets on my ass.* He quickly moved to check the next message and was surprised to find it was from his friend, Miss Dixie.

"Hey, Smitty," she began, her voice sounding rough and tired. "I'm in a bit of a pickle, and it seems like I'm going to need your help. They have me in lockup, and I have the feeling that I'm gonna be here for quite some time. They arrested loads of my girls and lots of clients too, but I am the only one left in this place. They let everyone else out, including the girls. The DA is threatening me with fifteen years for sex trafficking, so when you get a chance, please call Nigel Pope of the Practice. He can give you the scoop. I have been trying to call you for days, so I hope nothing's wrong. I don't know how you're gonna do it, but I need you to get me out of here. I'm beginning to get the heebie-jeebies. And, Smitty, the assistant DA wants me to go down hard. I don't know why Gallagher is not covering my back, but I get the feeling there is something bigger at play. Please, hon, don't take too long, or you may not be seeing my ass again for a long time." With a click, the line went dead.

Smith was pissed, barely believing what he had just heard. What happened while he was out of it? It seemed to him as if all hell had let loose. As much as he hated to do it, he knew he would have to deal with Miss Dixie's problem later. Pope's elimination came first.

As he had done so many times before, he began to dress in dark clothes, then strapped a small gun to his ankle, preparing himself for the assignment.

A little more than an hour later, he was on his way to the nursing home where Stewart Pope resided. He checked his watch and saw it was now 3:00 a.m. A first check of the facility showed nothing out of the ordinary. Everything seemed very quiet. After careful examination, he could tell the facility did not have any staff roaming around. He concluded that they probably had a lounge where they hung out at night. He hoped his assumption was correct. He waited a half hour, checking out whether security guards made rounds, but there did not seem to be any. He checked for alarm systems, and there didn't appear to be one of those either. *This is too easy*, he thought to himself. Picking the lock to a side door, Smith quickly slipped into the building and headed for Pope's room. The voice had left the room number on the machine during his earlier call. Faster than lightning, he grabbed a pillow from behind Pope's head and suffocated him. There was no struggle as Pope was an old and weak man. Smith placed the pillow neatly back behind Pope's head then exited as quickly as he had entered.

Once he was back in his home, he called the private number, which rang through to the only man he answered to. "It is done," he said, then hung up. It was all in a day's work for him. He was ruthless and cold, and he never showed any remorse for the executions he carried out. Long ago, he came to understand: kill or be killed.

The incidents leading up to the last few days came flooding back to him, including what had happened at Judge Poe's house. *Damn it, I hope I did not leave behind any clues*, he thought. He could not remember if the dude was dead. He thought he was. He would need to check that situation out later. Next, he needed to deal with the Doll's message that she left on the machine. Miss Dixie wanted him to get in contact with a Nigel Pope. He wondered if it was a coincidence that he had just snuffed out a Stewart Pope. He doubted it, then casually shrugged his shoulders, not giving the murder another second's thought. He needed to get the Doll out, and by god, the bastard who was trying to take her down had better run for his life. If he caught him, he'd make him pay. Miss Dixie had said something about the assistant district attorney; he needed to check out this character.

———————

It was ten o'clock in the morning when Harris walked up to Markita's desk.

"Are you ready to go pick up your mom, Markita?" Harris said, trying to sound as if he were helping her out.

"Yes, sir," she said as she watched Tara looking over at them.

"I'll have someone look at your car battery," he said trying to cover for her.

"Have a nice weekend, Tara," Markita said in her sweetest voice as she walked past the secretary's desk.

"You too, Markita. Enjoy the visit with your mom," Tara said, not caring one way or the other.

"I will, thanks." She followed Harris out of the office to his car.

"I think she is beginning to catch on, little boy."

"I think you are right, little girl. Don't worry about it. I love you too much to care. I'll give up everything in my life before I give you up." He kissed her cheek as he opened her car door and let her in.

"I love you too, little boy," she said as she buckled her seat belt then leaned over and kissed him back. "I waited all day for one of your kisses, LB. I have missed you."

"I missed you too, little girl. I thought about you all night and so did Russell." He was grinning.

"Who's Russell?" she asked, confused.

"Hmm . . . all men have a name, and his is Russell." He could feel himself blush at his bold humor.

"Ahem." She was blushing as well. "You're hilarious. What a strange name. That's just too much information, little boy." She was giggling now.

"Never mind, Chiquita, just know he was thinking about you."

"Hmmm . . . I was thinking about you too, little boy, and wished we had finished what we started the other night. I've never felt like this about anyone."

"Oh, I can assure you, me neither. We'll be together soon, I promise you."

"You are such a sexy bear," she said, squeezing his knee. Harris began blushing at her statement, went as red as a beet.

They arrived at Orlando International Airport and parked in short-term parking. Trudy appeared from the baggage claim area only moments after the couple had set foot in the terminal.

"Mommy, over here!" exclaimed Markita, waving her arms in the air to get her mom's attention.

"Hey, baby girl! How are you?" said her mother. "You look stunning."

"Mom, this is Harris Robertson." She said his name beaming with pride. Trudy's smile slipped from her face as she looked up to acknowledge Harris.

She started as if someone has just given her a small shock. "Hello" was all she could muster.

"He's my boss, Mom. They call him the Florida Hurricane attorney because he storms the bad guys and gets them to confess before they know what hit them," Markita explained to her mother, still smiling. She knew her mother would be pleased with her choice, not because he was an assistant DA, but because Harris was handsome, sweet, kind, and a gentleman.

Trudy was quite aware of Florida Hurricanes, and she was not impressed with the last one that had landed in her life. Trudy did not want her daughter having anything to do with any Hurricane that was for sure. Her mind raced; should she say something right now or wait until she had Markita alone? She was not expecting this encounter.

"I told you about him on the phone, Mom, he's brilliant."

"Yes, dear, I can only imagine, but you never mentioned his name."

"I'm sorry, Mom, I guess I wasn't thinking."

Trudy stared at Harris, not able to take her eyes off him. He looked exactly like his father, Mark; exactly like him. She shuddered.

"Are you OK, Mom? You really don't look too well."

"I am fine, baby girl, but I could do with something to eat."

"Let's go to our favorite restaurant," Harris suggested as he picked up Trudy's suitcase, carried it to the car, and placed it in the trunk. Harris glanced at Trudy and then over to Markita.

"I know where Markita gets her beauty from, ma'am," Harris said, trying to impress the mother of the woman he loved. They really did bear a striking resemblance to each other.

"Thank you, Harris. It's nice of you to say." Trudy sat in the backseat observing her daughter and Mark Robertson's son. What if he was the bastard his father was? Did he drink like him? Was he an abuser like his father?

Trudy remembered the night Mark tried to force himself on her, ripping her shirt open. She had fought back, hitting him with the night lamp and pushing him out of her apartment, locking the door on him. The next day she had called his father-in-law, Judge Harris, and asked him to get her the hell out of there. Judge Harris managed to get her a transfer and a position at the governor's offices in exchange for her silence.

The judge had been all too happy to oblige as he knew he might have a need of her later. And it didn't take long until he did. Not long after she'd moved to Tallahassee she'd received a call from the judge telling her to contact Mark and announce to him that she was pregnant with Mark's child. Judge Harris knew the news would put his son-in-law over the edge. Mark hated kids. He hadn't wanted Harris and wouldn't want a bastard child. In the end, it was how Judge Harris manipulated Mark and sent him to his demise.

What was she thinking when she sent her daughter to Orlando? Trudy never dreamed Mark's son would follow in his father's footsteps, especially with his hearing impairment. It was strange; she could not tell Harris had cochlear implants. His speech was exquisite. If she did not know the small device was located behind his ear, she would never have had a clue.

How was she going to handle this situation?

As Harris pulled into the parking lot of the Bistro, Trudy remembered this place all too well. It was Mark's and her favorite place to eat, and now her own daughter was coming here with his son. It was all too much to take in; Trudy needed time to process this awkward situation.

"Maybe I am not hungry after all," she said trying to avoid going inside.

"We can wait until we get to your apartment if you'd like. Markita?" Harris looked to Markita for guidance.

"It's OK, Mommy. We're here now, and the food is fabulous." Harris was already out of the car opening the door for Trudy and Markita. He had the looks, charm, and manners like his father, she had observed. It was Mark's other traits that scared her. What if Harris had inherited his father's alcoholism along with his abusive tendencies? She knew those traits could be hereditary.

She followed them reluctantly inside, and once there, the inevitable happened.

"'Ello, me lovies, 'ow are ya?" Brenda greeted them. She looked twice at Trudy, then her eyes opened wide in recognition. "Oh, looky 'ere if it ain't Trudy. I remember you, lovey! You used to come in 'ere with Master 'arris's father Mark, back in the day. Very 'andsome couple you two were indeed."

Trudy gave her a tight smile as the barmaid took them to a booth.

"I could tell 'ow in love you were even back then," she went on as she set their menus on the table. "Ain't it funny 'ow 'history is repeatin' itself as these two lovies are meant for each other as well?"

As Harris listened to Brenda rattle on, the memory of the argument his parents had had about his father's infidelities came racing back to his mind.

"You are having an affair with Trudy as well as Brandy?" he remembered his mother saying to his father.

"My god . . ." he muttered. His stomach began to tighten, and it wasn't butterflies floating around in it.

"What's Miss Brenda talking about, Mom?" asked Markita innocently. "Did you know Harris's father?"

"A long time ago, baby girl. I was his secretary when I lived here in Orlando."

Harris's head started to spin as more memories of his parents' fights came flooding back. His mother had also accused Mark of having an affair with his secretary. His stomach churned, and he felt a pulse beating on the side of his throat.

"God! It can't be, it just can't," he whispered.

He looked over at Markita as if seeing her for the first time. Did she look anything like his father? He could not tell as tears began to fill his eyes, clouding his vision like a heavy fog. Markita's eyes looked back at him, confused. She could see he was in pain; his sweet demeanor had turned to fierce scowls. Trudy said nothing, just observed the body language between Harris and her daughter.

"Why did you never mention to me you worked for the DA's office?" Markita asked, trying to get a sense for what was happening between Harris and her mother.

"I didn't work for Mark at the DA's office, baby girl. I met him at the Practice, a law firm." She was speaking to her daughter, but her eyes were on Harris.

"You worked at my grandfather's law firm?" Harris asked her slowly, trying to control his roiling emotions.

"Yes," Trudy answered him. "It's where I met your father. He begged me to go to the DA's office with him, but because of our circumstances, I thought it better if I stayed at the law firm. Later, I let him talk me into helping him obtain his judgeship by attending all of his social functions and that sort of thing," Trudy said, holding nothing back.

Harris had another flashback to a fight which occurred after a golf game between his grandfather and father. Mark had come home and threatened Mary Ellen; he accused her of telling her father to get rid of his secretary. His father then proceeded upstairs and antagonized his young son until he cried.

Trudy could see Harris was becoming agitated.

"I guess I didn't know this was going to be an issue, baby girl," Trudy said to her daughter, still not looking away from Harris.

"Were you having an affair with my father?" Harris asked, spitting the words out.

"Harris, it was not like what you are thinking," Trudy started to explain. "Your father and I were close."

"So you were . . . having an affair with him?" Harris said, banging his fist on the table, already knowing the answer. The churning in his stomach now burned; it felt like a volcano about to erupt. He tasted vomit, and his body shuddered. "You don't need to answer me," he nearly shouted. "I already know. My mother suffered because of you time and time again."

As much as it pained her to know how much her next words would hurt her daughter, Trudy thought now would be a good time to put the nail in the coffin and end this relationship between Harris and her Markita.

"I am truly sorry for your mother's suffering, young man, believe me. I was aware of what your father was capable of. It's why, when I found out I was pregnant, I left Orlando."

Trudy hated the lie, but it was necessary to keep her daughter safe.

In reality, she didn't get pregnant until she was living in Tallahassee, and the only reason she named Markita after Harris's father was because at one time she had been in love with him. She knew her lie was about to devastate her daughter, but Judge Harris was a powerful and dangerous man, and she would protect her daughter at all costs.

"Holy mother of god, Markita," Harris gasped, finally looking at the woman he had thought he loved. "Do you know what this means?" He continued looking over at her as if it would be the last time he would ever see her. She looked back at him with desperation in her own eyes.

"Your name is Markita—Mark. She was cheating with my rat bastard father and had the audacity to name you after him!" He pointed an accusing finger at Trudy. "Are you getting the same sick picture I am?"

Harris looked at her differently now, and his love was replaced with contempt. His eyes pierced through her as if it were all her fault. He had never felt hatred before; dislike, frustration, even anger, but never hatred. Right at that moment, he understood how his father could lash out at another person. He wanted to hurt Trudy and that scared him.

Markita's eyes began welling with tears; she was not quite sure what was happening around her, but it was all too much to take in, and Trudy was saying nothing.

Harris tried to get up from the booth, but his body was trembling and felt as if he had aged fifty years. His body did not want to move. He felt his stomach lurch— he had to get out of here. His conscience screamed out at him, *I nearly made love to her last night!*

It was that thought that finally got him moving. He ran to his car, thanking God it was parked just outside. Leaning over the edge of the hood into the gutter, he heaved and heaved, praying to God to tell him it wasn't true. None of this could be happening. He was thinking of his father as he vomited, wanting to rid himself of all his father's demons. He was trying to stand up straight, but all the while his legs just wanted to buckle from under him. His head was pounding, and he wasn't sure if he was sweating from the vomit or the hot Florida sun.

Suddenly, Markita was running out of the Bistro after him.

"Harris . . . Harris . . ." she cried, tears streaming down her face. She reached out to touch his arm, trying to help him.

"Stop," he snapped, pulling his arm back. "Don't touch me." He couldn't hold back his tears; they poured from his eyes, racing down his face, and he could taste the saltiness of them as they reached his lips. All he could do was stare at her in disbelief. How could he not have known? He was supposed to live by instincts! What the hell was wrong with him?

"Harris, I love you," Markita cried out in desperation.

His stomach was still trying to recover from the shock.

"Shut up!" he screamed at her.

"Harris, I know, I know, it all seems crazy, but we love each other! We were meant to be! You said so yourself." She was trying to find the right words to say to him, but there were none, not now, not ever.

"Stop saying those words," he screamed back at her again. "You're making me sick." He was trying to get his car key in the lock, but his hand was shaking so badly he could not keep it still long enough to get it to fit.

"Harris, please, please don't go like this," Markita begged him. "There has to be an explanation or something, please don't leave me." She grabbed his arm again, not wanting him to leave. "Please, please, Harris, don't."

He fiercely pulled his arm away from her. "I told you not to touch me," he said coldly. His own tears still clouded his vision. "Do you think I wanted this, Markita? You are my sister! What we had is gone . . . It's awful, an abomination, but is there anything we can do about it? No!" He was nearly screaming at her again. "It's a freaking reality, Markita, one we need to live with. The sooner you accept the truth, the better we will both be."

"Please, Harris, I love you," Markita cried again, refusing to let him go. "Don't, don't, Harris, please."

Her attempts at making him stay were failing miserably; she did not understand what had happened. It was all so quick and confusing. All she knew was she that loved him, unconditionally. She couldn't stop crying, and her breathing came in great gasping sobs. "I love you," she said again.

"I asked you to stop saying those words. I can't love you, and you can't love me. I have to go. I never wanted it to end this way, but it is time for me to leave you." He banged his fist against the roof of his Jaguar.

"Harris, last night we were about to make love. You told me you loved me! We are so good together," she said, making one final attempt to make him realize their love.

"My god, Markita! Don't the implications of what you are saying mean anything to you? How can you even say the words without them sticking in your throat? You still don't seem to understand: we are related! Do I have to spell it out for you? We are brother and sister. We would have been condemned by God if we had made love last night. It's called incest," he added cruelly. *I loved you so much,* he thought. *But now I will never know what making love to my beautiful Markita is like.* Harris could take no more; he was out of emotion, his body exhausted, his heart broken and empty.

"I have to get out of here. I'll send for a taxi for you and your . . . mother." He pushed by her and threw himself into the Jag, slamming the door shut behind him.

"Please, please, Harris, don't leave me," Markita begged, her hands on the window of his car. "I love you! This is so unfair, please."

She knew her pleas were hopeless, but she could not give up. She tried wiping the tears from her face, but as fast as she wiped them away, more appeared. When he refused to look at her and then finally drove away, it started to sink in, and she covered her face with her hands, realizing he was gone. She bent over taking her hands from her eyes and now holding her stomach, wanting to throw up herself, but couldn't.

Trudy waited to see that Harris had gone before she came out of the restaurant, then she ran toward her daughter, taking her into her arms and stroking the back of her head like a little girl.

"It will be OK, baby girl. I promise things will look better in the morning, trust me," she cooed.

"How could you do this to me, Mother?" Markita asked, sobbing.

"Sweetie, I did not do this to you. I would never hurt you. I love you, baby girl. It's just an unfortunate situation, that's all," Trudy said trying to console her daughter.

"That's all? That's all, Mom? Is that all you can say? I loved him, do you understand? I wanted to marry him. He was everything to me. I would have given up everything for him. I can't believe he is leaving me. God, what happened? Why? Why?" She turned her tearstained face to her mother. "Please bring him back to me."

"Now, now, Markita, you are getting yourself all worked up over nothing. This is your first serious relationship, after all. There are plenty more fish in the sea, trust me."

Markita couldn't believe her mother's cold and uncaring attitude. Feeling more lost and alone than she could ever remember, she put her face back in her hands and sobbed, not wanting to say another word to her mother.

As he drove slowly away, Harris had taken one last look at his beautiful Markita. He felt as if he suffered a heart attack. It was as if the doctor had torn his chest in two and taken out his heart; it didn't feel broken, it was just gone. Getting only as far as around the corner, he pulled over and stopped. He slammed his fist on the steering wheel, saying every curse word he knew. Opening his door, he leaned over, his body wanting to vomit again, but there was nothing left inside him. He sat in his car for what seemed like hours before driving on home. He had completely forgotten about calling the two women a cab.

When he at last dragged himself into his apartment, Harris threw his keys on the kitchen counter then went up and dropped onto his bed. His breathing began to quicken, along with a rush of adrenaline. *Of all women in the world, why did she have to be my sister?* He hated his father even more; he loathed him, despised him, and wished he were alive so he could hurt him like he was hurting. Even now, years after his death, the rat bastard affected his life. Wasn't it enough his father took his hearing for eight years of his life? Now his father had taken away the only love he had ever known, his beautiful Markita. His anger was starting to consume him. Leaping up from the bed, he paced back and forth in order to release his energy. His emotions exploded. He could not handle the pain or his anger any longer, so he hit the wall with his fist.

"Damn you!" he screamed out, his outburst intended for his father. He finally lay back down and tried to process his life until he finally fell into a fitful sleep.

———————

Trudy had finally gotten her daughter home and was busy calling the airport to make an extra reservation for her daughter, who stood at her dresser, woodenly laying clothing in a suitcase, saying nothing.

"We will send for the rest of your things later, Markita. Take the necessities. I'll call a friend and have them put your car in storage, and then we can come back together later and pick it all up."

Markita kept packing without uttering a word.

"I will call Hugh for you in the morning and make an excuse as to why you came back to Tallahassee with me. It will be OK, baby girl. You can finish interning at home."

Markita had tried to called Harris nineteen times. She now left the twentieth message.

"Harris, please call me. We need to talk. I have left my number in Tallahassee for you, and you know my cell number. I love you."

She believed if only they could talk, they could work everything out. How could they be brother and sister? She could not understand. Maybe she would wake up any minute, and it would all be a bad dream.

"We are booked on a flight this afternoon, baby girl," Trudy said hanging up with the airline.

It was not a dream. It was killing her inside knowing she might never see Harris again. The tears filled in her eyes again before slowly rolling down her face. It happened every time she thought about the man she loved.

"You need to stop, baby girl," Trudy said, seeing the tears starting again. "You are lucky you found out before it was too late. You will find someone else worthy of you soon."

Markita was furious at her mother. That was the last thing she needed to hear. She wanted answers from her mother, but she had not spoken a word to her since they left the restaurant. *Could things be any worse?* she said to herself.

———————

It was Sunday afternoon, and Harris should have been at his mom and Joshua's house; after all they were celebrating his birthday. Mary Ellen had been busy all morning preparing things for the occasion, making him a special chocolate birthday cake.

"It is not like Harris to not show up like this, Joshua. Could you please call him and find out what time he is planning on coming?"

"Of course, darling, right away." Joshua quickly dialed Harris's number, but only reached the machine.

"His machine picked up, darling. Maybe he's on his way."

"I hope so, Josh. It's getting late," Mary Ellen said, sounding a little concerned.

"I'm sure he will be here soon," Joshua tried to reassure her. "He always calls if something comes up."

"I know, Josh. You don't have to give me that look. I know I'm far too overprotective."

"No," he said, smiling. "You're just a good mother."

But the later it got and the more Josh called Harris's phone without an answer, the more worried they both became. Finally, Mary Ellen couldn't take the wondering any longer.

"Would you please drive over there, Josh, and check on him?" she asked, her eyes worried.

"Of course I will, darling." Joshua was glad she asked him. He did not want to show it, but he was a little concerned himself, especially with it being Harris's own birthday celebration. The boy would have known the trouble his mother would go through making sure everything was perfect for him.

When Joshua arrived at Harris's condo less than twenty minutes later, he knocked on the door several times, then rang the doorbell for a few minutes. After a moment, he gave up trying and took out the spare key he had and unlocked the door.

"Harris, are you in here?" Joshua called out. There was no answer. He turned the corner, and there in the living room was Harris, slouched in a chair, staring at a full bottle of brandy sitting on the table with a shot glass next to it.

"What the hell are you doing, son?" Joshua asked him softly, knowing something must be very wrong.

Harris said nothing, still staring at the bottle.

"Harris, I asked you a question," Joshua said, his voice rising. "What the hell do you think you are doing with that bottle of booze?" Harris still did not answer him, nor did he even look up.

"Son, there is nothing in this world a bottle of brandy is going to cure. Look what it did to your father."

"Do *not* mention that rat bastard to me!" Harris yelled, raising his voice to his uncle for the first time in his life.

"What is it, son?" Josh tried again. "I have never seen you this upset. Talk to me, please."

"I don't want to talk to you or anyone else for that matter. Why don't you get the fuck out of here?"

"Whoa, son." Josh actually took a step back in shock. "I don't care how angry you are, do not use that kind of language with me, do you understand?"

"If you don't want to hear it, then do as I ask and get out of here."

Joshua promptly sat down on the couch, letting Harris know he was not going anywhere.

"What is so awful you think booze will fix?" he asked, looking right into Harris's tortured face.

"You know, Uncle J, I love you, I really do, but you are really starting to piss me off. I want to be alone! Can you not understand me?"

"What I understand, son, is that there is a bottle of brandy sitting in front of you, and I am not leaving here until you pour it down the sink and then tell me what the hell has happened." Joshua saw his nephew's pain, and a thought suddenly occurred to him: this was the week Markita's mother, Trudy, was supposed to visit. He had hoped his fears were in vain and that she wasn't the same Trudy his brother had cheated on Mary Ellen with years before, but now he guessed that his fears had been on the money. He sat in silence with Harris, knowing now what the boy must be going through. His heart broke for his nephew. He knew he had fallen hard for the girl; he had never seen him happier. The memory of Mary Ellen's reaction to Markita's likeness to Mark became evident now. How was he going to tell Mary Ellen that Mark had another child? She was going to hurt all over again. After everything Mary Ellen had endured, all the lies, the beatings, the drinking, but most of all the kidnapping of Harris, which he was ultimately responsible for, how would she handle this? He never told Mary Ellen the truth about Trudy or the kidnapping. He had carried these secrets inside him all these years. He wondered how she would react if he had to tell her; would she forgive him? Joshua's stomach started feeling as sick as his nephew's.

"I guess from your silence, Uncle J, you have put the pieces together."

"I have, son, and I am so, so sorry for you."

"I hate him, Uncle J, I hate him."

It was hard to hear him berate his brother. Joshua always tried to see the good in Mark, remembering how he would try to shield him from their own father's abuse and alcoholism.

"'Hate' is a strong word, son. It is only for the Lord to judge us. There is a scripture in the Bible which states, 'Judge ye not, lest ye be judged.'"

"Then I am sure he went to hell."

"There is nothing I can say to console you, but I can assure you, that bottle is not going to do it for you either."

"Take the damn stuff and pour it out, I don't care," Harris said angrily, waving the bottle away.

Joshua quickly picked up the bottle and poured it down the sink in the kitchen, relieved Harris was strong enough to denounce the brandy before even drinking a single drop.

"Mom knew, you know. About *her*," Harris said, thinking back to his mother's cold attitude toward Markita.

"Yes, son, I think so."

"It's why she acted so strange towards Mar . . ." He could not finish saying Markita's name; it made him sick when he said it. "I thought it was because Mom was afraid of letting me go, but it wasn't, was it, Uncle J?"

"Your mother made mention of the likeness to your father" was all that Joshua could manage to say.

"She's beautiful, you know."

"Yes, son, Markita sure was a picture of perfection."

"No, not her, her mother Trudy." Harris nearly spat the name when he said it.

"I guess so," Joshua replied slowly. "But she has nothing on your mother. She is beautiful on the outside as well as the inside."

"You're right there, Uncle J. She is lucky to have you."

"No, no, son, I'm the lucky one."

"How could he have cheated on Mom? I don't understand," Harris asked, still bewildered by his father's behavior even after all this time.

"I know it's no consolation, but he hit Trudy as well. That's why she left town; she was afraid of him. He promised her he would leave your mother, but he never did. I think deep down inside he loved her, even though he didn't know how to show it."

"Don't ever say that again." Harris jumped up and started pacing around his condo.

"You don't hit someone you love, and you don't take their hearing away from them," he raged.

Joshua knew Harris's anger was intensifying and not just over the loss of Markita. His resentment toward his father for his hearing loss added to the situation. The last time Joshua had seen his nephew like this was when he was eight years old. It was the reason he kidnapped Harris all those years ago and had the cochlear implant surgery done without Mark knowing. Joshua wondered if Mark had ever heard Harris talking as eloquently as he did now, if their relationship would have become a loving one, or at least a stronger one. They would never know the answer to those questions, however, because Judge Harris made sure that after he shot Mark, the fire he set under the cabin would leave no evidence his brother ever lived.

"I am glad you kidnapped me and took me away from that rat bastard," said Harris, emotionally drained. He looked over toward his Uncle J. Suddenly, Harris's body stiffened up like a clay statue. His heart jumped out of his chest, not for himself, but for what he knew was about to happen.

"What did I hear?" Mary Ellen said softly, entering the room. She had driven over to Harris's condominium. Joshua had been gone a long time as well, and she had been worried about the two of them. Joshua jumped out of his skin at the sound of her voice. She stood just inside the doorway. His head turned toward her so fast it nearly spun off his neck. The guilt and fear he had carried around with him all these years was about to bite him in the ass. His throat gulped, gasping for air, his heart literally stopped for a second before racing as fast as a Thoroughbred winning a race. *This could not be happening,* he thought. *God could not be this cruel.*

It was not God, but his voice inside told him, *Today is your judgment day, Joshua Robertson, and you are the one who has lied to her all these years.* How was he going to make her understand? He was going to need time, but he knew he only had a split second. He could see the anger and rage all over her face as she scowled at him fiercely. The kidnapping of Harris had been torture for her.

Joshua tried to get up from the couch, but his body seemed frozen solid and as heavy as a elephant. Mary Ellen was now staring at Joshua waiting for an answer. Harris said the first thing that came to his mind.

"Mom, you need to sit down and stay calm." It was not the best thing to say right then.

"Son, the only thing I need right now is to hear your uncle say what I heard coming through the door is not true." Her eyes pierced through Joshua like daggers; her once-beautiful lips were so tight they could have split open. Again, Joshua tried to stand, but his poor, stunned body could not. He tried to speak, but words were not coming; all he could do was gasp for air and keep breathing. Mary Ellen started to raise her voice.

"I want an explanation, and I want it now, Joshua."

Finally, he was able to stand; he started to walk toward her with his hand out.

"Do not come near me or touch me, Joshua Robertson, until you tell me what I heard is a lie." Mary Ellen was becoming hysterical. Harris tried to defuse the situation, but nothing was working.

"Look, guys. It's late, and I have work in the morning," he tried. "It is obvious you two have a lot to talk about, so why don't you go home together? Mom, you need to listen to everything Uncle J has to tell you. Just remember he loves you and did everything because of his love for us."

Harris walked by his mother and kissed her on the cheek before going upstairs.

"Let us go home and discuss this calmly, darling," Joshua said in desperation.

"I am not going anywhere with you, Joshua, until you can tell me right here and now that you did not do this to me."

Chapter Eleven

The Confession

Joshua begged Mary Ellen to sit down; his explanation was going to take awhile. She, however, was in no mood to sit down. Her adrenaline was at the boiling point. Instead, she continued to stand, arms crossed, waiting for her husband to give her the explanation she demanded.

Joshua needed to sit; his body was already tired and worn out from anxiety and panic, his stomach tied in knots. Where should he begin? Looking up at her, he opened his mouth, and the words he prayed he would never have to say came tumbling out, heavy with sorrow.

"I had taken Harris to the lake one afternoon, wanting to teach him how to swim, but he wouldn't take off his shirt. I pleaded with him until he finally pulled off his shirt, and I saw his back. I couldn't believe the bruises, Mary Ellen! I didn't know what to do. I was so angry at my brother, so fearful for Harris. I loved Harris, and still do, like he's my own. I was appalled to know what my brother had done. It brought back memories of my own twisted childhood. Don't you remember the nightmares I endured, screaming out in the middle of the night? Your love and understanding are what helped me through those dark times and made my monsters disappear." He searched Mary Ellen's face for any trace of understanding, but seeing none, he went on.

"Then, there was the day I came to your house one morning unexpected, and you wore as much makeup as a clown trying to cover your own bruises. You begged me not to interfere, and I obeyed your wishes and stayed out of your business for as long as I could. But I couldn't have lived with myself if I'd allowed things to continue on the way they were going. I was afraid my brother was going to kill Harris if things went on like that for much longer.

"The last straw was the night Mark kicked Harris across the room like a football. That was when I made the decision to take things into my own hands. I can't claim I was thinking straight. I just wanted Harris to be safe."

Joshua looked at her in the eye, willing her to understand how fearful he had been for his young nephew. "You thought Harris was dying that night. You called your father over to the house, Mary Ellen, remember? You didn't know what to do, and you were so afraid you were going to lose your son. I couldn't stand seeing you, or Harris, in such pain any longer, and I knew that whatever your father could do might not happen soon enough to save the boy." Now came the difficult part, the part where he had to confess that he had caused the woman he loved even more pain. Joshua paused for a moment, taking a few deep breaths to regain his composure.

"I'm waiting." Mary Ellen's voice broke the momentary silence. "Don't stop now, Joshua Wayne Robertson. I'm sure you're getting to the part where you tell me the truth, the whole truth and nothing but the truth, so help you God, right? Unless of course you're incapable of telling the truth," she added coldly. She was getting angrier by the minute.

Joshua didn't want to go on with his explanation, but he knew he had no choice. If he didn't choose his words correctly, he could destroy everything they had together. He knew he had stalled long enough. Saying a silent prayer, he proceeded to tell her the truth, at least as much of it as he could safely tell, about what had happened to her son so many years ago.

"I had arranged for Barry, Mark's assistant DA at the time, to come by and get Mark drunk while I slipped upstairs and took Harris." He left out the part about her father being the one who actually made those arrangements; it turned out that Judge Harris wanted his grandson out of that awful situation nearly as badly as Joshua did. In that, they were united. It was on the question of what warranted murder that they were divided. But none of this was necessary for Mary Ellen to know. That was between her and her father, should he choose to share it, which he doubted he ever would.

"I took Harris to the lake house," Joshua continued. "He was so happy there. I purchased that puppy, Charlie, for him, and the two were inseparable. I think that dog had almost as much to do with the boy's recovery as the implants eventually did. I had obtained false documents and identification for us both and then set about arranging for Harris to get his cochlear implant surgery done. I felt Mark had taken too long to do this for his son, especially since he was the cause for his deafness. Mark's promises were empty. The boy was getting older and missing so much. I wanted him to catch up at school as well as hear the beautiful sounds this world has to offer."

"I can't believe this," Mary Ellen murmured, finally sinking down into a chair. "God, how could you?" she breathed, looking at her husband with accusing eyes.

"Look at him, darling. Your son has turned out a successful man. What I did hurt you, I know, but look at what it did for Harris. I love him, Mary Ellen, certainly more than his father ever did. You know I would have done anything for him, and you, if you'd have let me at the time."

"It wasn't your call, Joshua," Mary Ellen insisted. "He had a father and a mother! You had no right to take him." She was fuming.

"I did it out of love for him," he said in desperation, trying to get her to understand.

"No, Joshua. You loved me too much, and you knew it was wrong. You shouldn't have interfered in our marriage and taken things into your own hands. Harris's hearing was none of your concern. You were selfish. *You* loved Harris, *you* took him, and *you* thought about no one else's feelings except your own. He was *our* son, not yours, his hearing surgery was *our* decision to make. When you took Harris from me, you tortured my soul!" she was crying angry tears now, remembering how much Harris's disappearance had hurt her. "It was cruel! How could you betray me, Joshua?" Mary Ellen felt the tears streaming down her cheeks, her breathing uneven as she struggled to hold back the sobs that she knew would come. Joshua's heart broke as he struggled to tell Mary Ellen the truth and watched helplessly in the aftermath of the pain it inflicted.

"Darling, please don't misunderstand. Yes, I loved you, and yes, I loved Harris, but I would never dream of hurting either of you if it could have been avoided. My brother needed to be stopped, and I'm sorry if this hurts you, but I would do it all over again if I had to."

That was the last straw for Mary Ellen. She couldn't take any more of his words; she was furious with him.

"You would . . . would you?" she spat. "I don't ever want you to tell me you love me again. You couldn't really love someone and still put the person you love through the kind of hell you put me through. I spent night after sleepless night crying, aching for my son. I spent my days in my body while my mind was somewhere else, wondering if some pervert was hurting my child, or if he was even still alive. I didn't sleep or eat, Joshua. I took pills to make me sleep, pills to wake me up. I drank, I paced the floor night after night worried sick about Harris. So don't tell me you love me when it was you all along who tortured me. Then . . . then, Joshua, to make matters worse, you've kept lying to me day after day, and you encouraged my son to do the same! So much for our vows, huh? God, does this ever end?" she cried as she put her face in her hands. Joshua stood up to rush toward her, his instincts telling him to hold her and console her, but she pulled away from his touch and then blindly got up, turning to leave.

"I know this is a lot to take in, and we need to talk more, so let's go home so we can work this out," Joshua suggested gently.

"Oh, I'm going home, Joshua, but you can find somewhere else to sleep, as long as it's nowhere near me."

"Mary Ellen, please," Joshua begged. "We need to talk this out. I love you, darling."

Mary Ellen said nothing more; she simply rose from the chair and strode out of Harris's condo, slamming the door behind her.

Joshua stood in the living room alone. He was devastated; he had never felt so helpless in his life. Without her, what would he do with himself? They were a part of each other; they were meant to be. He dropped back down on the couch feeling lost and empty.

Harris had heard the door slam, so he went back downstairs, hoping the two of them had left together, but when he reached the living room, he saw his uncle sitting alone, staring into space. He immediately understood what had happened and went to sit next to Joshua.

"It will be OK," he said, trying to comfort the older man. "She just needs time to process it all. I know Mom loves you, Uncle J."

"I'm not so sure, son," Joshua said, shaking his head slowly. "I have ruined everything. I should have trusted her enough to tell her the truth a long time ago."

"Things will look better in the morning. I know she'll call you to come home, and then you guys can finish talking about everything."

"I don't think that's going to happen. Your mother was angrier than I have ever seen her. I put her through hell when I took you, son, and I am sorry for that, but I would do it all again if it meant saving your life."

"I know, Uncle J, you're the best father a son could ever have." Hearing Harris call him father made the whole ordeal worth all the risks.

"I don't believe it, son. Here you are, consoling me when today you lost the love of your life."

"I don't want to think about her, Uncle J, so please, could we not talk about her? I'm more concerned about you and Mom right now." Joshua felt a little better. At least Harris still loved him despite the agony he had caused his mother.

"Is it OK if I stay here the night?" he asked.

"You know it is. Take the spare room, there are clean sheets already on the bed." Harris turned to go back upstairs.

"I'm going to stay down here a while and think. I'll be up in a bit."

"I love you, Uncle J. Good night."

"I love you too, son." Hearing Harris talk so eloquently and telling him he loved him was helping keep Joshua sane.

Harris awoke at the usual time the next morning, but after everything that happened yesterday, he didn't feel like facing anyone, let alone getting out of bed. Leaning over to his left, he picked up his phone and called Tara.

"I won't be in today, Tara. I'm not feeling too well."

"You'll feel even worse when I tell you Markita is gone and not coming back. She went home to Tallahassee with her mother yesterday." Harris tried his best to sound surprised, which wasn't hard; he had no enthusiasm in his voice whatsoever.

"What happened, does anyone know?" he asked lethargically.

"No, 'personal reasons' is all Hugh told me."

"All we can do is wish her all the best. If Joe calls, refer him here please," said Harris, moving straight on to business.

"Of course, Mr. Robertson." Tara thought his unemotional attitude toward Markita's leaving was quite odd; she knew they both had feelings for each other. Her curiosity was going to nag at her until she found out the juicy details.

"Forget about Joe," Harris said, changing his mind. "I think I'm going to give him a call myself."

"OK, sir, I hope you get to feeling better tomorrow. I'll let Hugh know for you."

"Thanks, Tara." Harris hung up and went back to his thoughts. He had wanted to go to the nursing home this morning to interview Stewart Pope; he thought that maybe he could discover something helpful for his grandfather. Thinking of his grandfather, he had the unpleasant thought of how he was going to explain to him that he and his new girlfriend had already broken up. He knew his grandmother would be sad for him. And he had been planning to cheer her up when he visited, hoping to take her mind off everything her husband had to endure. So much for that idea. He couldn't face Stewart Pope or anyone else today, he decided. He needed to tell Joe he would go tomorrow. Leaning over to get the phone again, he dialed Joe's number

"Joe here."

"Joe, it's Harris."

"How's it going there, lover boy? What was your mother-in-law like? A real cracker, I bet."

"Oh yeah, she was a cracker all right," Harris replied.

"What the hell is wrong with you? You sound like a wet worm."

"Joe, I'm real sorry, but I'm in no mood to joke around with you. I wanted to tell you I'll go visit Stewart Pope tomorrow, I'm hanging at home today."

"Well, that's probably a good thing, since Stewart Pope is no longer with us."

"You're kidding!" Harris said, sitting up in bed. "What happened?"

"Appears to have died in his sleep, but I've got sources downtown that seem to think that an autopsy might show he was suffocated."

"No way," said Harris.

"Harris, what's up, man?" Joe asked again, hearing something wrong with his voice.

"Nothing, I just don't feel well."

"No, man, there is more going on, I can hear it in your voice. Whatever, you know you can talk to me."

"There is nothing to talk about."

"Is it the hot mama?"

"There is no more 'hot mama,' so I would appreciate it if we could stay away from the subject in the future and move forward."

"When you're ready, let's go get coffee, and you can tell me all about it, bubba."

"Did you not understand what I said, Marble? I don't want to discuss her with you, got it?" Harris hung up, pissed off.

Joe held the phone away from his ear, stunned. This was new. He guessed Harris would open up when he was ready.

Harris rolled back over, feeling guilty for snapping at his best friend, but how was he supposed to tell Joe that Markita was his sister? Suddenly, he felt queasy again. He needed to get his mind off her and concentrate on his grandfather.

Now that Stewart Pope was dead, there would be no need for a hearing. Short term, it was great for his grandfather. He wouldn't have to endure the humiliation of a trial now. On the other side of the coin, it wasn't so great for him as it would leave doubt and suspicion in minds of people, thus tainting his good name. His grandfather was still a strong man and could handle these kinds of affairs. The word "affairs" brought Trudy and his own father's affair back to his mind. He still couldn't comprehend that Markita was his half sister. He began thinking about last Thursday night when she was here in his bed when they were about to make love. His anger returned, causing him to leap out of bed in an attempt to put her out of his mind.

He went downstairs to make coffee and found his uncle J lying on the couch fast asleep. Harris headed into the kitchen and mechanically started the coffee brewing. Joshua awoke to the aroma, stretching out his stiff and aching back. He hadn't meant to fall asleep on the couch, but it got late, and he truly was exhausted. He'd tossed and turned all night thinking about how angry Mary Ellen was with him. He felt in his heart that she would never forgive him for taking Harris, no matter how much good it had done. He slowly dragged his tired body into the kitchen looking for Harris.

"Hey, son, good morning."

"Good morning, Uncle J, have you heard from Mom yet?"

"No, I told you last night, I don't expect to."

"I'll go by and talk to her later. I'll make her understand."

"That's really great of you, son, and I appreciate the offer, but the apology has to come from me. This has brought up painful memories for your mother. She has been forced to look back at the drinking, the beatings, and then she finds out that the man she married is a liar and the one who kidnapped her little boy. I don't think she'll forgive me for this one. I have lost everything."

"No, you've haven't, Uncle J. You haven't lost me and never will."

"I love you for saying that." Harris poured his uncle some coffee and sat down at the kitchen table with him.

"Are you going to tell me what happened with you and Markita?"

"I'm not going to dwell on it, Uncle J, but it wasn't a pretty picture. It killed me inside to see her so hurt. The desperation in her eyes made me want to reach out and hold her. I think if I hadn't walked away, she would have wanted us to stay together, and the thought of that made me want to heave."

"I'm so very, very sorry, son. It must have been painful for you as well. I know how much you loved her. It was plain for anyone around you to see. You fell fast and hard."

"I sure did, Uncle J, but it's in the past now, and I really would appreciate it if we could not mention her name ever again."

"Fine, son, but I do want to remind you that she is your half sister, and maybe down the road when the wounds have healed, you should try to form some kind of relationship with her."

Harris sighed heavily. "I don't ever see that happening," he said, shaking his head. "Never say never, Harris."

"Good, then don't say Mom will never forgive you. She'll come around. You two were meant for each other. Remember your vows and your favorite song? Uncle J, don't give up on her." Harris thought how ironic it was that his and Markita's song was the same song that connected Joshua and Mary Ellen.

"Who is supposed to be the one who gives the advice here, son?" Joshua said with a smile. Harris gave a small grin as he finished his coffee, rinsed the cup, and placed it in the dishwasher.

"I'm going to go back upstairs and lay down for a while," he said.

"Why are you not at work today anyway? A broken heart is no excuse to miss work."

"Oh really? I don't see you at the university today," Harris shot back.

"Actually, I'm getting ready to go. I was just trying to figure out how I'm going to go home to pick up some clothes without upsetting your mother."

"Let me call her, and I'll let her know you're coming and check out the situation at the same time."

"Thanks, son, you're the greatest."

"You bet your arse, I am," Harris said laughing for the first time in twenty-four hours. He went upstairs and crawled back under the covers, then reached over and picked up the phone to dial his mother. When she answered, he tried to sound upbeat, not knowing how she might respond.

"Hey, Mom, how are you this morning?"

"How do you think, son?" she snapped crisply.

"I wish you would hear Uncle J out. It was so long ago. It doesn't even really matter anymore."

There was a pause on the other end as his mother collected herself. "Harris, your father died the day you were returned home to me. He never knew you were safe. That's something your uncle Joshua is responsible for."

"Mom, he's also responsible for me hearing. Dad was never going to get around to having my surgery done. Something was always more important than me."

"That isn't true!" his mother responded hotly. "Your father was in the middle of a high-profile case at the time."

"Yes, Mother, and as I said, it took precedence over my hearing. What excuse did he have for all the other years he could have got it done?"

"How is your uncle?" Mary Ellen tried changing the subject.

"Miserable, lost, and missing you."

"I suppose he wants to come by to pick up his clothes? Tell him I have packed a suitcase for him, and I'll place it on the front porch when I know he's coming. You can tell him I'll make arrangements for him to pick up the rest of his stuff at another time when I'm not here."

"Mom, are you really going to punish him like this?" Harris asked in disbelief. He honestly didn't think she'd really take it this far. "I think you're going a bit overboard here, Mother. You shouldn't do anything rash that you might regret later."

"I have a lot of feelings to sort out, son. I don't appreciate the fact he has carried his lie around with him all these years. And I cannot believe he coerced you into keeping silent as well. You'll never understand the enormous pain and suffering a mother goes through when she loses a child. Your uncle took you from me. He should be in jail."

"No, you're wrong, Mom," Harris said, starting to lose his temper. "I *chose* not to say anything. I was glad Dad was out of the picture because he couldn't hurt me or you anymore. I still remember finding you on the bathroom floor covered in blood. The memory is so vivid in my mind, it's as if it happened yesterday. As far as Uncle J being in jail, I think he should have received a medal for saving my hearing and my life. You need to give him a break."

"Why did you not come to me, Harris, so we could have talked about all this? You've obviously been bottling up these feelings since you were a young boy."

"Mom, come off it. You were in denial back then, hell you still are. You have a great man in Uncle J. He loves you more than life itself. You're the first and only woman he has ever loved, and he treats you with respect. He has never even raised his voice to you, let alone a hand. He treats you as his equal and not his property."

"I know you love your uncle J, you always have. Maybe you loved him a little too much, and your father sensed and resented it."

"You know, Mom, you amaze me. Even now, after everything that bastard did, you stand up for him and defend his sorry ass."

"Harris, please, don't speak about your father that way. It's unfair to criticize him when he isn't around to defend himself."

"Why would he need to defend himself, Mom? He has you to do that for him." Harris was now getting extremely aggravated at his mother. "I'll tell Uncle J to go by the house and get his clothes and then bring them back here to mine. I hope you don't take too long sorting out whatever it is you need to sort out. Life is too short, and we only have this moment to live in. No one knows what will happen in the next five minutes, let alone what tomorrow may bring. Think about it, Mom."

"You're a wise young man for your age, my darling, but I'll not tolerate lies, not from anyone, not even you, Harris."

"Then stop lying to yourself about Dad. I didn't want to tell you about this as you've enough to deal with, but Markita and I have broken up."

Mary Ellen's heart didn't exactly break over the news; there had been something holding her back from liking Markita.

"What happened, darling?" Out of the love for her son, she tried to sound sincere.

"It was over the rat bastard whom you like to defend. Markita's mother Trudy enjoyed telling me yesterday that she'd had an affair with Dad, and that Markita is the result of that affair."

Now it was Mary Ellen's turn to be nauseated; she had always suspected they'd had an affair, but had never really known for sure. She guessed Markita was proof enough.

"I can only imagine how hurt you are, son," she said, trying to contain her own emotions at the news. "I'm sorry about your pain. I know you don't want to hear this right now, but believe me, you're better off finding out sooner rather than later. Look," she said abruptly, "I need to get going, son. I have to pack Joshua's things." Before Harris had a chance to say another word, Mary Ellen hung up the phone, not wanting Harris to know how much the news of the affair hurt her. She was a strong woman; back then, she had to be after everything Mark made her endure. No one understood why she loved him, but she knew he was a good man at one time, handsome, debonair, intellectual, and affectionate, and that's who she'd fallen in love with.

She hadn't felt this alone for a long time. First, Joshua's lies and now, the truth about Mark and Trudy. It was one of those days where you wish you hadn't gotten out of bed. She sat in her tall Queen Anne's chair in front of the fireplace and wept.

Harris sat staring at the silent phone in disbelief. He couldn't believe his mother had just hung up on him. He quickly dialed his uncle J's cell phone.

"What are you doing, calling me when you're just upstairs, you lazy arse?" his uncle answered in mock anger.

"I can't be bothered to get back out of bed, and besides, I'm comfortable right now. I just wanted to tell you I called Mom and—" Joshua cut him off.

"Is she OK?" he immediately asked, concerned more for her than himself.

"She's fine, don't worry, Uncle J."

"I'll always worry about her, and you, son."

Harris told him about the conversation with Mary Ellen.

"So she's still angry with me," he said glumly.

"She needs to sort some stuff out, that's all," Harris said, trying to give him confidence. "She'll be fine I promise." But inside, Harris wasn't quite so sure.

"I don't think so," Joshua said, seeming to mirror his nephew's thoughts. "But I need to get a shower and go get some clothes. I have a class at one this afternoon. Thanks for trying, son. I really do appreciate the effort."

"Anytime, Uncle J, as long as you promise not to tell the duck joke anymore."

"Never, son. You love that one too much. Love you, later, bye."

"Later alligator." Harris rolled over, lying on his back, looking up at the ceiling, and quickly returning to his troubled thoughts. He couldn't stop himself from thinking about Markita, now wondering if she was OK. His heart ached for her; she would always be the love of his life, even though they were no longer together. How could he have been so truly happy for the first time in his life, only to lose her so soon? It was unbelievably cruel and unfair. Markita's love had filled his heart with joy, excitement, laughter, and now he realized the butterflies were gone. His thoughts turned to sorrow and sadness again. Tired, he tried to get some sleep so he wouldn't have to think. He tossed and turned trying to get her out of his mind. His thoughts then turned to his mother and Uncle J. Surely she wouldn't leave him after all these years? There were no two people more in love with each other, except perhaps for himself and Markita, but that was over.

Harris was still tossing and turning, trying to clear his head, when the phone rang. He wasn't getting any sleep, so he decided to answer the damned thing. He had a moment's thought that it might be *her*, and desperately hoped it wasn't. Holding his breath, he glanced down at the caller ID.

It was Hugh.

"Hey, Harris," Hugh immediately jumped in. "Tara tells me you're not coming in today. Is everything OK?"

"Sure, I just don't feel very well. I must have come down with something."

"Well, whatever it is, you had better get over it in a hurry."

Hugh thought he knew what had caused Harris's "illness." The DA's predecessor, Harris's own father, had had an affair with his secretary, Trudy, when they were both at the Practice. When Markita applied for her internship, she listed her mother's name as an emergency contact. After seeing that name, Hugh had made some inquiries and realized Markita was Robertson's love child. He made a mental note of the fact, in case he needed to use her later. The rumors about Harris and Markita's flirting had been flying around the office, so when he heard the news of Markita's sudden departure, it didn't take much for Hugh to figure out what happened. Hugh didn't give a damn about either of them; he simply wanted Harris in the courtroom taking down Miss Dixie so the Executioner would go after him. This way Hugh could regain an advantage over Judge Harris and the escrow account. Hugh believed no actual harm would come to Harris; the judge had forbidden the Executioner to hurt anyone in the Robertson family. But it wouldn't hurt for Harris to be looking over his shoulder.

"I told you, Judge Poe is back at work and wants Miss Dixie's case in front of him," Hugh reminded Harris. "You've got a number of interviews to conduct before preparing for opening arguments. I want motion for bail denied, and I don't care how you get it done. I just want it done."

"That's the judge's decision, not mine, Hugh," Harris said sternly.

"Look, Harris, I put you on this case because you're quick and smart in the courtroom. There are going to be a lot of high-profile people involved in this trial, and I want it to go away as soon as possible. This son of a bitch is going to be on Court TV, and you're going to need to make an example out of her. We need people to know that we don't allow this kind of establishment here in our beautiful city."

"I appreciate your confidence in me, Hugh, but I can only go as fast as the system allows."

"Good then. You'll have all the interviews done by the end of this week, right?"

"I'll get right on it, Hugh." Harris's heart sank. As it was, he didn't even want to get out of bed, let alone deal with lying people and corruption. Hugh hung up before Harris could even say good-bye. Hugh seemed on edge as if the pressure was getting to him. It was a little disturbing. Harris decided he'd have Joe come with him on those interviews since he wasn't exactly at his best. He hoped Joe would catch anything he himself missed.

Harris finally decided to get up to shower and shave. Looking in the mirror and stretching his skin while shaving downward, he nicked his mustache when he thought he saw Markita's image in the mirror beside him, smiling. He shook his head from side to side trying to brush off the ghostly experience. He dressed quickly before calling Joe on his cell phone.

"Hey, man, Hugh wants me to interview everyone who was arrested at Miss Dixie's last week. Feel like tagging along?"

"Yeah, sounds great. Maybe we could tag team. Let's see if the medical examiner sticks with his story. I'll stay in the car while you conduct his interview, and then we can compare notes."

"OK, sounds like a wiener," Harris said trying to keep things light.

"A what?" said Joe.

"Never mind. It's one of my uncle J's sayings."

"You know he's nuts, don't you?"

"Yeah, but he's the best," Harris said, hoping his mother realized that as well. "I'll come by and pick you up in about a half an hour."

"What?" Joe exclaimed. "You want me to ride in that fancy piece of metal with you?"

"Well, I'm not riding in that great big old truck of yours, if that's what you mean. I'll feel like a hillbilly."

"Well, if you feel like one, I'll try and get one for you, now that you're a single man again."

"OK, Joe enough with the dating," Harris reminded him tersely. "I'll be right there, see ya."

"Later."

Harris stomped downstairs, picked up his car keys, and headed out, knowing he was going to dread the rest of the day.

Markita's return home to Tallahassee had been a long and grueling ordeal for her. During the flight back, tears slid down her face so often the flight attendant brought her extra tissues, repeatedly asking if she was OK. Trudy tried to console her as best she could, but Markita's heart was broken in two. Nothing her mother could say would change the fact that Harris was her brother and they could no longer be together.

Once home, she went straight to her room and put away the few items she had thrown together. Her room was just as she'd left it, and seeing its familiar decor, she was reminded of how she had been secretly planning to change Harris's condo once they moved in together. Her tears began to flow again thinking about him. She sat down on her bed and looked around the room through tear-blurred eyes. Markita loved everything tropical, and that love was reflected in the space around her, especially in the bamboo wallpaper, white wicker furniture, and palm tree-style lamps on either side of her bed. Above her headboard was an oil painting of a beach scene with lots of coconut trees. There was a tall palm tree behind one of their wicker chairs and a quilt with two flamingos sitting on a bench wearing neon green sunglasses and flip-flops. The pillows had pink hearts matching the flamingos. On the ceiling was a large white paddle fan with pineapples for lampshades. She glanced at a photo on the dresser of her and Trudy on the beach with Governor Mason. Next to the photo was a fiber optic lamp with an orchid inside; it changed colors as it rotated.

Markita had always loved the lamp. The governor had given it to her one year for her birthday. He'd regularly purchased expensive gifts for her for all kinds of occasions. Trudy had been seeing him off and on ever since she was a little girl, which always left Markita wondering. Her mother had always told Markita that her father was a powerful man who drank a lot and liked to cheat, a man who told her he would never leave his wife. Markita assumed that the governor was her father. Looking back now, knowing what she now knew, Harris's father was everything Trudy had told her about her own true father. It made her feel as if her whole life had been a lie. She felt strange knowing Harris's father was hers as well.

Just then, Trudy entered her room to check on her.

"Is there anything you want, baby girl?" she asked quietly, seeing the tears still standing in her daughter's eyes.

"Nothing, thank you."

"Are you sure?"

"Harris," Markita replied. Trudy left the room without saying another word, rolling her eyes so that Markita didn't see.

Markita lay on her bed and cried into her pillow. How was she going to live without him? He had been her whole world. He was so kind, loving, and gentle with her. His arms were warm and held her tight. When she was in them, she felt safe and secure. She flashed back to him telling her God made his shoulder to fit the perfect woman's head, and hers was the one. She already missed kissing him, nibbling at his lips, and the way he always smiled at her when she did this. He would close one eye and look out of the corner of the other one at her. She missed the way he ran his fingers through her hair and the way he stood behind her, holding her close. All she had left were memories; she swore she would carry them with her for the rest of her life. Markita cried herself to sleep, alone with her memories.

The next morning she awoke, still thinking about Harris. She got up and went to her computer, knowing what she planned to do was pointless, but determined to try anyway. She had already left him dozens of messages yesterday, and he hadn't returned any of them. She had decided to send him an e-mail.

> *Hey there, sexy bear,* she began. *I know I shouldn't call you that because you're my half brother, but you are, and always will be, a sexy bear, just not mine. Harris, I don't understand any of this. I cannot even ask my mother any questions because I'm so angry with her. Even though Mom never confirmed or denied it, I was always suspicious that Governor Mason was my father. I'm having a hard time wrapping my head around the truth that your father is mine as well.*
>
> *I remember you saying you disliked your father because he was a drunk and cheated on your mom; well, Governor Mason did the same to Mom, and I always believed he was my father. I always wanted to ask you more about your father, but I knew it was a sore subject for you.*

I knew when you were ready, you would talk to me about him. I noticed you had no photographs of your father on your mantel. You said, the day he became a judge, he died. Do you know how it happened? You never said. I guess I'm curious about him, but I know his memories are painful for you. There is no way I can ask Mom right now because, like I said, I'm just too angry with her. I feel like my whole life has been a lie, and she's been a big part of that lie.

When I came to Orlando to intern, the last thing I expected was to meet the love of my life. Growing up, I felt my destiny was always to become a judge. I'd watch crime dramas on TV and always identified more with the person on the bench doling out judgment and wisdom than with the regular lawyers. It was the reason I wanted to become a judge, but now I'm wondering if it's also because it's in my blood.

I could see the anger and contempt you had for my mother, and now that we know the truth about our parents, I guess I can hardly blame you. You and your mother are so close, so even the mere mention of mine has to be very painful for you. This is going to be awkward, but my mother must have loved your father to have named me after him. I have always loved my name, as it's so different. I never told you, but it means pearl in Greek. You probably hate it now.

How can any of this be real? It just doesn't seem possible. One minute we are starting a new chapter of our lives together, and now you're gone. We didn't even get to say good-bye. My body is here in my room on my computer writing to you, but my heart is there with you always. I know our lives have to go on in different directions, but I hope and pray maybe one day we can be together again. Some Harris is better than no Harris at all. I would give anything if we could talk once more. I need to know that even though you're gone, you still love me or at the very least, you don't resent me for what our parents did.

I'll miss working with you and Joe. I felt like we were becoming a great team. I'll even miss Tara grinning at us with that knowing look. Most of all, I'll miss you, Harris. Please, LB, I beg of you, please let me hear my phone ring, just once more. Let's talk or write. Please don't let things end this way with us never speaking again. I know you don't want to hear this, and you said I made you sick, but I cannot just turn my feelings off. I love you, LB, and always will. You'll be in my heart forever.

Always, Markita—your "little girl"

Markita sat back and read what she had written, fixing it here and there, making it perfect. Then, with a final glance at the last line, Markita hit the Send button.

Chapter Twelve

The Deal

No sooner had Hugh hung up with Harris when his private line rang. His stomach clenched, knowing who was calling. "Hugh Gallagher, DA's office. How may I help you?"

"You can start by telling me what the hell is going on down there, Gallagher? My phone has been ringing off the hook all damn weekend." Ronald Harris was furious.

"I expect you're referring to our wonderful chief of police, right?" Hugh said, knowing all too well the circumstances behind this call.

"James and a few others are not thrilled with you. You had better have a good explanation for me, Hugh. I am getting tired of your screwups."

"I'm not thrilled either, Ronald. I'm tired of defending myself for the incompetence of others. This crap started with your friend Judge Poe when he slapped around one of Dixie's girls, and Smith retaliated. You know that animal is sweet on Dixie. He called me and was screaming at me to allow him to teach Poe a lesson. He nearly killed Poe and actually did take down a couple of SWAT guys in the process. Then, the chief leaked the raid to the wrong person in his department, or pressed the button himself, sending in twenty officers to Miss Dixie's, turning the incident into a full-blown raid. Now once again, I have to clean up everyone's mess. James is pissed at me because I left his ass in jail over the weekend. He claims he had no knowledge of who could have pushed the button that night, which makes sense as his own pants were down, which leads back to the question of a leak in his department." Hugh took a breath, then went on. "He needs to chill out for a few days before he goes back to work chewing all kinds of ass. He's running at the mouth threatening me, saying that if I don't get him released immediately, he will squeal like a pig. Personally, we need to do something about him. This isn't the first time he has made threats to expose our organization."

"Who else in the Order was involved?" demanded Ronald, not liking any of what he was hearing.

"The mayor, but the media didn't seem to catch wind of him. We may get a lucky break where he's concerned. The fire chief is history. I can do nothing more to protect his ass. I spoke to Senator Johnson, and he's going to resign gracefully. They also arrested Joe Marble, my lead investigator. He was there that night interviewing one of Dixie's girls for a case of ours, so now Harris and his bloodhound are all over this. I am going to have to do some quick maneuvering where he's concerned," said Hugh, knowing he had pretty much thrown everyone under the bus.

"I'll have a word with Smith and get him back in line. I'll also have a conversation with Dixie. She had better keep her mouth shut. She knows far too much about the Order. We need to get her out of this mess. Take care of it, Hugh," the judge said with conviction.

"I understand," Hugh answered. "This screwup is going to be all over the TV. The senator is going to make a public announcement on Wednesday with his wife and kids by his side. He's just thankful his wife isn't going to leave him." Hugh was grateful to the senator for this gesture.

"Senator Johnson has always shown class. He's a good man. His resignation will be a great loss to the Senate, but I'll find a way to keep him on in the Order," Ronald said with a lighter tone in his voice.

"What do you want me to do with the chief? His biggest gripe is his pension."

"Leave his ass there for now. I know exactly how to shut him up." Suddenly a terrible thought crossed the judge's mind.

"My god, Hugh, was Hank there?" he said, fearful of the answer.

"No, sir, he was about the only damn official who wasn't."

"Thank God," said Ronald, relieved.

"About James, sir. I don't know what you have in mind, but whatever it is, it would be his own damn fault. This whole mess is his bungle," Hugh said, not caring about throwing the blame all his way.

"You may be right on this one, Hugh. We need to show a few people what consequences there will be if they continue giving me headaches. It seems I need to tighten the reins on Smith. I'll have a word in my friend Poe's ear as well. He seems to be getting out of hand himself."

"Don't worry about him, Ronald. I'll let him have his revenge in court with Dixie over Smith trying to suffocate him, but then I'll get her out on a technicality. I'll take care of everything for you, Ronald."

The judge was satisfied with this plan. If Hugh could keep Poe happy and get Miss Dixie off in one fell swoop, life would go back to being relatively uncomplicated.

"OK, Hugh, try not to give me any more headaches. I had a migraine dealing with those damn Johnsons. They never go away. It's time for Smith to make that particular problem disappear for me too. Anyway, Hugh, I'm glad we talked. Take care of my grandson."

"Will do, sir," said Hugh, a smirk on his face. He was elated that the phone call went his way for a change.

Hugh paged his secretary and informed her he was going out to lunch and he would return later that afternoon.

"If Harris calls, refer him to my cell phone, please."

"Of course, sir," she replied.

On his way to lunch, Hugh stopped at a local convenience store where he purchased a pay-as-you-go cell phone. They came in handy when he wanted to make untraceable calls. Once back in his car, he placed a call on his new phone to Henry Lane, an old friend and fraternity brother, as well as a fellow attorney. In fact, he and Henry had gone to law school together. He did well for himself and owned his own law firm. He was a player in the Order, but low on the totem pole. Hugh mainly used him for his private jobs and gave him a kickback out of his own pocket. Henry was a fairly straight guy, but he didn't mind bending the rules somewhat as long as he wasn't involved in anything *too* illegal.

"Henry Lane," spoke a deep Southern voice on the other end of the line.

"Hey, Henry, it's Hugh. Do you have a minute?"

"I always have a minute for you." Henry was a man of few words and always got straight to the point. "I have a job needing your personal attention."

"Go on," said Henry.

"I need you to represent a couple in a civil suit. Their son was sentenced to death and ultimately executed for the hanging of an African American forty years ago. Stewart Pope, formerly of the Practice, signed a sworn statement recently that he was a witness to the fact Johnson was framed. He said he had knowledge of who actually hanged the person, but then he up and died just a few days ago."

"Then the couple has no chance in hell of winning a civil suit," Henry stated, now curious about Hugh's request because he would have known this fact.

"This is where your personal attention to the Johnsons comes in," Hugh said. "I want you to offer your services free since you will tell them you believe they still have a case and feel they should be properly represented.

"Seems like a lot of time and trouble for something they can't win. What's in it for me?" Henry asked, knowing there had to be a catch coming.

"$250,000."

"You want to pay me that much for losing?" Henry asked, incredulous.

"You got it," Hugh replied.

"All right, but what's the catch?"

"The catch," Hugh told him, "is that you will be suing Ronald Harris."

There was a beat of silence before Henry spoke again.

"You want me to go up against Judge Harris?" Henry said slowly. "The same judge Harris who sits on the Supreme Court? Are you nuts? I don't have a death wish." Henry was not so amused now.

"Henry, it's OK. Judge Harris is aware of the lawsuit. His goal is to get rid of the Johnsons once and for all," Hugh said half-lying through his teeth. It was true Judge Harris wanted the Johnsons gone, but he knew nothing of the civil suit that Hugh hoped Henry was soon to suggest to the Johnsons.

"Well, if Ronald's OK with it, then I don't mind making a quick $250K for losing a case. I could take Lori Anne away for a few weeks."

"How is she doing?" asked Hugh sincerely caring. Hugh's wife had lost her brother recently, and he knew the two of them had been very close.

"Not so good, my friend, not so good."

"I am so sorry. I know how close they were."

"Lori Anne hears people say the word 'brokenhearted' all the time, but she wonders if they really understand the true meaning of the word like she does now."

"Please give her my best." Hugh was sympathetic, but needed to get right back to his own agenda. He went on to give Henry all the Johnsons' contact information and some of the details of the case. "The sooner you visit them and get the suit started, the better." Hugh was feeling good about the deal.

"OK," Henry said. "Is tomorrow too soon?"

"Nope, tomorrow will do just fine."

Hugh hung up and then pulled over to the side of the road. He dropped the phone onto the shoulder of the highway, ran over it with his car, and then headed back to the office.

Joe Marble was busy pursuing another lead; he had spent the better half of the morning stuck in the basement of the Orlando Police Department archive room going through old files. He had finally found the records for the fateful night of October 2, 1960. There was indeed a rape victim brought into the emergency room with a large wound on her right cheek. They listed her first name as Barbara, but no last name. The report showed trauma to the vaginal area and a soiled pair of panties with semen was taken from the victim as evidence.

"Great," said Joe. Finally a lead. He next needed to try to obtain a warrant to retrieve the panties from the archive evidence room and then look into getting an order to get a sample of DNA from Jake Johnson's parents. If the DNA in the panties matched Jake's, that would prove Jake could not have hanged the African American; he was clear across the other side of town raping the Jane Doe victim named Barbara. He took pictures of the folder and placed it back in the filing cabinet. He couldn't wait to report his findings to Harris. The results would be difficult for Harris to hear, if in fact, the semen belonged to Jake.

As Joe was leaving the room, his cell phone rang. It was Harris asking him to go on some interviews with him concerning the raid at Miss Dixie's the week before. The two of them agreed to hook up at Mama's.

"Harris, I finally got a damn lead," Joe told him as they sat down. "It looks as if Stewart Pope was right about Jake Johnson raping a woman the night of the hanging. The emergency room stitched up this woman's face and took a sample of the rapist's semen from her. I need to get a warrant to obtain the sample, but my bet is the DNA will match Jake Johnson's parents."

"Great, Joe, but if we can get a match, it still doesn't prove my grandfather had anything to do with the hanging. I say Pope was setting him up for some reason. There has to be an explanation somewhere."

Harris was still convinced Judge Harris was a good, honest, God-fearing man. He was, of course, pleased that Joe was finally able to obtain a lead on something, but his heart was saddened at the implications this again would put on his grandfather. Harris didn't dwell on the subject as he knew his grandfather was innocent of the Johnsons' allegations. "Did the medical examiner give you any more heads-up on the Eleanor Woodsworth case?" he now asked.

Joe couldn't resist his next comment. "'Heads-up,' Harris? Do you suppose that is how she lost it?" He cracked up. The expression on Harris's face was priceless, and he laughed so hard his sides hurt.

"Joe Marble, that isn't funny at all. In fact, it's pretty damn heartless."

"Heartless, Harris? I think it was only her head, buddy. You need to lighten up. You're the one who said heads-up, not me." Joe was doing everything he could to stop himself from laughing.

"Like I was saying," Harris continued, trying to ignore his friend's sick sense of humor, "Did you find out anything more from the medical examiner to give us an indication as to how she lost her head or where those expensive-looking earrings come from?"

"I found out her last known address was in Tallahassee, so I thought I would take a trip up there and do some digging." Harris was even more solemn after hearing the word "Tallahassee." He didn't need another reminder of his breakup with Markita. Joe felt bad for his friend, seeing the pain in his eyes when he mentioned the state capital. "Sorry, man, I know it's a sore subject."

"It's OK, Joe, move on," Harris snapped.

"Why don't we start at Miss Dixie's and see if we can get any of those girls to talk?" Joe suggested.

"Sounds like a winner to me," Harris replied.

"What? No wiener jokes?" said Joe, trying to cheer his friend up.

"Nope, not today. Let's get this job done and get this day over with. And by the way, please don't go getting yourself arrested like the last time you interviewed one of Miss Dixie's girls," Harris said in a serious voice. It was obvious he was not up to his usual self, let alone joking around.

"Harris, I know we're business associates, but we're also buds, and there is something eating you away inside. I know it involves the hot mama. Please, man, open up and share with me, maybe I can help," Joe said in one last effort to help his friend.

"She's my freakin' sister! Are you satisfied now, asshole?" Harris hissed at him through clenched teeth. "My father is her father!"

Joe stared at his friend stunned, not believing what he heard. His mind flashed back to one of their restaurant meetings when she'd told them that she thought Governor Mason might be her father. How could Harris's father be hers? He listened as Harris told him the whole story about his encounter with Trudy, "Markita's tramp of a mother," as Harris put it.

"My god, man, no wonder you're a flipping wreck," Joe said.

"Do you think we could get this day over with now that you know how messed up my life is?"

"Sure, man, sure," Joe said solemnly, knowing this was not the time to push him.

Things were not adding up in Joe's mind about this situation. He would have to give this issue more thought. There had to be some other explanation because something smelled like a seven-day-old fish story.

Harris was going through the motions of the day; his heart and thoughts were only with Markita. He wanted to go home, bury his head under his pillows, and sleep the time away.

Hank the Tank paid the chief of police a visit.

"Come with me," he said as he handcuffed him and led him from his cell.

"What the hell are you doing that for?" James said as he looked down at the restraints.

"Why don't you just shut it?" Hank said, dragging him out of the room.

"It's about time someone posted my damn bail. Was it Hugh?" asked James.

Hank was silent as he escorted the prisoner down the hallway to a secluded part of the jail.

"Where the hell are we going, Hank? This isn't the way to processing."

James was getting a little concerned now, especially since Hank wouldn't look at him. The burly sheriff unlocked a door and pushed the chief into the room, locking the door behind them. It didn't take James but two seconds to know what was about to happen. He tightened his stomach muscles as hard as he could, but still he was not prepared for what was about to take place. He had done the very same thing to criminals that he had arrested and interrogated behind closed doors. He never dreamed for one moment that he was about to receive the same terror that he had inflicted on others. Hank pulled a large thick nightstick from his belt. In a split second, the chief felt one swift blow to the back of his legs and fell to his knees. He screamed, but to no avail as no one could hear them. Another swift thump to his gut, and his body bent in two, vomit now spraying the floor. Before he could even catch his breath, there was another thump, this time to his kidneys. He let out a loud groan before barfing again. Hank took the chief's head and pushed it into the rank puddle of vomit on the floor, and then he lifted him back by his hair and swiftly gave another blow to his stomach.

"Had enough?" he asked the chief.

"Ya, ya," the chief replied weakly.

"Still wanna squeal, do ya?"

"No, never," the chief gasped, trying to breathe without pain.

"Then let this be a lesson to you. You better keep your big mouth shut if you want to leave this place in one piece. Do you understand me?"

"Ya, ya," he managed to say, still gasping for air.

"I don't think I quite heard you," Hank whispered right in his face.

"Yes, loud and clear!" he answered with every ounce of energy he had left. Hank pulled him up again by his hair to a standing position.

"This is a warning, James. Don't screw with them, man. It's not worth this, understand?"

"Got it," said James, thanking God to be alive. His body hurt in places he never knew could hurt.

Hank threw James a towel to wipe the puke from his face, then unlocked the door, and took the chief back down the long hallway into his holding cell. When he was done, he called Judge Harris.

"It's done."

"Did he get the message?"

"Yes, sir, loud and clear."

"Thanks, Hank, you're a good man. A nice bonus is headed your way." Judge Harris hung up and immediately placed a call to Hugh.

"You can let James out now. He won't be saying a word to anyone. I'll arrange to keep his name out of the media, but I want to know who leaked the raid. When you have a name, call me."

The judge promptly hung up before Hugh could even say anything to him. He wondered what could have happened to James to change his tune so quickly. He could only imagine whatever it was, it could not have been good. The thought certainly intensified his fear of both the judge and the Executioner. The thought of a blade across his neck made him rub his throat. He had not anticipated all these problems when he decided to go for the 150 mill. It made him wonder if the danger was worth the money. He hoped his new plan would go off without a hitch; with Miss Dixie on trial, Smith would certainly go after Harris. The judge would be all tied up with the civil suit the Johnsons were about to bring against him, making it necessary for the judge to step down from the Supreme Court and give up ownership of the Practice, leaving Hugh to run everything. He sat back in his chair dreaming about the money and smiling to himself.

Harris parked his Jag in the garage and stepped through the door of his condo. A wonderful aroma wafted toward him from the kitchen. Turning the corner, he beheld his uncle J wearing an apron and a chef's hat. Harris shook his head, laughing at him.

"What are you laughing at, young whippersnapper?"

"You're a riot, Uncle J."

"I am simply cooking us some supper."

"It smells fantastic. What is it?"

"It's spaghetti Italiano."

"Wow, perfecto, Uncle J'o," said Harris in his worst-sounding Italian accent.

"Wassa up, bambino? Letsa eata," Joshua replied in his own butchered accent. Harris went upstairs to change and wash up. It had been a day that Harris hadn't wanted to face, and neither had his uncle J, yet here they were together. It reminded him of when he was a little boy and his uncle J always made everything all right.

"I hope you don't mind me cooking and making all this mess in your kitchen, son," Joshua said as Harris came back into the kitchen. "I needed something to occupy my time after class today. I missed your mother more than life itself."

"Of course, it's OK," said Harris, knowing exactly how his uncle felt. Joshua tried to put on a brave face for Harris, knowing his nephew was in a lot of pain. As badly as Josh felt about his situation with Mary Ellen, his nephew's devastation was tearing Josh up inside as well.

"Howa wazza your day?" Josh said, still talking in a very bad Italian accent.

"Enough with the terrible accent," Harris said laughing at him.

"How was Mom when you went by the house to get some clothes?"

"She wouldn't even answer the door when I rang the bell. My suitcase was already on the porch when I arrived."

"Give her time, Uncle J, she will come around," Harris said, hopeful they would work things out and they would soon get back together. Not because he wanted his uncle to leave, especially if he cooked like this every night. It was because he knew his mom and uncle were meant for each other.

After the two of them finished supper and cleaned up the mess Joshua had made in the kitchen, Harris went upstairs and turned on his computer. He sat down then opened his e-mail. The first one in the queue was from Markita. His heart began to thump loudly in his chest as he kept staring at her name. His hands trembled. His head told him not to open it, but his heart was aching for her. What should he do? He got up from his chair and lay on the bed, looking at the ceiling fan. It was not long before he went back over to the computer. *No,* he said to himself, *it doesn't matter whatever she says, life cannot change.* Sitting down to delete the letter, his finger shook so badly that he felt he couldn't press the button. He got up from the chair again and started to pace, punching his right fist into his left palm, gritting his teeth. He needed a distraction so he flew downstairs and took out a bottle of green tea from the fridge.

"Harris, what's up?" Joshua called from the living room. When Harris didn't answer, Joshua got up and followed him into the kitchen. "Son, you flew down those stairs like a bat out of hell! What is wrong?"

"It's her," Harris said, his voice shaking.

"What do you mean 'her'?" asked Josh, seeing his nephew in pain again.

"Mar . . .," her name stuck in his throat.

"You mean Markita?" said Josh, knowing his nephew's pain had to be about her.

Harris nodded.

"Well, I didn't hear the phone ring, so you must have been on the computer."

Harris nodded again.

"Well, spit it out, boy, did she instant message you or e-mail?"

"E-mail," Harris replied.

"For all the love in China, what did it say?" asked Joshua, now wanting to strangle Harris as both his curiosity and concern were getting the better of him. At this point, he was almost praying that his nephew and Markita had worked something out.

"I don't know!" Harris exclaimed.

"What, you didn't open it?" asked Josh in disbelief.

No. Harris shook his head.

"If you don't answer me with more than one word or a head shake, I am going to come over there and kick your arse. What's wrong with you, boy?"

Harris finally cracked a smile. "I don't know if I should open it," he said weakly.

"Well, if you don't, you nincompoop, you won't know what it says, now will you?"

"I don't know if I want to know what is in it, Uncle J."

"Harris," Joshua sighed, laying a hand on the young man's shoulder. "Look at it this way. By reading it, you might get some closure. Like I said before, down the road a few years, maybe you and Markita could have some kind of sibling relationship."

Harris tightened his lips in anger and frustration; he didn't want a sibling relationship. He loved her and wanted her, and it hurt. He finished his bottle of green tea. Josh knew there was nothing he could do about his nephew's pain, and it tore him up inside.

"Harris, my advice is, don't delete the e-mail. You will always wonder what it said. Save it until you're ready to open and read it." Harris thought his uncle made sense.

"I love you, Uncle J. I am going to go watch some TV in my room and call it a night."

"Well, son, it's nine o'clock at night, so you wouldn't call it a day, would you?"

Harris cracked another small smile then shook his head, not knowing what to do with his goofy Uncle J. What would he ever do without him? He prayed to God he would never have to find out.

"Night, Harris, don't let the bedbugs bite."

"I am not four years old, Uncle J."

"No, you just act like it." Harris went back upstairs; he was feeling better about Markita's e-mail. He turned off his computer for the night. He didn't want to read anything from anyone right now. He turned on the TV and promptly fell asleep.

Hours later, the phone's insistent ringing awakened Harris. "Hey," he answered sleepily.

"Hey, bro, it's Joe, I am a poet, and you didn't know it."

"Damn, man, it's too flipping early in the morning to deal with your wit."

"I wanted you to know I won't be around today. You can reach me on my cell, but I am halfway to Tallahassee as we speak."

"Wow, you don't waste any time, do you?"

"No. I want to see what I can find out while the iron is hot, man."

"Careful you don't burn yourself," Harris mumbled sleepily.

"Wow, the Harris man is back! You actually cracked a joke, how about that! You know my mom always used to say better days to come, and yours are on their way, my friend."

Harris had no clue what he meant, but better days sure sounded good to him. It was too early in the morning to try to figure out how Joe Marble's mind worked.

"I'll catch up with you later," Joe said.

"OK," said Harris hanging up the phone and pulling the covers back up over his head.

The next few weeks were pretty much the same; Harris continued conducting interviews with suspects arrested at Miss Dixie's brothel house. He had subpoenaed her books, but on the surface, they looked clean. He was looking into the antique business she claimed on her taxes. Hugh notified him the pretrial hearing time was Friday morning in Judge Poe's courtroom.

Friday morning arrived, and Harris was ready.

The bailiff called the court to order. "Court is in session. The Right Honorable Judge Poe presiding, please be seated." The bailiff read the case number then proceeded to read the charges.

"The *State of Florida versus Dixie Jackson.* You are being charged on one count of sex trafficking, one count of contributing to a minor, and one count of possession."

"How do you plead?" Judge Poe asked, with an obvious smirk on his face.

"Not guilty, Your Honor," Dixie replied sarcastically.

"Trial will be set for July 29 at nine o'clock. Is that enough time for you both to prepare?" Judge Poe asked Harris and Nigel Pope. Both sides responded with a yes.

"Your Honor, if I may," Pope spoke up.

"Proceed, Mr. Pope."

"Your Honor, Miss Jackson has business to attend to and is not a flight risk. We ask that you set an appropriate bail amount."

"Bail denied." The judge banged down his gavel fiercely.

"Your Honor, if I may," Nigel interjected.

"Mr. Pope, would you like me to place you in contempt of court?"

"No, sir."

"Then I suggest the next time we meet is July 29."

"Yes, sir." Harris looked over at Nigel, and they both shrugged their shoulders.

"Court is adjourned," announced the judge. A stunned bailiff led Miss Jackson back to her cell. Outside the courtroom, there was the usual slew of reporters. Harris noticed a familiar face, but it looked like Amber Andrews had left Channel Nine local news and was reporting for Court TV. *That is all I need,* thought Harris.

"Mr. Robertson!" Andrews cried out. "How many of the city officials that were arrested will go to trial?"

"Miss Andrews, anyone who breaks the law and gets arrested will get a fair trial. It's the law."

"Then how do you explain why neither the chief of police, the medical examiner nor the mayor have yet to be formally charged? In fact they haven't even been served a subpoena, have they?" she asked belligerently.

"All in good time, Miss Andrews, all in good time."

"Mr. Robertson, is this case connected in any way to the mysterious death of Stewart Pope?"

"None whatsoever, Miss Andrews. You should do a better job of checking your facts." Harris didn't like her last question; he knew she was going to try to implicate his grandfather on national Court TV. He started pushing his way through the crowd before she could ask him any more questions.

"Mr. Robertson, isn't it true your grandfather is still somehow connected to the Practice? In addition, isn't Miss Jackson's brothel connected to the Practice?" Harris was beginning to despise this woman.

"My grandfather was absolved of all charges in a fair and unbiased hearing. I know it's your job to fantasize the truth, but you're going too far."

"You might want to check into the facts about your grandfather being the head of the KKK many years ago," she pressed. "I did, and I was right, Mr. Robertson. What do you have to say about that?" she asked forcefully.

Just then Nigel Pope stepped out toward the crowd; he'd apparently been observing the whole scene behind Harris. He grabbed a microphone from one of the reporter's hands.

"Let me just clear a few things up for all of you. Judge Harris has not owned nor been connected with our Practice for many years. Miss Jackson is simply a client. And, Miss Andrews, you're treading on thin ice." Nigel gave back the microphone and quickly walked away. Harris again pushed through the crowd of reporters and managed to catch up to Nigel in the parking lot.

"Thanks, Nigel. I appreciate what you said."

"It's the truth, isn't it?" said Nigel, knowing it wasn't.

"Yes, but you didn't have to defend my family honor the way you did."

"Anytime for a colleague," said Nigel, flashing him an uncharacteristic grin.

"I am sorry to hear about your father," Harris offered. "Our office is still waiting on the autopsy results."

"You and I both know how the system works. It takes forever to get anything done," Nigel said.

"You're right there, I guess. When I hear something, I'll be sure to contact you first, as a courtesy," Harris said.

"Thanks, man, I appreciate that. My father was already gone in his mind, you know. He didn't even recognize anyone, let alone know what was real and what was not." Poe stared at his shoes for a moment, then looked back up at Harris, all business again. "By the way, what the hell was up with Poe not giving my client bail? Any clue?" asked Nigel innocently, all the while knowing the exact reason why.

Harris shrugged. "Beats me. I was as stunned as you were."

Nigel doubted that, but gave nothing away. "Well, take it easy, Harris," he said. "I'll see you around, and in court." Nigel got in his car and drove away.

Harris sat in his own car thinking for a moment, trying to make sense of the day so far. So many things didn't add up in his mind. He needed to explain some of this stuff to his uncle J and maybe even run some of the discrepancies by his grandfather.

Joe had been gone a long time in Tallahassee without contacting him, he wondered how he was getting on and if he had uncovered anything yet. He would give him a call when he got home.

The Executioner was still nursing his shoulder wound, but it was slowly getting better. He had stayed pretty low and silent for a while, but was getting anxious worrying about his baby doll. He turned on the TV and started to flip through the channels. Suddenly, he saw Dixie's face on the screen. *What the hell?* He stopped and listened intently. It was that Amber Andrews reporting.

"Miss Dixie Jackson, of Orlando, Florida, and alleged madam, entered a plea of not guilty today. Her attorney asked for bail, which Judge Fredrick Poe denied. It was a strange denial as she's not a flight risk. Dixie Jackson is a well-known antique dealer, and according to preliminary investigations, her taxes and records are impeccable. It's going to be difficult for Assistant District Attorney Harris Robertson to prove she has been sex trafficking for years. In the usual arrogant Robertson fashion, he assures me he can get a conviction. I also raised the question to the so-called Florida Hurricane as to how his grandfather, the State Supreme Court Justice Judge Ronald Harris, fits into this arrest. It seems strange how Judge Harris, our chief justice, may have connections to the hanging of an African American forty years ago and the key witness in the case mysteriously dies from an early onset of Alzheimer's. Nigel Pope from the local law firm the Practice denied today that Chief Justice Harris has any connections to the Practice. I tend not to believe his denial. It feels like we're going back twenty years when there were allegations and more suspicions in Harris Robertson's families suggesting corruption and cover-ups. I recently had an extensive interview with Nancy Marble, who, in her prime, was a shark of an attorney. She was a well-respected reporter for our Court TV channel, but there has been speculation that her early retirement was not of her choosing. She would only comment that she might have gotten too close to the truth concerning conspiracy. I feel there will be a lot more to surface concerning this case. Stay tuned, viewers. I think you may be surprised at some of the outcomes concerning these proceedings. This is Amber Andrews reporting for Court TV. Good night."

Smith was furious. How was he going to get Dixie out of this mess? It was evident to him that he'd need to devise a plan to get rid of some annoying people. And right now, Harris Robertson was on the top of his list.

Chapter Thirteen

Tallahassee

Before Joe left for Tallahassee, he ran a background check on Eleanor Woodsworth and found she had a rap sheet showing several convictions for prostitution. He knew he needed a photograph of her to show around, but the ones he had in his possession of her head were just too gruesome. He guessed one of her mug shots would have to do. With a picture in hand, he headed out and was anxious to find out who last saw her alive and where.

He first visited Bourbon Street, the last known address of Eleanor Woodsworth. The street name lived up to its reputation; it was a small dead-end street in a highly undesirable neighborhood. An abundance of crack houses lined the surrounding streets and alleys, and all kinds of drunks and addicts slept on the streets. What was a woman wearing $10,000 or more diamond earrings doing and living in a neighborhood such as this? Joe showed her picture to anyone who looked at least half-sober, trying to get some answers. After three days with no success or anything remotely resembling a lead, he stopped in a rundown deli to get a soda.

"Have you seen this lady around here?" Joe asked the clerk, flashing the mug shot.

The scruffy clerk took a look, then pointed at the face and nodded. "Hey, that's Elley," he said to Joe in a heavy Spanish accent. "I haven't seen her around here for about two months now."

"How long did she live over on Bourbon Street, do you know?" Joe asked, trying not to spook the guy with his eagerness for information.

"Not long this time. She lived here on and off, thought she was one of those high-society chicks. She used to hook over there when she was younger, but she was beautiful looking, you know, gringo?" The clerk gave a lurid grin that showed a few gold teeth. "Her dreams were real big, you know? Like she would be a movie star or marry some rich guy. Those kinds always foolin' themselves." He shook his head. "Elley got too big for her boots, you know? She ran her mouth a lot."

"Do you know what happened to her?" Joe asked.

"Hey, gringo, are you some kind of cop or something?" the clerk asked, his eyes narrowing with suspicion.

"No, **señor**. She's just a friend of mine, and I'm looking for her," Joe lied. He knew where her *head* had been; he wondered if he'd be able to find the rest of her.

The clerk seemed to relax a bit. "You know," he said, "We heard from some of the other girls that she was all mixed up with the governor, and then we heard his wife found out, and so he needed to get rid of her ass. He left her with nothing and nowhere to go. She hooked over on Bourbon Street again for a while, then last I hear, she went back to Orlando to her daughter."

"Her daughter?" Joe sounded surprised.

The clerk's eyes narrowed again, and he took a step back from the counter. "If you're her friend, how come you do not know her daughter? Everyone knows about Elley's daughter. It's all she talked about when you met her. Are you sure you're not cop?"

"Oh yeah, **señor**, I'm quite sure. I guess she might have mentioned her daughter in Orlando once or twice. Don't remember her name though . . . what was it?" Joe waited, pretending to wrack his brain for a name, hope that his talkative new friend would help him out. This could be a critical lead.

"Bambi," the clerk finished for him.

"That's right, Bambi!" Joe said, slapping the counter, trying not to act stunned by this news; it had to be the same Bambi he interviewed the night of the raid. His mind was running a hundred miles an hour. They're both prostitutes—that can't be a coincidence.

"Now I remember," Joe said, trying to recover. "She works for Miss Dixie, right?" Joe took a calculated guess.

"OK, gringo," the clerk said, flashing his golden grin once more. "You're right, she works for Miss Dixie. Elley was going back to Orlando to see if she could get her job back with the big lady."

"Was that the last time you heard about her?" asked Joe, kicking himself for sounding too much like a detective.

"It's all I know, gringo, sorry. $1.25 for the soda please."

"Thanks, **señor**, you've been very helpful." Joe gave the man a fifty-dollar bill. "Keep the change, my friend." The golden grin got even wider.

"Thank *you*, gringo." The man accepted the fifty-dollar bill and quickly slipped it in his pocket. Joe left there a little wiser, but so many questions remained. The million-dollar one was, how was he going to get the rest of his answers?

There was another agenda to his visit to Tallahassee, and it concerned finding out the truth about Markita for his friend Harris. It seemed strange to him when she told him and Harris at the Bistro that as a little girl, she believed that Ex-Governor Mason was her father. Always being the predominant male in her life and continuously showering her with gifts, Markita told them there was no other man in her mother's life, so she thought it had to be him. Now all of a sudden, Trudy finds out her daughter is dating Mark's son, and the "truth" at last comes out. She claims Harris and her daughter have the same father. Joe smelled one of those rat bastard moments. While he was in Tallahassee, he was on a mission to investigate the situation for his friend. He knew the breakup devastated Harris, and he could only imagine what it must have been like for Markita. Joe knew from the way she talked about the young assistant district attorney there were sparks between them.

He paid a visit to the local county courthouse and looked up her birth certificate. It was as he suspected; her birth certificate, in fact, stated Governor Mason as her father.

Joe called 411 and asked for the number for Markita Mason. It was a long shot, since he'd never managed to get her last name. However, he was pleasantly surprised when the number started to ring. He was even happier when she was the one who answered the phone.

"Hello," said the familiar shy voice.

"Hey pretty lady! This is Joe, how are you?"

"Joe, is it really you?" Markita sounded so excited to hear his voice.

"Yes, hot mama, it really is me."

"Why are you calling? Is Harris OK?" she asked with concern.

"Yes, little lady, he's fine. I'm up here in Tallahassee on business and wondered if you would like to go to dinner with a lonely old friend?"

"I would love to, Joe." She was so happy to be even a little connected to Harris. She had grown fond of Joe even though he always teased her. Her heart was racing with excitement. Joe was the closest person to Harris. She wanted to hang on to anything and everything close to him; it was her only lifeline. It felt so right to her, like something was keeping them together. It was her fate, she told herself.

"So can I pick you up?" he asked

"Yes, you may, Joe Marble," and she gave him her address.

"How about I pick you up in an hour, is that OK?"

"Perfect," said Markita.

"I'll see you then." She hung up the phone, happier than she had been in days. It did not take her long to shower, clean up, and put on something plain but pretty. When the doorbell rang, Markita ran down the stairs to answer the door about the same time Trudy arrived there.

"It's all right, Mother, I'll get it."

"I wonder who it could be," said Trudy.

"It's a friend of mine, and I'm going out. I don't know what time I'll be home," she snapped before opening the door to Joe. Markita quickly exited the house, slamming the door behind her.

"Phew, I felt like I was in Alaska there, young lady," said Joe in his usual lighthearted mood.

"I'm so angry at my mother, Joe. I can barely stand to be in the same room with her."

"Ah, little lady, she's still your mother no matter what. You should have respect for her," Joe said as he opened the truck door for her.

"I don't want to talk about my mother," she snapped. "How is Harris? Is he OK?" she said, changing the subject. "Does he miss me, Joe?"

"Oh wow, pretty lady, so many questions all at once." Joe closed her door, walked around to the driver's side, and got in.

He changed the conversation by asking, "Is there a good pizza place around here?"

"Oh, Joe, you haven't changed. Pizza and Coke, huh?"

"Yep, you got it."

"There's one two blocks down, turn right, go another two blocks, and it's on the left."

"Great, let's hit it." Joe started the truck and did his best to divert her questions by trying several times to change the subject, but she always managed to turn the conversation back to questions about Harris. When they arrived at the restaurant, he walked around to her side and opened the door for her.

"You're such a gentleman, just like Harris," she commented.

"Whoa, I'm nothing like the assistant DA, pretty mama, he's one of the good guys."

"Don't fool yourself, Joe Marble, so are you. By the way, are you still seeing that new lady in your life? Robin, I think that's her name, the one with the big tubes." Markita tried her best to be funny.

"You bet, she's a knockout, we're going to make it, just like I hope you and Harris will," said Joe without thinking.

"There is no Harris and me anymore, Joe," she said sadly. "Can you believe he's my brother? I cannot come to grips with it. How can it be true? It makes me sick when I think about it. I have had other boyfriends in the past, but I have never felt anything like what I feel for him. Some people wait a lifetime to find the perfect one and others get lucky the first time. I thought we were one of those lucky ones. We often laughed until we cried together. We finished off each other's jokes, mainly because his were as bad as his uncle J's. It all is too much to take in. I hate what life has done to us. Oh god, Joe, did he even tell you about us? I assumed he did, as close as you were."

"Yes, he did, sweetie, and I must say I was blown away." Joe flashed back, remembering the bad language Harris used as well as his anger. "Never give up, pretty lady," Joe added.

"What do you mean by that? We can't ever change our DNA."

"No, but things are not always what they seem."

"I don't understand what you're trying to say, Joe," she said curiously.

"It's nothing, Markita, don't mind me. I'm an old hound dog who likes to get to the truth. I'm a Deputy Dawg with a curious sniffer."

Markita laughed at him. "You're so funny, Joe. No wonder you and Harris are such good friends. He's as humorous as you."

"He certainly does possess a different kind of humor, I'll give him that. He has to, to be friends with me." Joe smirked as they were led to their table.

The restaurant had authentic Italian decor. The tablecloths were red-and-white squares with red napkins. The chairs were white with red studs. Joe asked her if there was anything special she would like on the pizza.

"As long as there are no anchovies or olives, I'll be fine with whatever you want," she replied.

"How about squid and snails then?" he teased her.

"OK, Joe, always the joker," she laughed at him. They ordered one with everything on it and two Cokes.

"Have you discussed anything about what happened with your mother?" asked Joe.

"No, and right now, I can't. I'm too angry with her."

"Maybe if you give her a chance to explain things, you might learn something about what happened, did you ever think of that, pretty lady?" Joe said, always playing the detective.

"I will, Joe, but not right now." Her eyes started to well up with tears. Markita excused herself and headed to the bathroom. Joe noticed a long strand of her dark hair stuck against the white cushion on the back of her seat. He grabbed a napkin and pulled the hair from the chair, then placed the napkin in his pocket. She returned to the table a few minutes later, a little more composed, but quiet. They finished their pizza in relative silence.

"You know, I sent him e-mails and left tons of phone messages, but to no avail," she finally said. "I think he hates me, Joe." Markita started to cry again not able to control her emotions anymore.

"No, little lady, he doesn't hate you. That is the farthest thing from the truth." He was trying to get her to stop crying.

"I'm sorry I'm acting like a childish and immature schoolgirl." She was mad at herself now for being foolish, but it struck Joe as funny. Markita called herself childish and immature, which was something Harris called him frequently. Now would probably not be the right time to make a joke.

"It's OK, Markita. Anyone with eyes could see how in love the two of you were, and I dare say you both still are. I'm sure it's equally painful, and it's going to take a long time before either of you heal." Joe was being so kind and considerate toward her.

"Thank you, Joe."

"You're welcome, little lady," he said with a smile.

"I suppose we should get going. It's getting late," said Markita.

Joe pulled out her chair and let her walk in front of him. He quickly pulled her straw from her glass, wrapped it in a napkin, and put it into his other pocket. He took long strides to catch up to her. They sat in the truck talking for a little while.

"You said you were here on business. Does it have to do with the case you and Harris were working on?" she asked, wishing she were still helping them.

"I'm checking out a few things while I'm here, yes."

"If you need any help taking notes, I'm an excellent intern." She smiled.

"You sure are. Maybe you can help me with something. You said your mom walked away from the governor. Did you ever see him after that?"

"No, never. He was having an affair with someone else. It was all over the papers up here. Her name was Eleanor Woodsworth. My mom hated her. I remember one day we were in a department store, and Miss Woodsworth saw us and took a swing at my mom, saying she was trying to steal my father, I mean the governor, back. My mom whacked her good, telling her she could keep the lying, cheating bastard, that he wasn't worth it. It was nasty."

"I imagine it was," Joe said sympathetically. "Did you ever see her again?"

"No, but the last time I spoke with Mom about it, which is when she said she was coming to Orlando, she told me Governor Mason had washed his hands of Eleanor. Apparently, she talked a lot, and the governor's wife got wind of his affair and put a stop to it. I know my mother was furious with her and vowed to take her down one day. I asked my mom about the incident quite sometime after the event, and Mom said she was over it although I don't think you ever get over the embarrassment, do you?"

"I don't know about that, but boy, interesting lives these high-society people live, huh?"

"I guess so. There always seems to be a lot of drama going on with them. I think it's why Mom walked away from it all. I think it got too much for her. Eleanor Woodsworth was the last straw. I remember right after Mom dealt with her, it was all over." Markita was getting curious about all of Joe's questions.

"Does any of this have to do with the case?" she asked again.

"Determined, aren't we, little lady?" He grinned at her.

"You're asking a lot of questions, Joe Marble."

"It's because I'm a detective, and it's in my nature to ask people personal stuff." He was teasing with her now. She knew she wasn't going to get any more out of him, so she said good night before getting out of the truck to head inside.

She turned to face Joe as she closed the door. "It was good seeing you again, Joe."

"You too, pretty lady."

"Please tell Harris, I . . ." she paused before finishing.

"It's OK, I know what you wanted to say."

"I can't help myself, Joe. I'll never look at him as my brother. I fell in love with him."

"None of us can help what or who our hearts fall in love with. You can't help it. If it's wrong, it's too late for regrets."

"You're so special, Joe. That is exactly how it is. We can try to deny things all we want, but it is what it is, and maybe it's just not meant to be. But I don't understand why it has all gone wrong right now."

"Trust me, please," Joe said. "If you two are meant to be together, it will happen. It may not be today or tomorrow, but you will be together again if it's God's will."

Joe's words so inspired Markita she hung on every one of them. *One day,* she said to herself, *One day soon.*

Joe watched as she went inside. Once he knew she was safe, he drove to his hotel and called it a night.

Awakening early the next morning, Joe headed back to Orlando. Before making a call to Harris with his findings, he stopped by a lab where his friend Alberto worked. He handed Alberto the napkins with Markita's hair sample and straw.

"I'm going to meet with a friend in a few hours to collect his DNA. When I bring it back, I'll need to know if all those samples show that these two people are related. Do you have the time?"

"Well, I'm a bit busy," Alberto told him. "But if you don't mind waiting for a while, I'll get to it for you as soon as I can."

"Thanks, man, I'll be back. And, Alberto, this is just between you and me, OK?"

"Sure, Joe," Alberto said with a wink.

Once outside, Joe called Harris at the office. Tara answered and put him straight through.

"Hey, big man, do you have some time to spend with an old buddy?"

"Wow! If it's not Detective Marble back in town. You took your sweet time in Tallahassee. I hope you were successful in what you were looking for," Harris said, trying not to say too much on the phone.

"Well, yes and no. I would like to share, but it's also lunchtime, and I haven't had a good sub bought for me in quite some time," said Joe as his stomach growled.

"Oh, I see, it's not my company you want, it's my money."

"Certainly not, Mr. Ass . . . DA, it's only your company I seek." Joe was now cracking up at himself.

"Who is the ass I ask?" Harris jabbed back.

"Why, not I, sir. I'm a humble public servant assisting you through life's trials and tribulations." Joe was laughing hard now.

"Oh, and I guess me buying lunch assists your stomach."

"Well, if you insist, Mr. Robertson. How about we meet at your favorite place, the Bistro?" Joe did not realize everything that went down between Harris and Markita all took place there.

"*No!* Mama's in half an hour," Harris retorted sharply.

"Whoa, Mama's is fine. See you there." Joe heard Harris hang up seconds before he did. Joe could tell his friend was still angry.

He arrived at Mama's quite some time before Harris. He even ordered his own sub and Coke and paid for it himself, knowing Harris was still not in the best frame of mind.

By the time Harris got there, he saw that Joe was already eating, so he ordered himself a ham and pepper jack cheese sub and bottle of water, then walked over to sit with Joe. Things were awkward at first. Harris had a hard time looking at Joe, feeling bad that he paid for his own sub. Furthermore, he hated the fact that his friend knew about him and Markita; his face kept turning red with embarrassment.

"My trip to Tallahassee was interesting to say the least," Joe said, starting the conversation.

"Really, what did you learn?" Harris asked, glad to turn his thoughts somewhere other than Markita.

"Not to act like such a cop, for one thing." He laughed a little, and Harris cracked a smile.

Joe started to recount all he had learned from his talkative deli clerk friend, leaving nothing out. Harris listened intently, taking notes, then something clicked.

"Wait a minute," he interrupted Joe. "Markita told us her mother dated Governor Mason for six years, and Markita always thought Mason was her father. We know from Markita that her mother was with him for the first six years of her life. She also told me he showered her with expensive gifts. Of course we know now her mother was having an affair with my rat bastard father before the governor stepped into the sordid picture." Harris made this statement in anger. Why did the conversation always have to lead back to her?

Joe did some fast talking, getting Harris off his and Markita's problems and back onto the information he collected. "Apparently, Eleanor moved back to a neighborhood called Bourbon Street where she went back to hooking." He told Harris about Eleanor's connection with Miss Dixie. "My guess is the governor took her away from the kind of life she was living and took good care of her, but it sounds like something went terribly wrong to me, and she started talking too much."

"Wow! You got quite an education, Mr. Joe Cool, or should I say Joe the hottie?"

"Why, my friend Harris is back, nice to see you, buddy," Joe said, giving him a grin.

"Keep to our conversation, and we will be fine, Detective Snoop Dog." Harris was trying hard to lighten up, even though he was dying inside. He'd barely eaten any of his sub; in fact, he had hardly eaten anything since Markita left. He'd lost several pounds, which wasn't good as he was pretty thin to begin with.

"It actually gets more interesting. The clerk also told me she had a daughter here . . . named Bambi."

"Isn't she the girl you were interviewing when you got caught with your pants down?" Harris went straight for the jugular.

"Oh, not nice, my friend. My pants were secured tightly around my waist, trust me. But you're right. The clerk I talked too confirmed it. They're one and the same," said Joe.

"Do you feel like paying Bambi another visit after your long drive home?" asked Harris, wanting to interview her straight away. Joe was a little tired from the drive, but was as eager to get some more answers as Harris. They agreed to meet at the "antique dealership" that fronted for Miss Dixie's brothel in an hour. Joe let Harris leave first, pretending to finish off a few more nibbles of what remained of his sub. Then he picked up Harris's empty water bottle, wrapped it in a napkin, and put it in his pocket; he would drop it off at the lab where his friend worked later.

An hour later, they met at Miss Dixie's and headed for the front porch. Once at the door, they pressed the intercom button.

"Can I help you?" said a female voice from behind the door.

"Is Bambi home?" asked Harris.

"Do you have an appointment?"

"No, I'm here on official business. I'm Assistant District Attorney Harris Robertson, and this is Detective Joe Marble.

"Hold on a second please." The voice sounded quite nervous this time. A few moments passed, then the door opened, and Bambi appeared.

"Do I need an attorney present?" she asked warily.

"That is your right, miss, but really all I have are a few simple questions if you could spare the time," Harris said, his voice dripping Southern charm.

"OK, what do you want?" she asked.

"Is your last name Woodsworth by any chance?" Harris asked, smiling at her warmly.

"Yes."

"Is your mother Eleanor Woodsworth?" Harris asked.

"Yes, why?"

"I have been led to believe she was on her way back to Orlando to ask Miss Dixie if she could resume her position with her."

"I don't know what you mean," the girl said, playing dumb. She wasn't about to admit Miss Dixie hired people here.

"Well, let me put it another way. Did she come back here to visit with you?" Harris flashed another smile.

"Yes, she did."

"Have you seen her recently?" asked Harris craftily.

"Not since Miss Dixie . . .," she stopped.

"It's OK, Miss Woodsworth. This is off the record." He smiled sweetly at her again.

She hesitated for a moment, then thought how cute his smile was and answered him. "Miss Dixie wouldn't give her a job because a long time ago my mom stole some expensive diamond earrings from her." Bambi emphasized the "long time ago."

Harris decided not to tell her at this time that her mother was deceased. Currently, they had no real evidence proving anything except for the gruesome photos. Harris thought she could view them another time when he and Joe had something solid.

"You've been so helpful, Miss Woodsworth, I really appreciate all your assistance," Harris said, thinking he would nail her on the witness stand later.

"You're welcome, Mr. Robertson." She wanted to ask him to make an appointment with her, but knew it might not be wise. Joe and Harris stood by their cars talking before departing.

"Joe, I want you to look into Miss Dixie's records deeper than I have. You might catch something I have possibly missed. On the surface, the books look clean, but I know I'm missing something. The books are in my office. I subpoenaed them last week." Harris was hopeful Joe would find some evidence to incriminate Miss Dixie.

"OK, buddy, but is there anything in particular you want me to be looking for?" asked Joe curiously.

"I think the earrings are the link, but I can't put my finger on the answer yet."

"OK, man. I'll come by your office first thing in the morning and pick up her books, but right now, I'm beat and need some shut-eye before I drop," said Joe, yawning loudly.

"I'm sorry, Joe. I guess it's been a long few days for you."

"It sure has, buddy. I need to go home, call my girl, and then crash for as long as I can."

"Still seeing that Robin chick?" Harris asked, surprised.

"Yep, she's crazy about me," Joe said with a big smile on his face.

"Oh, I won't argue with you there, Marble. She must be crazy to keep seeing you."

"Ha, ha, ha, ha. Very funny, Mr. Ass DA."

"Have a good night, Joe. I'll see you tomorrow some time. Don't make it too late in the day. I want answers to this case. I need answers. Hugh wants me to take Miss Dixie down hard." It felt good to remind himself of that fact; it helped fuel his competitiveness.

"I know, man. I just need a few undisturbed hours of shut-eye, and I'll be as good as new."

"OK, Joe, tomorrow, man." Harris extended his hand for Joe to shake. Joe put his thumb to his nose, extended his pinky finger, and blew Harris a raspberry. Harris let out a loud chuckle.

"Joe Marble, you're too damn much, man. Childish and immature."

"I know, and that's why we're friends. Birds of a feather flock together."

"Whatever," said Harris, getting in his car shaking his head. He was lucky to have Joe as a friend. He didn't have any other real friends as his work schedule was grueling, and most guys did not understand. It was also why he had never dated. Harris usually kept long and frustrating hours. He drove home trying not to think about Markita.

Joe stopped at the lab and dropped off Harris's water bottle.

"Don't forget, buddy, this is between you and me," he said to Alberto. "No one else is to know you're running these tests, OK?"

"OK, man, your secret is safe with me. You're going to need to be patient, though. I'm really backed up," Alberto said.

"Do me a favor, and don't leave the results on my home machine or cell phone. When you have them, just leave me a message to call you, OK?" Joe said with some urgency in his voice.

"OK, man, I got it." Alberto could tell the results were quite important to his friend.

Joe thanked him and finally headed home. Joe was exhausted from the trip, but he wanted to call Robin.

"Hey there, hot lady," he said when she picked up the phone. "I just got back to town. How did you survive without my handsome face and sexy body hanging around?"

"Well, if it isn't Detective Joe Marble. I've been fine. How was your trip to Tallahassee? Everything you hoped it would be?" she asked.

"Yes, ma'am, it was, but I'm glad I'm home here in Orlando. The scenery is so much better, if you know what I mean."

"Joe Marble, I think you're flirting with me."

"Not me, pretty lady, never." He grinned into the phone.

"You were gone a lot longer than I expected." Robin was fishing a little, and Joe liked her missing him.

"Hmmm, how about I come pick you up tomorrow night, and we spend some quality time together?" Joe asked, praying she would accept.

"You betcha, Marble."

"Phew, you're such a hot one." Joe joked with her.

"Yep, too hot to trot," said Robin.

"Oh no, you're not a horse, are you?" Joe joked with her again.

"Well, I'm not a horse's ass, like you, Detective."

"Oh, you're too funny, missy. I'll pick you up around eight tomorrow night. Is that OK with you?"

"Perfect, Joe, see you then?"

"Hey, I missed you." Joe wasn't used to being open with a lady friend, but there was definitely something clicking between them.

"Good night," she said sweetly.

"Good night to you too, pretty lady." Joe couldn't believe it, but he blew her a kiss good night over the phone.

Chapter Fourteen

The Order

Joe was hoping to get a few extra hours' sleep after his long trip, but he awoke at his normal time. He stretched out his body and smiled, thinking how nice it was to wake up in his own bed. He showered, shaved, and dressed before going to his front door. It was a daily ritual: he picked up the newspaper, returned to the kitchen, grabbed a Coke from his refrigerator, and then sat down to read.

First, he read the headline news as sometimes this gave him a heads-up on the previous night's activities, as well as what might be in store for him that day. Next, he enjoyed the sports section, finishing off the paper by reading the classifieds. He loved his job and wasn't looking for another one, but in his line of work, he constantly bumped into someone who was looking for employment. He liked to help people out, and maybe something he saw in the job section could help someone looking. He'd just about finished reading when an advertisement caught his eye. The district attorney's office was looking for a new janitorial service.

"Interesting," he said aloud. What a great way to get into Hugh's office and do some snooping, he smiled. His thoughts turned devious. Obviously, he couldn't apply as Hugh knew him, so he would need someone whom he could trust. He picked up the phone and called Harris.

"District Attorney's Office, Tara speaking, how may I help you?" Joe missed Markita answering the phone; her voice was much softer and definitely sweeter than Tara's voice.

"It's Joe Marble, is the Harris-man there yet?" he asked in his normal jovial manner.

"Yes, he is, I'll tell him you're on the line." She put Joe on hold. *Man, she is cold,* thought Joe while he was waiting. Harris picked up a moment later.

"Howdy, pard'ner?" Harris greeted him.

"Howdy thar yourself, Mr. Ass . . . DA."

"Watch it, Marble, don't make me come kick your . . . *ahem.*" Harris coughed, pulling back, remembering he was at work.

"I was wondering if you could meet me for lunch today?" asked Joe. ""There's something I would like to run by you."

"What you really mean is you're broke and you want me to buy you lunch." Harris knew the drill.

"If you insist on paying, you know I don't like to argue with you. How about we meet at the Bistro?" said Joe, forgetting the bad memories it had for Harris . . . again.

"How about we never eat at the Bistro again and you quit bringing it up?" Harris snapped. "Does Mama's, about noonish, sound OK with you?"

Joe could tell Harris changed his tone for a moment. It let Joe know his friend was still not over Markita.

"Noonish sounds great. See you there, buddy." Joe hung up, finished his Coke, threw the newspaper in the recycling bin, and headed out for the day.

When lunchtime came around, Harris was already at Mama's waiting for Joe. He'd already placed their order.

"I hope you don't mind, but I knew you would have the pizza, so I took the liberty of ordering for you."

"You're too good to me, man," Joe said smiling.

"So what is it you want to run by me?"

"I have this crazy plan. If it pays off, we might become a tad wiser as to what is going on around here."

"Well, spit it out. It can't be any worse than some of your other screwups." Harris started cracking up.

"Hey, hey, hey! Some of my ideas have been masterpieces!"

"Really, you mean like when we went to the bank, and you asked the clerk with the large breasts to pay you with big ones? Another one of your brilliant ideas, Marble, especially when she called security on us."

"It's not my fault. She took it the wrong way. Seriously, Harris, this is a great idea, listen up," said Joe all excited about his plan.

"I'm sure you're going to tell me no matter what, so get on with it, and try telling me the short version, not the one which will last into next week." Harris was laughing again. Their food arrived, and they ate and talked.

"Who hires the janitor service in your building? Do you know?"

"Yes," Harris answered, a bit baffled. "The office manager interviews the potential employees, and then she sends me the best offer out of three. I then choose one and send it through to Hugh for approval. Why?" Harris was curious why Joe would want to know about their janitorial service. "I think you have finally lost all your marbles, Marble," Harris said, cracking up at his own joke again.

"Funny, Harris! Am I supposed to be laughing now? And maybe not all my marbles. This is a terrific plan, so listen. I have a hunch about Hugh. If I could get someone on the inside to let me into the building, I could go through his office and do some snooping."

"What does this have to do with our janitorial service?"

"Well, Mr. Wise Guy, this is why I get paid the big bucks. You pay me to think smart, right?"

Harris looked at him with one eyebrow cocked higher than the other.

Joe continued, "I'll draw up the perfect résumé, and the manager won't be able to pass up on the reference I give. Then you can sign off on it and give it to Hugh."

"Oh I see, it's my arse on the line again if you get caught," Harris said, not jumping at his idea right away.

"I won't get caught. I'm the famous Joe Marble."

Harris chuckled again. "How about I bring up your escapades at Miss Dixie's?"

"How about you don't?" said Joe not wanting to relive that nightmare.

"Hugh keeps everything locked up in the safe," Harris told him.

"That's OK, I've seen it. It's a combination safe. I can break the code with no problem. Don't you worry about the minor details. I'll take care of those."

"It might give us a heads-up, Joe," Harris said warming up to the idea a little.

"Now you're talking, buddy," Joe commented enthusiastically.

"Do you have someone picked out for this new scheme of yours?" asked Harris, always concerned when it came to one of Joe's brilliant ideas.

"I sure do, and I don't think the chick will turn me down."

"Oh mercy, you want to use one of your chicks?" said Harris, even more concerned now.

"Not any chick, buddy. This one is great," Joe said with a smile.

"So you have approached her with this?"

"Not yet, but she will be perfect, trust me."

"Oh shit, now I know we're doomed. I have never trusted anyone who tells me to trust them." Harris shook his head.

"Ah, give me a break. It will go great," Joe said as he gave Harris a high five.

"Well, I need to get back to the office."

"Yep, and I have a sexy little lady to go talk too."

"Wait a minute, are you talking about that chick Robin?"

"Sure am there, buddy. Why, do you have a problem with her?"

"I'm more concerned with the fact you haven't known her long. Are you sure you can trust her?" Harris asked, now more than a little nervous.

"Absolutely, man. This chick is one in a million," Joe said, bragging about his new girlfriend.

"OK, if you say so, but be careful, Joe. If you get caught, our asses are on the line here, and we will both get fired and end up in jail. This time I won't be able to free your arse as mine will be sitting right next to yours."

"I'll be careful, Harris. If my hunch is right, this thing is bigger than the both of us."

"Take care, Joe."

"You too, man, later." Joe headed out to his truck getting out his cell phone as he climbed into the seat.

"Hey there, sexy little lady, how are you today?"

"I'm fine, Joe Marble, and you?" Robin answered.

"I was hoping I could come by and see you. There's something I would like to run by you, is that OK?"

"Well, I'm not doing anything right at this moment, and you have my curiosity piqued."

"Oh, lady, you have me piqued too," Joe said in a deep devilish voice.

"Why, Joe Marble, you bad boy," Robin said with her Southern belle voice.

"I'll be right over baby, OK?"

"I'll be ready," Robin said flirtatiously.

"Hubba, hubba, hubba," Joe said before flipping off his cell phone. A few minutes later, Joe pulled his truck up into her driveway, got out, and headed to the front door. It was open, leaving just the screen.

"Is that you, Detective Marble?" Robin called out from the kitchen.

"Is sure is, ma'am," Joe replied.

"Well, come on in and make yourself at home."

"Thank you, ma'am," said Joe politely. He walked in and headed to the kitchen. Robin met him with her arms out ready for a hug. Joe took her hand and kissed it like the Southern gentlemen he was.

"It's nice to see you again, Miss Robin."

"Plain Robin will do just fine there, Joe Marble."

"There is nothing plain about you, pretty lady, that's for sure." Joe, still holding her hand, led her into the living room, and showed her to her couch.

"Now, you know how independent I am. Even though my vision is low I can find my way around, especially in my own home."

"I'm sorry, I didn't mean to offend you," Joe said sheepishly.

"You didn't offend me in any way, Joe Marble. I just don't want you fussing over me when I'm capable."

"Yes, ma'am, sure thing." The two of them sat together holding hands. It didn't bother Joe in the slightest that his girlfriend barely had vision. What drew him to her was her warm sense of hospitality. She was a beautiful-looking woman with long blond hair and blue eyes that searched for the sound of his voice when he spoke.

"I have something I would like to run by you."

"So you said, Joe Marble, so come on out with it." Her curiosity was about to get the better of her.

"Well, it's like this. I need someone to apply for the office cleaning job the district attorney's office is advertising."

"You think I fit the person?" she asked surprised.

"Of course! You said you're independent, and with your beauty and personality, there is no way they could turn you down."

"Why, flattery will get you everywhere, Joe Marble, but I can't see them hiring me, having the vision loss and all," she said, turning a little red.

"Well, actually, Robin, one of the reasons I think you will be perfect is *because* of your vision issue. You see, the government likes to give these kinds of jobs to people with disabilities and minorities before the rest of the public."

"I see, and what makes you think I need a job?" she asked, wondering if he thought badly of her.

"When I finish telling you my plan, you might want to turn me down, and if you do, I'll understand," Joe said, not wanting her to feel obligated to him.

"Why don't you let me be the judge?"

"OK, here goes. I'll prepare your résumé, and you will get the job. My friend Harris is going to see to it."

"He's the one who's the assistant district attorney you're always talking about, right?"

"Yep, that's right cutie-pie."

"You don't want me to steal anything or do something criminal, do you?"

"You won't be stealing anything, I promise."

"Then what is the catch, Joe Marble?" Robin was now suspicious.

"Hmmm . . . I need you to let me in, and that's all you need to know, little lady."

"Aha, so there is something not so legal here?"

"The less you know, the better. It isn't because I don't trust you. If I didn't, I wouldn't be here asking you to do this for me. I need you to let me in, and I'll take care of the rest. The less you know, the safer you will be."

"So if I say yes to this plan of yours, will it help you?"

"I think it will at least give Harris and me an advantage."

"Are you in any danger?"

"Not yet, but things aren't adding up. I have a hunch the closer we get to the truth, we might be."

"Then I'll help you, Joe Marble," she said smiling at him.

"I knew there was something special about you when I first set eyes on you and heard you sing."

"Your flattery is exciting me, Joe Marble."

"I have to get going, but would it be OK if I came back later, and we went to the club together?"

"That would be mighty fine, sir," Robin quipped. Joe loved it when she talked with her Southern accent; it sounded so sexy to him. He kissed her on her cheek and left to go home to start working on Robin's résumé. He would have to make sure her credentials were impeccable and make sure he had people in place to verify her services were excellent when they checked her references.

It didn't take long before Harris got the word back from Hugh; Robin's Rescue Cleaning Service was acceptable to him. Harris waited until he got home from work that night before calling Joe to tell him the news.

"Marble residence."

"So official, even after hours, Marble? You crack me up, man," Harris said with a chuckle.

"Oh, it's you, Robertson. What do you want?"

"Certainly not you, you're not my type."

"Hey, hey, hey," said Joe in the voice of Fat Albert.

"I have news for you, man. Hugh signed off on Robin's cleaning service, and you're in, buddy."

"Fantastic! Now all we have to do is put my plan into action," Joe said with excitement.

"Be careful, my friend. We're not playing with honest individuals. Missing bodies and evidence is unacceptable. I think you and I are being played by someone. I just hope that someone isn't Hugh," Harris said in a serious tone.

"I know that, man. I'll be in and out before anyone knows I was there. As for Robin, she can hand in her notice at the end of the week, claiming the job was too big for her."

"I caution you again, Joe, stay safe. And by the way, she's a nice-looking chick."

"Hey, hey, hey, keep your eyes to yourself, buddy, this one is mine."

"You don't have to worry about me, Marble. I've had enough of women to last me a lifetime." Joe could still hear the sorrow in his friend's voice and wondered if he would ever get over Markita. He hoped for his friend's sake the DNA tests he was having done would go Harris's way. If not, he knew his friend would be in pain for a long time to come.

"I'll be in touch," Joe remarked.

"Later," Harris replied.

Joe waited a week for Robin's training period to be over with and then decided it would be the following week before he would try out his plan. He chose a Wednesday night to put things into action since in the middle of the week people were always busy thinking about the upcoming weekend. In that state, they were less likely to observe what was going on around them.

On the appointed night, Joe tapped on the window of Hugh's office three times then quickly walked around the building to the back door. Robin had already turned the alarm system off, so she was able to let him into Hugh's office without any issues.

"Hey, pretty lady, are you OK?" he asked as he kissed her cheek.

"Yes, I'm fine, but please hurry, Joe. I don't feel right doing this," Robin said nervously.

"This won't take long at all. You go on about your business, and I'll come find you when I'm done," Joe said with confidence.

"No way, Joe Marble! I'm coming with you in case you need me, and don't argue with me. I can clean the office while you're busy doing whatever it is you're going to do." Joe didn't have time to argue with her; time was of the essence. He quickly walked down to Hugh's office, heading straight for the safe. He knew its exact location as he'd spent many hours in that office going over cases with the big guy. Hugh always put the files of the most serious offenders in the safe; the three cabinets behind his desk held all the other files.

Kneeling before the safe, Joe took out a stethoscope and put it on the metal door. He turned the knob left, then right, left and back right again, listening for the clicks. After a few moments of twisting, the door opened. Joe's heart was beating quite fast, and sweat was hanging on his brow. His hands shook a little with relief and nerves. He flipped through the case files inside the safe, taking special care to take photographs of Hugh's personal information; the most interesting file was the folder with his bank records in it. Joe didn't have time to study the folder for long, but from what he did see, there were some very large deposits. He didn't see anything else he deemed incriminating, so he closed the safe door, reset it, and then stood back for a moment. He moved Hugh's law books forward off the shelves, looking behind them for a secret panel, but there was none. *Only in the movies*, he told himself. Walking over to Hugh's desk, he picked the lock on the bottom drawer and once again looked for a false opening.

"Bingo! Jackpot," he whispered.

"Did you find what you were looking for?" asked Robin with a shaky voice.

"Yes, baby, won't be long now, and we will be out of here." Joe pulled a heavy maroon diary from the false drawer. At first glance, he could tell it was extremely old. On the front, it simply read "the Order" in an old English, gold font.

"The Order," Joe said aloud, intrigued. He moved quickly, taking his camera out of his pocket again and snapping photos of every page, wishing he had time to read each one, but he knew there was no time to spare.

"Finished," he exclaimed a few minutes later, happy to be done.

"OK, Joe, let's get going," Robin said urgently, pulling at his arm. They were about to leave when Robin heard footsteps coming down the hallway.

"Hide," she instructed Joe. He glanced around the room, but there was nowhere to hide. The footsteps grew closer. He pulled out Hugh's chair and got down on his knees squeezing into the space between the chair and the desk.

"Try to take his focus off Hugh's desk," he whispered softly to Robin, and then he started to pray. He would never forgive himself if she went to jail because of him. The door creaked as it opened. Robin let out a little surprised sound.

"Who's there?" asked a gruff voice.

"My name is Robin. I'm with the new janitorial service. Is something wrong?" she asked nervously.

"Oh no, miss, my name is Daniel. I work the night shift as a guard."

"Oh, yes, they told me about you, but you've been off sick," she said, trying not to sound so nervous.

"Right, missy, I had a touch of the flu, but I'm over it now."

"Wonderful, sir, glad to hear. It's nasty stuff. Was it the swine flu that's going around?"

"No, no, thank goodness, but thanks for asking, missy. Well, I'll let you get back to your cleaning. I'm going on my break now. I'll be in the back security room if you need me, OK?" He was touched and impressed she knew he had been sick. It was obvious to him she was genuinely concerned for him.

"Yes, sir, but I'll be fine. I'm just finishing up, and then I'll be out of here."

"Don't forget to reset the alarm when you leave, Miss Robin."

"No, no, I won't. It was nice to meet you, sir." He could tell her vision wasn't normal as she strained to focus on him; therefore, he had no reason to suspect that anything out of the ordinary was going on. He went on his merry way to get the coffee he had been brewing.

After Daniel left, Joe arose from behind the desk.

"Phew, that was a close one, baby. It's time you and I got out of here."

"You got it, Joe Marble. I don't fancy a jail cell bed tonight." Joe kissed her on the cheek and then left the building.

Robin finished up, set the alarm, and met Joe in the parking lot. On the drive back to Robin's, they talked about the night's events.

"We had a close call tonight, Joe Marble," Robin said with a sigh of relief.

"Yes, baby, but you were great, a real pro."

"Why thank you, sir," Robin said, blushing.

"I didn't get too much time to read what I found, but I'm telling you, Robbie, I think I hit the jackpot."

"I hope so, as I have grown quite fond of having you around."

"I like being around for you too." Joe was sincere; he really was attracted to her. Joe had only been in love one other time, and that relationship ended badly. He had come home from work early one day to find his girlfriend in bed with another man, and it damn near destroyed him. Joe always loved a woman's company, but after what happened, he was gun shy and kept women at arm's length. Robin was different though; there was something so honest and trustworthy about her.

Joe pulled into her driveway, got out of the truck, and rushed around to her side. Robin was already out of the truck, but Joe walked her to the front door. He waited while she unlocked it, then he took her in his arms as soon as they got inside and kissed her deeply.

"Why, Joe Marble, you make me feel like a high school teenager on her first date," she said giddily.

"And you make me feel the same way, Robbie," Joe said, feeling as giddy.

"Will you call me later and let me know what you found tonight, Joe?"

"I can let you know if it is helpful, but I don't want to tell you too much. It could be dangerous for you," Joe said, now sounding a little concerned.

"It's OK. I wanted to help you and Harris."

"You went above and beyond the call of duty for us, pretty lady. If it's OK with you, I'll call you tomorrow night."

"Yes, that will be fine," Robin said in her thick Southern accent.

"Whoa," Joe said, giving a loud wolf whistle. He turned around to head back to the truck smiling, happy with himself.

"Good night, lovely lady," he called to her as she stood on her porch.

"Good night yourself, Joe Marble," she called back as Joe started up the truck and left for home.

Joe arrived at his house and headed straight for the refrigerator, grabbing a Coke. He walked down the long hallway to his bedroom. He couldn't wait to kick off his shoes, change into his PJs, and hit the sack. As soon as his head hit the pillow, he was out, but as the night wore on, he dreamed about certain words that jumped out at him while he was taking photos of the book. He couldn't wait until he got the film developed. He knew the right person to take it to, as he wouldn't be able to let just anyone process a film with this much at stake.

The next morning Joe called an old college pal. "Hey, Randy, long time no see," he greeted his friend.

"Mercy me, if it isn't Joe Marble, the great Inspector Gadget."

"None other, my friend. How the heck are you?" Joe asked.

"Doing all right there, Joe, doing all right. How about yourself?"

"I can't grumble, I must say good, buddy."

"So to what do I owe the pleasure of this call? You must want something, Marble."

"Of course, you're right, Randy. I need a big favor, one I could only trust you with, my friend."

"Boy, it must be big. I need some bread to go with the butter that you're laying on thick, Marble."

"Funny guy. Do you still have your dark room there at home?"

"I sure do, Joe, what do you need?"

"I need a film developed, is that too much to ask?" Joe laughed trying not to make his favor sound like a big deal.

"There has to be more, Marble. With you it's never something small. You must need me to develop something illegal, some espionage secrets, or some jerk cheating on his missus," Randy smirked.

"Hmmm . . . none of the above," Joe said again, trying to downplay the favor.

"OK, Marble, you wanna come over now? It happens I don't have much going on this morning."

"Now would be perfect. I'll be over in a jiff," Joe said hanging up the phone.

He showered, shaved, and dressed in record time. He didn't even stop at the refrigerator for a Coke. He picked up his newspaper and threw it inside the house, locked the front door, then jumped in his truck and drove to his friend's.

After a quick hello, Randy got right to work as Joe waited patiently for the film to be developed.

"I have a feeling this one is going to be all over the news, big guy, right?" said Randy as he finished up.

"It might be, Randy, it might be." Joe thanked his buddy and drove home as fast as the speed limit would allow. This time Joe did stop at the refrigerator and grabbed a Coke. Randy must have gone through several reams of photo paper as the envelope he put the developed film into was thick. Joe opened the envelope and found that Randy had put all the pages into a binder. With extreme anticipation, he started to read the first page, which read like a diary.

It started with the words "the Order" in quotations centered at the top of the page. The first date was July 29, 1956. Joe sat down in his favorite chair, took a big swig of his Coke, and then started to read:

> *A strange thing happened today, something that would change many lives, especially mine. Judge Gary Alexander walked into my office with a proposal I could not refuse. Here was a tortured man, bitter because the system he took an oath to live and breathe by had failed him. He spent his life believing the judicial system protected the innocent, and then his beliefs were shattered. His son became the victim, and the judicial system let him down. The judge and the story he revealed to me were overwhelming. Even though I'm a man of little emotion, I teared up a time or two listening to the story of his tortured soul.*

He started with these chilling words: "I'll tip the scales of justice myself to protect the innocent."

The tale that followed then chilled me to my core and is painful for me to recount, but I will tell his story as he told it to me . . .

"My son, Cory, was a great kid, liked by everyone," the judge started off slowly. "His school attendance and grades were excellent. He was a good-looking kid, always well dressed and groomed, with manners to match. His personality was outgoing, and he possessed a unique wit, which kept his friends on their toes. It was a trait inherited from his uncle. Growing up, he always had a crowd of people surrounding him. It was when Cory entered middle school that his life, and our family's lives, changed forever.

"I found out most of this information much later, too late." The judge closed his eyes at this point and seemed to steady himself before he went on. "The principal of the school took an immediate liking to him, always making a point to say good morning, shaking his hand, and then eventually even hugging him, making my boy's life uncomfortable and embarrassing. The principal would seek him out in the hallway and greet him as if they were great friends. His true friends thought he was so lucky to have the principal favor him the way he did. The principal would summon Cory to his office offering him candy, sometimes detaining him for a whole period. He insinuated himself into his education, guiding and advising all his subjects, which we thought was all to our boy's benefit, but all the while that man was touching him in ways that made Cory feel uncomfortable. We just didn't know about these things until much later . . . .

"Things began to change when the principal started asking him awkward questions not relating to school, like who he was friends with, what he liked to sleep in, that sort of thing. But he never shared this with us. It wasn't long before he started to make obvious advances toward Cory. It started with shoulder rubs, then overly affectionate strokes to the back of the head. The principal found every opportunity to spend time with him.

"Cory told us about this last incident much later, and it pains me to tell it now. But here it is . . . It was a warm autumn day when the principal called for him to come to his office, offering him some lemonade. Being a polite boy, my son accepted. Then the man asked Cory to take off his shirt—it being so hot and all, he assured the boy that it was fine to do so. Then the principal approached him and started to unbutton my son's shirt. I'm sure the boy was terrified at that point.

"We found out after that this man, Richard Curtis, had been married for twelve years before all this. He'd had two little girls, six *and eight years old. But his wife left him two years before the incident with our son when she suspected her husband was molesting their own children. She realized it would be impossible to prove to anyone what a pervert her husband was, and she didn't want to embarrass and humiliate her girls, so she left town. If only we had known . . .*

"The principal instructed Cory to come closer and give him a hug to 'thank him' for the lemonade. When my son approached Curtis, he hoped to give the hug and get out, but Curtis was too strong for him. That man . . . ." Here, the poor judge actually had to steady himself against my desk before he went on, but go on he did . . .

"That man forced *himself on my son. The poor child was so scared and embarrassed that he didn't fight, that he couldn't get away. He felt it was all his fault. Why did this happen to my child?"* Judge Alexander whispered, his eyes staring at the floor.

"When it was over," the poor man forced himself to continue, *"Richard Curtis threatened Cory, said that if he uttered one word to anyone about what had taken place, he would expel him from school. He drilled into him no one would believe him.*

"Cory put his clothes back on and left that office, never to be the same boy again. He became withdrawn and solemn. His grades dropped, as well as his attitude. He lashed out, started to use foul language, and he fought with anyone who was bigger than he was, I guess to make up for the fact that he hadn't, or couldn't, fight off Mr. Curtis. I guess he fought so he could feel something. *For him, then, feeling something, even pain, was better than feeling nothing at all . . ."*

Joe couldn't believe what he was reading. It made him grit his teeth with anger. How could anyone entrusted with our most precious blessing from God do something so devastating and heinous to them? He needed to get up and shake off the anger he was feeling. He decided this would be a good time to run to the refrigerator and grab another Coke. He strode quickly to the kitchen and then rushed back to the diary. He couldn't wait to get back to see what happened to Cory and to the principal. He hoped he got twenty years. Assholes like Curtis were the reason Joe had become a detective; he wanted to expose perverts and criminals, then turn them over to guys like Harris Robertson who could put them away.

Before returning to the book, he took a quick bathroom break. He was hurrying back to the diary when the phone rang.

"Shit," he said aloud. Then, he said, "Marble speaking."

It was Forensics, calling to tell him the blood he recovered from Judge Poe's house matched a P. Smith. There was no other information regarding the suspect. They didn't even have a first name.

"Thanks," said Joe as he hung up the phone. He made a quick note in his own notebook and then got back to the diary. He began intensely reading again.

"At the time, we couldn't understand the drastic change in him. His mother and I were at a loss. He repeatedly started to wet the bed and experienced excruciating nightmares. His older brother told us about one night in particular that he screamed out, and while still asleep, he started to beat on the wall. When his older brother found him, Cory was lying in a pool of urine, crying uncontrollably, and curled up into a fetal position.

"His brother begged Cory to let him help him, whatever it was, but Cory wouldn't have it. My older son told me later that Cory kept crying out, 'You can't help me, no one can help me, and it is my own fault. I should have fought harder and tried to get away. You need to get away from me. I want to die!' He was screaming through his tears.

"His brother tried to reason with him, but Cory just screamed at him again, 'Shut the hell up. Don't ever tell me you love me. I hate you, I hate my life, and I hate the principal. I want to die. Get out, get out!'

"The next morning Cory's brother finally pulled me aside and explained what happened the previous night and also shared with me his suspicions. I was horrified. If what he suspected was correct, it was a nightmare no child or parent should have to endure. As a judge, I had presided over enough molestation cases to know the signs, and yet it appeared I'd missed them in my own son.

"At work, it was different. I learned to shut off my personal feelings. Some of the cases brought in front of me were horrific. Especially the kind I feared my son had been subjected too. I never imagined it would happen to one of my children. I prayed to God that my older son's suspicions were wrong.

"I kept Cory home from school that day, and we talked for hours. I was finally able to coerce my son into revealing the cruel and sickening truth about what took place. I told him I loved him, then gently hugged him, telling him everything would be OK, and that Mr. Curtis wouldn't be going anywhere near him or any other child. I would see to it. I spent hours reassuring my boy that what happened wasn't his fault, that he had done nothing wrong.

"Of course, I had to tell my wife. Cory's mother is a Christian woman, soft, quiet, and compassionate, but now her life had been changed forever too. She listened to what I had to say and then went to kiss Cory. Then, without another word, she went to Cory's school to pay a visit to Principal Curtis.

"She revealed to me what happened after her visit, and I couldn't have been more proud. She calmly walked past his secretary, ignoring her protests, and made her way straight into the office. Principal Curtis showed an obvious nervousness when she approached his desk. Her words to him were like an inscription on a tomb.

"'You'd better get life in prison,' she told him. 'Because if you get out in my lifetime, I'll hunt you down like the dog you are, and I'll kill you myself.' She turned to leave, and then, looking back for the last time, she spat toward his feet. 'God will judge you as I'll be judged,' she told him. 'God will have mercy on my soul, but you do not possess a soul, and therefore you will get no mercy. Look into my eyes and remember what you see. It will be the last thing you will see before you die, I promise you. It must be a cold day in hell because that is where you are going.' And she left.

"I, of course, reported this poor excuse for a human being, and he was arrested. The following months were excruciating. The trial seemed like it took forever. It was almost unbearable for us to enter the courtroom every day and look at the monster that hurt our son. It was especially awful for me, as I was normally the one who heard the evidence and handed out the sentence. The rush of anger bursting inside of me every time I heard what happened to my son was killing me. I wanted to scream out to my colleagues, 'Enough, hang the bastard, kill him, wipe him off the face of this earth! People like him do not deserve to live!' I had faith in the system though. I knew that Curtis's life was about to take a drastic turn as inmates didn't take too kindly to men who abused children. They would take care of him in their way, I said to myself, but I had nothing but hatred left in my heart."

He looked at me then with so much pain as he related the end of his tale. The days, weeks, and months went by, and he and his wife became estranged; they could no longer relate to each other. Cory's mother was no longer a soft, compassionate woman. She was angry with God and ugly to everyone else around her. Gary Alexander still loved his wife, but he no longer knew how to reach her, console her, or how to alleviate her pain. Cory's brother was mocked at school, the children calling him and his brother names. The town looked at Cory's parents as if they were the criminals. "How could they ruin Principal Curtis's life with this ridiculous lawsuit?" they whispered. "He has taught in our community for over twenty years," they said. "He was a good Christian man who went to church every Sunday, always helping the community whenever there was a crisis," they insisted. They didn't know why his wife left him, but he always told everyone she'd found love in another man's bed. It made people feel more sympathetic toward him . . .

The phone rang, again. "Shit, now what?" Joe muttered. He was so into the diary and wanted to know how the trial ended. He was furious at the principal, and the cop in him wanted to see him go down hard. *I need to get the max,* said Joe to himself as he picked up the phone.

"Marble, can I help you?" It was Forensics again, this time telling Joe that on the night of Judge Poe's assault, both SWAT team guys fired two bullets each, but only three bullets were recovered. That let Joe know his hunch about the suspect's injury was correct.

Joe needed to stretch his legs, so he paced for a while before going to get himself another Coke. He couldn't wait to get back to the diary.

Chapter Fifteen

The Harrises

Joe settled back into his chair and started to read again, hoping for no further interruptions. He hoped the diary would soon reveal who was telling the judge's tale and why Hugh might have been keeping it in a hidden drawer in his desk . . .

> *The community could not understand why or how the Alexander family, an upstanding family themselves, could charge another upstanding citizen with these outrageous allegations.*
>
> *Finally, the judge told me, the trial was over. With the closing arguments delivered, he felt it was just a matter of time now before the principal would receive his sentence. Judge Alexander was praying for at least twenty years. Then the verdict was read.*
>
> *"Not guilty," said the jury foreman. The words rang out in the courtroom. There was a silence for a moment, and then the room filled with applause.*
>
> *"How could this be?" Alexander had wondered.*
>
> *"There must be a mistake," Gary Alexander said to his wife and son.*
>
> *As a judge, he could not understand the verdict. The bastard was guilty, and he knew it; all the evidence was there! How could the jury get it wrong?*
>
> *As Cory's father, he was stunned, shocked, furious, and confused. What could have happened? What were they thinking? Something was definitely wrong with this verdict; he looked at his wife, who appeared fragile and pale. He saw a look in her eyes which he had never seen before, and it frightened him.*
>
> *The courtroom started to empty. Judge Alexander stared at his colleague presiding over the trial, trying to get some sort of justification*

from him. As Richard Curtis walked past the Alexander family a free man, he looked over at Cory and mouthed the words: "I love you," taunting him, letting him know he would see Cory soon.

It was all too much for Cory's mother, and something inside of her snapped. She opened her purse and pulled out a small handgun. In an instant, she pointed the gun at Curtis. The explosion of gunfire was deafening. One . . . two . . . three . . . four . . . five shots rang out as she continuously pulled the trigger. Cory's mother watched as Curtis's legs buckled from under him; he went down on his knees, and his body started to quiver. Suddenly, she felt her own body falling to the floor. One of the bailiffs had taken out his gun and shot her. Judge Alexander told me that he heard her whisper a prayer as she fell. She prayed to God, "Give me strength, dear Lord. There is one more bullet left. Please, God. Let me pull this trigger just one more time, please, God, please."

The people in the courtroom were screaming and fleeing. Judge Alexander said he knew he should have tried to stop his wife, but he froze, and his conscience could not let him stop her.

At last, Cory's mother screamed out, "Look into my eyes, you son of a bitch, and remember the words I told you in your office. Winter began in hell today." Her finger pulled back with every ounce of energy that her body had left. There was one last loud explosion, and the last bullet exited her gun and entered Curtis's heart. His body hit the ground with a final thump.

Her limp, bleeding body lay on the floor. Alexander dropped beside her, picking up his wife's bloodied body and holding her against him.

"I love you," he told her through the tears that were streaming down his face, his voice trembling as he sobbed. Then he screamed out, "Someone get an ambulance here now." His voice was quivering and desperate. She gasped with one last breath of air.

"I got him, didn't I?" his wife asked him, exhaling her last breath of life.

"You sure did, sweetheart, you sure did." He brushed back her hair from her face, his own hands now stained with his wife's blood. He cupped her lifeless body with his arms and held her against his aching heart. He was crying out to the Lord to forgive her and to forgive him for not stopping her.

He was yelling out, "No, God, no, how could you? Please, God, please do not let this be. Why, why, why is this happening?" He leaned over and then rocked back and forth, his tears dripping on what was once his beautiful wife. His groans and sobs echoed throughout the emptying courthouse. He saw his son Cory run out of the courtroom.

He didn't want to leave his wife's side, but knew he needed to run after his son to console him and tell him it was not his fault. None of this was his fault. He ran down the corridor after him, needing to convince his son everything would be OK, when even he knew it was a lie.

Finally, the judge told me, he caught up with Cory, dropping to his knees and holding him as tight as he could. The boy struggled to get free, but his father wouldn't let go. Cory beat his fists against his father's chest, but still he held on to his son until Cory ran out of energy.

"It's OK, son, it's going to be OK. I know you don't believe me right now, but I promise you it will be OK." Judge Alexander carried his son to the car and took him home to tell Cory's brother the sad news. That night, while alone in his room, the judge plotted his revenge, and he called it "the Order."

His own life, along with his sons', would never be the same again. Their lives were now shattered, and his new chosen path would lead him into a life of darkness and corruption. He vowed to avenge his wife and son by creating an elite membership of men who would act as the judge and jury. It would be his own judicial system, and everyone would play by his rules. He would no longer uphold the oath he had taken, to be unbiased and fair. The Order would need corruptible prosecutors as well as defense attorneys who would poorly represent accused criminals. There would also need to be corruptible judges who would hand down the maximum sentence, all designed to allow him to exact revenge on the judicial system which had failed his son and his wife. He knew this made him no better than the people he put away, but after what happened to his family, he simply did not care.

Joe looked over at the clock and noticed it was getting late. He remembered he'd promised Robin he would be back to pick her up and take her to the club. He threw on a clean pair of jeans and his Bass Pro shirt; he loved to go fishing. Taking the heavy binder containing the secrets of the Order, he placed it in his safe in the closet.

He could not wait until he could return to read more. The diary was both riveting and intriguing. He was still angry inside at what happened to Judge Alexander's son, but he knew this sort of thing still happened all the time. When he was a cop on the beat, he'd see a husband who went to work and treated his kids OK. But after having one too many drinks on a weekend, he'd turn into a violent ass that would beat up on his old lady. At other times, he would meet a mother with her kids in a grocery store, and then later that night, after she shot herself up on drugs, he would see her down on the corner hooking. It was easy to see why someone like Judge Alexander could turn into the very opposite of everything he ever believed in. Joe's heart started to thump a little harder, his lips tightened and his body movements were tense and stiff as he remembered his own childhood.

He was twelve years old and in the Boy Scouts. He needed his Polar Bear badge, which meant he would have to go camping. Joe thought this was going to be cool since he loved camping and fishing. His scoutmaster was a cop, and this impressed Joe because he knew one day when he was older, he was going to be a cop himself.

After kissing his mother good-bye, his scoutmaster picked him up, and they were off, just the two of them. The scoutmaster brought the tent, and all the food and equipment they would need for two days of camping. The woods they would be camping out in were five miles away from Joe's home, so it didn't take long for them to get to their destination. They set up the tent and threw their sleeping bags inside. Joe collected branches and broke them up into small pieces so they could make a fire. The scoutmaster brought premade sloppy joes, which they only needed to heat up before placing it on the buns. After supper, they cleaned up and sat around the fire talking until bedtime.

It was not as cold as a winter's night, but there was a chill in the air, with a brisk wind blowing. Joe kept on his jeans and T-shirt before slipping into his sleeping bag. The scoutmaster climbed into his sleeping bag as well, and Joe noticed him scooting closer and closer.

"How about we sleep in the same bag?" suggested the scoutmaster. "It's a cool evening, and we could stay warmer if we use our body heat." He placed his arm across Joe's body.

"No," said Joe, sternly slapping the scoutmaster's arm away. Joe scooted as far away from the scoutmaster's sleeping bag as he could; he was scared knowing what the scoutmaster had in mind. All he could do was pray to God that the man had gotten the message. He kept his body as stiff as possible and pretended to be asleep. The next morning Joe made excuses, saying he was not feeling well and asked to go home. The scoutmaster did as he asked, and the two drove home in silence.

Joe never did get his Polar Bear badge; he never went back to the Boy Scouts. He also never told a soul about what happened, and he could totally relate to the Alexander family's sense of anger and betrayal. He'd buried the memory of what happened to him for all these years, but now, reading the diary had brought those fearful hours back to his mind. He always swore that when he became a cop, he would take out scum like the perverted principals and scoutmasters of the world. He was glad he was able to believe in the system.

He thought of Harris, another crusader. They were like the dynamic duo, taking on the world of bad guys, and he chuckled aloud at the thought. *Sounds like a comic-book life to me.* Joe laughed again. His friendship with Harris meant a lot to him, finding they had so much in common. It was cool having someone like himself to exchange wits with.

He was glad he was taking a break to go pick up Robin; he needed to shrug off the old unpleasant memories he'd just relived. It was one of the reasons Joe was in his early forties and still not married. He was always uncomfortable in long-term relationships, but there was something different about Robin. He felt like himself with her. She had a great sense of humor, which was important to him. Something else struck him about her that he could not quite put his finger on yet. Maybe it was her intuition about people; she had this unique ability to tell the phony people from the honest ones. Whatever it was, it made her more attractive to him. It made him think about Harris and Markita. He was saddened for his friend as he noticed a great change for the better in Harris when Markita entered into his life; his friend had seemed more content, just like himself and Robin.

Joe managed to get to Robin on time, and they had a great time at the club. He enjoyed hearing Robin sing. She did a couple of numbers and, as always, won the karaoke competition. It made him proud when she told people she was his girlfriend.

It was getting late, and Joe needed to get home, eager to learn more about the Order. He dropped Robin off at home, giving her a lingering good-night kiss. Before leaving, he thanked her again for her recent help in retrieving what he called the answers to a friend's prayers, which really pricked Robin's curiosity, although she knew that in his kind of work he could tell her nothing.

He regrettably left her and returned home. As always, he grabbed a Coke out of the refrigerator and then made it to his room. He took the binder from the safe and placed it on the bed, looking at it with intrigue while changing into his night shorts. First fluffing up his pillows, and then turning on the night lamp, he picked up the diary to continue reading. The diary now read more like a history, with more dates and lists of notable names and events. The next section began after that fateful revelation from July of 1956.

What follows, began the next section of the diary, *is the history of the Order established by Judge Gary Alexander.*

> *July 4, 1956: Alexander spent months checking out various local and regional law professionals, along with other powerful men, carefully compiling a list of those he felt would be sympathetic to, and enthusiastic for, his cause. One of the first men he recruited was John Harris, the head of a powerful local law firm. He was also the head of the local KKK, which meant he was a man who would bend the rules to suit his own purpose. His grown son, Ronald, a young lawyer in his father's firm, was of a similar mind to the senior Harris, and Alexander felt that both men would be perfect members for the Order. Judge Alexander also knew he needed a safe place for the money the Order was bringing in from the lawsuits they were fixing, so the Harris and Harris law firm*

would be a perfect base from which to run the whole operation. Judge Alexander approached them with an offer neither man could refuse.

July 23, 1956: In a private meeting with the two lawyers, Alexander revealed damning information about the son, Ronald, that his father had thought was the tightest of secrets. He revealed that he knew what had happened with Ronald's young wife when he was off fighting in the war, and he also revealed that he knew about a certain racial hanging, for which Ronald was also responsible, along with the young man he'd framed for the crime. The elder Mr. Harris listened intently to what Judge Alexander knew, wondering what the judge's intentions were going to be. He didn't know how the man had found out about what Ronald had done, but he prayed that he wouldn't exploit Ronald's indiscretions.

Surprisingly to both Harris men, Alexander made them a generous offer: to be the judge presiding over the Johnson murder case, promising to ensure the boy was executed for his "crime" . . . in exchange for their loyalty to what he was calling the Order. All he asked of them then was that Mr. Harris send Ronald away for a while after the trial, so as not to bring attention to the law firm. Ronald's father agreed, believing it was a small price to pay for keeping his son out of prison. He felt that some of what his son had done was wrong, but because of his racial views, he wouldn't allow this event to cause the family a major scandal. He didn't let what his son did keep him awake at night.

Judge Alexander explained to John Harris that 10 percent of all the funds collected from lawsuits they were connected with would be set aside and put into an escrow for future use. This money would be used to pay off anyone who was needed to help the cause, and another 10 percent would go to John Harris for running the Order. The high-level officials and politicians who would be a part of the Order would require handsome pay for their favors, and the Harris and Harris law firm ensured the Order's success and survival.

Alexander told John Harris it would be his responsibility to initiate the members and use anything deemed necessary to keep them quiet and loyal. He would need to find out what skeletons were in their closets and use that information to his advantage to induce them into the Order. Once initiated, he would need to have enough dirt on them to keep them loyal and the Order a secret. He would need to use the dirt against the members just as Judge Alexander was using his own son's crimes against him. John Harris felt that Alexander was setting a fine example on how to run such a ruthless organization.

Jan 23, 1958: From there, things progressed quickly. Judge Alexander let the Harris's law firm win many cases and ensured

Ronald's case went as planned. It was not long before the word got out that if you had money and wanted to beat a rap, then you needed to hire the law firm of Harris and Harris. It gained a great reputation, as well as ruthless attorneys who were not afraid to do anything to win their trials.

May 14, 1961: The escrow fund accumulated a lot of money, fast. In the five years Ronald was gone, as per Alexander's instructions, his father grew the Order as well as their own firm, to triple its original size. The members now consisted of judges, lawyers, law enforcement, mayors, and even the governor. The Order garnered support from people in Washington, with a few contacts reaching as high as the White House. John Harris had enough power to influence the election of mayors, law enforcement, and senators, as well as other high-ranking officials that were a part of the growing list of elite membership.

August 27, 1962: Gary Alexander decided that revenge was no longer gratifying. It was time to get out. He was impressed at the way John Harris ran things and so offered him the whole organization. His only request was a promise to make the guilty pay. Ronald's father was ecstatic and honored, vowing to keep Judge Alexander's ethics and conditions of the Order in good standing. Not one child molester was to go free, not one; Alexander made that point very clear. It was, in fact, the motto of the Order.

November 28, 1962: It was around this time that young Ronald Harris returned home with his new wife and young daughter, Mary Ellen, along with an explosive secret: Mary Ellen was not the only child Ronald's second wife had borne him, but she was the only one that had returned home with them. It is part of Order records that Ronald delivered their first child at home, a son, telling his wife that the child was stillborn. His grief-stricken wife believed him, and life went on, but in reality, the son lived. Immediately after the "still birth," Ronald instructed his wife never to tell anyone about the first pregnancy or the dead son she had given birth to, or he would disgrace and desert her. She agreed, and she went on with their life, with no clue that her son had lived.

Order records show that Ronald sent the infant away, planning to transfer their son to Orlando later . . .

Joe stopped for a moment and rubbed his tired eyes. This information was proving to almost more than he could handle. He'd had no idea he would be seeing into a part of his friend Harris's life that he was sure Harris himself didn't know about. If this record were true, it meant that Harris might still have an uncle out there he knew nothing about. This was wild and getting uglier by the minute. Joe was worried about how Harris was going to take all this information, and he knew he'd have to be careful, as he didn't want to lose his friend.

His mind quickly went into detective mode, devising a plan of action. First thing in the morning, he would need to investigate to see if either of the Alexander boys was still alive. He would start searching the Internet, and with any luck, they would still be local. Time would be of the essence; Joe could not go to Harris without solid proof. The implications of the diary would devastate his friend, but he needed corroborating evidence to ensure Harris would believe that his grandfather was, and pretty much always had been, corrupt. He quickly read on, wanting to learn as much as he could before falling asleep.

February 1, 1963: Ronald Harris rejoined the firm as a lawyer upon his return to Orlando, but his main goal was to become a judge.

October 6, 1966: Judge Gary Alexander took his own life. He downed a bottle of sleeping tablets and left this world peacefully, leaving a note on his bedside table that read: "Judge ye not lest ye be judged, as I'll be."

March 29, 1967: In his time, John Harris was not only a good lawyer, but also a good businessman. He grew the firm by adding two senior partners, one of which was named Stewart Pope. He was the only other person who knew Ronald had hanged a young black man and framed Jake Johnson for the crime. John Harris knew Stewart was loyal and trustworthy, and he never told a soul about what his son Ronald had done. The other partner was a good bit older than Stewart and had been fired from his previous law firm under suspicion of money laundering. His skeletons made him a good match for the Order, and he came on board with a lot of wealthy clientele. His name was Joseph Masino, and he handled mostly real estate law and limited trust funds. The escrow account grew into a healthy pile of cash, thanks in great part to the addition of these two men to the Order.

December 21, 1967 Even though Ronald's father kept him up-to-date, the young man was amazed at how his father had grown the Order. Before his return, he had never dreamed for one minute how tight the network had become, nor how smoothly it ran. In the next five years after Ronald's return, the law firm took on two other senior partners, and now boasted a team of fifty lawyers and paralegals.

November 11, 1968: John Harris died of a heart attack. Control of the Order now went to his son, Ronald Harris. Ronald took the passing of his father hard, but accepted his new role with enthusiasm. It was an overwhelming responsibility, but one that Ronald embraced. He quickly added many other aspects of business to the Order, including an upscale brothel named Miss Bea's. Her girls all called her "Queen B," as she ruled her roost with a sharp tongue. It was a large house, which boarded numerous ladies of the night, and was perfect for the Order, as all its members were men. With this newest addition, the Order no longer had to pay for their favors in cash only; often, they could get a break by simply sending out a beautiful woman to accompany a member for the night or on a weekend getaway.

August 2, 1969: The Order enjoyed having Miss Bea as part of the organization, and when she died, they searched for a long time for a new madam. When they found a young brothel owner named Miss Dixie, she was more than willing to add her services to the Order in exchange for their protection.

April 7, 1970: Although Ronald had returned to the firm to work alongside his father, he had also been busy pursuing his dream of becoming a judge, and after the passing of his father, he felt that now, more than ever, it would be beneficial for him to leave the firm and run the Order from the bench. He planned to leave Stewart Pope in charge, while still running the firm as a silent partner. This way, he believed, his judgeship wouldn't be a conflict of interest and bring unwanted attention to him or his business dealings.

During his transition into his judgeship, however, his other most senior partner, Joseph Masino, double-crossed him out of his shares at the law firm. It happened during the time Disney announced it would be building a new theme park in Orlando. The location was a secret, and Joseph conveyed to Ronald that he was privy as to the location of the park. He told Ronald he should buy up as much land in Apopka as he could and that Disney would pay a premium for that land. Little did Ronald know that the land Joseph convinced him to buy in Apopka would be worthless to him until years later. Ronald had used his shares as collateral for the land, but when Disney announced that Kissimmee, Florida, was to be the new location of Disney World and not Apopka, Ronald's land was nearly worthless. His note became due, but when he didn't have the funds to cover the payment, Joseph offered to cover the amount of the loan in exchange for his shares of the firm. Ronald had no choice but to sell. It was evident in his writings, a copy of which are documented below, that Ronald snapped over the loss of his shares, and his life took on an eerie parallel to Gary Alexander's. He was now bitter and vowed his own kind of justice.

June 21, 1973: Ronald wrote in his own records: "The Executioner's first assignment was to assassinate Joseph Masino. The effect this portrayed to the other members solidified my power in their eyes. Any more disloyalty would result in dire consequences and possibly a visit from the Executioner."

: Order records show the origin of the Executioner, who became Ronald's enforcer. Soon after his birth, Ronald had transferred his unknown firstborn son from the Pennsylvania orphanage where he had been placed, to Orlando, training him to use a gun in secret. The boy grew up in an orphanage in Oakmont for his first eighteen years of life. When he was old enough to leave, Ronald set him up in a remote cabin and gave him the nickname the Executioner.

The ways of a loyal assassin were brainwashed into the boy's mind until he became the cold empty shell of a human that he was trained to be. Soon, it was not a job to the Executioner; it was a hunger that he sought. He didn't just kill his victims, he hunted them, he stalked them, and he jeered at them before he engaged in the final blow.

Once he fully trained the Executioner, Ronald moved him from out of the woods and into a small house on a quiet street in Orlando, where he would try to live a normal life until his services were needed.

March 19, 1976: Ronald soon secured his position as a judge, and his wealth, as well as his power became increasingly more predominant. The Harris and Harris law firm changed its name to the Practice, and he made sure their cases took first priority in his courtroom. They won most of them, thus still affording him a close association with the firm. He knew that one day, when the time was right, he would take back what was rightfully his. He wined and dined four senior partners, making two of them a part of the Order. A short time later, in December of 1982, his daughter married Mark Robertson, a young and upcoming lawyer whom Judge Ronald Harris had manipulated for his entire career, bringing him into a powerful position at the Practice. The judge made sure Mark won every one of his cases, including the expensive Bellamy trial in which Mark was able to buy out the other three senior partners' shares on his new father-in-law's orders. He then returned control of the firm, secretly, to Ronald.

In his famous case against accused child molester, Jonathon Bellamy, Mark Robertson took the Order back to its roots and followed through with its founding purpose: to convict and put away all child molesters, one way or another.

"Not one was to go free," Gary Alexander had ordered so many years before. "Not one."

In the case of Jonathon Bellamy, with Mark's help, Ronald made sure that he paid for his child molesting with his life. In his own turn, however, Ronald was cunning enough to make his own son-in-law pay ultimate price for hurting his daughter and young grandson . . .

"Oh my freaking god!" Joe shouted aloud, violently snapping the binder shut. "Harris's grandfather had his father killed!" He sat there stunned for a moment, then leaned back heavily on his pillow, the binder falling to the floor.

"Jesus Christ! That is too much. I can't tell Harris about this," exclaimed Joe. "What the hell am I supposed to do with this bloody information? God!" he exclaimed again. He jumped up out of bed and began pacing the floor.

"No freaking way, no freaking way," he kept repeating to himself. "What the hell am I supposed to do?" He was shaking his head, and his thoughts raced at a hundred miles an hour.

"My god, how did his grandfather ever get to be on our Supreme Court? What the hell is up with our judicial system?" Joe was beside himself. He couldn't wait to get back to the diary, but man, this was all too much, even for him! Joe began to think he was reading a script from a TV show like *Law and Order*, or even *Perry Mason*! *This shit cannot happen here in Orlando*, thought Joe. *This is the Sunshine State!* What he was reading only happened in the movies for God's sake, or a fiction book. There's no way this could be happening to his best friend.

Joe grabbed the book off the floor, flopped back into bed, punched his pillows into shape, and continued reading, determined to get to the bottom of this mystery.

> *August 6, 1983: In addition to his son-in-law, Ronald Harris also manipulated Governor Mason's career for years, mainly with large amounts of campaign contributions. It would be Governor Mason who would make Mark Robertson a judge, however briefly, so he could adequately provide for his wife and son. Ronald didn't foresee that his son-in-law would turn out to be a cheat and betray his precious daughter, but he made Mark pay for that mistake, judgeship or no.*
>
> *Ronald accomplished this by making sure that one of the women Mark chose to bed would be the woman who would destroy him. Ronald had Trudy Collins removed from Mark's life with a transfer to Tallahassee and into the governor's mansion. In return for her silence, on Ronald's orders, Governor Mason would take extremely good care of her. He was to make sure he bedded her himself, a chore to which he offered little protest; Trudy was a beautiful woman. It didn't take a lot of persuasion on the part of the governor to convince Trudy either; he was generous with his money and showered her with expensive jewelry, as well as other luxuries. What she did not know, however, was that another woman named Eleanor Woodsworth was also in the governor's bed for similar reasons.*
>
> *August 16, 1983: Eleanor once dated an Officer Parker, who was close to exposing the Order, along with Eleanor's help. In order to silence*

*the lawman, they framed Officer Parker's son in a drug raid and then
had Officer Parker himself executed. Eleanor's silence cost a steep price,
but then she found out about Trudy. Her tongue started to wag, and
the Executioner was brought in to silence her for good. Eleanor died
with many secrets.*

Joe was now frustrated. The diary had revealed so much, but on the issue
of what more Eleanor could have possibly known, it was not explicit as to what
secrets she was sworn to keep. Could it have something to do with Markita?

Joe banged his fist on the bed then growled. Joe could not believe what he
was reading about Officer Parker. He was stunned to read he was a part of this
sordid mess. Then there was Harris's father. He knew that Harris had always
hated him, but he wondered if Harris would feel differently about his father
when he realized how his grandfather had manipulated Mark's whole career.
How was he going to tell him that it was his own grandfather who had ordered
his father killed?

Joe was so worked up, he thought he was having a panic attack. How could
all this be?

Joe was even more convinced than ever that he would have to find some
solid proof that everything in the diary he was reading was true before telling
anyone anything, especially before telling Harris. Tomorrow wouldn't be soon
enough for the great Joe Marble to start his fact-finding mission. Joe's eyes
were becoming heavy; he was frustrated and exhausted, but found he could
not put the diary down.

"A few more pages and then I'll put it away," he said out loud, then continued
reading.

*October 2, 1984: Toward the end of his term, Governor Mason
started to become a problem. He had been making regular trips to
Orlando to visit with a special escort. He broke the rules by letting
himself have feelings for the woman. In addition to flapping her lips
too much, Eleanor Woodsworth had stolen a pair of earrings, valued at
$50,000, from Miss Dixie. The Executioner received instructions to kill
her and return the earrings, but Governor Mason stepped in by paying
the Order for the earrings in exchange for Eleanor's life. He could not
understand why she had done such a thing; he showered her with gifts
all the time. He didn't know she'd found out about Trudy. He was also
unaware that his wife had discovered the other two women in his life or
how it had devastated her. But he would soon know as his wife went on
to meet and confront both women, effectively ending both affairs.*

*January 1, 1985: Judge Harris vowed when Governor Mason was done
with Eleanor, the contract would be reinstated, and she would be history.*

"My god," said Joe. Harris's grandfather had had Eleanor Executed as well. *How many deaths had the man been responsible for?* Joe wondered.

"Damn," Joe was in disbelief with each page he read. Again, how the hell was he going to tell Harris his grandfather offed people whenever they got in his way? Joe knew Harris was devoted to his grandparents, and he was already devastated over Markita; how could Joe destroy more of his life by telling him that his grandfather was a racist and murderer? *My god*, thought Joe, *Could this get any worse?*

On the bright side, if he could call it that, at least now Joe now had the answer to Eleanor's decapitation. It didn't explain the head's location or the identity of the Executioner, so he'd have to read on, but he was sure that this diary was the answer to everything. Joe was beyond exhausted, so he closed the book, and then set it down beside him on the bed. He would get up early in the morning to see what else he could discover.

Chapter Sixteen

The Civil Suit

The next morning, Hugh called Harris into his office.

"Good morning, Harris. How are you today?" Hugh greeted him.

"I'm fine, sir, thank you for asking," said Harris politely.

"Well, now, son, have a seat. There is something I must go over with you." There went Hugh with the "son" again, thought Harris, as he gritted his teeth and bit his tongue.

"Oh, and what is that?" Harris asked, curious.

"I've been informed that the civil suit against Ronald will be heard today."

"But my grandfather never mentioned it," Harris said, unsure of what to think.

"I'm sure he didn't want to worry you. Henry Lane is a damn good attorney," Hugh said rather smugly.

"I'm not worried at all, sir, since my grandfather has nothing to hide. Someone is obviously trying to bring grief to my family with all these frivolous allegations," Harris snapped.

"Right, right, son, I'm sure that's all it is," Hugh said, knowing full well that was exactly what it was, especially as he was the one who orchestrated the suit. He would do anything to keep Ronald Harris distracted.

"It wouldn't surprise me if that bloodhound of a reporter Amber Andrews is all over this again today, and I wanted to warn you so you could stay close to the office. If you want, that is." Hugh tried to sound as sincere as possible.

"Thank you for your concern, sir, but I'll be fine. I can handle Andrews. She's a power-hungry reporter who doesn't always get her facts in order." Again, the distaste for the media showed in Harris's tone.

"Right, right," Hugh said repeating himself. "By the way, Harris, have you received a report from Marble yet concerning Judge Poe's assault?"

"No, sir, but I expect a full one any day now."

"Yes, yes, nasty business that, you know? The forensics people are taking their sweet time. They always seem to be backed up these days. Makes it hard for us, right, son?"

Harris gritted his teeth before answering.

"Yes, sir, they sure do. Marble is a good man, so I'm sure he's on top of things."

"Right, right, I'm sure he is." *Hugh was acting strangely*, thought Harris, as if he was there in the room, but his mind was elsewhere. Harris started to rise from his seat when Hugh spoke up again.

"While I've got you here, have you and Pope seated a jury for the Dixie Jackson case yet?" Harris sat back down.

"We have been in contact with each other."

"Well, you'd better speed things up. I received advanced word from Judge Poe yesterday, and the case is on his docket for two weeks from today."

"My word, that was quick, don't you think, sir?" Harris asked, curious to know how Hugh managed to get the case heard so quickly.

"That's why they keep electing him, son. The taxpayers feel like they are getting their money's worth out of him," Hugh managed a small laugh.

"I suppose so," Harris replied, not convinced of Hugh's theory.

"Why don't you get with Pope today, if you can, and get this trial moving?"

"Of course, sir," Harris started to stand again.

"Oh and if you talk to Ronald today, give him my best." Hugh tried again to sound as sincere as possible.

"Thank you, I will," Harris said as he left Hugh's office. As soon as he got back to his office, he called Nigel Pope.

"Nigel speaking, how may I help you?"

"Hey, Nigel, it's Harris Robertson from the DA's office."

"To what do I owe this pleasure?" asked Nigel, curious to know why Harris would be calling him although he had his suspicions.

"I was told by Hugh this morning that Dixie Jackson's case is going in front of Judge Poe two weeks from today," Harris explained to him, not happy with the idea they had to hurry and seat a jury in two weeks.

"Hell, man, the big guys didn't waste any time on this one, did they?" said Nigel pretending to sound surprised.

"I guess this is the part in the Constitution where one gets a speedy trial," Harris said, trying to make light of the situation.

"Hold on one second while I check my schedule, would you please?" asked Nigel.

"Sure thing, man," Harris was hoping he wouldn't take too long, as he wanted to call his grandfather and see if they could get together after his case was heard. He also wanted to call Joe to see what he was up to today. Nigel came back on the line.

"Harris, someone must be looking out for me. My schedule is pretty light for the rest of this week. How does tomorrow morning sound?"

"Perfect, how about we meet at the courthouse around nine?" Harris proposed.

"Great, see you then."

Judge Harris landed at Herndon Executive Airport in downtown Orlando, flying in on a private jet. Hugh was supposed to pick him up. It would give the two men time to talk about the upcoming annual meeting of the Order. When Ronald moved to Tallahassee to sit on the Supreme Court, he'd left the running of the Order to Hugh.

Hugh certainly was not looking forward to the meeting this year. It was his responsibility to make all the necessary arrangements for people attending, from flights, hotels, and rental cars, to all the plans for the meetings, catering, and entertainment. This year, the entertainment for the members would be a trying task for him, what with Miss Dixie in jail. The Order consisted only of men, and her boardinghouse was always a highlight for many of the members.

Dixie would always throw a lavish but discreet party for the Order's meetings. Only the most beautiful, as well as the most trustworthy, of her women received invitations to attend. It was a function they looked forward to all year because the compensation exceeded what they made annually.

When they were both safely on their way out of the airport, Hugh made sure he made his hardships well known to the judge.

"Don't worry, Hugh. We will have to fix the trial so she gets off in time for the meeting. I'm sure Fredrick Poe will be on board with our plan."

That statement scared the living daylights out of Hugh since he was the one helping Poe to put her away. *This is all getting so complicated and messy,* he thought.

Ronald's cell phone rang, and a smile spread across his face as he answered. "Why! Hello, Harris how are you, son?" said the judge, excited to talk to his grandson.

"I'm fine, sir, how about you?"

"Oh, not too bad. I'll be glad when these pesky Johnsons realize I had nothing to do with their son Jake. Maybe they will finally go away after today." Judge Harris knew they would be leaving this world after today no matter what; he was going to make sure of it.

"I hope so, sir. I think your peers should make a public apology to you as well. It's not right when people like the Johnsons can ruin a great man's reputation," said Harris proudly.

"Well, thank you, son. It's good to know I can count on my family."

"Yes, sir, always."

"How is your mother these days? Is she still having her lovers' spat with Joshua?"

"Yes, sir, but Uncle J grovels every day," Harris said with a little laugh.

"You and he are always the jokers. I must say Mary Ellen is being a bit stubborn, if you ask me."

"She certainly is, Grandfather. Maybe you could have a word on behalf of Uncle J. Everyone respects your opinion, sir."

"Oh, I wouldn't say that, Harris, but I'll do my best." The judge laughed from deep in his belly. "Hugh and I will soon be at the courthouse, son. Is there anything I can do for you? Or did you call to give me that special support of yours?"

Harris was stunned to hear the two men were together. Hugh never mentioned to him at that morning's meeting anything about picking up his grandfather today. In fact, his recollection was that Hugh had referred to Harris telling his grandfather good luck at the trial from Hugh. Now he finds out Hugh picked him up from the airport? *Something is not quite right with this picture*, thought Harris.

"Well, sir, I was wondering if we could get together after the hearing."

"Unfortunately not, son. I'm on a tight schedule, and I have to be back in Tallahassee this afternoon, but I'll return soon for a visit. If I have the time, I would have loved to spend it with you. Hugh tells me you're doing a fantastic job for him," he said, changing the subject.

"Thank you, Grandfather, I'll do my best. I can't wait for your next visit," said Harris a little disappointed.

"Tell your mother I owe her a phone call, and hug her on Sunday for me, please."

Harris felt a little guilty; he hadn't visited with his mother the previous Sunday because of the fight between his mother and Uncle J. Instead he'd shot hoops with Joshua. He made a mental note to make sure he went out there this Sunday.

"I will, Grandfather. I love you and good luck today."

"I love you as well, son."

"Oh, and tell Grandmother, I love her," Harris started, but he was too late; Ronald had already hung up.

Darnik, Harris said to himself as he grinned, thinking about his uncle J. Harris's next call was to Joe. The phone rang several times before he answered.

"Marble speaking," said a tired voice.

"Hey, Marble, you sound as if you're still in bed."

"As a matter of fact I am," Joe said yawning and now stretching out his body.

"What the hell are you still doing in bed at this hour? It's so not like you, early bird."

Joe yawned in his ear again. "Shit, man, I was up late last night reading." Joe rubbed his eyes with his free hand.

"Reading . . . is that what they call it now?" said Harris, laughing.

"I'm serious, man, I fell asleep reading." Joe stretched out again.

"Sure thing, Marble. I believe you. Thousands wouldn't. I could have sworn you told me you were taking Miss Robin out on a date last night. All I can say is it must be one hell of a book," Harris said, still laughing and not quite believing him.

"Let's put it this way, it's thicker than all the *Godfather* books put together, twice as heavy, definitely more attention grabbing, and more surreal." Joe decided he was not going to tell Harris about any of the things he read in the book until he could follow up on some of the facts. His friend was in enough pain as it was.

"I called to tell you I have two weeks to seat a jury in the Dixie Jackson case," said Harris.

"Damn it, man, that's quick, isn't it?"

"Yep, sure is. Hugh had me in his office this morning to tell me."

"It's OK, buddy, we'll be ready," Joe said with confidence.

This news was not coming at the best of times for Joe. It would limit the time he could devote to his "other activities." He would have to get an immediate start on finding out if either of the Alexander boys were still around, as well as help Harris prepare for the upcoming trial.

All in a day's work. Joe smiled to himself.

"By the way, Hugh wants me to find out if we can speed up forensics. He's waiting on a full report on Judge Poe's assault."

"I was going to call you about that this morning," Joe said, cutting him off.

"That would have been cool, Marble, but it's noon," said Harris teasing him.

"OK, jerk, I can screw up once every now and again, give me a break," Joe said yawning again.

"Give you a break? You must be kidding me, With the amount it costs the department to feed you every week? I don't think so. Not only that, it gives me great pleasure pulling your plonker."

"My what?" exclaimed Joe.

"Never mind, Marble, what were you going to tell me about Forensics?"

"I received two calls yesterday."

"Oh, I'm only now finding out?"

"Hold your horses there, big guy, they called pretty late. The SWAT team guys fired two bullets each, and we only recovered three, meaning the other bullet likely hit our suspect. I'll check with the hospitals to see if anyone came in that night to have a bullet extracted. The blood samples I took from the outside grounds showed they matched to a P. Smith, but that's the only information they had on him. They couldn't even give me a first name."

Harris listened in silence. It made sense; suffocation and decapitation were the Executioner's MOs. But why would he want to kill Judge Poe?

"Are you still there, Robertson?" asked Joe.

"Yes, sorry. I'll have to check this Smith character out," Harris answered, trying to say as little as possible about him.

"That's OK buddy, I'll start on it today."

"No, it's OK, Joe. I'll get this one. You continue looking into Dixie Jackson's business, please. I'm going to need some more information on her in a hurry," Harris snapped. He didn't want his friend anywhere near the Executioner, and he couldn't divulge any info about him to Joe because of his promise to Hugh.

"Well, Harris, it's been swell talking to you, but I need to get my lazy ass up out of bed and get this day started," Joe said, stretching out for the last time before throwing back the bed covers, forgetting about the diary.

"I'm going to be a bit busy for the rest of the week, but you know how to get a hold of me if you need to," Harris said.

"Later," said Joe.

"Later."

Joe needed to get a shower and head out to his office. He couldn't believe half the day had already gone. He was behind schedule and backed up like a cheap suit, he told himself. He didn't even have time to read the newspaper. He did grab his Coke on the way out though.

Amber Andrews, along with her camera crew, had already set up their equipment in anticipation of the judge's arrival. When he approached the courthouse, she was ready for him.

"Judge Harris, isn't it true your father was the head of the KKK and you were also a member before becoming the Grand Dragon of the Realm here in Florida?" she demanded, shoving a mic in his face.

The judge made no comment. He didn't even look at her.

"Isn't it also true you hanged an African American man and framed another man, Jake Johnson, for the crime?"

Still the judge made no comment. Amber Andrews sped up, trying desperately to get into the judge's face.

"And isn't it true that Stewart Pope knew about what you did and now he's dead?"

Amber was getting more brutal with every question. Although his face didn't show it, Judge Harris had a few questions of his own. The first among them being how did she know all that she did?

"I would like to ask you one more question, Judge Harris." Andrews was back in his face. He would have loved to shove her down the stairs, but instead, he continued to ignore her. She didn't give up.

"Are you the head of some secret society club?" She finally hit a nerve, and Judge Harris now retorted.

"Miss Andrews, you have tried persecuting my family for years, just as Miss Nancy Marble did many years ago. I'll tell you like I told her: I've no idea from where you get these ludicrous allegations, and if you continue down this path, your news station will be entering the court system—as a defendant. Have a good day." He ended the conversation and entered the courthouse as quickly as he could.

"That was too close for comfort," Hugh quipped.

"You're damn right it was," Judge Harris hissed back at him. "I want her gone! You understand me, Gallagher?"

"Yes, sir, loud and clear."

Ronald Harris entered the courtroom.

Henry Lane was sitting with the Johnsons. Ronald went to sit down as the judge entered.

"All rise, the Right Honorable Judge Peacemaker," The judge entered and immediately sat down.

"Please be seated," the bailiff announced.

The bailiff read the case number and then announced that they were here for the civil suit against Ronald Harris for $250,000. Judge Peacemaker was well aware of who Ronald Harris was and greeted him with respect. The judge looked over at Henry.

"Good morning, Mr. Lane."

"Good morning, sir," Henry responded.

"I've read the suit which you bring forth before this court, Mr. Lane, and quite frankly, I'm a little surprised. You state here your only witness is deceased. A first year law student knows that is hearsay, Mr. Lane, so I'm sure you have something else up your sleeve, am I right?"

When Henry didn't answer right away, Judge Peacemaker spoke to him more sternly.

"Mr. Lane, please don't tell me you have wasted the court's time with a frivolous lawsuit. I'm sure it is not your intention to try my patience, am I correct?"

"Yes, Your Honor. If you please I would like to explain to the court."

"Oh Mr. Lane you have my full attention, but I'm warning you, your explanation better be good, or I'm going to charge you with contempt of court."

"Yes, Your Honor." Henry was not happy about this, but $250,000 was too much money to pass up on for losing.

"Your Honor, I beg the court's indulgence. Stewart Pope was a well-respected attorney. I have the letter he wrote to the Johnsons, begging them to come to his retirement home. He told them he was there, in the room, when their son Jake told Ronald Harris he couldn't have hanged the African American man since he was elsewhere, committing a rape."

"Mr. Lane, surely you're not basing your civil suit on the ramblings of an Alzheimer's patient, because so far, what you have presented here continues to try my patience. You have dragged one of our most prestigious and honored judges here with no evidence whatsoever to support your allegations."

"I beg Your Honor's pardon, but again, the Johnsons would like to have their son's name cleared for a crime he didn't commit."

"I've heard enough, Mr. Lane. Your case is dismissed. You can pay the clerk $5,000 on your way out for wasting the court's time and mine. You know better than this, Mr. Lane. You surprise me." Judge Peacemaker turned to Judge Harris and smiled apologetically. "Ronald, I apologize for the court's indiscretion, and I appreciate your indulgence."

"It's fine, Judge Peacemaker," Ronald responded with benevolence. "I've always believed in upholding the law, and I understand the overzealousness of some attorneys. It seems they prefer grandstanding rather than getting to the truth. Perhaps they should get an acting job." He gave a sly look in Henry's direction. Turning back to Judge Peacemaker, he said, "I don't hold you responsible, Judge Peacemaker. You have been most tolerant about the situation."

Judge Peacemaker gave a friendly nod to Ronald as if to say thank you. He looked over at Henry Lane, giving him a final lecture warning him never to bring forth such a ridiculous case, especially to his courtroom. If he ever did, next time Judge Peacemaker promised to throw him in jail for criminal stupidity.

The bailiff announced, "The court is adjourned." Judge Harris was relieved that finally the Johnsons could no longer go after him. But Amber Andrews was eagerly waiting for him outside the courtroom.

"Judge Harris, are you going to step down from the Supreme Court?"

"No, Miss Andrews, I'm not. The Johnsons proved nothing. The case was thrown out, and I was acquitted as I should have been all along."

"That may be so, Judge Harris, but you know you're guilty."

"Miss Andrews, you'd better be careful of the accusations you're throwing around, or you might find yourself in the middle of a lawsuit for slander," Ronald Harris snapped.

Andrews refused to back down. "I'm not afraid of you, Judge Harris. I can and will prove you're guilty."

"Well, you keep wasting your time trying, Miss Andrews. It seems to me you have no other excitement in your life. Maybe you should look for a man." Judge Harris pushed her and her cameras out of his face. He was getting angry now and was trying to contain himself, but she was pushing all his buttons.

"That was quite a sexist remark, Judge Harris," she shouted out at him.

"That's right, Miss Andrews, and that's exactly what I said you needed." He was so furious with her, he was not thinking about what he was saying.

"You went a bit too far there, Ronald," Hugh said, getting him into the car as soon as he could. "I have a feeling that remark is going to come back and bite you in the ass."

"Bitches like her shouldn't be allowed on our streets, let alone be reporters," Judge Harris said with a snarl. "Like I said earlier, Gallagher, I want her gone permanently. You understand me perfectly, right?"

Hugh knew exactly what he meant.

They drove back to the airport in silence as Hugh pondered his firsthand knowledge of the kind of venom Judge Harris was capable of spitting.

Harris made a late stop and picked up his favorite chili cheese dog, light on the onions, with a thin whipped strawberry milkshake, then took it home to eat. He went into the living room with his meal, sat down, turned on the news, and begun to eat.

"There was more controversy concerning Supreme Court Justice Judge Harris today. Amber Andrews will give us her report when we return," said the news anchor. *Oh, boy,* thought Harris, *What now?* He found Amber Andrews as bad as Nancy Marble. He had a sneaking suspicion that these two women simply liked hounding his family. Just then, Harris heard the kitchen door close.

"Hey, Uncle J, is that you?"

"No, it's the boogeyman," Joshua said.

"Quick, come watch the news. It's about Grandfather's case today," Harris said. He was expecting huge apologies from everyone, as his grandfather was a great man, but when Joshua saw Amber Andrews's face, he knew it was not going to be the good news his nephew was hoping for.

"So, Amber, what happened with the civil suit against Judge Harris today?" asked the news anchor.

Andrews's face filled the screen, and she began her rant. "You will be totally surprised and outraged at our Supreme Court justice's behavior," she said. "He showed his true colors today." Amber ran the tape with Ronald telling her she needed a man to have sex with since she had no life.

"Oh my gosh," gasped Harris. "I can't believe he said that! The media will crucify him. She must have pushed him to his limits for him to say something like that to her, don't you think?"

Joshua was not surprised in the least at anything the judge said or did, not after what he had done to Mark. He didn't want to hurt Harris's feelings though by running his grandfather down, so he kept these thoughts to himself.

"I'm sure you're right, son," is all that Joshua could muster up to say.

"By the way, Uncle J, Grandfather is going to talk to Mom about you and her. Even he thinks she's carrying things a bit too far and is being extremely stubborn."

"You should have told him to stay out of our business," snapped Joshua to Harris's surprise.

"I'm sorry, Uncle J, I thought we needed all the help we can get."

"Your mother has every right to be angry with me. I deserve it. I also know our love will survive anything. Even after death, she will love me as I loved her."

That was a strange thing to say to Harris though; what on earth did his uncle J mean?

"Are you going to visit with your mother this weekend, young whippersnapper?" said Joshua trying to change the subject.

"Sure am there, pardner," said Harris in a bad Southern accent.

"Good thing, son. Your mother needs to know you support and love her."

"You know, Uncle J, that's what makes you so precious. You're a hopeless romantic."

"Only when it comes to your mother. My life didn't come alive until I met her. She woke up every emotion in me, even ones I didn't know I had."

"Like what, Uncle J?" Harris loved to hear stories about him and his mother.

"Well, let's see. There was this one time we were staying in a hotel waiting for someone to pick us up to take us to the airport. I wanted to christen the room one last time, and of course, your mother thought I was crazy, but she agreed. We finished moments before our driver knocked on the door. Only someone who truly loved me would do that." Joshua had a tear in his eye telling Harris that story.

"Uncle J," Harris choked out, a look of horror on his face. "That was *way* too much information. You guys are like teenagers, I swear." Harris started laughing, helping to relieve some of the awkwardness of the situation.

"You wait, young 'un. When the right woman comes along, she will be able to make you do things you never thought possible."

"I thought I had found her, Uncle J." Harris lowered his voice, turning sad.

Joshua's heart ached for him at that moment. How could he have been so inconsiderate, talking about being in love when Harris was still in so much pain?

"I'm sorry, Harris. I'm so thoughtless sometimes."

"No, you're not, Uncle J. You're one in a million and the kindest individual I know. You know I love you with all of my heart. It's not your fault, it's that tramp Trudy." Harris was seething as he spoke her name.

"Now, son, it is not nice to call people names. We all make mistakes, well, except me of course." Harris's grin returned. Only his uncle J could make that happen.

"Well, Uncle J, I think I'm going to call it a night and turn in."

"Oh yeah, what you going to turn into, an ugly frog?" Harris got up from his chair, walked past Joshua to take his trash out to the kitchen, and mocked him.

"Gribbit, gribbit."

"Do you need a handsome prince to kiss you, Froggy?" his uncle J started to walk toward him.

"Ah, no, no, don't you dare try it," Harris said, running quickly toward the stairs. Joshua watched him as he climbed the stairs. Josh had tried not to be, but he was angry that the only true love his nephew found was his brother's tramp daughter. Now he was mad at himself because he called Trudy the very name he told his nephew not to use. He called himself a hypocrite and went to bed.

Harris lay in bed thinking about Markita and how close they had come to making love. His heart still ached for her. He was angry with himself because he should not be having these feelings for his own sister. *Stop it*, he told himself. He rolled over trying to clear his mind of her so he could sleep.

Judge Harris was in his chambers early the next morning going over the previous day's events, smiling smugly at the thought of defeating the Johnsons once again. He was slightly aggravated with himself for letting Amber Andrews get under his skin. He noticed the older he got, the quicker he lost his temper. He was startled when his private line rang as it was still early. He was even more surprised at the voice on the other end of the line.

"Hello, Judge Harris."

"Well, well, well, if it isn't Trudy Spencer or is it Mason? You sleep around so much who knows what name you go by today. To what do I owe the pleasure of this call?"

"It is a courtesy call."

"Forgive me for being coy, Trudy, but you have never been courteous, so you must want something. How much is it going to cost me?" he asked sarcastically.

"You know, I didn't have to call you, so if you want to be kept in the loop, you might want to try a little harder to be nice to me."

Judge Harris had little to no use for Trudy, and as far as he was concerned, she was lucky to be alive after the pain she caused his daughter with her sordid affair with Mark. He had many fires to put out today, so he certainly was in no mood to be nice to her.

"Well, woman, spit out whatever it is you think I need to know. I'm a busy man."

"Markita received a visit from a Joe Marble," she began, but the judge cut her off.

"Joe Marble lives in Orlando, what would he be doing in Tallahassee, visiting your brat?"

Trudy was angry at the way he talked about her daughter, but that was one of the reasons for calling him: to let him know about her and Harris. She wanted her daughter to have nothing further to do with him or his family.

Trudy knew exactly how dangerous Ronald Harris could be and to what lengths he would go whenever a situation didn't suit him.

Once he found out about her and Mark, he used her not only to betray him, but because of her, Mark lost his life. Trudy shuddered at the thought of even talking to the judge, but knew she had no choice, especially if she wanted to keep Markita safe.

"While Markita was interning down in Orlando," she tried again, but the judge cut her off once more.

"What the hell do you mean 'interning in Orlando'?" He was almost screaming at her.

"I know it was a bad idea, but I didn't dream Harris would be walking in his father's footsteps, and Markita wanted desperately to intern there."

"You stupid, stupid woman! No wonder you're a blond! You haven't a thing in that head of yours. Of course, Harris is following in our family footsteps. He's a brilliant attorney and one day will replace me as a Supreme Court judge."

He was livid now and couldn't believe Hugh had not uttered a word of this to him. He would deal with him later.

"So pray tell me, what the hell Marble was doing there?"

"Apparently, Harris and Markita were seeing each other, and before you explode," she cautioned him as she heard him gasp, "I took care of their relationship. I implied to Harris that Markita was his sister, and it broke them up immediately."

Judge Harris was coming unglued; he couldn't believe what he was hearing. He remembered Harris saying he was going to bring a girlfriend for a visit with him and his grandmother, who was so happy for him, but Trudy's brat? It couldn't be. Although he had to admit, it was fortunate for her that she had intervened, or he would have taken matters into his own hands. Hugh was going to need a good explanation for this one, or his head will be next.

"I think this Marble fellow was here checking birth records. A friend of mine from the hospital gave me a call and said someone had been asking around for information. I called you immediately."

"That's the first smart move you have made in your life. Leave things with me. I'll take care of Marble. You keep that brat of yours away from my grandson, or you know what will happen to her. Do you hear me, woman?"

"Loud and clear," said Trudy.

"Is this conversation concluded?" Judge Harris asked, still extremely irritated with her.

"Actually, no, it isn't." *I wish it were*, thought Trudy, but she knew she had to tell him everything she knew, or it could come back to haunt her.

"I also overheard a conversation in a deli over on Bourbon Street. Something about a guy, likely Joe Marble, who had been in there asking questions about Eleanor Woodsworth."

"Well, don't beat about the bush, woman. I know you despised the whore, so tell me what you know." The judge's voice was getting even more agitated with her.

"I don't know any specific details. All I heard him say was some friend of Eleanor's from Orlando was looking for her, and his name was Joe."

"That doesn't tell me a damn thing, woman, but I guess I should thank you for at least keeping me in the loop, which is more than I can say for some people." He was referring to Hugh. "You know, if you hear anything more, you are to let me know immediately, right?" he instructed her.

"Yes, sir," she said as she heard the phone disconnect, glad the conversation with him was over.

Judge Harris was not used to unexpected surprises such as the one he'd just received. He was accustomed to knowing everything happening around him before it happened. It was the only way to keep things in control. Heads would roll with this one, the first being Hugh if he had anything to do with this matter.

Harris was busy interviewing potential jurors all week. It was going to be hard to find an unbiased jury for this case. The women seemed to want to crucify Dixie Jackson, and the men wanted a piece of her body. Harris was glad when the week was finally over; he planned to spend some quality time with his uncle J, as well as his mother over the weekend.

Saturday morning, Harris and Josh cleaned the condo. The maintenance workers mowed the little bit of lawn out front, then Harris ran to the store. He picked up a couple of different frozen pizzas for the football game playing that afternoon, which he planned on watching with his uncle J. The Dallas Cowboys were playing the Miami Dolphins; it should be a good game, especially since his uncle always rooted for the Cowboys.

They enjoyed watching the game together and ribbed each other all afternoon as they cooked and ate the pizza. Before they knew it, Saturday had flown by.

"I think I'm going to call it an early night, Uncle J. I'm going over to see Mom tomorrow, so I need to look rested, or she'll worry," said Harris.

"Why call it a night, maybe it doesn't like that name," said Joshua, always with the groan-inducing wit.

"OK, OK, I get it. I love you, Uncle J, and hopefully I'll see you for a bit in the morning before going over to Mom's," Harris said, slapping the high-five hand extended out to him.

"I love you too, son, and tell your mother I love her for me tomorrow, please."

"Oh, you want me to tell her you love her? I would have thought you would have wanted me to tell her the duck joke." Harris ducked as he saw a pillow flying his way.

"You're the only duck around here," jeered Joshua.

"Night, Uncle J."

"Night, son," said Josh.

Harris lay in bed for quite a while, starting to write his opening arguments for Miss Dixie's trial. His mind wandered to Markita several times before he finally fell asleep.

Chapter Seventeen

Rocky Road

Harris awoke early Sunday morning, showered, shaved, then dressed in some casual clothes. He ran downstairs to the smell of coffee, which Joshua had already brewed.

"Thanks, Uncle J, you're a gem."

"You're right there, son, a diamond in the rough I would say."

"Man, how do you come up with that stuff so early in the morning?" asked Harris, taking his first sip of the tasty coffee.

"I'm a born natural." Josh smirked.

"A natural nut," Harris laughed.

"Thought you got me there, did you, whippersnapper?"

"Well, Uncle J, you are so much like the nutty professor." Harris was now cracking up, knowing he had outwitted his uncle.

"Well, talking of nuts, did you hear the one about the squirrel that went to the pharmacy to buy nuts?" said Josh with a straight face.

"No way, Uncle J. You cannot tell that joke with a squirrel." Harris was having a hard time drinking his coffee as he was laughing so hard.

"The clerk took him over to the nuts and proceeded to ask the squirrel how he would like to pay for them."

"Squirrels don't have bills, Uncle J, so the joke isn't going to work," Harris warned him.

"That's right, son, the squirrel scurried out without paying."

"That isn't even funny," said Harris, cracking up anyway.

"Well, I don't know how you can say that. It looks to me as if you need to change your underwear, you're laughing so hard."

"It's because you're such a riot." With a wave, Harris picked up his car keys, placed his coffee cup in the sink, and headed out to his mother's.

"Later, Uncle J. Be good."

Mary Ellen was happy to see her son. She hugged him tight for several minutes after he arrived.

"I've missed you," she said.

"I've missed you too, Mom." He gently disentangled himself from his mother's embrace. "I'll be right back. Let me put the rocky road ice cream in the freezer."

"You didn't have to bring that, son," she said with a frown. "We only ever had it for your Uncle J more than anything else."

"I know, Mom, but I thought we could have some for dessert anyway."

Mary Ellen looked closely at her son for a moment, then took his hand. "Come sit with me please," she said, pulling him toward the two Queen Anne chairs, which sat in front of the fireplace facing each other.

"I went to visit your father's resting place yesterday," she stated solemnly.

"That's nice," was all Harris could think to say.

"I straightened up the fence and placed some new flowers around the stone."

Again, all Harris could say was, "That's nice."

"Your uncle J would be proud of me," she said with a small smile. "I put my cell phone down on his headstone and told him I would leave it there if he would just call me once in a while."

He agreed that his uncle J *would* find that funny, but he started to wonder where she was going with all this talk of his father. She knew he didn't like her talking about him, but she continued anyway.

"He was a good man when I met him, son, full of life and ambition. We went to every rally and high-society function there was. We were known as MME: Mark and Mary Ellen, together forever." Harris sat in his chair listening intently.

"I don't know what happened to him, son. But I feel it was my fault the marriage failed. When we met, when we first got married, I was so young and free-spirited, maybe even a little on the wild side, so independent and carefree. But when I got pregnant with you, I became needy. My hormones were raging. My blood pressure rose to extreme highs, and I started to get massive migraine headaches. One night I screamed out at your father just for breathing." Mary Ellen paused for a moment, thinking back to that night and how scared she'd made Mark.

Harris thought it a little on the humorous side, but didn't laugh for his mother's sake. He continued to listen without comment.

"The pressures of the judicial system started to get to him, you know? He was the finest attorney Orlando ever had. He was suave and debonair, like an award-winning actor on his own stage." She shook her head sadly. "He really believed that rat Jonathon Bellamy was innocent. It destroyed your father when he started to realize that the man was nothing more than a con artist. A very good one, at that. It even made your father start to doubt himself."

Harris was intrigued. This was the most his mother had ever spoken to him about his father.

Tears started to fill Mary Ellen's eyes as she continued. "Something changed with him, and I don't know why. He became violent, arrogant, conceited, and ugly. We grew distant, spending more and more time alone in different rooms of the house, and I became so lonely. I know he loved me, Harris, but I turned to your uncle Joshua because he was so kind and gentle. I could feel his love and compassion through the phone line whenever we talked. He was always there to help me pick up the pieces after one of your father's drunken nights. I don't know what I would have done without him." She had said his name with a little smile.

"Joshua was always there for me," she went on. "I knew he loved me from our first hello. I tried to discourage him many times, but something always pulled me back to him. He was always the prankster. One summer I was in the pool floating on my lounge chair, soaking up the sun when the phone rang, and I answered it. It was Joshua wanting to talk to your father, so I handed him the phone. The two of them conspired together, and next thing I know, your father turned my lounge chair upside down, and I went under. We all laughed so hard. I swore I would get your uncle back for that one." Harris laughed out loud. He could imagine his uncle doing that, but it surprised him that his father went along with the plan. Harris had always thought of him as the stuffy kind.

Mary Ellen continued, but it seemed her mind was all over the place.

"I knew about Trudy, you know. Your mother isn't a stupid woman, just naive," she said, looking him in the eye. "She was an evil woman. We were at a huge function for your father this one night. He got up to make his acceptance speech for some award when I received an emergency message to go to the front desk. When I arrived, they gave me a message that you were sick. I found out later that Trudy left the message, knowing I would immediately leave without a moment's notice. She also knew how angry it would make your father. Trudy was right. He was livid with me and embarrassed that I was suddenly no longer at his side. The governor was there after all. When he didn't come home that night, I knew exactly where, and with whom, he was for the night. I smelled her on his clothes the next day. I could always smell her," she said, wrinkling her nose.

Harris was getting angry inside; he had no empathy for Trudy himself, and he knew exactly how his mother felt when it came to that woman.

"As soon as I saw Markita, chills ran down my spine. I saw Trudy in her, and I wanted to scream it out, but I knew how much you liked her." She looked at him, her eyes begging for him to understand.

Harris felt so badly for his mother. He could feel her pain, and he realized how much it must have hurt her when he brought Markita to the house.

"It doesn't matter, Mom, she's in the past, and it's over between us," he said, trying to console her.

"Trust me, son, it's never over when it comes to Trudy. Look how she's still intruding into our lives."

"You're wrong, Mom. They will *never* be a part of our lives."

"Markita is your half sister, Harris." Mary Ellen winced at the words, but she knew he had to hear her say this. "Once you have gotten over the initial shock, you will have questions and maybe even want a sibling relationship."

"Never," snapped Harris.

"Never," Mary Ellen repeated. She moved on, determined to leave the subject alone, at least for now.

"It was about then when your father started to get worse. He hurt me more and more. I started to withdraw. I had to stop seeing your grandparents, my own parents! I didn't want them to see the bruises your father left on me."

Mary Ellen pulled a handkerchief from the pockets of her shorts, as if she knew she would need it today. "I poured all my love into you, Harris. You were my world. I felt I had failed your father, so I wanted to make everything right by giving you all of me. When your father began taking his anger out on you, I retreated from him completely, spending all my time with you. I even moved into the spare room. The nights I knew he was drinking, I slept with you so I could protect you.

"Then your Uncle Joshua left for a mission in Africa with his church, or so I thought. I was all alone. How was I going to protect you and myself against your father? I couldn't tell anyone. It would have ruined his career, which would have ruined your future. I couldn't tell your grandfather because I feared what he would have done to your father. I don't know if you know this, but my father is the one who guided Mark's career and helped him get where he was in life. But instead of being grateful to your grandfather, he resented him. To this day I don't know why."

Mary Ellen wiped away her tears. Harris felt so many emotions; he was uneasy, awkward, angry, and sympathetic all at once. He wasn't sure what to do or say to his mother at this point. He had never seen her open up like this.

Mary Ellen's voice suddenly turned angry. "It was then that you were *taken*." She emphasized the last word with bitterness in her voice. "I thought I was going to go crazy. Harris, you don't know, could never know, how devastated I was. I was a shell of a person here on earth, but my thoughts and heart were somewhere else. I hated your father, I wanted him dead, and I never felt those kinds of feelings before. I needed your uncle Joshua so much, but he left me alone as well. Now I come to find out he was the one who took you. Son, I don't know where to put all those feelings."

Harris promptly took over. "You put them where they should go, Mom, and that is in the past. He saved my life! He helped make me the man I am today! I know you loved Dad, but he could never have stepped up to the plate as Uncle J did. He restored my hearing and made sure I not only caught up with life, but also excelled at it. You have to let it go, Mother." Harris went to his mother and hugged her.

Mary Ellen placed her tearstained face on Harris's shoulder. "I'm so sorry for the mess I've made of things, son."

"You haven't made a mess of anything, Mom. You needed to put things into perspective and sort out your feelings. Uncle J is the best thing that happened to us. God blessed us by putting him in our lives. I wouldn't change a thing, Mom. I love him dearly."

"As do I, son," said Mary Ellen.

"Then why don't you pick up the phone and tell him? He has been a wet willy without you."

"A wet what?" Mary Ellen asked, trying not to laugh through her tears.

"It's OK, Mom, it's one of those Uncle J sayings. As much as I love him, I sure will be happy when you take him back. He's a pain in the arse to live with."

"Now, Harris, how can you say that? Your uncle J is perfect to live with. He does everything. He doesn't let me lift a finger."

"Exactly," Harris said with exaggeration. "That's what I mean, Mom. My condo is as clean as a whistle."

"You should thank your lucky stars he helps out around the place. Most men are not like him." Harris was so happy to hear his mother defending his crazy uncle again. He smiled at his mother.

"Why are you smiling at me?" she asked, smiling back.

"Because you are a beautiful woman, and you and Joshua belong together."

Mary Ellen gave him a smile and wiped away the last of her tears. "I've babbled on for so long, and it's late, Harris. Are you hungry?"

"Not at all, Mother. I'm ecstatic, and I want you to call Uncle J and get him home with you where he belongs. I'll pick up a hamburger on the way home."

"Would you at least like a bowl of rocky road?"

"No way! Save it for Uncle J. He's going to want a bowl when he gets here." He leaned in and gave her another hug. "You know, Mom, I love you so much."

"I love you too, son, and thank you so much for listening to me."

"No problem. I'm glad I was able to help you put everything in its rightful place. You needed time to sort everything out in order to reach the right decision for everyone."

"You are a wonderful son. You have the love and compassion of your uncle Joshua, and I'm truly grateful for that."

Giving his mother a huge smile, Harris hugged her once more and rushed out the door. He couldn't wait to get home to tell his uncle J the good news.

Harris nearly flew into the condo, calling for his uncle. "Hey, Uncle J, where are you? I'm home."

"Darnik, boy! I'm in the living room, not in Texas! What the heck is up with you, boy?"

"You know, Uncle J, I hate to tell you this, but I'm a man now, not a boy."

Joshua bent over holding his stomach. "A man are you, huh? That's a good one," he chuckled. "So do you have something to tell me?" Joshua asked with a huge grin on his face.

"Oh, darnik, she called you first," Harris said, faking a pout. "I wanted to be the one." Joshua cut him off. "Oh, you are the one, all right. I don't know what you said to convince your mother, but you are my hero. I never thought she would budge. She's a stubborn lady."

"Yes, she is, but she loves you more than she is stubborn. I'm so elated for the both of you. You belong together. You are a match made in heaven."

"No truer words were ever spoken, Harris. I'll love her with all of my heart even from heaven."

Harris's brows furrowed; he wasn't sure quite how to take his uncle's last statement, but chose to let it go. He wanted to savor the moment of his parents getting back together.

"Wow, Uncle J," Harris said, looking around. "I can't believe you are not packed yet."

"Who says I'm not? What do you think I was doing while you took your sweet time in getting here? My case is on the edge of the bed waiting for me."

"Then why don't you get the heck out of here and go home?"

"Are you trying to get rid of me, young man?" asked Joshua, a little sad at the thought of leaving him.

"Not at all. I'm going to miss you, but don't take that as an invitation to stay." Harris walked toward Joshua and held out his arms.

"I've enjoyed your company and will miss you dearly, Uncle J, but please go get Mom before she changes her mind." They hugged each other tight, then as always, they high-fived.

"I'll miss you too, whippersnapper. Thank you so much for having me. I know I can be an annoying old man and you tolerate me, but I love you like my own, you know that," Joshua said, tearing up.

"Get out of here before I beat you, old man," Harris said mockingly, doing everything he could to hold back his own tears. "You know how much I love you, Uncle J. You are welcome here anytime, but I know you won't be staying again. Mom and you are going to spend eternity together, right?"

"You got that right, sonny boy."

Joshua went upstairs and looked around his temporary room once more. Even though he was ecstatic to be going home, he'd enjoyed his time with his nephew; it brought back memories of the two of them in staying at the cabin. He quickly put those thoughts out of his mind. Those actions got him into this mess in the first place. He picked up his suitcase, then left to go downstairs where Harris was waiting on him.

"Drive home safely, old man, and give Mom a big hug for me when you get there. And just to let you know," he whispered, giving his uncle a wink, "there's a tub of rocky road ice cream in the freezer with your name on it."

Joshua hugged Harris again, holding him tight. "You are the best nephew an uncle could ever have."

"I know," Harris said.

Joshua gave him a parting wink and headed out through the kitchen to his car. Harris heard the garage door open and then close and smiled with relief that all was right with his parents once again.

He sat in his chair in his living room, turned on his stereo, and listened to some music. His thoughts, as usual, turned to Markita; he wished they could reunite just as his mother and Joshua were doing. He couldn't believe his ears when the song playing on the radio was "Reunited."

The words rang out, *Reunited and it feels so good.* The coincidence was almost unbearable for him. How could this song play right now? He wished more than anything he could reunite with Markita and once again feel good.

Me minus you, the next words rang out. Those words felt like a dagger being twisted into his heart. He was so alone without her. *Please, God, give me one more moment with her,* he prayed. *I want to tell her everything I didn't get to say. Life is so unfair. Our hearts touched each other's and ignited, but for only such a short time. We had so much more to discover about each other.* Harris thought about her lips, her soft skin, and his mind wandered to the day in the park where they swam and their bodies came alive. They laughed so much when they were together. They had shared so much in such a short time, only to have their love ripped apart like this. Was he going to have to spend the rest of his life alone? How would he live without her? How do you walk through this life without the one that you love? His eyes welled with tears, and soon they began to slide down his face. He wiped them away with his hand, devastated and angry, then slowly drifted off to sleep.

He dreamed of the two of them. He took her in his arms, and they danced the night away on a sandy beach in Mexico. He touched her beautiful lips with his tongue, then slowly licked them. He brushed back her hair with his hand, looking into her big beautiful eyes. Her body felt good so close to his, and his heart began to pound hard for her. This time they would explode together in passion, and nothing, and no one, would stop them from reaching the ecstasy they deserved.

Harris subconsciously heard himself making little groaning sounds; his body felt warm, and he ached so hard for her. Suddenly he jerked in the chair, realizing he'd dozed off. This time he took his tired and depressed body to bed, allowing his dreams to continue of the only woman he ever loved.

Early Monday, Joe finished getting ready and threw a duffel bag together with a few things he would need for a road trip. Once at his office, he began his search for Cory Alexander, hoping he could catch a break and find him as the binder didn't reveal the name of Cory's brother.

"Bingo," exclaimed Joe, happy with himself. The Google search revealed a Cory Alexander living in Dahlonega, Georgia. The age seemed right, and there was also a phone number listed. Joe didn't want to chance the phone because of the Order's secrecy. He was afraid a call might alarm Cory. Bringing up these kinds of memories wasn't only painful, but also embarrassing. Joe began making airline reservations along with ones for a rental car. Once he finished confirming everything, he made another set of reservations to Pennsylvania. He was going to check out all the orphanages there, and maybe with a little luck, he could help uncover the mystery as to whom the child was that Ronald Harris concealed in secrecy.

This dilemma really concerned him because of the ramifications it could present for Harris. He wondered how his friend would react to finding out he had another uncle. Joe was also suspicious as to why Judge Harris would lie to his wife about their first child being stillborn and then placing him in an orphanage. Although after some of the things he had been reading, he guessed the judge was capable of just about anything. Although he realized this whole venture was like looking for a needle in a haystack, whatever he could find out, he needed to do quickly. He needed to get back to help Harris with the trial.

Part of *that* puzzle was starting to come together. Eleanor was Bambi's mother, the governor's lover, and worked for Miss Dixie. Judge Poe hired Bambi's services from Miss Dixie. He had a hunch that the same person who attempted to kill Judge Poe could have killed Eleanor. He was beginning to realize his friend Harris was a part of this mess as well. He was hoping once he got the DNA results from his friend at the lab, he would be able to piece together how Governor Mason, Trudy, Markita, Harris, and this mysterious uncle fit into this warped puzzle. Somehow, he knew he would find at least some of his answers on this trip.

Before leaving, he made one last phone call.

"Hey, Robbie, how are you, darlin'?"

"Well, if it isn't the elusive detective, Joe Marble. I'm fine, kind sir, and how are you this fine day?" Robin asked in her usual thick Southern accent. Joe had goose bumps just listening to her sweet, sexy voice.

"I'm fine, baby, but I wanted to call to let you know I'm leaving town for a few days. I'm going to Georgia, then on to Pennsylvania."

"Why, Joe Marble, you make sure you take good care of yourself, do ya hear me now?"

"Oh, baby, I hear you loud and clear," he said having naughty thoughts.

"I know I'm not supposed to ask, but does this have anything to do with the case I helped you work on?" she asked, a little concerned.

"Now, baby, you know if I told you, I'd have to shoot you," he laughed.

"My, my, my, Joe Marble, you'd really shoot lil' ole me?" she asked playing along with him.

"You need to stop that, lady, or I'll never get out of here." He smiled widely at the thoughts of her again.

"Will you call me when you can, handsome?"

"You betcha, and when I get back, you and I are going to have one of those special talks."

"Oh my, Joe Marble, you intrigue me." Robin was now anticipating his return, a thrill running through her as to what he might want to talk to her about. She hoped it might be about their future together.

"I love you, lil' lady," he said quickly as his heart skipped a beat.

"Why, I love you too, Joe Marble. How do you feel about that?" she asked, taunting him again.

"I feel like the man." His smile broadened, and he blushed. "Take care, lil' lady," he managed to utter.

"You too, Joe . . . bye now."

Joe sat back in his chair for a moment, thinking how lucky he was after all these years to finally find someone he truly cared about again. *Phew, she's a hot one*, he laughed to himself as he got up, locked his office, and left.

Even though it was a short flight to Georgia, it was quite late when he arrived since he'd gotten such a late start. Picking up his rental car, he searched for a small motel close to the airport. Once he found one, he checked in, went to his room, and crawled into bed, calling it a night. He planned to head out early the next morning, knowing it would only take him about an hour to get where he was going.

He arrived in Dahlonega promptly at nine the next morning. His first objective was to get himself another motel as he made his reservations to Pennsylvania for the day after tomorrow. He didn't know how long it would take him to get to talk to Cory, or if he would even see him. He figured if things went quicker, he could always check with the airlines and see if he could move up his flight. After he found a Motel 6 and checked in, he pulled out the number he had for Cory Alexander and dialed, waiting patiently for an answer.

"Hello," said a voice. Joe hung up and decided now would be the time to go see him.

When Joe arrived at the address, he drove down a long driveway which ended at an old-style plantation-looking piece of Georgia property. The house was on concrete blocks and had what looked like a new front porch. It contained only one rocking chair, which led Joe to believe that whoever lived here lived alone. He pulled into the circular graveled area and parked the car, then proceeded to walk up to the front door. There was a rather large old-fashioned iron doorknocker, but no bell, he noticed. He knocked loudly, making sure that if there was anyone home, they would definitely hear him. After a moment, a slender and well-dressed man opened the door. He was around five foot nine or ten and looked to be in his seventies, with distinguished-looking silver hair.

"Hello," Joe greeted him.

"How can I help you?" the man asked.

"I'm looking for Cory Alexander," Joe said in his best investigator voice.

"Who is looking for him?"

"My name is Joe Marble." Joe saw no reason to lie, at least not yet. "I'm an investigator for the district attorney's office in Orlando, Florida, but I'm not here on official business. I'm here for a friend."

"I don't have any friends in Florida, so why would you be looking for Cory?"

"Ahem, I don't mean to be rude, sir, but you said you didn't have any friends in Florida and then mentioned Cory like you knew him, which leads me to believe you are indeed the Cory I'm looking for," Joe said, catching him out.

"So what if I am? I told you I don't know anyone in Florida," the man stated firmly. It appeared he was slightly agitated.

"I'm sorry, sir. I didn't mean to imply that you did. I'm here on behalf of a friend of mine," Joe repeated.

"Again, Mr. Marble, I wouldn't know any of your friends," and he started to shut the door.

"Please, Mr. Alexander, it's about the Order," Joe quickly piped up.

The man went as white as a ghost and stopped in his tracks.

"The what?" he whispered.

"I came across a diary called 'the Order' and wanted to talk to you about some things I found in it. I would really appreciate it if we could just talk."

"Did Hugh send you?" the man, whom Joe now was certain was Cory Alexander, sounded even more nervous now, but Joe could tell he'd piqued his curiosity.

"To be totally honest with you, no, sir, he didn't." Joe knew he was risking blowing his one chance, but he didn't want Cory catching him out in a lie because then surely he wouldn't talk to him.

"Hmmm, an honest man," Alexander remarked. "I'll give you five minutes," he told Joe. "But don't try my patience. Why don't you come inside?"

Joe appreciated the fact that he offered even five minutes. Cory opened the door wide for him to enter. At first glance, Joe could see the decorations of the house were impeccable. He followed the older man down the hallway, which led into a beautiful and expansive living room. There was an expensive crystal chandelier hanging in the middle of the ceiling. A huge fireplace was the definite focal point of the room, complete with what looked like a hand-carved mantel. There were four low hanging paddle fans made of rattan surrounding the chandelier, two to the right of it and two to the left. The design let them cover all four corners of the large room. On either side of the fireplace were two expensive-looking Georgian chairs with velvet green upholstery. There were no carpets, just brilliantly shiny wooden floors. To the left of the chandelier was a huge window, which looked out to the rear of the house. It overlooked a long narrow river, bordered by a perfectly landscaped garden. Along the opposite wall of the living room were rows and rows of law library books. *He must have inherited them from his father,* thought Joe.

"Please be seated," Cory said, pointing to one of the chairs in front of the fireplace. Joe walked over and sat down.

"Would you like some ice tea?" Cory asked politely.

"No thanks, sir, I'm fine for now." Cory sat in the chair opposite him. The two men stared at each other for a few moments, neither saying a word.

"So, Mr. Marble," Alexander started, "Why don't you tell me about this book you say you found?" His eyes pierced Joe's as he tried to sound vague.

"Well, sir, how I came across the book isn't important, but what I found in it was unbelievable, to say the least." Joe was trying to get Cory to loosen up before getting into the details of the book. He didn't want him to feel uncomfortable when Joe disclosed what he knew. Cory listened intently to everything Joe had to say, not uttering a word himself and finished telling him what he knew, adding his fears and concerns for his friend Harris.

"You are a good friend," Cory said quietly.

"I'd like to think I am," said Joe, realizing that simply telling the tale had taken more than his five minutes, and yet Mr. Alexander did not seem ready to throw him out. A good sign, he thought.

"What exactly is it you want from me, Mr. Marble?"

"I would like you to stand up in court and expose the Order and all their wrongdoings," he started to say, but Cory stopped Joe hastily.

"That will never happen, so I'm sorry you have wasted a visit."

"Mr. Alexander," Joe tried again.

"It's OK, Mr. Marble, you may call me Cory."

"If you won't testify, Cory, then would you at least help me by giving me something to prove the Order exists? If you have anything you can tell me about Ronald Harris's and Hugh Gallagher's involvement, I would be even more grateful." Joe sighed with relief; he'd finally asked the man the question he most wanted the answer to.

"How long are you staying in Georgia?" Cory asked, seeming to change the subject.

"At least two days," Joe replied.

"I need to think about some things if you don't mind, Mr. Marble."

"No, no, sir, I don't mind at all. I'm staying at the Motel 6 down the road, room 103," Joe told him, excited that Cory hadn't shut him out.

"I'm not saying I can help you with your dilemma," he cautioned, "but like I said, I'll think about a few things, OK?" Cory rose from his chair letting Joe know his time was up.

"Cory, I know this is difficult for you. Please trust me when I tell you I can relate to what happened to you. I'm not here to destroy your father's or your own reputation. I only want to help my friend Harris to find out the truth about his grandfather. I know it puts the Order at risk, but it's time for the corruption and the killings to end," Joe said sincerely.

"I'll agree with some of what you are saying, Mr. Marble. I've not often agreed with the way Ronald Harris has handled certain matters. They are things my father wouldn't have approved of, if you know what I mean. I hope you are a man of your word when you tell me you won't bring me or my father into your quest for the truth or into any part of your investigation."

"You have my word, sir." Joe held out his hand to shake Cory's as if to seal his promise. Cory Alexander decided he liked Joe Marble; there was something sincere about him, and he liked the concern he had for his friend. He himself couldn't relate to friendship, not anymore. After what had happened to him as a child, he'd lost every friend he'd ever had. They shied away from him as if he were the guilty person.

Joe returned to his motel room feeling positive about his visit with Cory. He felt that now it would only be a matter of time before he could tell Harris everything. Once back in his room, he flopped down on the bed and proceeded to call Robin.

"Hey, Miss Robbie, it's your favorite investigator, Inspector Gadget."

Robin laughed. "You are my only Inspector Gadget, Joe Marble." He was happy to hear her wonderful voice, and her oh, so sexy Southern accent; he smiled.

"How is your trip going? I hope you are close to coming home," she said, hopeful it would be soon.

"All I can tell you is I think my meeting went better than expected today."

"Well, Joe Marble, that's a good thing."

"It sure is, lil' lady. It means I'm one step closer to coming home to you." His thoughts turned to the talk he wanted to have with her when he returned.

"I like the sound of that," she said in a sultry tone.

"Have you been behavin' while I've been gone, pretty lady?" Joe asked, already knowing the answer to his question.

"Of course I have, Joe Marble, you shouldn't expect any less," she sounded surprised by his question. He should know she was as pure as they come.

"You know I don't, Miss Robbie, and I apologize for the question," he said, feeling a little guilty. He couldn't help but be insecure after what happened to his last relationship.

"Apology accepted, Joe Marble, don't give it another mind, ya hear?"

"I guess I'd better get going, pretty lady. I have some reports I'd like to get started on while I've got some down time. I'm hoping my contact doesn't take too long in making a decision," he said wanting to get this part of his trip over with and move on to the next. That trip was going to take a lot of luck.

"Well, Joe Marble, you take care now and call me before you go to sleep tonight," she said, a little sad they had to hang up.

"I will, lil' lady, I promise. I love you." Joe said the last three words quickly before hanging up, not giving her a chance to respond.

Robin smiled a big smile as she hung up on her end.

Joe called the front desk and asked for the phone number to the nearest pizza place that delivered. He ordered lunch and then pulled out his laptop and dove into writing up some much-delayed reports. He spent the rest of the afternoon and early evening stuck on his computer. Around nine that night, he stopped to eat the rest of the cold pizza. He was a little disappointed; Cory Alexander had not called him yet.

The computer had mentally exhausted him so he thought he would call it an early night, hoping Cory would call early the next morning. But before going to sleep, he kept his promise to Robin and gave her a good night call.

Chapter Eighteen

Secrets Unfold

On Wednesday morning, Joe awoke, took his shower, then sat down on the bed and stared at the phone, wishing it would ring. He wasn't sure what he was going to do if Cory didn't call today since he was supposed to be on a flight to Pennsylvania at noon the next day. *I suppose I'll have to cancel my flight and wait,* thought Joe. He had come too far not to obtain the proof he needed for Harris. He paced the room for a while and then decided to do a few more reports, trying to stay occupied. He wondered several times if he should call Cory, but he didn't want to blow things by being pushy. He needed to be patient.

Evening arrived, and Cory had still not called. Joe started to pace—again—having finished all his reports. He gave Robin a quick call to say good night, explaining to her that he didn't want to miss an incoming call. She totally understood. Joe turned on the TV and then lay down for a while, still hoping the phone would ring. He didn't realize he had fallen asleep until the warmth of the sun hit his face early the next morning.

"Damn it," he said aloud. He was disappointed Cory hadn't called. He decided he would take his shower then call the airlines and change his reservations, moving them forward another day.

"Damn it," he said again. He showered, shaved, and then sat down on the bed, ready to call the airline when, at last, the phone rang.

"Joe Marble," he said as his heart skipped a beat.

"Joe, it's Cory Alexander."

"Yes, sir," Joe said anxiously.

"Can you come back out to the house in about half an hour?"

Joe looked over at the clock, not even knowing what time it was. It was only 8:00 a.m. If their meeting didn't take too long, he could still make his flight at noon.

"Yes, sir, of course," he replied. "I do so appreciate this, Cory, I'll be right there." Joe started throwing his stuff in his duffel bag as they were speaking. This way he could check out and then leave for the airport as soon as he completed the interview.

"I'll see you soon," Cory said and then hung up.

Joe paid his bill then left. He parked in the graveled area again, then proceeded to the front door. Cory was already waiting for him.

"Come on in, Mr. Marble," he said. Just like before, Joe followed him down the long hallway into the large living room. "If you have read the diary, then you already know why my father started the Order," Cory said, getting right into the conversation.

"Yes, sir, and I have no intention of divulging that information to anyone," Joe said, reassuring him.

"I appreciate it, Joe. I live a private life and wish to keep it that way." Cory sounded frail when talking about his private life.

"I understand," said Joe, making sure Cory knew he was sincere when he spoke.

"I want you to know my father's intentions for the Order were not to kill people, but to put criminals away when the system failed the innocent children. I want you to understand that fact before we go any further, Joe, OK?" Cory's voice was quiet and subdued when talking about his father. Joe could see the pain in his eyes as he was obviously flashing back to what happened to himself all those years ago.

Cory cleared his throat, then sat back comfortably in his chair, as if he knew his story was going to take awhile.

"He was a good and pure man before what happened to me and my mother. It broke him, you know."

Joe interrupted. "Under the circumstances, it's easy to see how someone can snap when it concerns the ones you love and swear to protect."

Cory liked his response. He could already sense Joe's sincerity to the situation.

"My father was pleased with the way Ronald Harris's father ran things," he went on, "but he would turn over in his grave if he knew Ronald was having people killed who got in his way. That wasn't the purpose of the Order." Cory paused, then seemed to change topics. "You know, Ronald went away to war after being married only a short time. His wife was a beautiful woman until her face was scarred."

"How was she scarred?" asked Joe, stunned and amazed at what he was hearing. He slid to the edge of the seat so he could listen even more intently.

"She thought Ronald died while he was away since his letters stopped coming. She was distraught, then turned reckless. She had an affair with a black man. Another man, a white man, by the name of Johnson, found out about the affair and raped her in revenge. He apparently meant to kill her afterward, but they were disturbed, so he fled. Before leaving, he gouged her face with his thumb, intentionally scarring her right cheek to make sure no other man would ever look at her."

"Oh, holy mother of god," Joe said, completely shocked. He was appalled, his mouth hanging open in disbelief. Thinking of Harris, Joe could only imagine the pain this was going to cause him. How was he going to tell him someone raped his grandmother?

Cory saw the look of shock on Joe's face, but went on. "When Ronald finally returned, he of course found out about the affair. He searched out her lover and hanged him on a tree. Ronald's wife told him about the rape. He was furious with her, and they didn't speak for months. Jake Johnson sought his defense from the Harris's law firm. He had no idea the defense attorney he confided in was none other than Ronald himself. I heard him tell the Order his revenge would be as sweet. He was able to frame Jake Johnson for a murder he himself committed on his wife's black lover. He made sure the Johnson boy received the death sentence for the murder. This way Johnson couldn't tell anyone the truth. Ronald knew Jake wasn't a well-educated man, and so it was easy to tell him he stood a better chance of getting off if he pleaded guilty. It was after that when Ronald became a KKK member. He wanted to punish every black man for what happened to his wife. I guess to him it was easier than blaming her for her infidelity."

Joe was in total disbelief now. How was he ever going to explain the cold truth about Harris's grandfather? Harris was no racist and deplored anyone who was; even more so, he knew Harris believed in the justice system to the extent that he would turn his own grandfather over to the authorities when he found out. His friend would be devastated. How would Harris handle all this on top of losing Markita? No one should have to endure so much pain. Joe was even more concerned at having to be the one to relay all this to him. It was a task he certainly wasn't looking forward to.

Cory continued while Joe's mind tried to deal with what he was hearing. "It was clear to the Klan Ronald's hatred for the black community. When integration first started in Florida, a group of black teenagers staged a protest at Jones High School. Ronald had them arrested and thrown in jail.

"The girls occupied one basement cell and the boys another. There was laughing heard from the girls' cell, and so late one night, they were loaded into a police van and taken to Orange County, where they were transferred to a prison farm on Colonial Drive. They had to work off their sentences milking the cows and working the fields. Once there, they received brutal whippings. The laughter soon turned into tears.

"In those days, the Shiloh Baptist ministry's youth minister had a reputation as a rabble-rouser. Ronald didn't take kindly to anyone trying to integrate Orlando, and so he had the Klan burn a cross in front of the mission and hanged an effigy of the youth minister on the tree outside. He ordered the police chief to pass it off as pranksters. He organized many other incidents where the Klan would rally against the protests of young black men and women. He didn't care how old they were, he wanted them killed or locked up. This hatred of the black community got increasingly worse, with Ronald organizing more and more rallies until the KKK made him The Grand Dragon of the Realm, presiding over all Klans in Florida. Ronald had so many city commissioners and officials in the Order that his rise to power was unstoppable." Cory paused a moment seeing Joe was looking a bit pale.

"Are you OK, Mr. Marble?" he asked.

"I must admit, I'm feeling a little sick," Joe admitted, "but things are starting to make a whole lot of sense now," he finished, trying not to throw up in Cory's living room. He flashed back to his mother, Nancy, remembering how angry she used to get when he was younger.

"I know Judge Harris is corrupt," she would say. "There is no way I should have lost that case."

He remembered how it peeved her. It seemed every time Ronald Harris presided over a case where she was defending an African American, she would lose every time. Joe always knew there was more to her retirement than she let on. She was, after all, an ambitious and determined woman. Nancy Marble wasn't someone who was scared away easily. He later found out she gave up her job on the Court TV channel due to threats against her life, but he never found out who sent the threats. It was one of the reasons he was so determined to become an investigator; his goal was always to find out who could have wanted to hurt his mother so badly. Now he suspected it was because she'd defended African Americans.

The words of Amber Andrews stuck out in his mind from the night of the attack on Judge Poe. Andrews was sure Ronald was a part of the KKK. He knew Harris was angry about that, so how was he going to tell him it was all true? He tried to clear his head as Cory continued.

"The worst of it was while the Harrises were away trying to put their marriage back together, his wife bore a son. Knowing the boy wasn't his, Ronald put him in an orphanage, but you know that already. What you do not know is his name is Philip Smith. I don't know this for sure, but I have heard rumors that the person doing the executions for Ronald is his wife's bastard son."

Cory paused again, looking over at Joe, seeing he didn't look too good. This time Joe had to ask to use the bathroom. Cory showed him to down the hall, and as soon as the door was closed, his throat welled and began to pulse, until at last he emptied his stomach into the bowl. He splashed some water on his cheeks and then looked at his pale white face in the mirror.

P. Smith was the name the lab technicians gave him in reference to Judge Poe's assault. Could this be Philip Smith? Harris's mysterious uncle? He looked over at the toilet bowl again, getting the queasy feeling back in his stomach. He splashed some more water on his face before returning to the living room.

"Are you OK, son?" Cory asked, genuinely concerned.

"I am now, sir, thank you."

"I guess this is a bit more than you bargained for when you read the book?"

"I'm more concerned for my friend, sir, that's all."

"A good friend, is he?" Cory asked, not unkindly.

Joe, always on the side of caution, answered with as few words as possible.

"He has overcome a lot in his life, sir, and recently lost the love of his life. I hope he is able to handle these recent revelations on top of everything else he is going through." Cory raised his left brow at Joe before he continued.

"If you want proof, you will have to go to Oakmont, Pennsylvania," Cory told him.

"I have reservations to go there tomorrow," said Joe.

"There is an orphanage called Saint Michael's. Ask for a priest named Father Jimmy. I'll call him to let him know you're coming. He will show you the records you need for your proof." Joe started thank him, but Cory held up a hand.

"There is one more thing you need to know, Joe Marble. Hugh Gallagher is now running the Order for Ronald Harris, and this makes him a dangerous man. I heard from a reliable source that there are rumors surfacing about him, that he is a corrupt DA, only out for himself. It appears he is trying to take over the Practice. Ronald is getting old, and if he dies, his grandson will inherit the secrets of the Order along with the power that goes with it. He will inherit the escrow, which is a great deal of money, but from what I hear, the grandson is as straight as a die. If that is the case, he needs to watch his back. They'll come after him faster than flies."

Joe could have told him his friend Harris and Ronald's grandson was the same person, and he was watching his back for him. But he didn't. Joe didn't want to let Cory know too much. Cory continued again.

"Apparently, there was a big bungle involving a madam named Miss Dixie."

Joe didn't want to divulge he was there for that debacle.

"I have suspected his actions for quite some time, but I do not take an active role in the Order anymore," Cory said, speaking of Hugh again.

"I have had my suspicions too for a while. That's actually how I happened to come across the diary," Joe said.

"Hmmm, so where exactly did you obtain it?" Cory was curious as the diary was never to be discovered by anyone.

"I would rather not tell you, sir, as the less people know, the safer they may be." Joe hoped his explanation would be enough.

"Well, Joe Marble, I have told you all I know, except to be very careful, because if P. Smith is the one and the same Executioner as they call him, you could be in grave danger."

Cory stood up, letting Joe know the conversation was over. Joe shook Cory's hand and thanked him for all his help. As they walked back down the long hallway to the front door, Cory told him his friend was a lucky man to have him in his corner. He gave him one last warning, as if he had known his friend was Harris all along.

"If he were my friend, I would warn him about Smith and also to not to trust his family members."

The front door closed, and Joe headed for his car wondering if Cory really did know Harris was the friend he was trying to protect.

Joe glanced at his watch and saw that it was only 10:00 a.m. If he hurried, he could still catch his flight. He hopped in his rental car and sped out of the drive and onto the highway. After a few moments, he looked over at the speedometer, realizing he was traveling too fast. He slowed down, wanting to avoid situations with the local police as he couldn't afford to waste any time.

When he arrived at the airport, he returned the rental car, then made a rush for the gate; he made it with only minutes to spare. At last, he was on his way to Pennsylvania, where he knew the rest of his answers and the proof he needed would be.

As soon as he landed in Pennsylvania, Joe rushed to pick up another rental car and then headed toward the 102-year-old town of Oakmont. It was a town about eight miles from Pittsburg, with a population of approximately eight thousand people. Life here looked pretty much the same as it was back in the '50s and '60s. He looked around for a small motel and quickly found one that didn't look too expensive. It was quaintly named *The Oakmonter*. After checking in, he proceeded to his room.

He was pleasantly surprised. For such a small motel, it was immaculate. The room was quite large, and the sliding glass doors looked out onto the Allegheny River. Smiling at the view, he threw his duffel bag on the bed, then called Robin, letting her know he arrived.

"Hey, baby, I'm in Pennsylvania. My room is quite quaint, but lonely without you."

"Why, Joe Marble, anyone would think you're missing me," Robin replied.

"It feels like forever since I held you in my arms," he said bashfully.

"I'm lonely without you too, Inspector Gadget," she teased.

"I shouldn't be too much longer, Robbie. Things are falling into place. I'm getting all the answers I need before going to Harris," he said with some relief.

"That is a good thing, Joe Marble, as Orlando isn't quite the same without you in it."

"Don't you worry your little self, missy. I'll be back before the end of the week for sure," he said, smiling and thinking about his return and the two of them getting together.

"I'm not worried, Joe Marble. You're the best at what you do, and I know we will be together again real soon."

She said the words encouragingly, but even though she had no idea about what he was working on, something was definitely nagging at her subconscious; it was one of those intuitive feelings she often got.

"I'm not supposed to meet with my contact until tomorrow, so I'll rest up for what is left of the day. I think I'm going to grab a pizza and a Coke and then call it a night," he said, now realizing how hungry he was.

"I swear, Joe Marble, all you think about sometimes is your stomach."

"It's a beautiful one though, don't you think?"

Robin laughed at him. "I sure do," she drawled.

"I'll call you as soon as my meeting is over tomorrow, OK? It shouldn't take too long, then I'll be flying home to you, baby, if that is OK with you," he teased.

"I cannot wait for you to return to my arms and hold me, kind sir."

Robin was now blushing at the thoughts she was having about them being together. His voice turned serious. Robin could sense the pain in it as he shared his concerns with her.

"Robbie, there is something I'm not looking forward to when I get home. I'll have to reveal to Harris despicable truths about his grandfather, which are going to crush my friend. In my line of work, I have had to tell people about the loss of loved ones, but you tend to distance yourself from those feelings when you're relaying devastating news to relatives. The truth I have discovered concerning Harris, although not fatal in the sense of the word for him, it will feel worse than losing Markita."

"Oh, Joe, that is awful for you and for your friend. I cannot imagine what it could be that could pain you so much. I can hear it in your voice, you know," Robin spoke with a heavy heart herself.

"It's OK, lil' lady, I probably shouldn't have burdened you with this, but it's certainly affecting me."

"Now, Joseph Marble, we know each other well enough now to know we can share anything, right?"

She'd never called him Joseph before, and it made him smile.

"I guess so, Robbie. Thanks for listening and not asking me for details. I'll give you all of those once I have revealed my findings to Harris."

"That's fine with me. Now you go get something to eat and rest for your meeting. Please call me tomorrow night and let me know you're OK."

"Of course I will. I can't go to sleep without getting my good-night kiss from you." He grinned. Robin blew a kiss through the phone.

"Thank ya, darling. Sweet dreams," he said.

"You too, Joe Marble. I love you." They both hung up, and Joe rolled over onto his back and lay there looking up at the ceiling, picturing her beautiful face. It would soon be over, he told himself, and they would be together.

The next morning, he awoke, got ready, and then pulled the local directory out of the nightstand drawer. He looked up the number to Saint Michael's. He thought it strange when the listing noted them as being an orphanage for the blind and deaf. It was something he wasn't expecting. He knew if P. Smith was blind, it couldn't be the same one who suffocated the security guard at the impound lot or who tried to suffocate Judge Poe. He would not have been able to decapitate Eleanor's or shoot the two SWAT team guys between the eyes. That would blow his whole theory. If he were indeed deaf, maybe there was a correlation between him and Harris, with both of them being deaf. Since Smith and Harris were related, the deafness could run in the family . . . but then he remembered Harris telling him he became deaf because of something his father did. That blew his theory out of the water. He dialed the number telling himself he needed to meet with the priest and then he would get all the answers he needed.

"Saint Michael's," a sweet elderly lady's voice answered the phone.

"Yes, ma'am, I'm looking for a priest named Father Jimmy, would he be around?"

"He is with the children in the playground right now, is there something I could help you with?"

"Not really, ma'am, I'm supposed to meet with him today."

"Why don't you give me your name, and I'll let him know you're on the phone."

"That is most kind of you, ma'am. It's Joseph Marble."

"Hold on a moment. I'll be right back." Joe didn't like giving her his name over the phone, but he didn't have another option, except to just show up, and he didn't want to do that. The lady returned after just a few moments.

"Mr. Marble, could you give me a number where he could call you back? He is rather busy with the children at the moment." Joe hesitated, then went ahead and gave her the number.

"I'm staying at the Oakmonter Hotel in room number 729. I'm sorry. I don't know the direct number."

"It's OK, I'm sure Father Jimmy can get it. Are you sure there's nothing I can help you with?" she asked again.

"Not really, but I do appreciate your help." Joe hung up the phone, disappointed. He wished he could have talked to the priest right away; he had hoped to get his visit with him over so he would know everything and then return home to Robin. He was about to get up when the phone rang. It made him jump as he wasn't expecting a call, and it was too soon for the priest to call back.

"Hello."

"Is this Joe Marble?" a man's voice asked.

"Yes." Joe was now on full alert, not knowing who the man could be.

"Is this the Joe Marble that Cory Alexander told to call me?" the voice asked, sounding hesitant.

"It's one and the same. Is this Father Jimmy?" Joe replied.

"It is," the man answered with a thick Irish accent, which Joe could now distinguish.

"Is two o'clock this afternoon OK with you to come to the orphanage?" asked Father Jimmy.

"That would be fine, sir. I'll be there."

Joe heard the dial tone. He looked down at the phone. *Hmm, strange,* he thought. The priest returned his call so quickly, especially as the woman said he was busy. *I think I need to watch myself* he thought. Before leaving the hotel, he packed his pistol in his ankle holster.

It wasn't long before two o'clock came around and Joe arrived at the orphanage. It was an old decrepit building, with a cross on the left side of the front wall. He could tell it lit up at night. The sign outside read "Saint Michael's Orphanage."

He opened the large oak door and entered into a cold tiled foyer. There were two long wooden benches against either side of the walls. The only other furniture was a desk with an old-fashioned telephone sitting on it in the middle of the foyer. An elderly woman dressed in a nun's habit greeted him, and he guessed she was the same one who answered the phone.

"Welcome to Saint Michael's," she said in a pleasant tone.

"Thank you, ma'am. I'm here to see Father Jimmy."

"You must be Joseph Marble."

"Yes, ma'am, that would be me," Joe said, trying to be humorous.

"Please take a seat while I go and fetch him for you." He sat down on one of the long wooden benches and waited. The nun returned after a few moments and sat back down at her desk, staring at him the whole time. It was quite awhile before Father Jimmy came out.

"What brings you to our orphanage?" the nun asked. Joe wasn't quite sure how to answer her question when the priest came out of a door located behind her desk. He was glad he appeared when he did as he certainly didn't want to lie to a nun.

"Welcome to Saint Michael's, you must be Joseph Marble."

"I'm indeed, sir, and you must be Father Jimmy."

"I am, son, I am," he responded in his warm Irish accent, even more pronounced in person.

"Follow me, son, I'll show you our facility. I think the child you will be bringing here will be very happy."

Father Jimmy looked over at the nun making sure she heard every word he said. Joe did as instructed, and saying nothing, he followed the priest back through the door from where he had first appeared.

"My office is back here, Joe. Don't say another word until we are in it."

Joe obeyed him, not feeling comfortable at his request. Once inside the room, Father Jimmy showed Joe to a chair.

"Have a seat here for a few minutes. We will need to conduct an interview, concerning the child you wish to leave here at Saint Michael's." Father Jimmy winked at him. "We will then look around the orphanage. Together you will meet some of the children. We will then return here to this room, which is where I'll give you a package. You will need to look it over carefully. It will contain everything you need, do you understand?"

The priest made several hand motions toward the envelope in his hands before putting it back in his drawer.

"It will tell you everything you need to know about Saint Michael's. Do you understand this, son?"

"I understand perfectly, sir," replied Joe.

Father Jimmy stood up and instructed Joe to follow him again. As Father Jimmy closed his office door, he began the conversation.

"Little Sammy, you said the boy's name was, did ya?"

"Yes, I did, sir," replied Joe.

"I'm terrible at names, son, but don't you worry—there isn't a child here I don't recognize. I have nicknames for them all."

Father Jimmy took Joe through two more large oak doors; they were quite heavy, and he wondered how the children had the strength to open them.

"There is someone with the children at all times," Father Jimmy said. That answered Joe's question, and he smiled to himself.

As the men walked out into the playground, Joe noticed how many children there were. It was quite sad there were so many kids without parents. Suddenly, there were at least ten little ones all over Father Jimmy; their faces lit up seeing him. They called out for him to hug them first. They were laughing, tugging at him and holding onto his leg. The priest started naming some of them to Joe.

"This little rascal here is Jayden. We call her Rascal as she is always into mischief. Alicia is the quiet one around here. Oh, and this one here would be Hailey. She is our oldest 'favorite one.'"

Joe noticed she was quite a bit older than most of the other children, and she had certainly had eyesight.

"This lil'un here is Alexandria," the old priest went on, "but we call her Precious Little One because she is so little and a precious little cutie-pie, don't you think, Joe?"

"Who is he?" asked one of the girls.

"Ah, this one here is Adrianna, and we call her Nosy Rosy, I'm sure you can guess why."

The priest laughed along with the children. It was obvious he loved all them all.

"Well, kids, we have to be going now. Father Jimmy has work to do, but you know I'll be there for supper and prayers with you all."

The children hugged and kissed his hand good-bye, and they even shook hands with Joe. Father Jimmy thanked the nun in charge of this group for allowing them to disturb her. The men walked around the rest of the building, then finally returned to Father Jimmy's office. Once inside, they sat down, the priest leaning over to talk to Joe. He spoke quietly now as he pulled out an envelope and handed it to him.

"Inside you will find everything you need."

"I noticed one or two of the children were not deaf or blind," he remarked to the priest.

"They are the lost souls, son. Some of the older ones are delinquents, some have been abused, and the others were left here on our doorstep. We don't typically take on nondisabled kids unless there are mitigating circumstances."

"Was Philip Smith one of those?" asked Joe.

The priest coughed loudly.

"Take your package, son, fill out the information, and return it to us at the orphanage, and we will see if we can consider your child."

The priest looked at Joe sternly for even mentioning Smith's name.

"As a matter of fact, son, you might want to consider another facility for your child, as I'm not sure we can accommodate any more children at this time." Father Jimmy didn't realize it at the time, but that statement is what saved him from losing his own life.

Joe could tell he had made the priest uncomfortable. Father Jimmy stood up and motioned for Joe to head toward the door.

"You have a nice day now, son, and may God be with you." The priest led Joe back down the hallways through the doors back into the foyer. Once Joe left, he looked at the elderly nun who now had a scowl on her face. He said nothing to her as he headed back inside the door. The nun immediately dialed the phone.

"Judge Harris's office, how may I help you?" the receptionist answered.

"This is Sister Sheila from Saint Michael's in Oakmont. Is the judge available?" the nun asked.

"Hold on a second, ma'am, let me see if I can reach him." The receptionist put her on hold then paged through to the judge.

"Judge Harris, there is a Sister Sheila calling you from Saint Michael's in Oakmont, did you want to talk to her?"

"Put her through, Susan, if you would please," the judge replied quietly.

"Yes, sir, right away."

"Sister Sheila, how are you? It has been a long time. How is the orphanage doing?"

"It's doing well, sir, thanks to you."

"Oh, Sister, you're too kind. Saint Michael's is a wonderful facility, and every city should have one. What is the reason for your call today, Sister?" asked the judge, concerned.

"The orphanage had a strange visitor today, sir. His name was Joseph Marble. He wanted an appointment with Father Jimmy."

"Is that right?" said the judge not letting out his anger.

"Father Jimmy showed him around our humble facility, and then they went into his office. I listened at the door."

"Pray tell, what did you hear, Sister?"

"I heard the Marble gentleman ask about Philip Smith." The judge was now outraged. He had to put a stop to this Joe Marble; he was starting to ask too many questions, and interfering in his business was going to get Joe Marble killed.

"What did Father Jimmy reply?" inquired the judge.

"He told the man he needed to take his child elsewhere and we had no room here."

"Father Jimmy was very wise. I'm truly indebted to you, Sister. As you know, I do not need people checking into Philip's background. I pay the orphanage well for its discretion."

"Oh, I know, Judge, and that is why I called you. Philip is no one's business but your own."

"You're right, Sister, and I thank you so much for your loyalty, dear."

"Oh, you're so welcome, sir, and the children appreciate your donations."

"Don't worry yourself about this situation, Sister. I'll take care of things from my end. I don't think we will have to worry about Joe Marble."

"OK, Judge Harris, you have a good day, sir."

"You too, Sister, and there will be a nice bonus check for you this month."

"Oh, thank you so much, Judge. You're so kind."

Ronald hung up, furious. He was at his wits' end with Marble. It was time to take him out. He made a few phone calls making it clear what the outcome was to be.

Once Joe Marble was gone, the priest returned to his office and sat back in his chair. He began to pray.

"God be with you, Joe Marble, and with me." He put his hands together and prayed for hours. He had known the meeting would be a risky one, but he had no idea Joe would ask about Philip Smith aloud. He would need to call

Cory Alexander and warn him as to what happened. If the judge found out it was he who sent Marble, his life could be in jeopardy as well.

Joe couldn't wait to get back to the hotel and open up the envelope. He threw himself on the bed, ripped the envelope apart, and started to read the contents. He was right. "P. Smith" and Philip were the same. Judge Harris had dropped Smith off at the orphanage. He also wrote some large donation checks to the orphanage; there were copies of old checks signed by the judge.

The documents showed that Barbara Harris, the judge's wife, was the child's mother. Her date of birth and distinguishing marks were the only two things listed about her. It noted a large scar on her right cheek. Joe gulped as he looked down at the print. The child's ethnic background was listed as "Negro." Joe dropped the papers; he couldn't believe his eyes. He had not even thought about Harris's uncle being an African American. This meant Jake Johnson was telling the truth.

"Oh my freaking god!" Joe exclaimed aloud. "The man Ronald hanged was Philip's father! Judge Harris murdered him and framed Jake." Joe was so shaken, he was nearly unable to grasp it all. "This is freaking incredible, nuts, freaking crazy, man," Joe continued to mutter. He felt like he'd had the wind knocked out of him.

Joe finished reading everything that was in the envelope. This certainly was the proof he needed to present to Harris although now he didn't want to at all. Suddenly the room phone rang.

"Yes," answered Joe.

"It's the front desk, sir. The last people who stayed in your room complained about the air conditioner, and we need to know if it would be OK if maintenance came by now to fix it."

"Sure," said Joe, not thinking. He was so engrossed at what he was reading he wasn't on guard. He did, however, hide the envelope and contents under the mattress as he didn't want the maintenance man looking at it. There was a knock on the door a moment later. Joe unlatched the lock and opened it. There were two huge men dressed in black with ski masks over their faces.

Suddenly the two men burst into the room, lunging at him. Joe felt only the first blow of a baseball bat to his head. When he tried to bend down to get his pistol, he heard a gunshot, and that is the last thing that he remembered.

Chapter Nineteen

Opening Arguments

Harris was glad it was the weekend. He had spent Saturday cleaning his condo, doing small chores like placing clean sheets on the bed in the spare room and vacuuming. He was a neat and orderly individual and didn't like things out of place. His mother taught him there was a place for everything and everything had its place. "There is nothing worse than a dirty house," she would say.

He had stayed busy most of the day and then kicked back, relaxing, to catch up on last week's recorded football games until late in the afternoon. Today was Sunday though; it would be the first time he returned to his parents' house with both his mom and Uncle J. He was thrilled to be going there and seeing them together. This time when he purchased the rocky road ice cream, he smiled thinking, *All is right with the world today*. His mom and Joshua together made him happy. The song "Reunited Again" popped back into his head; he sang it all the way to the house.

"Hey, guys, I'm here," he called as he walked in the front door.

There was no answer from anyone.

"Hey, Uncle J, the rocky road ice cream is melting," he tried again. Harris turned the corner into the living room, but there was no one there. He looked in the kitchen; there was no one there either. He placed the ice cream in the freezer and then continued to look for his parents. They couldn't have gone out since they knew he was coming. *This is so odd,* he thought. He walked over to the sliding glass doors, and his eyes nearly popped out of his head. There stood Mary Ellen and Joshua, in stupid-looking birthday hats, both wearing the same T-shirt, which had his picture on it with the words "Happy Birthday, Harris" printed on them. The patio had streamers and banners hanging everywhere. He could see the patio table had birthday plates and cups with ducks printed on them.

Only his uncle J could do this to him, he thought. On a table lay a large decorated chocolate birthday cake with all the trimmings. He slid open the doors, and the singing began.

"Happy birthday to you, happy birthday to you, happy birthday, dear Harris," they sang, although he was almost positive that his uncle, the usual prankster, sang the words, "whippersnapper" instead of his name.

"You guys never cease to amaze me," Harris said with a grin when they finished singing. "You crack me up."

He stood there smiling, along with a tear in each corner of his eyes. Before he knew it, his mother placed another T-shirt with his picture on it over his head. He slid his arms into it and pulled it down, beaming with happiness. Meanwhile, Joshua put one of the ridiculous-looking hats on his head. On the chocolate cake, there was a bright yellow duck face with cherry icing on its bill, along with thirty brightly colored candles. Harris had to endure his uncle J's torturous teasing as he lit every one of them.

"Now, kiddo, it's time for you to burn down the house with all these candles. Gosh, you're so old. In fact, I haven't seen nanny goats as old as you," Josh harassed him.

Harris was filled with so much emotion, he couldn't even summon the words for a comeback, much less the air to blow out his candles. "Now take a big breath, son. We know you're full of hot air, so you can do it."

Harris had to do it in a couple of blows as he was now laughing at his uncle, but he managed to get them all out. Joshua and his mother applauded and then proceeded with all the kisses and hugs.

"Thanks, guys, you're the best. I know you're both crazy, but it's not my birthday."

"We feel so bad your birthday was ruined with everything that happened, so we wanted to make up for it today."

Mary Ellen gave her son another hug.

"You didn't have to do this, guys."

"Yeppers, you're right, young 'un, but then we wouldn't have had the pleasure of embarrassing you with your stupid hat on that head!" His uncle J cracked Harris up again.

"We're having your favorite chili cheese dog too," Mary Ellen told him. Harris gave her a look. "I know, I know, light on the onions, just like you like it, along with strawberry milk shakes, thinly whipped."

"Aw, Mom, you didn't have to go to all this trouble."

"Aw, yes, only the best for you, whippersnapper," jeered Josh.

His mother handed him gifts to open. His uncle got him two expensive sheepskin car seat covers, and as always, his mother bought him his favorite Kenneth Cole cologne, along with three new polos and three dress shirts

"Thank you, guys—not just for the gifts, but for being so . . ." he paused for a moment then blurted out, "You! So together and so very crazy!" They had a wonderful afternoon together, with everyone laughing, eating, and of course enduring Uncle J's duck joke.

Mary Ellen took the leftovers to the kitchen and made care packages for Harris to take home.

"So the big trial starts tomorrow?" asked Josh as he and Harris sat around the table outside.

"It sure does. I'm a bit concerned though," Harris confided.

"Oh, and why is that?" asked his uncle, now listening intently.

"It's Joe. He hasn't called me in a week. He went on a fact-finding mission and should have called in by now."

"When did he say he would be back?"

"He said before the trial started."

"Well, son, that's not until tomorrow. Maybe he'll be in late tonight."

"Yeah, I'm sure you're right," Harris said, still sounding unconvinced. Joshua took the opportunity to try to lighten up his nephew's mood.

"The word is 'yes,' not 'yeah.' I taught you better than that, whippersnapper."

He always made sure his nephew pronounced his words correctly. He spent years making sure he spoke eloquently, pronouncing each word with perfection, never letting up on him, not even in adult years. Hearing Harris speak gave Joshua great pleasure. He thanked God every day for his nephew's miracle.

Harris chuckled; trust his uncle to get off track.

"If he doesn't get back tonight, son, why don't you give me a call? I can always make some calls for you since I know you're going to be busy."

"Thanks, Uncle J. I might have to take you up on that offer. I guess I should get going. The next few weeks, maybe even months, are going to be hectic."

"Yes, it's going to be heck on the rest of us poor schmucks who are going to have to watch your ugly mug on the tube day in and day out."

"Gee thanks, I love you too," Harris said, chuckling.

"I didn't say I didn't love you, but do I have to look at you every day?" Josh teased again.

"You could always turn the box off."

"Oh, and miss your performance? Never, son. You always provide me with some good material." Harris grabbed his uncle's arm and punched it.

"Is that all you got?" Joshua took his nephew's arm, and they started arm wrestling on the table.

"Look at these biceps, Uncle J. Don't you wish you had some like these?"

"That's not what the hot chicks go for, son. Look at my calves, strong and thick, that's what they look for." Mary Ellen returned from the kitchen.

"Oh no, you guys are at it again," she said, rolling her eyes. "I can't leave the two of you alone for two minutes."

"I don't ever want you to leave me alone again for one minute," Joshua said as he jumped up and grabbed his wife from behind, hugging her.

"I want to buy fifty mirrors for the house," he whispered loudly in her ear.

"Oh, and why is that, pray tell?" said Mary Ellen playing along.

"That way every time you look in one I can come behind you like this and get a hold of you and tickle you."

"Last time you wanted to buy mirrors, it was only twelve. You're too silly, Joshua, but I love you any way. You're such the romantic," Mary Ellen said.

"Yes, he's quite the mush, isn't he, Mom?"

"Mush? Mush? I'll show you mush," his uncle piped up.

"Now, Joshua Robertson, you stop that. I think you've teased our son enough for one day. It's time for him to leave. You two have done enough playing around for now. Get over here and give us both a hug, son."

Harris was happy to obey. It had been such a perfect day.

"I've one question, guys," Harris said as he headed for the door.

"And what would that be, son?" Josh asked.

"Can I take this ridiculous hat off now?"

"No! You have to drive all the way home with it on." Josh high-fived him as Harris took the hat off, placing it on the table.

"I hope we didn't embarrass you too much today, Harris," his mother said with a smile.

"I had a fantastic day, Mom, and I wouldn't have changed a thing, You guys are the best parents a guy could have. I'm blessed beyond belief."

"We feel the same, son."

They walked Harris out to his car, taking the opportunity to get in a few more hugs before their son left. Once home, Harris put his care packages in the fridge then took his gifts upstairs. He hung his birthday T-shirt in his closet, smiling. He would have the other shirts cleaned first because he didn't like to wear stuff that was new. He liked his clothes to be soft before he wore them. He placed his cologne in the bathroom, along with the other two bottles he still had left from Christmas, changed into his pajamas, and called it a night. His big day in the courtroom started tomorrow, and he wanted to be fresh and ready for the days, or even weeks, ahead. Even Markita didn't enter into his thoughts. It still concerned him, however, that he had not heard from Joe.

The two thugs hastily gathered up Joe's belongings, including his cell phone and the files he had been working on, and threw them into the duffel bag on the bed. They searched his body, then found and removed his wallet. They undid the ankle holster and took it, along with the pistol, leaving his limp, bloodied body lying in a pool of blood on the floor. One of the gunmen wanted to shoot him one more time, just to make sure they had completed their assignment, but there were already guests starting to come out of their rooms into the hallway. Apparently, some of the guests heard the shots and wondered what all the commotion was about. Before anyone could stop them, the two men fled the room as fast as they could. Once in the car, they made the phone call to the judge, informing him of their success. They rode off into the night while Joe Marble lay bleeding on his hotel room floor.

The night manager's switchboard started to light up like a Christmas tree. Guests were calling in with complaints of what they thought sounded like gunshots. The manager was horrified; nothing like this had ever happened in his hotel before. He called 911 requesting the police along with an ambulance, both of which arrived in moments. Joe was rushed to the hospital six miles away in Pittsburg. Once they were there, the doctors in the ER sent Joe directly to surgery. By the time the cops arrived at the hospital to see if they could question him, Joe was out of surgery and in intensive care. The surgeon informed the police that the patient had fallen into a deep coma and the next twenty-four hours would be crucial. They wouldn't be able to question him for a while, if ever. One of the doctors asked the officers if they knew the name of their patient.

"All we know is he checked into the hotel under the name Joseph Marble. We haven't received any official confirmation on the victim as of yet."

"Do you have any additional information on him?" the doctor asked.

"Only what he wrote in the hotel register. Says he's from Orlando, Florida. We found no wallet, no other forms of ID on the victim, so we're not even sure this is his true information."

"Well," the doctor said. "Please, could you let the hospital know once you find out something, in case we have to notify a next of kin?"

"We would be more than happy to," the officer replied. "Please give us a call when he regains consciousness, Doc. Hopefully he'll be able to help us in our investigation."

"Of course, Officer."

One of the officers reached into his wallet and pulled out a card and wrote a case number on it for the doctor's reference. Then two officers assigned to the case left; they knew there wasn't anything more they could do that night. They would check with the investigators who were working the motel room in the morning and see what more they could uncover. For now, they headed home, leaving Joe alone in his hospital bed.

It didn't seem long before the next morning arrived. As Harris got himself ready for the day, he rehearsed his opening arguments as he had been doing for the last two weeks. He dressed conservatively for court, wanting to make sure the likes of Amber Andrews couldn't call him flashy or flamboyant. He grabbed his briefcase and headed out. As he drove closer to the courthouse, he could see the expected hordes of cameras and news anchors. He was, however, surprised at how many members of the public seemed to be gathered on the courthouse steps. He literally had to push his way through the crowds. He was hoping to avoid any contact or interviews with Amber Andrews, but of course, no such luck.

"Mr. Robertson, are you feeling confident today, sir?" Andrews called breathlessly behind him, seeming to appear out of nowhere.

He was surprised at her politeness.

"I think the state has a solid case, Miss Andrews," he replied, pleased with her first question.

"You've become known as the new Florida Hurricane. Do you think you can blow Miss Dixie's theory of being an antique dealer out of the water?"

"Again, Miss Andrews, I think the state has a solid case." Harris felt a pleasant rush when being called the Florida Hurricane; no matter what their relationship had been like, the reference to his father made him proud.

"The big question is . . ." Andrews started.

Oh, here it comes, thought Harris. He should have known he couldn't get away from an interview with her without her throwing some sort of dagger at him.

"Are you going to call *all* of the city and state officials caught with the madam or just the chosen few?"

It took every effort inside of him to maintain a professional demeanor as he answered her.

"The state will call anyone who is directly involved in this case, and that includes any officials, Miss Andrews," he retorted sharply. "The state will undoubtedly prove its case with any means necessary, as long as it's within the boundaries of the law. Have a nice day, Miss Andrews." He turned away from her and continued to make his way up the courthouse steps, effectively dismissing the troublesome reporter. Harris had already had enough of her cat and mouse game. He was going to have to see what he could do to avoid her each day; he didn't want to endure her intolerable interviews for the next several weeks, or even months.

Going through the courthouse security, many of the officers wished him luck with this case. They, along with others, knew this was going to be a hard case to prosecute, let alone win. Harris didn't think he needed luck; he believed his case was solid. It would be a slam dunk if Joe would get back with the proof he needed. He actually wondered for one second how his father would have handled this one. He even wondered if his father would have been proud of him. He supposed that didn't matter now. With a slight shrug to clear his mind, Harris strode into the courtroom, as ready for his case as he could be.

The courtroom was packed; there wasn't one empty seat. The bailiff brought the courtroom to silence.

"All rise," said the bailiff. First, the jury was seated and then the judge. The bailiff began, "The Right Honorable Judge Poe, presiding."

"Case number 0729-O1220C-0610-ORL, the *State versus Dixie Jackson*. Please be seated," announced the bailiff. There was a quick buzz in the air, but silence soon filled the room. The judge gave the jury their instructions, and the bailiff made the announcement for the people in the gallery to take their seats. Judge Poe addressed Harris and Nigel, taking care of all the usual formalities before beginning.

"Mr. Robertson, is the state ready with its opening arguments?" asked Judge Poe.

"Yes, Your Honor."

"Then you may proceed," Poe said with a nod.

Harris took the stage.

"Ladies and gentlemen of the jury, good morning," Harris said confidently as he looked at each member in the eye, making sure they acknowledged his glare. It helped to see which jurors were paying attention. "The State of Florida will prove beyond a shadow of doubt that on the night of Thursday June 9, at approximately nine p.m., Orlando law enforcement raided the home of Dixie Jackson, located at 555 North Chesterfield Avenue. The prosecution will prove that Miss Jackson knowingly ran a sex trafficking ring, contributed to the delinquency of a minor, and had contraband and drugs confiscated from her home. Miss Jackson claims her income is derived from an alleged antique business, but the State will prove otherwise." Harris took up the whole morning with his opening arguments and his introduction of items into evidence. He was relieved when the judge announced an adjournment for lunch.

Harris was ready for the break as he wanted to give Joe another call. He couldn't understand why he had not heard from him. It wasn't like Joe not to keep Harris apprised of things; he especially was concerned because the information Joe was supposed to deliver was so crucial to the case. As the courtroom emptied out, Harris sat alone for a few moments, then he dialed Joe's cell phone. It rang for what seemed forever, but there was no answer. Harris slammed the lid of the phone down.

"Darnik, where could he be?" He closed his briefcase and left for lunch.

Smith knew Dixie was going on trial today. In anticipation of the dreaded event, he had gotten a little drunk the night before. Now he was mad at himself; he'd wanted to watch the Court TV channel's live coverage to see what was going on, but he'd overslept. Instead, since it was already noon, he'd had to catch the local news update.

"On another note," the anchor was saying, "the trial of the alleged madam Dixie Jackson started here in Orlando today." The program then switched to Amber Andrews live at the courthouse.

"The charges against Miss Dixie Jackson are sex trafficking, contributing toward the delinquency of a minor, and possessing drugs and contraband on her premises. The state vows they have a solid case. The question remains, however, will the prosecution call to the stand state and city officials arrested on the premises of Miss Dixie's? This is Amber Andrews, reporting for Court TV."

"Amber Andrews asked that question of the Assistant District Attorney Harris Robertson this morning," the Orlando news anchor continued. "He assured her that the State would indeed call anyone who, and I quote," he said, glancing at his notes, "'is directly involved in this case, and that includes any officials.'" The anchor looked back up at the camera. "Harris Robertson, who'll be prosecuting this case, is the youngest assistant district attorney in Florida history. He has been dubbed the new Florida Hurricane, a direct reference to his late father Mark Robertson, who was found dead twenty years ago under suspicious circumstances." The news anchor completed his report, and the show switched to commercial.

Smith pointed his finger and thumb at the TV as if it were a gun. He uttered the words "bang" and then blew his finger. *I think it's time I showed this clown a lesson,* he said to himself. *If he wants to hurt the only family I have, I think it's time I find out who his family is and hurt one of them.*

After lunch, court was back in session. It was Nigel's turn to address the jury.

"Good afternoon," Nigel said pleasantly, walking close to the jury box. "During the course of this trial, we will prove Dixie Jackson is an upstanding citizen, someone who contributes positively toward the community.

"On the night in question, she was throwing an elaborate party for her wealthy clientele, some of which were state and city officials who buy and sell antique items. She had no knowledge of the drugs recovered from the premises, and no way was she involved in any kind of sex trafficking. The state has also fabricated charges against her for contributing toward the delinquency of a minor. Bambi Woodsworth, the minor in question, is the daughter of a dear friend and was at the party by invitation." Nigel knew this wasn't true, but he also knew Bambi's mother, Eleanor Woodsworth, couldn't be called on to testify for the prosecution to refute this "fact" as she was no longer living.

When court was finally adjourned for the day, Harris was relieved. It had been a long day in court, and he was glad the first day was out of the way. He couldn't wait to get home and see if Joe left him a message on his answering machine, but when he got home, there wasn't a thing from him. There was only a good luck message from his uncle and his mother. He tried Joe's cell phone again, but this time it went straight to voice mail. Harris knew something was wrong. He remembered Robin's last name from when she filled out the application form to work at the DA's office. He called information and got her number.

"Hello," answered Robin.

"Hello, Robin, this is Harris Robertson from the district attorney's office. How are you this evening?"

"Oh, Mr. Robertson, I'm so glad you called. I'm beside myself with worry. Have you heard from Joe? Is he OK? He was calling me twice a day, but then stopped. I haven't heard from him since Thursday. He was supposed to be home Sunday night." Harris interrupted her as she was talking a mile a minute.

"No, Robin, I haven't heard from him either. That's why I'm calling you. He didn't show up for court today, and it's most unusual for him not to stay in contact with me. I was hoping you had heard from him."

"No, like I said, he was supposed to be home on Sunday. I'm so worried, Mr. Robertson."

"Please, call me, Harris," he said. "Do you know where he was?" he asked her.

"No, I'm afraid all he said was he was heading to Pennsylvania and that he would explain everything else after he had informed you." Harris thought that was a little strange; what was it about Miss Dixie's case that could have led him all the way to Pennsylvania?

"Harris, is there something you could do? I don't understand what could have happened to him. Joe Marble is a good man."

"Yes, he is, Miss Robin. Try not to worry. I'll start checking out the situation right away. I'll call down to the Orlando Police Department right now and put out an all-points bulletin on him. I'll have them get in touch with local law enforcement in Pennsylvania as well. I probably won't hear anything back tonight, but I'll let you know tomorrow at the latest. I'm in court again all day, but I'll get in touch with you as soon as I hear something."

"Yes, I've been watching you on Court TV. I can see how you get your name. You sure don't pull any punches. You're like a fierce storm. Joe admires you so much. He tells me all about you. I already feel as if I know you."

"I hope it's all good," replied Harris, knowing how Joe liked to tease him. He could tell what a charming and humble person Robin was; he could see why Joe was head over heels for her. "I promise I'll call you at some point tomorrow, Miss Robin."

"OK, I appreciate that, and you have a good night, y'hear now?"

"I hear you, Miss Robin," he said with a smile, enjoying her accent.

Harris hung up, then called in a missing person report, explaining that Joe was working for the district attorney's office and was due in court to testify in a major case. After waiting on hold for what seemed forever, he gave them all Joe's information. The officer taking the call said he would contact him if they had any updates. Harris went to bed that night with a sick feeling in his stomach; he didn't like not knowing what happened to his friend.

The next day, he did his best to concentrate all day in court. He knew he'd missed some crucial objections and that infuriated him. He didn't enjoy looking over at Nigel and seeing him smirk. He would need to bring his game on tomorrow, or he would be in trouble. Of course, Amber Andrews was all over the news with his inconsistencies, and she of course proposed the question that maybe he was throwing his case, just as his father did twenty years ago in the Bellamy trial. He wanted so badly to respond to her, but it was more important to get home and call Robin. Maybe she had heard something.

"Have you heard anything from Joe today?" he asked her as she answered her phone.

"Not a thing," she said softly; she had obviously been crying.

"Robin, how about I come and pick you up and we go over to Joe's house? Maybe we could find some clues." She was ecstatic; it was better than sitting at home pacing the floor, putting herself through agony with bad thoughts swimming around in her head.

"I would love to, Harris. How soon can you be here?"

"Give me your address, and I'll head over right now," he said.

She relayed her address to him, and he took off from the courthouse to go get her. Once he picked her up, they headed for Joe's condo. It was funny that they both knew he kept the front door key under the mat. Robin tapped her white cane along the hallway walls, guiding herself while following Harris. She observed some newspapers stacked on the floor with her cane, and she could tell there was more than one. They looked around and found nothing out of place or out of the ordinary.

When they got to his bedroom, Harris noticed the phone and answering machine next to the bed on the nightstand. He started to rewind the messages.

Tuesday, 9:15 a.m.: "Hi, Joe, it's Ma. It occurred to me you told me yesterday you were going out of town, but you neglected to tell me exactly where you were going. Please give me a call so I don't worry. I want to talk to you before you testify for Harris next week. Maybe I can offer you some motherly advice. Love you, son." *Beep.*

Tuesday, 2:37 p.m.: "Mr. Marble, this is Leslie. I'm calling from Dr. Ebner's office. I'm calling to remind you have a dentist appointment Thursday at 11:00 a.m." *Beep. Typical Joe*, thought Harris. *He's always forgetting something.*

Wednesday, 9:20 a.m.: "Hey, Joe, it's Alberto, give me a call. Your results are in." *Beep.*

Wednesday, 11:37 a.m.: "Hey, Joe, it's Alberto again. I thought you wanted these results as soon as possible. Give me a call. I'll be leaving early today. I have a hot date." *Beep.*

Wednesday, 4:20 p.m.: "Hey, Marble. It's Alberto from the lab again. Those DNA samples you dropped off for Robertson and Mason? The results were 99.9 percent negative. There is no genetic relationship to each other whatsoever. Sorry to call and leave a message, but I haven't been able to catch you. Later, bud." *Beep.*

Harris couldn't believe what he heard. He immediately rewound the machine and had to listen again. The only words embedded in his head were "99.9 percent negative." He wanted to rewind the machine repeatedly until the words could sink in, but he didn't want Robin to think he was obsessive or concerned.

"Oh, Harris, what wonderful news," she said, breaking the silence. "I'm guessing she's the lady you thought was your sister?"

"Yes, it's," Harris said, feeling dizzy from the news and wondering how Robin knew so much. What the hell was going on? Could this be true? Trudy had confirmed they were siblings. He was so confused. Where the hell was Marble? He wanted some answers.

"I had no idea Joe was having this done," he finally managed.

He didn't know whether to be mad at him for going behind his back or grateful to find out the love of his life wasn't his sister after all. He wondered when Joe collected the DNA from both of them; boy, did his friend have some explaining to do.

"You can listen to it again if you like, Harris," Robin said smiling at him. He blushed, hoping she wouldn't notice.

"No, I think it's OK. I don't think I'll forget what it said."

Harris's heart pulsed with so many emotions. He was glad Robin couldn't see the tears in his eyes. His hands were shaking, his legs were weak, the butterflies returned to his stomach. He wanted so badly to revel in the news and enjoy the moment, but he knew it was more important to find Joe. He turned the machine on once more.

Sunday, 7:00 p.m.: "Hey there, Joseph Marble, this is Robin. You were supposed to be home at five p.m. It's now seven o'clock. Please call me and let me know you arrived home safely. I missed you, baby, and cannot wait to see you again. I love you." *Beep.*

This time it was Robin's turn to blush.

Sunday, 11:00 p.m.: "Mr. Marble, this is Budget Rent a Car. Our records show you didn't return your rental car to our Pittsburg terminal by the required time of 5:00 p.m. Please call our reservation department immediately to update us on the status of your car. The number is 1-800-555-0729. *Beep.*

"Bingo," Harris said with excitement. There was another call from Joe's mom and several more from Robin, then nothing more. At least now, Harris had a lead on his whereabouts. What he couldn't figure out was what he was doing in Pittsburgh. He looked around the room one last time, making sure they had not missed anything, but everything seemed in order. He noticed Joe had not made his bed before he left and made a mental note to tease him about it when they caught up with each other.

The two of them locked up Joe's house and replaced the key under the mat. Harris opened the car door for Robin, and they started to drive back to her house.

"Did Joe say anything else to you that might possibly help me find him?" he asked her.

"Well, I know on Wednesday he was distraught after the meeting he had. He said it concerned you, and he wasn't looking forward to telling you what he found out. I could tell whatever it was pained him."

What could anything to do with Eleanor Woodsworth's case have to do with him? He was now even more confused.

"Are you sure that's all?" he asked her again.

"Yes, he said nothing else about his trip. Only that he would tell me the details after he explained them to you, and I already told you that."

"I guess we're both in the dark here, Miss Robin." As soon as the words were out of his mouth, he felt awful.

"Oh, Robin, I'm so sorry. I didn't mean anything by that. I hope you didn't take offense."

"Of course not. It's always quite cute when someone uses a phrase or saying which pertains to my sight. I'm not the sensitive type. I would like you to feel comfortable around me since I think Joe and I may be taking our relationship a bit more seriously when he returns. So hopefully we will be spending a lot of time together," she said trying to stay positive.

"Hey, that's great!" Harris responded happily. "It's about time that scoundrel found a good lady."

"Well, I can assure you, he has," Robin told him, smiling.

Harris drove into Robin's driveway and ran to the other side of the car.

"It's OK, I can manage from here," Robin said, being her usual independent self.

"No, ma'am. I wouldn't be a gentleman if I didn't escort you to the door, and then I'd have Marble on my ass."

The two of them laughed trying to lighten the situation.

"I'll make some phone calls in the morning, and then I promise no matter what I find out, I'll call you, OK?"

"Thank you, Harris, that's so kind of you. I won't rest well until I know Joe is OK."

"Good night, Robin."

"Good night, Harris," she said, then turned and headed in the front door.

Harris got back in his car then drove home. *Joe is a lucky man,* he thought to himself. It was about time he got a break. He stopped at a drive-through and grabbed something to eat. He was trying to force himself not to think about Markita or the test results on his drive home, but his stomach was already feeling the return of the butterflies.

Once inside, he ran upstairs and threw on his pajamas, then returned downstairs to eat. He grabbed a green tea and fixed a plate of his leftover birthday cake before heading to his favorite fat boy chair. He didn't even turn on the music; he just wanted to sit in silence and reflect on the day.

He was having trouble focusing on Markita. There was a time when if he heard the news about them not being siblings he would have driven up to Tallahassee at a moment's notice. But slowly, the memories of the two of them returned. He thought about the e-mails they sent to each other every day when she was at the office. He remembered the songs he would send to her, each one of them representing something the two of them shared. He'd revealed to her his most intimate secrets, telling her he had never felt true love or experienced intimacy with a woman before her. He had finally found the love of his life. There were so many memories in just a short period.

He remembered her long soft hair. How perfectly her head had fit into his shoulder, the one God created just for her. Suddenly the butterflies disappeared again. His thoughts went back to their breakup. He stood up and walked around the condo, then went upstairs to his room and sat down at his computer. He looked up the e-mail she had sent, which now seemed so long ago. He stared at it for a while before clicking on it.

In it, she expressed her sadness at the thought that it would be the last e-mail she would ever send him. She told him her heart would never ever be the same after that night. Her whole world had turned upside down. Life without Harris, she'd said, was like no life at all. How could God have been this cruel to the two of them?

"Hey there, sexy bear." He greeted her words with tears that rolled down his face immediately, remembering how he'd felt when she used to call him that.

"You will always be a sexy bear, just not mine," she'd continued.

He read on. His heart ached as he thought back to the love they once shared. As he read, he could feel the tenderness of her heart, along with the pain in her words. It was her softness and sweetness that made him fall in love with her. The butterflies now consumed his stomach again. It was as if his heart stopped and restarted with a defibrillator. He felt as if it ignited his blood and he had the circulation back in his body. No sooner could he wipe away his tears, that more would fall in their place.

As he read on, his anger returned. How could Markita's own mother lie to her, telling her his father was hers when she knew he wasn't? This bewildered him. How could any mother do that to her daughter? He was even angrier at the thought of the pain Trudy's lies caused his own mother. It wasn't long before his emotions hit another high.

"A little Harris is better than no Harris at all." He was devastated reading her words, knowing how much he had hurt her. His tears flowed heavier now. He had to get up and go to the bathroom to grab a tissue. He returned to the computer, staring at the screen for a while. So many things were running through his mind.

He finished reading her letter. He saw the words "LB" at the end of the e-mail; they made him smile. He had not heard LB since they broke up. There was more; it ended with the words "always, ylg," which stood for "your little girl." How could a love so pure and so perfect have ended so soon? It wasn't right. Harris shouted angry words at the Lord, but then realized he should be counting his blessings as they might be together again one day. But he felt he needed to consider his mother's feelings. How would she react to Markita and him being together again? Trudy was still Markita's mother. Mary Ellen would still have to endure the pain of the lies. Then suddenly the butterflies left again, and he gasped for breath. What if Markita had moved on and found someone new? He had been so cruel to her at the end. He'd told her she made him sick and that he never wanted to talk to her again. All the feelings he was having could be for nothing. What if she had moved on? He would be devastated all over again. His head swimming, he got up and paced around the room, filled with anxiety. He tried contemplating whether he should call her or not. He looked over at the clock and saw that it was already 11:00 p.m.

"Darnik," he said to himself. *It's too late to call now, and I'm in court all day again tomorrow.* He turned off his computer and got into bed. How was he ever going to sleep tonight? He wished he had something to help him. He needed to be refreshed for court tomorrow. He then thought about Joe and his disappearance. Why had he not heard anything about him yet? Too much was happening in his life all at once right now. He wished he could talk to his uncle J; he would be able to help him. His eyes were finally getting heavy as he thought about calling him during the trial tomorrow.

Chapter Twenty

The Trial

Harris was back in court, calling Ex-Senator Franklyn to the stand. The bailiff swore him in. Harris had spent tedious hours laying out the foundation of the case before he could continue with the obvious line of questioning. It was important to establish a time line of the events that took place on the night of the raid. He was slow and methodical at first, asking easy questions, getting the witness to feel comfortable with him. He wanted to give the jury the impression he cared about the senator and his reputation. He showed compassion when he asked about the ex-senator's family, making sure to acknowledge his wife's battle with breast cancer.

"Senator, please explain to the jury the circumstances leading up to your resignation."

"Objection, Your Honor," Nigel Pope interjected. "The senator resigned for personal family reasons, which Mr. Robertson just bought to the jury's attention."

"Your Honor, his resignation is extremely pertinent to this line of questioning," Harris explained.

"Mr. Robertson, I'm quite capable of making a ruling without your help."

"Sorry, Your Honor," said Harris, not sorry at all.

"Overruled, you may answer the question, Senator."

The senator replied, "I knew there would be a scandal over the raid, and I thought I would save my family the embarrassment."

Harris nodded, then continued. "Very admirable, Senator. What were you doing at Miss Jackson's brothel on the night in question?"

"Objection, Your Honor," Nigel interrupted again. "It hasn't been established that Miss Jackson's home is a brothel."

"Sustained. You know better, Mr. Robertson."

"Yes, Your Honor. I'll rephrase the question. Senator, what were you doing at Miss Jackson's home on the night of the raid?"

"I was selling a piece of my wife's jewelry."

"I see, and for what reason were you selling this piece of jewelry?" asked Harris, knowing the senator was going to again use his wife's illness as an excuse.

"To pay for medical expenses," replied the senator.

Aha, there it is, chuckled Harris to himself.

"So you want us to believe you and your family are without medical insurance?" Harris asked sarcastically.

"Objection, Your Honor! Not everyone possesses medical insurance, even in senatorial positions," retorted Nigel.

"Sustained. Move on, Mr. Robertson."

Harris shook off the objection. Now that he'd made the jury believe he was concerned and sympathetic, it was time for him to become more direct. He would need to prove to the jury that this witness wasn't buying or selling jewelry, but was instead engaging in illegal prostitution.

"On the night in question, what were you wearing when the Orlando Police Department raided the premises and arrested you?"

"Objection. Irrelevant, Your Honor. What he was wearing has no relevance to the case," Nigel argued.

"Your Honor, I'm establishing a pattern," Harris snapped back.

"Overruled. You may answer the question," Judge Poe said.

The senator hesitated.

"Please answer the question," Harris pressed.

"Nothing," the senator said softly.

"I'm sorry, I didn't quite hear you. Could you please speak up, so the jury can hear you?" Harris badgered him.

"Nothing," the senator said louder.

There was a snicker from the courtroom; the sound of the gavel could be heard.

"Silence," demanded the judge.

Harris continued.

"Again, on the night in question, what was the woman in the room wearing when she was arrested alongside of you?"

"Objection, Your Honor. Again, irrelevant," pleaded Nigel.

"Mr. Pope, same objection. Again overruled. You're trying my patience."

"Please answer the question, Senator," Harris urged.

"Nothing," he again said in a soft voice.

"Senator, you're going to have to speak up. The jury needs to be very certain of your answers.

"Nothing!" snapped the senator, feeling like the Florida Hurricane had just hailed down on him.

"So, Senator, it is your testimony that you would have the jury believe you were selling antique jewelry at a party in a private room, while naked with a woman?"

"Objection, Your Honor. Nowhere does it state you have to be wearing a business suit to sell jewelry." Nigel knew he was grasping at straws, but he had no other defense to offer. The courtroom snickered again. Once more, the judge banged down his gavel and called for silence.

"If indeed you were selling jewelry to the young naked lady in the room with you, could you explain to the jury how come no jewelry was recovered from the room when you were arrested?" said Harris, going for the kill.

Suddenly, before the senator could answer the question, the bailiff walked over and handed the judge a note. Judge Poe instructed Harris to approach the bench. The note was from Hugh telling Harris to ask for an adjournment as there was word on Joe. It explained how he would be unable to testify that afternoon due to injuries received from a gunshot. He neglected to tell Harris the intense details surrounding the incident; he would leave those details to Hugh. The judge told Harris to file the appropriate paperwork. Harris returned to his table.

"Your Honor, I have no further questions for this witness. I reserve the right to recall him."

The senator could not believe his luck; he was so relieved. Harris then begged the court's indulgence as he asked for the adjournment. The judge explained the mitigating circumstances to the jury and thanked them for their service. He gave them instructions not to discuss the case with anyone.

"This case will be resumed at nine o'clock sharp Monday morning. That is all."

The bailiff instructed the court to rise, while first the jury and then the judge left the room. Nigel walked over to Harris.

"What the hell is this all about, Robertson?" he asked, pissed off.

"Our lead investigator who was going to testify this afternoon was shot."

"Wow, man, that sucks," Nigel said. "I'm surprised the old man indulged you."

"Maybe he does have a heart after all," Harris sneered.

"I guess I'll see you back on Monday."

"Sure," said Harris as he closed his briefcase. They walked out together.

Harris immediately drove back to the DA's office and headed straight for Hugh.

"Is he available?" he asked Hugh's secretary.

"He is waiting for you, Mr. Robertson. Hold on one second while I let him know you're here." Hugh instructed her to bring Harris into the office.

"Hey there, son, have a seat."

Harris cringed at him calling him son, yet again.

"I received a personal call from William Hall, the district attorney in Pittsburgh, Pennsylvania. He informs me that on Sunday night, hotel guests reported seeing two armed men leaving Joe's hotel room shortly after hearing a single gunshot. An ambulance rushed Joe to the nearest hospital from Oakmont to Shady Lane in Pittsburgh, where he had immediate surgery. The surgery was successful, but Joe remains in a coma."

Harris pinched his own leg. He needed to feel pain so he could process the reality of Hugh's words. Hugh could see Harris had turned pale and looked sick, but it did not affect him in the slightest.

"So do you want to tell me what the hell Marble was doing in Oakmont? I thought you said he was going over Dixie Jackson's books."

Harris was angry at the callous way he talked about Joe, but remained calm.

"I don't know why he was there," he replied without emotion.

Hugh had a good hunch he was snooping around trying to gain information on the Executioner. It was the only logical reason Hugh could come up with as to why Marble would be in Oakmont. The town and the secrets it held were too coincidental. He tried to rack his brain as to how Marble could have gotten wind of the Executioner and, if indeed he had, that begged the question as to whether Harris shared the knowledge of him with Joe, because that would be a disaster. He could not figure out what other possible reason Marble could have for being there. Hugh knew he would need to get some answers in a hurry since he could not afford another plan of his to go awry. If Joe was getting too close to the truth, it could mess everything up for Hugh again. *Thank God, Marble is in a coma*, Hugh thought to himself.

"Have you notified his mother, Nancy, or would you like me to do it?" Harris asked.

"No, you go ahead. It might be easier coming from his friend." Hugh had no time or sympathy for either Harris or Joe—or the man's mother.

Harris was more worried about how Robin was going to take the news; it was obvious she loved him, so this was not going to be a conversation he looked forward to. It wasn't something he wanted to tell her over the phone either. He figured after leaving Hugh's office, he would see if he could go visit with her.

This would be fine with Hugh. He wanted to get Harris out of his office so he could contact Judge Poe and find out how the trial was going. He needed Poe to put the pressure on Harris to go after Dixie, so the Executioner would in turn go after Harris. He was tired of waiting around for things to happen. He wanted the money he felt was due to him sooner rather than later. Hugh also wanted to call Ronald; Joe's shooting had him very uneasy, and he needed to know what Judge Harris knew about Marble's visit, and if, in fact, he had ordered the shooting.

"Well, Harris," Hugh said. "When you return to court on Monday, you make sure you put the pressure on the defense. We can't have trash like Jackson in our city beautiful."

"Yes, sir," Harris said getting up, knowing that was his cue to leave.

"Have one of the girls in the office send some flowers and a get-well card from the office to Nancy Marble, as well as to Joe, will you, Harris?" piped up Hugh, playing the all too sympathetic employer.

"Yes, sir," replied Harris, knowing how phony the gesture was. He turned and walked quickly out the door.

He strode back to his office and sat down in his chair. He rummaged through some messages, making sure there wasn't anything that needed his immediate attention, then paged through to Tara, asking her to get the number to the district attorney's office in Pittsburgh. He told her he wanted to talk to a William Hall. Maybe if he talked to the district attorney himself, he might learn something new; even the smallest of clues could be helpful.

Tara paged back just a few moments later. "He's on the line, sir."

Harris picked up the line. "Hello, Mr. Hall," he greeted the Pittsburg DA. "Harris Robertson from the district attorney's office here in Orlando, Florida. How are you today, sir?"

"I'm fine, Mr. Robertson. You must be calling about your lead investigator?"

"Yes, sir, I was hoping you could spare me a moment of your time."

"Of course, Mr. Robertson, how can I help you?"

"Was anyone able to identify the suspects?" Harris asked, being blunt and not wasting a moment of the district attorney's time.

"No, apparently they were wearing ski masks."

"Did anyone get a description of the vehicle or a tag number?"

"All we know is it was a burgundy Grand Am." Harris wasn't happy at the information he was getting, as nothing so far would help him to find out who might have done this to Joe.

"Could you have his personal items mailed directly to me here at the office?"

"I can't do that, Mr. Robertson. There were no personal items recovered. Do you know if he wore any jewelry, such as a wedding ring?"

"No, sir, he wasn't married. He did, however, wear a Rolex watch, which had an inscription from his father. Also he had an ankle holster, with a pistol."

"I'm sorry, Mr. Robertson, none of those items were recovered." Harris felt badly for Joe after learning this information. He knew Joe's mother had purchased the ankle pistol for Joe on his birthday, and he had loved that watch; it was the only gift he ever received from his father, who had passed away years ago. Losing it would piss Joe off more than the bullet he took, Harris suspected.

"Well, I do appreciate your time, sir."

"No problem, Mr. Robertson, I wish I could have been more helpful."

"Here is the number to my direct line if you find out anything more," Harris told him, giving him the number. "Would you please call me, sir, when you receive any updates?"

"Certainly, Mr. Robertson, my pleasure."

"You have a great day, Mr. Hall."

"You, too," Harris said politely and hung up. He then paged Tara again and asked her to get in touch with the doctor at Shady Lane hospital who was in charge of Joe's case. After forty-five minutes and several phone calls, she had to leave a message. She hoped it was OK she'd left Harris's cell phone number, as well as the office number. When she gave Harris the update, he thanked her for taking the initiative; he wanted to talk to the doctors as soon as they were free to find out if there was any update on Joe's condition. He then had the unpleasant task of calling Joe's mom.

"Hi, Mrs. Marble, it's Harris. How are you?"

"If you're calling me, Harris, I guess I'm not going to be well at all, am I?"

"I'm so sorry to inform you of this, but Joe has been shot. But," Harris added quickly, hearing the catch in Nancy Marble's voice, "he is OK, to a point."

"What the hell does that mean, Harris? 'To a point?' Is he or isn't he OK?" She did not mean to snip, but the news put her into a state of shock.

"I haven't heard back from the hospital yet to get all the details, but I've left messages with my phone number for the doctor to return my call."

"How bad is it, Harris?" Mrs. Marble was crying.

"From what I understand, two men stormed into his hotel room. They must have robbed him as none of his personal items were recovered." He knew this news would upset her.

"He'll be so mad they took his watch, along with his pistol. He loved those two items. They were his pride and joy, you know," she said, trying to be distracted herself, but Harris knew his call was a mother's nightmare. His stomach tightened before he told her the rest.

"Mrs. Marble, it pains me so much to tell you this, but there is more. There's no easy way to tell you, so I'll come right out with it. Joe is in a coma."

"Oh my god, no, no, Harris," she started to sob harder.

"I'm so, so sorry. If there is anything I can do for you, please don't hesitate to call me."

"Do you know how long they expect him to be . . . asleep?" she asked in desperation, not able to say the word "coma."

"I'm sure it won't be long." He was at least praying for that. Joe was the only friend he'd ever had, and he wasn't ready to lose him.

"I'm going to call the hospital right now," Nancy said, trying to pull herself together. Can you give me the number?"

"Yes, of course. It's Shady Lane Hospital in Pittsburgh." He gave her the number, hoping she would be better able to get through than he had been.

"Thank you, Harris, I appreciate you calling me. I know it wasn't easy."

Harris told her again to call if she needed anything, then hung up to move on to his next call. This one was to Robin, and he wasn't looking forward to this call either.

"Hey, Robin, it's Harris."

"Oh, Harris, have you heard anything yet? I still haven't. I have been pacing the floor all day again. I cannot understand why he hasn't called me. Something must be so wrong."

"Robin, Robin, calm down." He couldn't get a word in edgewise with her talking a mile a minute; he was starting to realize she did this when she was anxious.

"Oh, Harris, I'm sorry. It's just I'm so worried about Joe."

"I know you are, but you must stay positive, remember that . . . I was wondering if I could come by and see you on my way home."

"Oh my god, he's dead, isn't he? I can hear it in your voice." Harris could hear the air huff out of her lungs as she must have dropped into the closest chair. "No, no, no, Robin. Why don't I come by?"

"No way, Mr. Robertson," she demanded. "You tell me what has happened to my Joe. I need to know right now, please," she begged him. Harris hesitated for a moment, then tightened his stomach again, deciding it would be best if he came straight out and informed her of what had happened.

He took a deep breath and told her everything. "He was shot, and he had surgery, and the doctors were able to remove the bullet successfully, but he is in a coma."

"Oh my, ever loving Father in heaven . . ." Robin gasped.

"Robin . . . take some deep breaths and try to stay calm. He'll be OK, he's got to be. He's Joe Marble, right?" Harris said, trying to help her remain positive.

Robin tried to take Harris's advice and calm down, but she felt this news may have hit her harder than he could have guessed. She may not have known Joe long, but there was something special about their relationship, something she had never felt before. He was a rock she knew she could lean on one day, especially if her eyesight failed her. Even though she never wanted to give up her independence, if it was inevitable, she knew she could trust Joe. Robin was in a frenzy of worry. She wanted to get off the phone and call her mother to ask if she would pray for him. Her mother's prayers always helped her in times of crisis, and she felt she needed her more now than ever.

"Harris, I need to ask a large favor of you. I'm going to make reservations to go to Pittsburgh this evening to be with Joe. Do you think when I have made all the arrangements you could drive me to the airport?"

"Of course I can, Miss Robin, but are you sure it's safe for you to travel alone?"

"Of course I can, Harris. The airlines are wonderful at assisting me."

"OK, then you call me whenever you're ready, and it will be my pleasure to take you there."

"Oh thank you, Harris. I need to call my mother, but you're such a sweetheart. I know Joe will need me when he wakes up," Robin said, overwrought with worry. At this moment, nothing else mattered; she knew she needed to be by Joe's side.

"I think you're right. He's at Shady Lane Hospital, but I don't even know the room number, Robin, I'm so sorry." He hoped Joe would recognize her when he did wake up.

Harris was weary from all the day's events, so he told Tara he was going home. He instructed her to call him if there was any news on Joe. He wanted to go home and relax awhile until Robin called him to go pick her up. Once home, he threw himself into his fat boy chair and closed his eyes, reflecting on all the things that were happening around him: his current case, the secret investigation of the Executioner, accusations against his grandfather, the short-lived breakup of his mother and Uncle J, and of course, Markita. With a sigh, he opened his eyes, pushed himself out of his chair, and headed for the stairs. Once in his room, he took off his business suit and laid it on the chair, ready for the dry cleaners. He happened to look over at the clock, thinking he should call Markita to tell her about Joe. It would be the perfect icebreaker. He could then proceed with caution to see if she was seeing anyone new. His reasoning was that if she had indeed found a new boyfriend, then it would be pointless in telling her that her mother was a liar. But even if she *was* seeing someone, he argued with himself, she had the right to know.

A spark of anger entered his mind thinking about her with someone else. Deep down, if he was honest with himself, he had never stopped loving her and never would. True love never died, he believed, even if the person you love isn't in your life anymore. Eventually all true loves reunite and their journeys continue; he truly believed this.

Determined to end the suspense once and for all, he went to grab the phone to call Markita, when suddenly it rang. It was Robin calling. She had already booked herself on a flight and was ready to go to the airport. He sighed, telling her he would be right over. It was starting to bother him that he had known for more than twenty-four hours that he and Markita were not siblings and yet he had not managed to call her yet; it seemed something was always stopping him from making the call.

As he drove over to Robin's, he began to fantasize about seeing Markita again. He had dreamed the same dream over a thousand times. He would be waiting for her at the airport gate when she walked off the plane. They would both be nervous, their bodies shaking with anticipation, their knees weak. Their hands would reach out for each other's, gently touching, first the palm and then the fingers, like two blind people meeting for the first time. They would embrace, and he would never let her out of his arms again. He always woke up before they kissed. As this familiar scene played again in his mind, the butterflies returned to his stomach.

Robin was already waiting for him at the door with one small suitcase. He placed it in the trunk of his car, then opened her door for her. They talked very little on the way to the airport. Once he had escorted her through security, he realized they had an hour before her flight left, so he sat with her and waited.

"Did you make any arrangements to stay somewhere while you're up there?" he asked.

"No, I thought I would figure that out once I find out more about Joe." He was her main concern.

"If you need any help while you're there, please don't hesitate to call me."

"Oh, Harris, you're so sweet. No wonder Joe thinks the world of you." Harris blushed a little at her statement.

"Please call me when you arrive and let me know you got there safely. I want to know how Joe is as soon as possible."

"Of course I will. I hope when he hears my voice he'll wake up and everything will be OK."

"I'm sure it will all turn out OK. He's a strong and determined guy. I don't know if he told you," he added, trying to lighten the mood, "but I call him Inspector Gadget."

Robin actually gave a smile. "Yes, he did tell me, actually, and he loves it."

"I'll bet he does," Harris said with a wry grin, trying to cheer her up.

"Is there any word on who could have done this to my Joe?" she asked.

"No, not yet, but the district attorney in Pittsburgh is working on it. He promised to call me direct if they heard anything."

"I hope they catch whoever did this to him."

"Me too, Robin, me too."

The airline attendant announced Robin's flight and requested all early borders to go to the gate. Harris took her up to the podium, where an airline official helped her onto the plane. He watched while she took off before leaving to go home. It was now late, and he realized he had not eaten, but he was so tired he thought he would call it a night.

The phone rang early the next morning. It was his uncle J.

"Morning, thar whippersnapper, how be you this day?" he said cheerfully.

"Oh . . . my gosh . . . not you this early in the morning?" Harris said, rubbing the sleep out of his eyes.

"Yeppers, it's me, your favorite uncle."

"You're my only uncle, thank God," Harris said.

"Hey, hey, hey, I'm the best, and don't forget it, sonny boy." Joshua was in a good mood.

"How could I ever forget? You would never let me." Harris stretched and started to sit up. "It must be very important for you to call me this early, right, Uncle J?"

"Well, of course it is, laddie. I need a huge favor today."

"Only a huge one? That's not much, coming from you."

"Ha, ha, very funny. I have classes all day so I cannot do it myself, or you know I would. Your mother needs some work done on her car, and it'll be in the shop for several hours. Do you think you could pick her up and take her home, then return her back to the shop when her car is done?"

"Of course, I can. It will be my pleasure. It will give me a chance to spend some extra quality time with her, especially since I don't have court again until Monday."

"Oh, why is that?" asked Joshua, surprised.

"Oh gosh, I haven't had chance to call and tell you."

"Tell me what, son?" Josh was now concerned.

"Joe was up in Pittsburgh, actually Oakmont, Pennsylvania, and he was shot. He's in a coma."

"Oh my god, Harris! Is he going to be OK?"

"He had surgery, and they removed the bullet successfully, but he never woke up."

"That is awful, son. I know you and he have become good friends, as well as colleagues." Joshua was a little hurt Harris had not called and told him any of this earlier.

"I know, and I'm sorry I didn't tell you earlier. I dropped his girlfriend off at the airport last night. She has gone to be with him."

"Hmmm, you didn't even tell me he was seeing anyone."

"I know, Uncle J. Things have been so hectic lately."

Joshua's mind was already running a mile a minute as to why the town of Oakmont rang a bell with him. He was racking his brain, and then it came to him. He remembered Judge Harris and his wife lived there for a while after he got back from the war. *This has rat bastard written all over it*, he said to himself.

"Are you still there, Uncle J?"

"Yeah, yeah, I'm here."

"You went all quiet on me," Harris said.

"How is the trial going by the way?" Joshua said, changing the subject.

"I was destroying the senator's testimony when I got the word about Joe. Hugh must have some pull with Judge Poe as he adjourned the case until Monday morning."

"Damn. Did they catch whoever shot Joe?"

Harris told him what he knew.

"What was he doing in Oakmont?" Joshua asked.

That was the million-dollar question Harris wanted answered as well. "That's it, Uncle J. I don't know. He was supposed to be working on Dixie Jackson's alleged antique jewelry business. He was supposed to testify about a pair of earrings recovered from a decapitated prostitute's head, a woman who used to work for Miss Dixie. When Joe was arrested in the raid, he was questioning the woman's daughter. Her name was Bambi, of all things."

"Oh really? Son, there seems to be a lot here you haven't been filling me in on. Is there a reason for that?"

"No, no, Uncle J. I told you a while back, it's been one nightmare after another. I did fill you in on most of it, but I still have unanswered questions myself. I know there is one piece of the puzzle that connects everything together somewhere, I just haven't put my finger on it yet."

"Do you suppose Joe found those answers you were looking for and someone knew it?"

"What on earth makes you ask me that?"

The hair on the back of Harris's neck stood up. Could that be it? Did Joe find the missing piece of the puzzle? If that was the case, then it wasn't a robbery. Someone was obviously trying to kill him.

"It's a hunch, son. How about this Sunday when you come over, you tell me everything from the beginning, maybe together we can figure this mess out."

"OK, Uncle J. No problem. It'll be good to unload everything. Oh, and here is another shocker," he decided to add. "This one will really floor you."

"No more bad news. My heart can't take it," Joshua cautioned him.

"Markita isn't my biological sister."

"What?" Joshua exclaimed.

"Stomach puncher, huh?" Harris explained to his uncle the circumstances surrounding this discovery.

"My god, Harris, that is incredible." Joshua did not know if he should be happy or not. His first thought was of Mary Ellen's feelings. He decided to be cautious. "How do you feel about that, son?"

"That is another million-dollar question, Uncle J. I'm not sure."

"Wow, I can honestly say for the first time in my life I'm speechless."

"Oh no, not you, Uncle J, that could never happen," Harris said with a chuckle.

"Look, I need you to get your mother to the mechanic's by nine a.m. If you need to talk tonight, I can call you."

"No, it's OK. We'll talk more on Sunday. Maybe by then I'll have some more answers for you. I'll make sure Mom gets home, and I'll pick her up when the car is finished."

"OK, but please be careful, Harris. I don't like any of what I'm hearing. Like I always tell you, I can always smell a rat bastard, and this one stinks."

"Uncle J, everything is OK," Harris reassured him. "I love you."

"I love you too, son, and don't ever forget it." The two of them hung up. Joshua was left with a ton of questions, ones he did not like. Like why Trudy had lied about Markita came to mind first. Why would she name another man's daughter after his brother? He was now in the same boat as Harris, trying to piece this sordid puzzle together. He knew how his nephew must have been feeling about Markita because he knew Harris loved her as much as he loved Mary Ellen. The issue was still going to be that Trudy was her mother and if nothing else, she still had an affair with his brother. Those scars would never heal, but why continue with the lie? Joshua had a sinking feeling in his stomach; he could not shake the feeling that Ronald Harris was behind all this somehow, and that scared the living daylights out of him.

Later that morning, Harris met his mother at the mechanic's and took her home.

"Call me when your car is ready, and I'll come and get you," he told her as he dropped her off.

"You're such a good son. I don't know what I would do without you," she said, smiling at him.

"You're never going to find out, so don't worry your little self about it," he responded, smiling back.

She waited for him to go around to her side of the car to open the door for her. He was so like his father when it came to being a gentleman. He kissed his mother's cheek before hopping back into his car and heading for the office. Once there he called Robin.

"Hey, Miss Robin, is there any news?" he asked anxiously.

"There is no change, Harris," she said, then started to cry.

"It's OK, Robin," he tried to reassure her. "Give it time. I know he'll be fine."

"I'm so glad you're positive, Harris. I feel like I'm letting him down when my negative thoughts take over."

"It's only natural, Robin. You're a strong woman. I'm sure your strength is one of the things that attracted Inspector Gadget to you in the first place," he joked, once again trying to lighten her mood.

"Do you think so?" she asked insecurely.

"I'm quite sure of it. Joe told Markita and me how much he admired your strength and determination. Of course, he loves to hear you sing as well. I'd like to hear you sing soon myself."

Robin blushed, feeling a little more at ease after Harris's encouraging words. "Thank you, Harris. You don't know how much those kind words mean to me."

"You're welcome, Robin, but it's the truth. You hang in there, and let me know if there are any changes."

"OK, I will," she assured him.

When he hung up, Harris paged through to Tara.

"Please do me a favor, Tara. I need to wire some cash to Shady Lane hospital in care of Joe's girlfriend, Robin. Could you arrange that for me?"

"Of course, sir," she replied.

Just as Harris was about to tackle the paperwork on his desk, Tara paged Harris back unexpectedly.

"Sir, it's your grandfather on the line."

"Thank you, Tara, put him right through."

"Grandfather, how are you?" Harris asked immediately.

"Very well and you?"

"Ah, not so good," Harris replied.

"Why? What's going on?"

"Joe Marble, our lead investigator, was shot last Sunday."

"Oh my goodness, Harris, that's awful," the judge exclaimed, trying to sound as surprised as possible.

"He wasn't just my lead investigator, Grandfather. He was becoming a close friend."

"Well, son, I know it's devastating when one loses a friend, but you will meet others."

"Oh, he isn't dead, Grandfather, but he is in a coma," Harris informed him.

Ronald nearly choked on his morning coffee midsip.

"He survived?" The judge was furious and frantically tried to cover his surprise by sounding happy for Harris.

"Yes, sir. He was taken to the hospital, and they removed a bullet, but he remains in a coma."

"Thank God," the judge said, lying through his teeth.

Ronald was beside himself. After he had the two numbskulls responsible taken out, he would need to find a way to make sure Marble never woke up.

"Not to change the subject, sir, but are you calling to say hi, or are you calling on official business?"

"Actually, son, I wanted to call and tell you that you were a pleasure to watch on TV. I'm so proud of you. You continue to handle that Amber Andrews beautifully, and you made the senator look like a fool. My only concern, Harris, is the senator is still loved by the people of this state. Even if he isn't in office, he's still a powerful man, so be careful where he is concerned, will you?"

"What are you trying to imply, Grandfather?"

"I'm not trying to imply anything, Harris, I'm informing you. Senator Franklin can cause you problems in your career."

Ronald knew all too well how powerful Senator Franklin was. Even though he removed himself from his position, he was applying a lot of pressure to the members of the Order.

"Thank you, sir, but I'm not afraid of the likes of him, and I certainly can't be influenced. My reputation speaks for itself."

"You're absolutely right, son. Your integrity is impeccable."

His grandfather's words were the highest compliment he could have received, but Harris wasn't quite sure how to take the comments he made about the senator.

"Please know I'm not saying this because I'm your grandfather, Harris," the judge was saying. "You're truly a brilliant prosecutor."

"Thank you again, sir."

"Oh, don't thank me. I enjoy watching you blow the bad guys away." The old man laughed from his belly. "How is your mother?" he asked, trying to change the subject.

"Good, thanks. Her car is in the shop today, and I have to go pick her up and take her to get it when it's ready."

"Good job, son. I like the way you take care of my daughter. She is so precious to me."

"I know. I plan on keeping her around forever," Harris teased.

"Well, son, I'd better get going. I have laws to uphold, you know."

Even though he knew they were meant as humor, those words filled Harris with such pride for his grandfather.

"Say hello to Grandmother, and tell her I love her, sir."

"I will. Oh, and, Harris? Let me know if Joe wakes up, will you?"

"Of course, sir." Hanging up, Harris reflected on how good it felt talking to his grandfather; he wished they could see more of each other.

Harris's cell phone rang. He glanced down at the caller ID and saw that his mother was calling.

"Hello, Mother," he greeted her brightly.

"Hi, son. My car is ready, so will you be able to stop by and pick me up soon?"

"Sure, I'll be there in a jiffy. By the way, I just got off the phone with Grandfather."

"Oh? How is Daddy?" Mary Ellen asked.

"Fine. He was calling to tell me he saw me on Court TV and said I looked good. I think he reckons I remind him of my father."

"I know you don't like to talk about your father, Harris, but when it comes to the courtroom, it's eerie. You really are just like him in that respect, and he truly was brilliant."

"It's OK, Mom," Harris replied. "I don't mind being compared to him as a prosecutor. His reputation was as impeccable as mine when it came to upholding the law. I only wish he could have had that kind of passion, and compassion, for me."

"I know, son." There was a pause, and then Mary Ellen gently reminded him of the purpose of her call. "Not to change the subject, but my car is ready, so if you would like to come and get your old mother . . . ?"

"Ah, Mom, you will never be old. Your heart is too young, and besides, Uncle J's is right next to yours, so you have two lives."

Mary Ellen chuckled. "See you soon."

Harris told Tara he would be leaving for the afternoon, but if there was any news on Joe, to go ahead and call him. He would be back in the morning. When he arrived at the house, Mary Ellen was waiting at the door with keys in her hand.

"What took you so long?" She smiled, settling down into the passenger seat as Harris held the door for her.

"Hey! I have enough teasing from Uncle J without you starting on me," he replied, sounding shocked for her benefit. She smiled at him, shaking her head slightly as climbed in the car and headed downtown.

"Did you want me to follow you home once you pick up the car, or will you be OK?" he asked her as they neared the dealership.

"Oh, Harris," she chided him. "I'll be fine. I'm sure you have lots of work to get done," she said as Harris pulled into the dealership lot.

"Actually, Mom, if you have a second, there is something I have to tell you about before you go and get your car."

"Oh, boy, I don't like the sound of this. It's not bad news, is it?"

"I'm not quite sure. You'll have to let me know after I tell you."

"Now you really have me intrigued," she said, looking him in the eye and waiting for him to go on.

"I'm not sure how you're going to react to the news. I don't quite know how I feel about it myself."

"OK, son, why don't you get it out in the open and we can go from there?"

Harris was nervous about telling her. The last thing he wanted to do was hurt his mother. Right now, Trudy was a bad memory to her, and the mention of her name would bring up the same ugly feelings in his mother as they did for him. He decided to just tell her and figure out his next move from there.

"Markita isn't my sister," he blurted out.

Mary Ellen stared at him, not saying a word.

"Please say something, Mom," Harris begged her softly.

Mary Ellen still sat in silence, just looking at him.

"Please stop staring at me that way," he said, feeling uneasy. He felt a little reassured, however, that he did not seem to see pain in her eyes; it was more like relief or surprise.

"How do you know this?" she asked.

Harris told her about Joe's secret investigation and the resulting discovery. Mary Ellen again sat in silence. He couldn't tell what his mother was thinking, but he wished she would say something.

"Tell me, son," she finally said. "I know you loved this girl, so what does this news mean to you?"

"Honestly, Mom, I can't answer that at the moment. I have only just found out myself and haven't fully processed it yet." He paused, then asked her the question that had been on his mind.

"Would it bother you, Mom, if we got back together?" He didn't know if he wanted an honest answer or not.

"It isn't up to me, son. You have to follow your heart. We cannot help whom our hearts fall in love with." She smiled at him and touched his cheek. "It may not always be right for everyone, but it must be right for you."

He wasn't quite sure how to respond to what she said. Was she avoiding telling him that it would hurt her, or was she really saying to follow his heart? He knew his heart loved Markita and only Markita.

Mary Ellen kissed her son on the cheek and told him she knew he would make the right decision. He watched as she got out of his car and went inside the dealership to collect her own vehicle. He gave her a little wave and headed for home.

Mary Ellen paid the cashier and drove her vehicle onto the main road. Her thoughts were of her son and his dilemma when the light suddenly changed to red on her. She was traveling forty-five miles an hour and tried frantically to slow down. Her foot kept hitting the brake pedal, but the car wasn't responding. Her heart started to race, what was she going to do? Even though it was in vain, she kept stomping on the brake, hoping for a miracle. It never came. Her car rear-ended the vehicle in front of her going full speed. The last thing she remembered was lunging forward and feeling a hard thump to her chest as the air bag deployed. Then, nothing.

Harris was almost home when his cell phone rang. It was his uncle again.

"Hey, Uncle J," he said, not waiting for Joshua to say hello. "Yes," he rushed on. "I picked her up, and yes, she got her car, so don't go giving me a hard time." He finally paused, waiting for his uncle to crack a joke right back. The response he got was not at all what he had expected.

"Harris," his uncle said in a choked voice. "You need to get to the hospital immediately. Your mother has been in an accident."

Harris was horrified. Goose bumps made his body shiver as he slammed on his own brakes, pulling over as soon as he could, his heart pumping and his whole body shaking.

"What happened?" he managed to blurt out. "I just left her!"

"Her brakes didn't work from what the officer on the scene could guess," his uncle told him, his voice shaking with emotion.

"Oh, holy mother of god!" Harris cried. "Is . . . is she OK?" he stuttered, not sure if he could take it if the answer was no.

"So far all I know is she's unconscious."

Harris leaned forward onto the steering wheel of the Jag, shaking his head back and forth. How could this be happening? "First Joe, and now Mom . . . Uncle J, it's all too much."

"I know it is, son, but your mother will be OK. She has to be. Do you understand me?" Joshua spoke with conviction.

"Yes, sir," was all he could answer.

"I'll meet you at the hospital," Joshua said "Are you OK to drive, son?"

"Yes, yes, sir. I'll be fine," Harris muttered. "I'll see you there."

The minutes seemed to drag by with painful slowness as Harris made his way to the hospital as quickly as he could. He tried not to think about what might be awaiting him there.

When Harris arrived at the ER, Joshua met him with open arms, the two men patting each other on the back in an attempt to make the other feel better.

"Where is she? Is she OK?" asked Harris, trying to hold back tears.

"It's going to be OK, son, it has to be." Joshua was now crying himself as he tried to convince them both that everything would truly be all right. "She is in surgery," he told Harris. "There was some internal bleeding, that's all I was told."

Harris led his uncle to a pair of open seats near the back of the ER waiting room. As they sat down, he placed a trembling hand on Joshua's shoulder, giving it a squeeze and trying to stay strong for the both of them.

"I can't lose her, Harris. I just can't," Joshua kept muttering.

"You're not going to, Uncle J." Harris reassured him. "Mom is a strong woman. No one knows that better than you. And," he added, looking at his uncle in the eye, "her love for you is even stronger." Still, the wait was excruciating.

Chapter Twenty-One

Mary Ellen

It was hours before a doctor finally appeared.

"Mr. Robertson?" Both Joshua and Harris stood up.

"Yes, Doctor?" Joshua replied anxiously.

"Mrs. Robertson is going to be fine. We needed to use quite a few stitches to stop the bleeding, but there appears to be no permanent damage. We'll move her up to a room and keep her for a few days while she recovers. You can visit with her as soon as she's settled in her room, OK?"

"Oh thank God!" Joshua said with relief. "And thank you, Doctor, so much." The two men shook hands, then Joshua turned to Harris, and they hugged once more, patting each other on the back, so thankful that she was OK. Still their stomachs felt the anxiety. They couldn't wait to see how she was for themselves.

Once again, it seemed like they waited forever before being allowed to enter her room. Joshua's first thought was how pale his wife looked lying on the bed, tubes in her arm. He noticed the oxygen tube in her nose and the many monitors, which kept beeping. He rushed over to her side and brushed back her hair.

"Hi there, beautiful, how are you feeling?" he said softly. Mary Ellen opened her eyes and smiled weakly at seeing both her men, and then fell back into a deep sleep.

The nurse explained she would be in and out of sleep for quite some time until the anesthesia wore off. Joshua sat faithfully by her side holding her hand, looking at her adoringly the whole time, telling himself how lucky he was to have someone so beautiful in his life. Harris stood on the other side of the bed and gently kissed his mother's cheek as he held onto her other hand. His eyes filled with tears seeing her lying there so helplessly. Suddenly, his cell phone rang, breaking through the silence; he had forgotten to turn it off when he got to the hospital.

"Mr. Robertson," said an unfamiliar voice when Harris mumbled a quick hello. "I hope you don't mind. I got your number from your secretary, Tara. She thought you would want this information immediately."

He knew if Tara had given an officer his cell phone number, it had to be important. "Please hold for a moment, sir," he instructed the officer, then told his uncle J he was going to take the call outside, so as not to disturb his mother. He walked down the hallway to the small waiting room, relieved there was no one else in there.

"I'm back," he informed the officer.

"Yes, sir. My name is Detective Gary Snoke with the Orange County police investigations department."

"Yes, Officer, how can I help you?"

"I'm calling in reference to . . . I believe it's your mother, Mary Ellen Robertson?"

"Yes, yes, sir, that's my mother. I'm actually here at the hospital with her right now. What have you found out?"

"It seems your mother's accident was not so straightforward, and so I was called to the scene. I know you're the assistant district attorney, so I did a thorough investigation of the accident."

"Well, Officer Snoke, I surely appreciate you being thorough, but was it necessary?"

"Well," the officer started. "After a long talk with the towing company driver, although he's not a mechanic, he mentioned he'd noticed the excessive amount of brake fluid on the road. He got under the vehicle, and it appears, sir, at first glance, someone may have cut her brake line."

Officer Snoke paused for a moment, then went on. "With you being a city official, we like to rule out foul play, sir. I'm going to have to impound the car as evidence."

Harris stood still, not fully digesting what the officer was telling him.

"My mother just picked up the car from the mechanic's," Harris heard himself say. "It had some repair work done to it. Do you think the brakes could have accidently been cut or damaged at the mechanic's shop?"

"Was she having the work done to the brakes?" the officer asked.

"I'm not sure what she had done. I'll have to ask my uncle and get back with you."

The officer gave Harris the case number, along with his badge identification information, as well as his private cell phone number. Harris went back into his mother's room and asked Joshua what she had had done to the car.

"Your mother noticed the check engine light was coming on a lot, why?"

"Did she have the brakes looked at or worked on?"

"Not that I'm aware of. Why, son, what's up?"

"It probably is nothing, Uncle J."

"Don't give me that crap, son, let's go outside." They went out into the hallway.

"I don't want you to get all upset, but the police think her brake line was cut," Harris told him.

"What the hell are you telling me, Harris?" Joshua said, raising his voice. Harris explained to him about the phone call from the police.

Joshua started to pace, then looked sharply up at Harris. "Could this have anything to do with this mess that you can't figure out?"

"Why would anyone want to hurt Mom?" Harris asked, confused.

"I don't know, son, but I'm worried about you *and* your mother now. I think it's time you filled me in on what has been going on in your life."

Harris knew his uncle was right, so he dropped down into an empty chair in the hallway and brought him up-to-date on everything he knew. Joshua continued to pace back and forth while Harris talked.

"It certainly seems to be getting messier, son," Joshua said when he had finished. "Now that I know more, I'll think on some of the things we have discussed, and I'll see what I can come up with to help you."

Harris nodded and gave his uncle a grateful smile as the two of them returned to Mary Ellen's room. Joshua sat back down and held Mary Ellen's hand again. Suddenly a nurse entered the room. She looked from one man to the next and quietly asked for Harris Robertson.

"That's me," Harris replied.

She walked over to him and held out an envelope. "This was handed to me by some man in the hallway," she said. "He asked me if I would hand it to you."

"Thank you," said Harris taking the envelope. The nurse smiled faintly, checked Mary Ellen's chart, and then left the room as quietly as she had entered.

Once she had gone, Harris opened the envelope and started to read. Joshua became alarmed when he looked up and noticed that Harris had turned pale.

"What is it, son?" he asked, not sure he wanted to know.

"It's a message, a threat," Harris said, still staring at the opened letter in his hand. "It says the next time I won't be as lucky. It says if I continue to hurt his family, whoever 'he' is, the next time he will kill one of mine." Harris looked up at his uncle. "He's telling me to get Dixie Jackson off on a technicality, or I'll be next."

"My god, Harris. This *was* done to your mother on purpose!" Joshua was beside himself. "You have to recuse yourself from the case, son."

"I can't do that, Uncle J, besides Hugh would never allow it. This is my job, it's what I do," Harris said, some of the strength coming back to his voice. "I cannot let people like this sway me, or I'll never win another case."

"I don't care about you winning, son, I care about you and your mother being alive."

"This comes with the territory, Uncle J. It's probably an idle threat, anyway, but I'll have Hugh take care of it when I get back to the office."

Harris remembered the newspaper article he'd received about his grandfather and how he overreacted then. He knew now that he needed to be better prepared for stunts like this if he expected to move forward in his career. Criminals always thought they could intimidate people in his line of work; if he gave in, he'd never get anywhere.

"I wish I possessed your confidence, son, but I'm telling you I don't like any of this. I'm telling you I smell a rat bastard."

"It will be OK," Harris said, trying to reassure his uncle.

Where was Joe when Harris needed him? He sure could do with his help right about now. Joe could find out if Dixie Jackson had any family members in town, but as far as Harris knew right now, his investigation hadn't revealed any family.

He realized he needed Hugh to get him an investigator to take over for Joe. "Uncle J, I need to get going. I want to go see Hugh and show him this note. I need to shed some light on whether Dixie Jackson has family members in town since I was led to believe she was alone."

"I guess you gotta do what you gotta do." His uncle looked unconvinced.

"Uncle J," Harris said, trying to reassure Joshua, "I'll be back as soon as I can, I promise. I won't be gone long. I just want to get Hugh's take on this."

"OK, Harris, but hurry back. I'm sure your mother will want to see you when she wakes up."

"I know. I'll be as quick as possible." He gave his mother a quick kiss on the forehead before he turned to go.

Harris stopped by the nurse's station on his way out to speak with the young woman who had given him the envelope.

"Excuse me, ma'am, do you remember what the man who gave you this note looked like?" He showed it to her.

"Not really," she said apologetically. "It was so quick. I know he was an African American, and he was wearing jeans, but that's about all I can tell you. Wait," she said. "There is one other thing, but you're going to think it's silly. I remember his eyes. They were just . . . scary. They seemed to pierce right through me when he talked to me, like he had no soul. It kind of gave me the creeps."

Harris didn't think she was being silly at all. "What exactly did he say, if you don't mind me asking?"

"'Give this to Harris Robertson,' that's it."

"Well, thank you for your time, I do appreciate your help."

He left the hospital and headed back to the district attorney's office. He instructed Hugh's secretary to tell him he needed to see his boss this instant, it was urgent. Hugh told her to send him right in.

"Harris, how is your mother? I heard about the accident."

"She's going to be fine, sir. Thank you for asking. That's why I'm here."

"What's so important about it that you made me hang up on the governor?"

"I'm sorry, sir, but I received a phone call from the police while I was in the hospital, and it appears my mother's accident might have been intentional."

"Oh, and why do you say that?" Hugh remarked.

"It appears her brake line was cut," Harris told him, watching for Hugh's reaction. "An officer, Gary Snoke, said the towing mechanic could tell the brake line was cut."

"Who on earth would want to hurt your mother? Mary Ellen is one of the most compassionate and kindest ladies I have ever had the pleasure of meeting."

Harris liked what he said about his mother, but he was not so sure how sincere he was.

"If that's true," Hugh went on, "then give me the case number along with the officer's badge number, and I'll personally call the chief of police and have him thoroughly look into this matter for you."

"Thank you, sir, but there is more." He handed him the note. Hugh read it intently.

When he finished, Hugh shook his head. "I warned you, son, about getting used to shit like this," he told him. "Don't feel too badly. It means you're doing your job well, and you have the bad guys worried. When court is back in session, you need to get through your witnesses as quickly as possible so you can get vermin like Jackson off our streets. Once you get her on the stand, you can take her down. I have complete faith in your ability to apply that Florida Hurricane pressure to win this case."

Hugh relished the thought of him taking down Miss Dixie. He knew it would piss off the Executioner more than he already was. His plan was finally working out.

"You're doing a fine job, son," Hugh encouraged him, trying to hide the scorn in his voice. "I'm proud of you. Let's clean up our city beautiful." Harris felt good about the confidence he showed in him, but he always felt like Hugh had a hidden agenda where he was concerned. Although with everything he had on his plate, he would appreciate his assistance. Hugh could probably get things moving faster than he could anyway.

"The nurse at the hospital said the man who gave her the note was an African American with creepy eyes. Said he seemed to look right through her. There is only one person I've met in my life who fits that description—the Executioner."

"Harris, don't let your imagination run away with you. He's long gone, probably back underground. He wouldn't risk showing himself in a public place, let alone a hospital. Furthermore, he certainly wouldn't risk running into you, since you know what he looks like." Hugh felt like he'd covered Smith's tracks well.

"I'm not so sure. I wonder if he's connected to Miss Dixie in any way?" Harris mused, wishing Joe were around again to help him.

"Like I said, Harris, don't let your imagination go wild. You have other issues to concern yourself with, such as your beautiful mother's recovery. Please give her my best when you see her."

"Yes, thank you, sir." Harris knew that was his cue to leave.

As soon as Harris was gone, Hugh got straight on the phone to the chief of police. He gave him the officer's name and badge number and told James to make sure the report on Mary Ellen's accident conveniently got lost. Hugh then made a call to the Executioner.

"Hey, Smith, it's Hugh Gallagher."

"Yeah, what do you want?" Smith said, sounding like he could really care less what Hugh wanted.

"I wanted to let you know I'm doing everything I can to get Robertson to throw Dixie's case. I'm also working on a mistrial with the judge."

"Yeah, well, you better do something, or your errand boy will be meeting with a stainless steel blade, get my drift?" Smith slammed down the phone.

Hugh felt chills run down his spine; even talking to that man through the phone line got to him.

Harris arrived back at the hospital where Joshua was still sitting by his mother's side holding her hand.

"I'm glad you're back, son, she's starting to wake up."

"Hi, Mom," Harris said as he kissed her on the cheek.

"Hi, son," she managed to say with a groan of pain.

"It's OK, darling, don't try to talk too much," Joshua said tenderly. "I love you, my darling," he told her.

"Me too, Mom," Harris added.

"What happened? Why am I in so much pain?"

"Try to lie still, sweetheart. You were in a car accident, do you remember?"

"I remember seeing the light turn red." Both men could see that Mary Ellen was in pain; her lips were pressed together in a thin line as she tried not to let them see how much.

"Harris, could you please tell the nurse to get the doctor? Tell her your mother is awake and in pain."

Harris nodded and quickly left the room in search of the doctor. Joshua looked into Mary Ellen's eyes then, kissed her lips gently.

"I love you, darling," he said again, his voice shaking a little.

"What are you not telling me, Joshua Robertson?" She knew him like the back of her hand. "I have been married to you for too long not to know when there is sadness in your eyes, Joshua. Please tell me what you're keeping from me."

"It's nothing, really, I'm concerned, that's all. You had some internal bleeding, and they had to put some stitches in you."

He didn't want to worry her about the note Harris had received.

"Are you sure that's all?"

"Yes, my darling. You know that you're the love of my life, and I worry about you."

"You're a good man, Joshua. I'm one lucky lady to have you in my life." She smiled at him. His eyes filled with tears.

"I don't know what I would have done if I'd lost you. I have always lost everything I let myself love. First, my mother, then we lost Charlie. I'm always scared one day I'll lose you too."

"Joshua, you will not lose me. I'm not going anywhere," she said trying to reassure him.

"You know I've loved you from the first time I heard your voice. You were with my brother then, and I knew it was wrong to have the feelings I had for you. I wanted so many times to tell you how much I loved you, but you had a child I adored like my own. I didn't want to interfere with the beautiful home you made with him. Even though I knew my brother was hurting you, I felt like you deserved so much more than I could offer. Mark could provide you with things I never could."

"Joshua Robertson!" Mary Ellen cried, struggling to sit up. "What's the point of money and a beautiful house when there is no love inside of it? Life should be shared with the person you love and who loves you." She smiled at him once more as she reached out to touch his cheek.

"How did I get so lucky?" he murmured as he gently settled his wife back into her pillows. He'd waited all his life for someone this special, and now he felt as blessed as anyone could ever be.

The doctor and Harris returned to the room.

"Hi there, Mrs. Robertson, how are you feeling?"

"I'm in a little pain, Doctor."

"That's to be expected. I've put in an order for some pain medication so you will be more comfortable."

"Thank you, Doctor."

"When can she come home?" Joshua inquired eagerly.

"Not for a few days. I want to make sure everything is OK before we release her. Then it will be bed rest for about ten days. You can do light things, but no stretching or lifting."

"That's OK, Doctor, I'll take good care of her," said Joshua.

"OK, Mrs. Robertson, I'll be back in the morning to check on you."

Mary Ellen thanked him again, and then she was alone with her family.

"I'm so glad to wake up to the two of you," she said. "I'm sorry to have caused you both so much trouble."

Both men protested as she knew they would, but she still felt so guilty for causing them so much worry.

"How is my car? Have either of you seen it?" she asked changing the subject.

"No, Mom, it was—" *Impounded for further investigation*, Harris started to say, but Joshua jumped in and stopped him.

"Towed to a garage," he finished.

"Was there much damage?" Mary Ellen asked.

"We don't know as of yet, darling. We'll have to wait and see what the insurance company says. Don't you worry about any of that stuff," Joshua said, patting her hand. "I'll take care of all those arrangements." Joshua's eyes pierced Harris, telling him not to say a word to his mother. Mary Ellen caught the stare he gave their son. "Joshua Robertson, there is something you're not telling me. Don't lie," she interrupted when she saw he was about to protest. "I saw the look you gave Harris."

"OK, I'll come clean. The car is probably totaled, but it's OK. We can get you a new one."

Mary Ellen turned her head painfully and eyed her son. "Harris, is your uncle J lying to me?"

Harris had never lied to his mother before, but he figured telling her the car was totaled was not actually a lie.

"No, Mom, it's true, the car is probably totaled."

"We can always get a new car, but we can never replace you, my sweet Mary Ellen."

"Gosh, Uncle J, there you go again with all that mushy stuff," Harris said, trying to lighten up the mood in the room.

"Son, what are you going to do about the dilemma you told me about in the car shop?" Mary Ellen asked unexpectedly.

Harris seemed shocked by her question; he certainly didn't expect her to bring it up, considering the pain she was in. It must have really bothered her.

"What dilemma might that be?" asked Joshua, looking curiously at his nephew.

"Harris told me that he and Markita are not siblings after all."

"Oh, he told you about that?" Joshua raised an eyebrow.

"You knew and didn't tell me?"

"I only found out myself today, darling," Joshua soothed.

Harris thought fast. He wasn't ready to think about this himself, much less discuss it with his parents. "Why don't we concentrate on you getting better first, Mother, and then I'll think about what I'm going to do?"

"You might not want to wait too long, son. Sometimes true love only comes along once in a lifetime. Right, darling?" Joshua looked over at Mary Ellen affectionately.

"Absolutely," she replied, once again flashing him her beautiful smile.

"There you two go, getting all mushy again. I think I'm going to get out of here and give you lovebirds some time alone. There are some things I need to take care of."

"Anything we need to know about, son?" Mary Ellen asked.

"You're as bad as Uncle J, always worrying about me."

"It's called love," Joshua said, laughing at him.

"I'll be back later, Mom. You get some rest and no hanky-panky while I'm gone."

As he was about to leave, the nurse came into the room with Mary Ellen's medication. She also took her blood pressure and temperature.

"Are you hungry, Mrs. Robertson?" the nurse asked.

"Yes, a little." Mary Ellen had not given food a thought.

"The doctor said you could have some Jell-O and ice cream if you like."

"If you have rocky road, I'll have some too," Joshua told her.

"Sorry, sir, it's for patients only," she said with a small smile.

"Oh, I have plenty of patience," he said joking.

The nurse gave him a funny look as she left the room.

"Too much, Uncle J, too much. I'll see you both later," Harris said waving over his shoulder as he left.

Harris stopped at a drive-through and picked up something to eat, then headed home. He didn't think he could go in to the office today. The nerves in his stomach were only now starting to calm down. He threw the Styrofoam carton from his fast food in the garbage, grabbed a bottle of ice tea, and went to his fat boy chair to unwind, turning his music down low so he could lightly hear it in the background. *What another rotten day,* he thought to himself. When would this whole nightmare be over? Thinking about nightmares, he picked up the phone and called Robin.

"Hi there, missy, any news on Joe?"

"I'm afraid not, Harris. There's no change. The doctor told me today the longer he stays in the coma, the worse it will be for him when he wakes up."

He could tell she had been crying.

"Oh, Robin, I'm so sorry to hear that. I wish there was something I could do."

"Me too, Harris, but he has to wake up on his own."

"I'll call the district attorney's office in Pittsburgh in the morning and see if they have come up with anything yet. I didn't get a chance to today."

"Oh, is everything OK with you?" Robin asked, genuinely concerned.

"My mother was in a bad car accident today. She's in the hospital recovering from surgery."

"Oh my goodness, Harris! Is she going to be OK?" Robin felt so badly for him. First his best friend, now his mother.

"There was some internal bleeding, but they got it stopped, and now it's a matter of her healing."

"What happened, if I may ask?"

"She was coming up to a red light and tried to brake, but her brakes didn't work." He didn't want to alarm her by telling her about the brake lines.

"That's awful. Please give your mother my best."

"Thank you, Robin, I will."

"The doctors told me today Joe's mother will be arriving tomorrow. It will be nice to meet her, but I wish it could have been under different circumstances."

Robin wondered how Joe's mother would feel about her being by her son's side. She didn't want his mother to think she was intruding.

"Oh, yes, I guess that will be a bit awkward."

"Have you met her?" she asked, hoping he had and maybe he could shed some light on what she was like.

"No, actually I have not, but she has quite the reputation in the courtroom."

"Oh really? Joe never mentioned it." Robin was nervous about meeting his mother, and she hoped the woman approved of her.

"Hmmm, I don't want to spook you, but she was called the Shark."

"Oh my, Harris! Should I be concerned?" she asked nervously.

"I'm sure it will be OK. You're a wonderful lady, and we all have bad lawyer jokes told about us. Look at me, I'm no Hurricane."

"I beg to differ with you, Harris Robertson. You're quite the storm in the courtroom."

"Maybe so, but I'm a pussycat at home."

Robin laughed at him. "I certainly didn't think I could laugh today, thank you."

"You're welcome. I'll call again tomorrow. Maybe we'll get lucky, and he will wake up when he hears his ma's voice."

"Oh, I sure hope so. It would be the miracle I'm praying for."

"Remember," he said. "Call me anytime, night or day, if Inspector Gadget decides to wake up from his nap." He wanted to try to make her laugh a little more before he ended the call with her.

"OK, I will. You take it easy and best regards to your mom."

"Please tell Joe's mom I said hi, and I'm praying for him."

They said their good-byes, and Harris put the phone back in its cradle, leaning in the comfort of his fat boy chair.

He thought back to the first big case he and Joe worked together. They had realized right away there was a humorous connection between the two of them. The jesting back and forth came naturally to them; it was if they already knew what the other one was going to say before they said it. It reminded him of the bond he and his uncle J shared. He remembered how good he and Joe felt when that first bust finally went down. They'd spent six months working closely together, day and night, and were ecstatic when they had gotten all those guns and ammunition, as well as drugs, off the streets. The two men went out and celebrated together, sharing the fact they both believed in making the streets safer, as well as in the justice system.

Harris was, in fact, now starting to have major concerns about the legal system, especially where Hugh was concerned.

The phone rang, breaking into his thoughts and making him jump.

"Harris, it's Hugh." He wanted to say "Speak of the devil," but he bit his lip.

"Hi, sir, how are you?" He looked over at his clock; it was rather late for him to be calling. Maybe he had word on what happened to Joe or better yet who cut his mother's brakes. He had not given the threat to his life another thought since Hugh told him it was probably a hoax or maybe even one of her customers trying to get him to back off Miss Dixie.

"I called the officer who investigated your mother's accident. It appears he was wrong. The brakes were not cut, they were just leaking. I took the liberty of having the insurance adjuster look at the car for you, and he wrote it off for your parents. He said he would have the car taken away first thing in the morning, since it's totaled, and he'll offer you a settlement after you file the appropriate insurance claim. You should get a settlement check pretty soon after that."

"What about the note though? It said if I didn't let Dixie Jackson go, I would be next, insinuating my mother's accident was obviously intentional."

"I don't know how to answer that, Harris. These crackpots get wind of something like her accident, then when they associate the news with a government official such as yourself, and they fabricate whatever they can to intimidate you. It happens all the time. I told you that when you received that dreadful article about your grandfather."

"Right," Harris replied shortly.

"Well, son, I'll see you in the office bright and early tomorrow morning."

"Yes, sir," he said, barely able to contain his anger as he hung up.

Something is definitely wrong, he thought. He started to place the chain of events in order. Things were not adding up.

The officer had been adamant about the evidence: someone cut the brake lines to his mother's car. That's why he impounded the vehicle for evidence. Hugh's conclusion was there was only a leak in the brake line. He couldn't believe Hugh was able to get the insurance adjuster to total the car as well as dispose of it the next day. If things looked suspicious, then it usually meant someone was trying to cover something up. It was evident to him at this point that Hugh was involved with his mother's accident somehow, but why? His uncle J's words came to mind: *"I smell a rat bastard."* Those words had Hugh Gallagher written all over his mother's accident.

The phone rang again.

"Hello," said Harris.

"Hey, son, your mom is asking for you. How long are you going to be?"

"I'm on my way, Uncle J."

"Good, your mother needs us right now," Joshua said.

"I know. I promise I'll be there as soon as possible. I was on my way out. Tell Mom she's beautiful, and I'll be there in a heartbeat."

"OK, son, but there is one thing I think you need to do before returning to the hospital."

"What's that?"

"I think you should call your grandfather and explain to him what happened to your mother."

"Oh! You're right. It never occurred to me that I hadn't called him yet. Thanks for reminding me."

"No problem. I know I'm not a big fan of your grandfather when it comes to your career, but in this instance, I recommend you inform him of your mother's accident along with its suspicious surroundings."

"OK, Uncle J, I'll do that."

"When you're done, please don't be too long in returning to see your mother."

"I promise, I won't be."

He hung up with his uncle then immediately called his grandfather. Ronald's secretary put Harris straight through to him.

"Well, son, to what do I owe this pleasure?"

"It's not such good news, sir."

"I don't like the sounds of that."

"Mom was in a car accident."

"Is she OK?" the judge said, sounding deeply concerned.

"She will be fine, Grandfather, but it's the circumstances surrounding her accident that have me worried."

"What do you mean?" Judge Harris asked, growing suspicious.

"Well, an officer called me in the hospital to inform me that after investigating the accident, it appeared her brake line was cut."

"What! Are you sure?"

"The officer seemed pretty confident that it was done on purpose. I, of course, reported this to Hugh."

"What was his take on this?" the judge asked calmly.

"That's the million-dollar question, Grandfather. I gave him the case number, along with the other information, and he offered to take care of things personally for me. He felt my first priority should be taking care of Mother. At first, I was grateful to him, until he called me to let me know the officer recanted his statement about Mom's brakes, saying they were only leaking, not purposefully cut. Hugh even called the adjuster to come out and total the car, and the insurance company is all ready to write an insurance check."

"Wow, that's a lot to digest, son."

"Right, sir. I'm beginning to suspect Hugh has a lot to do with many discrepancies around here."

"What are you insinuating, son?"

"Well, I received a note in the hospital saying that if I put Dixie Jackson on the stand Monday morning, either I, or another family member of mine, will meet with an accident, but next time, they won't be as lucky as Mom."

"Jesus Christ, son! What the hell is going on down there?" The judge couldn't believe what he was hearing.

"That's a good question, sir."

"Harris, I'm glad you called me. You leave this with me. I'm going to make some phone calls, and trust me, I'll get to the bottom of all this."

"Thank you, Grandfather. I'd like to think that I'm experienced enough to take on corruption, but it's good to know I have someone like you on my side."

"Thank you for your confidence, son. Please give your mother my love and let her know I'll be there this weekend. I'll stop by on Sunday and see the both of you."

Harris thanked his grandfather again as they said good-byes.

Judge Harris was furious. He immediately tried to call Hugh, but couldn't get a hold of him. He left a message telling him they needed to talk. He then called Smith, who was also unavailable. He left him a message as well.

"I have told you in no uncertain terms that you're not to go anywhere *near* the Robertson family," he stormed to the answering machine. "Not ever. Don't cross me, do you understand? I'll be there this weekend, so you had better have a good explanation for your actions, or you will meet with an uncertain ending."

Harris returned to the hospital.

"Harris, there you are," his mother greeted him. "Joshua tells me I was in an accident today. You must have been in court all day since you haven't been to see me."

Harris looked at his mother strangely, then glanced over at Joshua, who shrugged his shoulders in confusion.

"I was here earlier, Mom, don't you remember?"

"Oh, son, I'm sorry, I didn't know." Mary Ellen looked confused herself.

"It's OK, darling," Joshua told her soothingly as he stroked her cheek with the back of his hand. "You're still groggy from the surgery."

"Oh silly me," his mother laughed quietly. "Yes, now I remember. You were telling me about Markita."

"Right, Mom," Harris said not wanting to revisit the subject right now. There was a moment of awkward silence, then his uncle spoke up, breaking the tension.

"Your mother ate a little Jell-O, and I ate her ice cream. She said she didn't want it," Joshua said defensively, a shamefaced grin on his face.

"Are you sure she didn't want it, or did you steal it from a sick woman?" Harris asked, trying to hold back his own grin.

"Would I do that to your mother?" Joshua asked, his grin turning sly.

"Hmmm, I wouldn't put anything past you." Both men chuckled.

"I'm sorry if I kept you from court today, son," Mary Ellen said. "I hope you don't get into any trouble."

"It's OK, Mom, court is adjourned until Monday."

"Oh, why is that?" she asked.

"It's a long story."

"Then tell me the short version."

"You need to rest, Mom. I'll tell you all about it when you're stronger."

"You will tell me about it right now, son. What is it?" Mary Ellen sounded worried, and he didn't want getting herself upset, so he thought he had better tell her something.

"My friend Joe was involved in an investigation for me and wound up shot. He was supposed to testify but couldn't, so the judge adjourned the case."

"Oh, Harris! Is he going to be OK?"

"He will be, Mom," Harris said, trying not to tell her too much. He certainly didn't want to bring up the town of Oakmont; otherwise, he knew she would interrogate him. Joshua helped him out by changing the subject.

"We probably should go in a bit, darling, so you can rest. We want you to come home as soon as possible."

"Yes, baby, you've been here all day hovering over me. You need to get some rest yourself."

"I will, darling, as soon as I know you're comfortable. It should be time for the nurse to bring you some more pain medication," Joshua said. "Do you want me to get her for you?"

"Yes, please, Joshua."

"It's OK, Uncle J. I'll go, you stay with Mom." Harris left the room to go find the nurse and returned with her a few moments later.

"The doctor said you were allowed to have a sleeping pill if you feel like you need one with your pain meds," she told her patient.

"Thank you, but just the pain medication please."

The nurse nodded and checked Mary Ellen's chart and machinery, then left with another brief nod as she went to retrieve Mary Ellen's medication.

"I think it's time we let your mother rest, don't you, son?"

"Yes, sir, she looks tired." Harris walked over, held his mother's hand, and kissed her cheek several times.

"I love you, Mom, and hope you get to feeling better soon."

"I will, Harris, and I'll be up and home in no time."

"I'm going to walk out with Harris, darling," Joshua said. "But I'll be back in the morning." He also kissed her cheek, but then he gave her a soft one on the lips.

"I'll be back first thing in the morning as well, Mom."

"I love you, guys. Drive home safely, both of you."

"Yes, dear," said Josh.

"Yes, Mom," said Harris, and the two men left the room together. Once outside, Joshua couldn't wait to ask Harris what he found out from Hugh.

Harris filled him in, including his suspicions about Hugh.

"My god, son, what's going on?"

"I don't quite know, but whatever it is, I don't like it one bit. I think you're right, Uncle J. It sounds like a rat bastard, and I think its name is Hugh Gallagher."

"You need to watch your back very carefully, son, until you can get some more answers."

"Oh, I will, don't you worry."

"Of course I worry, son. I couldn't love you more even if you were truly my son."

"I know. I feel the same, Uncle J."

"I'm going to see what I can find out tomorrow, then I'll call and let you know," Joshua told him.

"I had best be your first call, do you hear me?"

"I hear you loud and clear." Joshua laughed, clapping Harris on the back as they headed for the parking lot.

"Uh-huh, good. I'm glad we have that straight."

The two of them hugged before parting for their separate cars.

Chapter Twenty-Two

Reunited

Harris awoke and looked at the clock; it was 6:10 a.m., far too early for him to be conscious. He rolled over and tried to go back to sleep, but found himself half-awake, dreaming of Markita, flashing through every moment they had spent together. Harris thought it seemed so long ago, and when the alarm went off at seven thirty, he kept his eyes closed, his thoughts still consumed with the memories of Markita.

Today was Friday, the day he would tell her what he had known for the past few days. His stomach was doing double flips at the thought of calling to tell her they were not brother and sister. Under normal circumstances, he should have been thrilled to tell her so they could reunite and have the perfect storybook ending, but Harris's lawyer instincts took over. He knew there were other mitigating circumstances to consider now: her lying cheat of a mother, for one, as well as how that woman's actions would color how his own mother might treat Markita. And what about Markita herself? Would her reaction be a happy one or had too much time passed for her? He hadn't exactly been kind to her when they parted, and maybe she had moved on with someone else.

The anticipation was killing him. He looked over at the clock again; this time it was 8:02 a.m., still too early to call her. His mind wandered to the thought of movies with great love story endings. He thought about two lovers running along the beach seeing each other after being apart for a long time. The music would start to get loud, the two lovers would finally reach each other, then they would embrace, kiss, cry, and then speak the undying words, "I love you." Then the movie would end, and the credits would roll.

He wondered if his own reunion with Markita would be as sensational as a movie ending. He looked over at the clock again; now it was 8:27 a.m. He felt he could not wait a moment longer. He'd wanted to wait until at least 9:00 a.m. before calling, but his butterflies were fluttering inside so badly that he felt if he did not call now he might never have the nerve. He reached out to pick up the phone when suddenly it rang. His body made an involuntary leap into the air, and he felt one of the butterflies occupying his stomach turn over his heart, then fly up to his throat where it leapt out of his mouth, causing a hiccup.

"Hell-hic-o," he said.

"Hello, is this Harris?" Robin asked, not quite sure of the sound that she heard. She wasn't sure she had the right number.

"Yes-hic, it's me, Robin. I have the-hic-hiccups. Let me go down-hic—stairs and get a drink of wa-hic-ter and I'll call you ri-hic-ght back."

Robin laughed and told him to go ahead. "But don't be long. I've got news for you."

"OK will-hic-do."

He hung up the phone and threw the bed covers back, growling. He was not sure what made him angrier, the darn hiccups or the fact that every time he wanted to call Markita, something happened to keep them apart. He returned to his bed with a glass of water and drank it while holding his breath for long periods until at last the hiccups went away. He called Robin back hoping her news was good.

"Hello, Robin, it's me—all better. What's your news?"

"It is fantastic news, Harris," she gushed. "I was sitting near Joe, as usual, and just quietly singing 'Blue Bayou' when suddenly he opened his eyes! It was only for a moment, but I'm sure he heard me!"

Harris was not as excited as Robin; he'd heard about coma patients having a muscle reaction that might mimic the patient opening his eyes, but he wanted to sound positive for her.

"That is wonderful, Robin. What did the doctors say?"

"They told me to keep singing to him, so that's what I'll keep doing. I have the faith."

"Well, Robin, I guess the best any of us can do is to keep the faith strong for as long as necessary. We need to get Joe to wake up."

"I'll sing my heart out to him if it's what will make him wake up," she said, sounding determined.

He did not want to sound cold or uncaring, but he wanted to make his call to Markita. He started to wrap up the conversation. "Robin, this news is really fantastic. Please make sure you let me know if he opens his eyes again, or better still, when he wakes up, OK?"

"Of course I will. I'm hoping the news will be a comfort to Joe's mom when she arrives today."

"Yes, let's hope so. Please give her my regards."

"I will, and say hi to your mom for me."

"Will do," Harris said and hung up as quickly as he could. Now that she'd mentioned his mother, he debated whether to call her first, and he growled again. Nope, he told himself. If he did not call the love of his life right now, it was not going to happen. He looked over at the clock; it read 10:02 a.m. Time seemed to be flying by.

Once more, thoughts of Markita consumed him; she was always the first and last thing on his mind. After he made the call to tell her he still loved her, he prayed they would not be the last words he would ever get to say to her. As he went to dial her number, the phone rang—*again*. He was so anxious at this point when it rang that he jumped, throwing the phone into the air.

"Darnik," he muttered, truly pissed. "At this rate I'm never going to get this call made," he said aloud, frustrated.

"Whippersnapper, it's ten o'clock in the morning!" his uncle called from the other end of the line. "Are you ever going to come and visit your beautiful mother?"

"Yes, sir, I'll definitely be visiting Mom today."

"The day is nearly over, sonny," Joshua snapped.

Harris thought fast, he needed to hold off his uncle J until he'd had time to talk to Markita. "I've been dealing with the hiccups," Harris said, not lying.

"Oh rea-hic-lly? Well, that's just too—hic-bad," his uncle said, mocking him.

"OK, it's not funny, but I do have some good news to share," Harris said, trying to quickly change the topic. "Joe's girlfriend Robin called me this morning. It seems she was singing to him, and he opened his eyes."

"Wow, what fantastic news!" Joshua replied. "It's, at the least, a step in the right direction, son."

"I'm optimistic, but I worry it may have been a muscle spasm or something like that," Harris said feeling guilty about his negativity.

"God moves in mysterious ways, son, so keep your prayers coming and have faith."

"That is what Robin said, Uncle J. 'Keep the faith.'"

"Well, she has the right attitude. So what time should I tell your mother to expect you?" he heard Joshua say.

"I need to make one quick phone call, and then I'll be on my way, OK?"

"Okeydoke, then I'll see you soon."

Harris hung up and yet again looked over at the clock and couldn't believe how late it had gotten. So much for calling early. *This is it*, he thought. He swore he would not answer the phone again if it rang, no matter who it was. He prayed luck would be with him this time. "It has to be," he said aloud, desperate to call her.

He dialed the number, and the moment it started to ring, his stomach turned upside down. His heart felt ready to leap out of his chest, and a lump had formed in his throat. He prayed to God his hiccups would not return.

Suddenly a despairing thought hit him. What if Trudy answered the phone? *I'll hang up*, he thought crazily. If she answered, he felt it would be a sign that he should never tell Markita the truth.

To his relief, a familiar voice said, "Hello."

All his feelings for her came rushing back to him. It seemed like a lifetime since he had heard her sexy, angelic voice. His hands started to tremble, and he broke out in a cold clammy sweat. It was all he could do to hold onto the phone.

"Markita, it's Harris." His voice cracked with fear and nerves he cleared his throat.

"Harris! I can't believe it's you!" Markita cried. She sounded excited, but seemed only moderately excited, not overly excited, he thought. *Stop it,* he told himself as his brain tried to rationalize the situation.

"Ahem, yes, me, it's Harris." Now he felt stupid. There he went, mixing up his words already. *Why do I have to do this every time I talk to her?*

"Why . . . why are you calling?" Markita asked hesitantly. "Is everything OK?"

"Well, yes, but not everything," he stumbled. He knew he would need to tell her about Joe and his mother, but right now, he did not feel he could convey the information to her correctly; as always he stuttered and jumbled his words.

"What is wrong? You're not sick, are you?"

"No, no, I'm fine." He paused for quite some time.

"Well, if you're not sick, then why are you calling me?" He was not sure how to take her tone. Maybe she did not even want him to call her again after the things he'd said to her. He was now thinking of kicking himself for making the call.

"Harris, are you still there?"

"Yes, yes, I'm sorry. It's about Joe."

"What is it about Joe, is he OK? Is he the one who is sick?" His insecurities about her and Joe returned; she seemed more concerned about Joe than she did his call.

He managed to tell her about Joe's attack without stumbling too badly, although he obviously missed something in the telling.

"Oh, Harris, you must be devastated. I know how much his friendship meant to you. I'm so sorry for your loss."

"Oh no, that didn't come out right. He's not dead, Markita, but he *is* in a coma." He was not explaining things to her well at all.

"Oh, thank goodness, but what about you, Harris? Do you need me?" Those words were the ones his heart longed to hear. It was all too much for him, and he accidently dropped the phone onto the bed. He fumbled around like a football player who'd fumbled the ball. Finally, he grasped the phone in his hand, and then he returned it to his ear.

"Harris? Harris, are you there?" he heard her voice calling out.

"Yes, I'm here, I just accidently dropped the phone," he admitted to her, embarrassed.

"As I was saying, do you need me to come and support you? I promise I'll keep my feelings inside. I just want to help you if I can."

Relief seemed to wash over him. "Well, that's the other reason I called."

"There's more?" He wished she would let him get out what he needed to say without interrupting him. This was harder than questioning a witness on the stand. He was far more comfortable doing that than trying to explain this to her now.

"Actually, you would not have to hide your feelings, if you didn't want to." He paused.

"I don't understand? Are you saying you are OK about us being siblings?" This confused her; his last words to her were about how sick she made him because of their relationship.

There she went again, said Harris to himself. *I'm never going to get to tell her the truth. Maybe that is my sign. What if I'm tempting fate?* He began to get nervous, and then the cold, clammy sweat returned.

"Harris, if it doesn't bother you that we are brother and sister, maybe we could just be close, loving friends," Markita suggested hesitantly. She was utterly baffled as to how to proceed.

He could tell now she still had feelings for him and knew he needed to tell her the truth right now, this minute, no more waiting or excuses. No more stumbling, he growled to himself; this had to come out, perfect or not.

"Markita, that's just it, we are *not* siblings." There, he'd told her. It was all up to her now.

This time, she was the one who dropped the phone. Markita stared at it for a few moments before picking it up. Harris had been about to hang up, thinking that she didn't care anymore, when he heard a gasp and her sweet voice reaching out to him across the phone line.

"Harris," she breathed, her voice quivering and near tears "Do you know what this means?"

Harris was stumped. How was he to answer her? He didn't know if she still loved him like he loved her, so he was unsure how to respond. Unfortunately, he said the first thing that popped into his head:

"It means your mother told us a whole bunch of lies."

He could have kicked himself blurting out those words. Trudy was still her mother; he didn't know if Markita had forgiven her. Maybe they had gotten past the lies.

"I'm sorry about the choices my mother made in her life," Markita said quietly. "I don't condone any of them. It kills me that she hurt your mother."

"You have nothing to be sorry about," Harris told her. "I don't blame you for your mother's actions."

"Harris, I need you to know that I've prayed to God every night to hear the words that we are not related." She took a deep breath, then burst out,

"My god, Harris, are you sure it's true?" She was crying now, tears of joy and of relief. God had finally answered her prayers.

"Yes, I'm as sure as I can be. Apparently, Joe got some of your DNA, and mine, and took it to a lab for testing. The results were 99.9 percent negative."

"Harris, what wonderful news! I love you so much. I never thought I would ever get to say those words to you again. I can't believe this." Her words came tumbling out.

She sniffed as the tears streamed down her face. Harris let out a sigh of relief himself as his own tears of joy began to flow.

"I wasn't sure if you'd found someone else," he admitted.

"How could I have ever done that, LB? I was prepared to spend the rest of my life alone if we couldn't be together. I meant it when I told you I'd found true and everlasting love in you."

"I love you too, little girl. I never stopped. I was just too stubborn to admit it to myself."

"Harris, I'm shaking inside. If you were here, I would make you pinch me. We have been truly blessed."

"I know, little girl, I'm still trying to process the news myself. I don't know how Joe got our DNA, but I thank God he did."

"Did Joe tell you he came to Tallahassee on some business? He came and took me out to a restaurant, and I interrogated him about you. I wanted to know if you were missing me as much as I was missing you. I wonder if that is when he got my DNA."

Harris was now even more ecstatic knowing Joe had made a special visit there to do this wonderful act for them. "That is true friendship," he told Markita.

"Is he going to be OK?" She was talking to him as if nothing had ever come between them, and it felt so good.

"I'm not sure. Robin called me this morning and told me she was singing to him, and he opened his eyes."

"Well, that's at least encouraging. LB, we owe him so much." It felt so wonderful to call him that again.

"I don't think I've ever been happier in my life . . . Well, I can think of one time, but I'd rather show you than tell you," he hinted, shocked that he could slip back into such familiar conversation with her so quickly.

"Why, whatever do you mean, little boy?" she asked in her sexiest Southern accent. Changing the subject, she asked more seriously, "What are we going to do now?" She was eager to hear his answer.

"That's up to you."

"What would you say if I made a plane reservation right now and got on the first one that flies me into your arms?"

"I would say you would make me the happiest man in the world, little girl." He, like Markita, could not believe he was calling her little girl again.

He'd never dreamed for a moment either of them would ever get to use those pet names with each other.

"I don't want to hang up with you, LB, but if I don't, it will be longer before I get to you."

Harris needed to think logically now, if that was at all possible. "You'll need to give me a few hours, sweetheart. I want to pick you up from the airport, but I need to go visit my mom in the hospital for a little while, or Uncle J will have me killed."

"Harris, I'm sorry," Markita exclaimed. "Is your mom OK? I never thought to ask if it was your parents who were sick when you called."

"It is a long story, little girl, one which I haven't fully uncovered yet, but it appears someone cut her brakes."

"Oh, Harris, that is simply awful! Who would want to hurt your mother? She's just the sweetest person." His heart melted to hear her say that since his mother had not exactly been nice to her the first time they'd met.

"As much as I hate to wait," she went on, "how about I make the flight for later this afternoon, around five, or would seven tonight be better?"

"Oh no, five will be fine. I don't want to wait a minute longer than necessary to hold you in my arms. My shoulder has missed your beautiful head on it."

Markita's tears of joy continued to flow. "I love you, LB," she whispered.

"I love you too, my darling. See you soon." Those words were like magic rolling off his tongue.

"See you soon, sexy bear," she said and hung up as giddy as a schoolgirl who'd just accepted an invitation to the prom by the most popular boy in school. Her head was so light and airy, she felt she was floating as she proceeded to pack up the few clothes she would need for the trip. She would worry about the rest of her stuff later. All she could think about right then was that she was going to be with Harris. That is what mattered to her. She would figure out the rest later.

Harris finally headed for the shower. He could not believe he was singing in there; he was so happy! It seemed every cell in his body was reacting to his happy thoughts of her. Suddenly an idea popped into his head. He wanted her return to be special as it should have been the night they'd nearly made love. He would stop by the jeweler on his way to the airport and pick up a promise ring for her. She wouldn't be able to resist his charm. He grinned, happy with himself. Reuniting with the love of his life had been the only thing that could make him come alive again; without her, his insides felt dead.

He got dressed floating on air, taking special care when making his bed, making sure it looked especially good, just in case. He grinned from ear to ear. He realized his high cheek bones where aching from all the grinning he was doing. He looked in the mirror combing his hair to perfection. He flew down the stairs and out of the door to his car, the one that would be picking up his beautiful Markita later today.

Harris tore out of his garage, and even though the hospital was quite a long way from his home, it seemed like only minutes before he arrived there.

"Well, good evening, young man, it's about time you got here," Joshua greeted him.

"Don't start, it's early yet."

"Hmmm, seems to me half the day is over, son. What could have kept you from your mother's side?"

Harris went straight over to her and kissed her cheek, ignoring his uncle's dig.

"How are you feeling, Mom? You look a lot better than yesterday."

"I *am* feeling a lot better today," she agreed. "The pain has subsided enough that I can handle it without the pain medication."

"That's great news."

Mary Ellen looked at her son and could tell immediately that he looked different today too.

"Harris, what has you glowing like a Christmas candle?" she asked, the ghost of a smile playing at the corners of her mouth.

"Yes, you're grinning like the darn Cheshire cat. What's all this about?" Joshua chimed in.

"It shows, does it?" Harris knew this would get their curiosity sparked even more.

"Do I have to come over there and beat it out of you, whippersnapper?" Joshua smiled through his threat.

"Not at all," Harris responded gleefully. "I'll be happy to tell you." He paused for a moment, and then really got his uncle J good. "Tomorrow that is." He cracked himself up, laughing while Mary Ellen smiled, knowing her son had wound up his uncle Joshua.

"Hm, think you have one over on me, do you? Well, get this. I don't want to know now," Joshua said, about to burst wondering why his nephew was so happy.

"Oh then, I guess I'll wait," Harris said calmly. He sat down in a chair next to his mother's side and held her hand. Joshua waited no more than three minutes.

"You have until right this second to spill the beans or I'll explode," Joshua demanded.

"I knew I could get you going, Uncle J."

He was now nervous again, and the butterflies started to flutter; only this time he was ecstatic they were there.

"I called Markita this morning."

"Oh, so that's what took you so long to get here?" said Josh.

"It must have gone the way you wanted it to, son. I haven't seen you this happy since you were with her before," Mary Ellen said, sounding a little concerned.

"I hope you will both be happy for me. I've asked Markita to come and be with me. I plan on giving her a promise ring when she gets here later this afternoon."

"Oh boy! You don't waste any time, do you?" Joshua asked. "Ha, no wonder they call you the Florida Hurricane." His uncle J laughed.

Harris was more concerned about his mother's feelings.

"So you talked about what happened?" Mary Ellen asked.

"If you mean about her mother, yes. Markita is not happy with any of the choices the woman has made. By the way, she told me to give you her best regards, Mom."

"That was very sweet of her, especially since I was not exactly warm towards the girl."

"You had your reasons, and they were all warranted," he reassured her. "Are you going to be OK with us being together, Mom? Because I want to ask her to marry me."

"Wow, it's a good thing I'm lying down," Mary Ellen responded, giving her son a small smile.

Harris now felt terrible that his mother felt that way.

Seeing his face, his mother instantly clarified her reaction. "No, son, I didn't mean it disrespectfully. I meant you could have knocked me over. I'm fine with your decision. I guess I'm not prepared to lose you to another woman, no matter who she is. To me you're still my baby and always will be. It would not be fair to blame Markita for her mother's indiscretions."

"So you're OK with all this?" he asked hopefully.

"I told you to follow your heart, Harris, and it is obviously with Markita."

"I could not be happier, Mom. I've always felt from the moment I heard her voice, I knew I wanted to be with her for the rest of my life." He was glowing again, grinning from ear to ear.

"Congratulations, son, you got yourself a good cookie there," Joshua chimed in.

"Uncle J, if you say anything about chocolate chips or sugar cookies, I swear I'll rough you up."

"Ah, you wouldn't hurt a poor old man, would you?"

"Only if I have to." They all laughed, and it felt good. Harris felt complete inside; he had not felt this good in what seemed forever.

He kept looking down at his watch, and the time felt like it was at a standstill. He could not wait to reunite with the love of his life. His parents could tell how anxious he was; it was like watching someone itching to start a race in the Olympics. Finally, they let him off the hook.

"Why don't you get going, darling?" Mary Ellen suggested. "I'm sure there are many little details you want to take care of before Markita arrives."

"Oh, are you sure? Thank you, Mom."

Harris could not have gotten up any more quickly. He leaned over and kissed his mother's cheek with a little more pressure, showing her how grateful he was to her.

"Now, whippersnapper," Joshua told him. "Do I need to give you the birds and bees talk before you leave? It seems to me you might need it for tonight."

His uncle cracked himself up.

"Ha, ha, very funny, Uncle J. You're cruising."

"No, actually, I'm sitting right here with the most beautiful girl in the world."

"One of them," Harris said proudly.

"When am I going to see Markita?"

Harris could not believe his mother had asked him that. She really did seem supportive.

"If it is OK with you, I could bring her by in the morning."

"I think that would be lovely. It will give me a chance to redeem myself."

"You have nothing to redeem yourself for. You will love her as much as I do, given half the chance."

"If she makes you happy, then I'm happy."

"Thanks, Mom. I didn't know today could get any better, but you made it perfect."

"Of course she did, son. Your mother is the kindest, most compassionate, and of course sexiest, woman I know."

"I had better be the only woman you know, Joshua Robertson."

"Hmmm, hmmm, hmmm, of course, my darling." Joshua had a sly grin on his own face now.

"Did the doctor say when you could go home?" Harris asked before he left.

"Monday, after he makes his rounds."

"Cool beans," Harris said, excited for her.

"No, beans are better warmed up."

Harris shook his head; trust his uncle J to get in the last joke.

"Bye, guys."

"Be good tonight, son," Joshua winked at him with the thumbs-up. Harris left smiling.

Now that Harris was gone, Joshua wanted to know how Mary Ellen really felt about her son reuniting with Markita.

"Well, Joshua, I want Harris to be happy, and I know Markita makes him feel happy. He couldn't hide that fact if he wanted too."

"So then you're 100 percent OK with them?" he asked, wanting to make quite sure his wife would be OK.

"Yes, darling, I'm fine with the two of them, but if he marries her, that changes things somewhat, don't you think?"

"What do you mean, Chiquita?"

"Well, Trudy is still her mother and not only did she have an affair with Mark, but she also lied about Harris and Markita. It feels like she's deliberately trying to hurt me. If they marry, it would mean Trudy would become an in-law, and I don't know how I'll handle that, if at all." She looked up at her husband, doubt clouding her eyes. "Is that wrong of me, Joshua?"

"Oh, my darling, please. Don't let what she did to you rest one single second in your head. If she becomes an in-law, we will never be doing the family gatherings, that's all."

"I have to be honest, baby," Mary Ellen told him. "Thoughts of her stir up some pretty painful memories for me."

"That is totally understandable, darling. She was one of the reasons your marriage to my brother was torn apart."

"Yes, but it takes two to tango."

"Yes, it does. You know you will never have to worry about that with me, right? Because darling, I don't tango, I only cha-cha with you."

"Always, Joshua, always." She grinned, knowing in her heart she would never have to worry about him straying. He was old-fashioned when it came to that sort of thing.

"Do you think I should discuss how I feel about Trudy with Harris?"

"That is a tough one," Joshua responded thoughtfully. "It would tear him up if he knew his relationship hurt you in any way. At the same time, darling, if it is going to upset you, then you should discuss it with him."

"I dread the thought of seeing her in a church on the happiest day of our son's life."

"Hmm, an interesting thought. Mary Ellen, you bring up a good point. I don't think I'm comfortable with that scenario either."

"I wonder if we should just cross that bridge if we come to it. You know it might not even happen. He might not like living with her. Maybe she doesn't put the cap back on the toothpaste." Mary Ellen smiled.

"You really are grasping at straws now, sweetheart." He smiled back, knowing a little hope crept into her voice.

"Let's leave it for now, Joshua, and see how things go. Right now they deserve to get back the time Trudy stole from them."

"As usual, my darling, you're right. That's why I love you so much."

"Hmmm, me too, Joshua Robertson, so kiss me right here." She pointed to her lips.

"My pleasure, Chiquita," he said, enjoying her request.

Harris turned his cell phone back on as he hopped into his car.

"Good, there's a message," he said aloud, hoping it was Markita letting him know what time she would be back in his arms.

"Hey there, sexy bear. I'm sure you're drooling to find out what time I'll be back in your arms," the message began, and he sighed, amazed he had the same thought as her. How poetic he told himself. He continued to grin as he listened to the rest of the message.

"I'll be in your loving arms shortly after eight p.m. tonight. My flight arrives at 8:02 p.m. Harris, I'm so giddy with happiness. I hope I can make it until that time. By the way, my flight number is 1966. See you then, sexy bear." He sat back, relishing in the thought of her being in his arms soon. It would not be too much longer, so he needed to get to a jewelry store quick.

It was then that he realized he had no idea what to buy. Ironically, he went to the same jewelry store where his father had bought his mother's wedding ring. As he opened the door, a little bell tinkled, letting the clerk know there was someone in the store. A short older man appeared.

"You're looking for something unique for a special person in your life, right?" the little man asked. At first, Harris thought, *Whoa, how did he know?* but it occurred to him that is why most men probably went to a jeweler's in the first place.

"Yes, I am," Harris beamed.

"I can tell you're looking for something very exquisite and, hmmm, dainty."

"You're spot on," Harris said. He had no clue that this man had sold his father the wedding ring for his mother. The man, however, had known Mark from the TV, and he now recognized this was his son, the new Florida Hurricane. The man cleverly pulled out a ring almost identical to his mother's. Harris took one look at it and knew immediately that this was the perfect stone.

"How did you know?" he asked curiously, not a little weirded out by the man's uncanny knowledge.

"It is my business to know, sir."

"Well, I'm extremely impressed. Please gift wrap it."

"Did you know your father didn't ask the price either?" the salesmen asked as he carefully wrapped up the velvet box.

"Wait! You knew my father?"

"How else would I know that this ring is perfect for you and your girl?" he asked with a smile.

"Whew, thank goodness for that!" Harris said, somewhat relieved. "I thought I was in the *Twilight Zone*."

"You're a bit young to remember that show."

"I work late nights sometimes and have the reruns on in the background," Harris said, glad he'd at least solved this mystery. He wished the others in his life were so easy.

"I'm sure the little lady will love it."

"Oh, I know she will, especially if it looks as good on her finger as my mother's looks on hers."

"I thought I heard your mother remarried?"

"She did, but she wears the ring on the right hand ring finger. It is still one of her favorite pieces."

"I'm pleased to hear that. It tells me I did my job right for your father as well as you."

"I'm grateful to you, sir." The man handed over the tiny box, gift wrapped with a small bow attached. He saw Harris's face as he looked at the bow.

"It's a neat touch." The man smiled, happy with himself.

"It sure is. Thank you so much. You have a great day!"

He could not wait to put it on Markita's finger.

It was getting close to the time to pick her up. He popped home for a short while to freshen up. Just as he was about to head out the door, the phone rang. It was Robin, so he stopped to answer it.

"Hello," he said. All he could hear was crying.

"Hello," he said again, concerned.

"Oh, Harris," Robin cried. "It's Joe." Harris's heart jumped into his throat. *Please,* he prayed, *please let him be all right.*

"Harris," Robin said again. "He's awake. God has answered our prayers!"

"Whoa, Robin, when did this happen?"

"About an hour ago. I would have called you sooner, but Joe's mom and I wanted to hear what the doctors said first. We wanted to make sure it was going to be permanent."

"Wow, Robin, this is fantastic news!" Harris was ecstatic. "What a day this is turning out to be."

"What do you mean?" she asked, puzzled.

"Oh, it's nothing to worry about. I'll fill you in more later, but I called Markita today, and she's on her way back to Orlando."

"Congratulations, Harris! I'm so happy for you. You're right, we have both received miracles today," Robin said through her tears.

"It must have been your angelic voice that did it after all, missy."

"I have to be honest with you. I've been singing my heart out to him all day. I even sang in front of his mom."

"Wow, I bet that was nerve-racking," he said hoping he would never have to do something like that. "I bet she thought your voice was amazing though."

"You're too kind, Harris."

"Nope, Robin, just as honest as they come."

"There is something I have to warn you about though, but please don't be discouraged. The Lord has answered our first prayer, and he will answer this one for us as well."

"What is it?" Harris asked, concerned again.

"Well, Joe does not remember anything," she said. When Harris didn't respond immediately, she hurried on. "But it's likely only short term, the doctors say."

"What do you mean? Does he know his name?"

"Yes, he knows his name, he remembers me, and of course his mother. The doctor said this is temporary though," she repeated.

"Oh, how awful," he exclaimed. He was flabbergasted.

"When did the doctors say he might regain his full memories?" He thought himself very selfish at that particular moment, but so many things were running through his mind. What details did he find out concerning the Dixie Jackson case? How did Eleanor Woodsworth fit into the picture? He wanted to know if Joe knew who the suspect was who tried to suffocate Judge Poe. The most intriguing question was what made him go to Oakmont. He asked the Lord to forgive him for his selfishness and then thanked him for watching over his friend making sure he came back to them.

"The doctors say there is no reason why he should not remember everything eventually, but they can't give an exact time. It might take some time and coaxing. His mother and I will do everything in our power to get him to remember."

He asked the next question, almost afraid of the answer.

"Robin, did you ask him if he remembered me?"

She paused a moment before answering, and that told Harris all he needed to know. "I did ask him, Harris, and I'm sorry, but he didn't. It is OK, though, he will soon, I'm sure of it. I called my mother and told her about the news, and she's praying for him as well. I know God will answer our prayers, you wait and see."

"OK, Robin," Harris said, trying not to sound too disappointed. "I'll keep you and Joe in my prayers. And tell his mother I said hello. I hate to chat and run, but I have the most beautiful girl in the world to pick up from the airport."

"Aw, Harris, you're such a good person. You deserve to be happy. Markita is a lucky lady."

"Oh no, missy, I'm the lucky one, trust me on that."

"You're both lucky, Mr. Robertson."

"I'll call you in the morning, Robin, but if there are any more changes, please don't hesitate to call me. You have my cell phone number, OK?"

"OK, Harris, and say hi to Markita. Please tell her I hope to meet her real soon. I know we will be the best of friends."

"I'm sure she will love that, Robin. You're both good Southern people." Robin laughed as they hung up.

Chapter Twenty-Three

The Promise

Harris was bursting with energy, but it felt like it was taking forever to get to the airport. He swore he hit every red light there was along the way. He followed the signs to the A side of the terminal and then pulled up outside the baggage claim area. He looked down at his watch, smiling. It was exactly 8:27 p.m. He looked anxiously over to the doors and could not believe his eyes.

He had seen pictures of the Seven Wonders of the World. If there were an eighth, it would definitely be the elegant picture of beauty he watched walking in his direction. He grinned; she was right on time. He hit the button to open the trunk and then jumped out of the car to greet her.

Markita put her suitcase down on the sidewalk, and they stood there, looking into each other's eyes. Their trembling hands reached out at and touched fingertips, and then suddenly they were in each other's arms. Harris held Markita tight as she laid her head on his shoulder, right where it was meant to be. They stood this way for quite some time, hugging each other, tears gently streaming down both of their faces.

They had waited for what seemed like a lifetime for this moment, had dreamed about it, a thousand times over. What would their first kiss be like? Who would talk first? Whatever the outcome, they both knew it was what they wanted more than anything else in the world. This time, nothing or no one would ever keep them apart.

She looked up at him, still staring into his eyes, neither of them quite believing they were at last together. She reached up and had a moment to rub her finger lightly along his top lip, before Harris pulled her close again and kissed her passionately. It took a few moments before both of them realized they were standing there on the sidewalk, locked in each other's arms in front of the whole world.

"Maybe we should continue this at home, little girl?" Harris asked her, his voice rough with emotion. They looked at each other, giggling. He grabbed her suitcase, put it in the trunk, and then opened her door. He stood behind her and slipped his arms around her waist, and after holding on tight for a moment, he tickled her under her chin.

"Gully, gully, gully," he said with a grin.

"Oh, Harris, I never thought I would ever hear those words again," Markita laughed. "You are still the silliest, and I love you."

"I love you too, little girl," he told her as he helped her into the passenger seat. Once inside, they held hands as Harris leaned over to give her one more kiss before starting the car.

"I couldn't believe it when I heard your voice on the phone," Markita was saying as they left the airport. "I never thought I would hear from you again, and now here I am. It's unbelievable, Harris."

"I know just how you feel. After hearing the results of our DNA test, I needed to rewind the message and listen a second time. I wanted to listen to it again and again, but I was afraid Robin would think I was a nut." Markita was confused at the statement.

"Wasn't it on your machine?" she asked.

"No, it was on Joe's. When Robin and I hadn't heard from Joe in several days, we went to his house to see if we could find any clues as to where he might be. That message was one of several on his machine."

"Wow! How amazing, LB."

"It sure is, little girl. I thought I had lost the love of my life forever. Having you here is like a dream." He glanced over at her. "I'm so scared I'm going to wake up and it won't be real."

"I know what you mean," she said, squeezing his hand. "I feel the same way." Markita turned a little more serious. "Harris," she said. "I'm so sorry about my mother. I don't have a clue as to why she lied to us."

"Don't worry about it," Harris comforted her. "Like my mom said today, you are not to blame for the decisions your mother made."

"Your mother said that?"

"Yes, little girl, and she wants me to bring you by the hospital tomorrow to see her."

Markita gave a little gasp. "Is she going to torture me?" she asked, only half-jokingly.

"Of course not! She doesn't blame you."

"I wouldn't blame her if she did. I don't know how my mom could be so cruel to me."

"With your mom, I think it is more about my family than hurting you, little girl."

"You think so?"

"Absolutely. I'm not sure about her motives, but I'm sure it had something to do with my father and their affair."

"Let's not talk about them, sexy bear. Let's concentrate on us."

"That suits me fine, my little lover girl."

He looked over again and smiled at her. The ride home was far quicker than the ride to the airport. As soon as he'd parked in the driveway, Harris opened the trunk and went to get her suitcase.

"Welcome home," he said to her as he reached out to take her hand.

When they got to the door, he put the suitcase down. He opened the door and surprised Markita by picking her up and carrying her across the threshold.

"I know we're not married, but I want you to feel like this is your home, little girl," Harris told her.

Markita could not believe how romantic he was. Her heart gave a double beat, and she kissed him passionately. Finally, he put her down and got her suitcase, then carried it upstairs, leading her by the hand behind him.

"You will have to be patient with me, my little angel," Harris said apologetically. "I've been a bachelor for a long time, and I'm not used to sharing."

"It's OK," she assured him as they reached the top of the stairs. "I'll take over right now and rearrange everything to my liking. I hope you like white wicker, tropical patterns, and palm trees."

He cracked up, laughing at her. Harris got a feeling that she was going to be the boss around here.

His CD player sat on the dresser, and he turned it on, putting in a favorite CD, and then turning it down low.

"Come over here," he said, looking at her with more longing than he had ever felt before.

Markita walked into his arms without hesitation. They danced slowly to the song. He remembered the last time they had done this together. It was on his birthday when they came so close to making love that night. This night would be different; he was going to entrust the rest of his life to her.

"I taught you how to dance well, little boy. You are a fast learner," Markita told him, murmuring against his shoulder as they swayed gently back and forth.

He pulled her body closer into his, running one hand down her back and holding her hand with the other.

"I had the best teacher."

He flipped back her hair and kissed her neck, then gently pulled her blouse to the side and kissed her shoulder. She touched her finger to the corner of his mouth and then followed with her lips. Her tongue sought out his. He held her tight as their lips pressed together, her hands exploring his body. His heart beat against his chest like a wild animal. She held his face with both hands, kissing the end of his nose before her tongue licked his lips and entered his mouth again.

They started to undress each other, their clothes falling to the floor. They slowly moved over to the bed, still dancing, and lay down. Their naked bodies seemed to scream out to each other as they gently caressed. Harris was so anxious, his stomach was tied up in knots, and not with the butterflies he was used to around her, but the kind which fluttered around, tightening his stomach in knots of nerves. He knew it was a man's job to please her, and he was so concerned he might not. What then? Would he lose her? He needed to clear his mind and just love her.

"Markita, what if . . . ?" he tried, but she stopped his talking by kissing him with every ounce of passion she possessed. Her body was ready for him.

"Little girl," he whispered in her ear. "I'm scared. I never want to lose you, but what if I don't live up to your expectations?"

"I love you, sexy bear, and nothing else matters," she gently assured him. "And I'm scared too."

Their bodies moved on their own, pushing hard against each other. Markita let out a groan of pleasure, her body telling him to take her. Harris felt on fire from wanting her. She felt his heat against her, and it excited her.

"I want to satisfy you completely, like a woman should be satisfied, little girl. What if . . . ?" he started to falter as his paranoid insecurities consumed his thoughts. She took over, feeling his nervousness and letting him know what felt good to her. He loved the way she talked to him, her sexy voice turning him on, helping to soothe his fears.

Markita nibbled on his ear, then sucked on his neck, and finally kissed his bottom lip, taunting him, letting him know that she had wanted and waited so long for him. Her tongue inserted itself inside his mouth again, and this time she sucked on his, then pulled back, wanting him to play. He gently sucked back, then felt himself responding to her touch, thrusting himself into her hard. He could feel her body tightening up with pleasure as he touched her, his hands cupping her gently, his tongue and teeth lightly licking and nibbling her. She felt her ecstasy build as she responded to him; he felt his own body respond as he let out groans of pleasure.

"We are meant to be, LB," she breathed. "Oh, baby, that feels so good." Her voice quivered with passion. His body embraced hers, holding it tightly against him, the heat between them growing. They both began breathing harder as their passion intensified. Neither of them could control anything they were now experiencing.

"Take me, baby, take me," Markita cried out, her arms wrapped tight around Harris. He could not hold off any longer; his breathing quickened as he felt his body moving beyond his control. He groaned hard and loud, his emotions all over the place.

Markita cried out again, her body pulsating with the same emotions. Their bodies exploded together like fireworks lighting up the sky on the Fourth of July as they both let go of the desire they had felt for each other for so long. The ecstasy of it all left them both breathless.

As their breathing slowed, Harris held her close to his body, not wanting to let her go. The moment was so beautiful; their hearts, along with their bodies, seemed entwined forever.

"I love you so much, little girl," he said through tears of happiness and joy.

"Oh, LB, I love you too," she answered breathlessly. "I cannot believe this is happening. This is more than I could ever have hoped. You are a fantastic lover."

"No, no, no, little girl, it was all you," Harris said, actually feeling himself blush at her words. "My heart, body, and soul are now yours forever. Your love amazed me. I never dreamt what you did could ever happen that way for me."

Suddenly, he remembered the ring and jumped up off the bed. Poor Markita wondered what was wrong. He pulled the box from his shorts pocket and returned to her in the bed. He put her back in his arms.

"I hope you like this, little girl."

"What is it, LB?" she asked, curious.

"Well, why don't you open it and find out?" he said, teasing her.

Markita unwrapped the box, rushing to see what was inside, her heart pounding faster.

"Oh, Harris, it's beautiful," she exclaimed when she saw the ring. "Oh my gosh, I can't believe it."

"It is a promise ring," Harris explained. "I would like you to promise to marry me. I love you more than life itself. My life was so empty until you came into it. I didn't know what love felt like until you. Little girl, would you do me the honor of marrying me?"

The tears were flowing down Markita's face; they poured out faster than she could wipe them away. "LB, you have made me the happiest girl in the world. I'm so honored you have asked me . . ." she hesitated, then went on, "but I must decline."

Harris's body froze. He could not believe what he'd just heard. He never even thought about what he would do if she said no. He couldn't think of what to say next.

"I can't marry you, LB," she explained, "because you are naked and not down on one knee." She finally saw the look on his face and took pity on him. "I'm kidding, sexy bear," she said, smiling up at him. "I love you and have from the moment we met. Of course I'll marry you."

Harris's heart had stopped beating for a second, but after he got over the shock of her declining, it started up again. He grabbed a hold of her and tickled her until she asked for mercy.

"Good, googa mooga, Chiquita, are you trying to give me a heart attack? You need to beg me for mercy. I love your unpredictability, but, darling, don't scare me like that. I guess you'll keep me on my toes."

"Hmmm, on your toes . . . that would be different," she mused mischievously.

"Ooo, you are a bad girl, but I love you anyway." Markita placed the ring on her finger.

"LB, it looks perfect on my hand. It is a little big, but it doesn't matter. Thank you darling! I love it, and I love you."

"It does look perfect on your hand, just like you. I'll take it back to the jeweler tomorrow and have the man resize it for you."

"No, no, LB, I don't want to part with it, not even for a second."

"You are so adorable, but it will be OK. They won't take too long." She pouted sadly. He did not want her to be sad. He had no clue where the next words out of his mouth came from, but they seemed to come naturally to him. "I have seen some of the most beautiful diamonds and pearls in the world, but none of them compare to you," he said. "Your beauty is as perfect as a morning sunrise and an evening sunset. Your love amazes me, little girl."

He felt as if he had written the world's best poetic line. He looked into her eyes hoping she could tell how sincere his love for her was. She burst into tears.

"Oh my god, Harris, how could I have ever gotten this lucky? God has blessed me with you."

"And me with you, my love."

He could not wait to tell her the story behind her ring.

"Something strange happened today, Chiquita, when I went to purchase your ring." He started to tell her as he held her close again. "Can you believe that of all the jewelry stores there are here in town, I chose the same one my father did when purchasing my mother's promise ring?"

"What a coincidence," she said, sounding surprised.

"That's not all the owner of the shop remembered. Along with my father, he remembered the ring he picked out for her."

"Whoa! That does sound strange." She smiled.

"He helped me choose this ring for you, telling me it was almost identical to hers. As soon as I saw it, I knew it was the perfect ring."

"Harris Robertson, you are such a romantic. We can tell our kids and friends this story for years to come."

He pulled her close again, relishing in the thought of having children with her. His mind started thinking about them making love again, and his body began to yearn for her. He felt himself starting to respond once more.

This time he took over, kissing her passionately, teasing and taunting her body. She was in ecstasy, wanting him as well. They made love again, totally in tune with each other. After, they snuggled under the covers, drifting off to sleep together, happier than they had ever been in their lives.

The next morning, Harris lay sleeping on his back while Markita crawled up and nibbled on his top lip; she then licked it sexily with her tongue. Not getting any response, she nibbled at him again, this time kissing his mustache. He opened one eye and looked over at her.

"What is it you want, little girl?" he murmured, still half-asleep. He loved her playfulness first thing in the morning and wanted to wake up every day with her.

He grinned at her, and she purred like a pussycat. She now had his full attention. He turned on his side facing her, then gently kissed her face and then her bare neck. He pulled her into him. She purred more seductively this time. His body began responding yet again. She pushed her body hard into his, beginning to wrap her legs around him. Harris would never forget this morning.

"I love you so much, LB," she said after, almost tearfully, her emotions getting the best of her.

"Ooh, I certainly love you too, little girl, especially if you wake me up like this for the rest of our lives." They lay for hours with her head on his shoulder, catching up on the time they'd spent apart.

Markita told Harris that she'd finished her internship at another law firm there in Tallahassee. She had taken the bar exam and was patiently awaiting the results. She told him she would call the law firm on Monday morning and inform them her plans had changed—she would now reside in Orlando. The sound of that made both of them feel good.

"What did you tell your mother?" he asked inquisitively.

"I didn't," she said. "I left her a note."

Harris was surprised. "Do you think that was the right thing to do, Chiquita?"

"Not really, baby, but I did not want to give her a chance to mess things up for us again."

"Maybe you did do the right thing!" He smiled at her.

"What is happening with the supersecret case you wouldn't share with me?" she asked, sarcastic but grinning.

"It is a total mystery, but I can tell you, Chiquita, there are so many dead leads and coincidences, even the great Inspector Gadget was having a hard time piecing everything together."

"Harris, you and I are going to be a team, and in my book, that means we are going to be one person. We need to share everything if we are going to last forever. It's secrets that tear people apart."

"You are so wise, my angel," he teased her.

"I'm serious, LB, if you can't trust me with every aspect of your life, we won't make it."

"I agree with you, Chiquita, and I know I can trust you with anything, but I must warn you—whatever it is I'm involved with is turning out dangerous."

"What do you mean?" She was intrigued but also concerned. "I'm listening, Mr. Robertson, and let me tell you, your closing arguments better be worthy." She eyed him sternly as he laughed at her gently.

"Hmmm, you are so damn, cute little girl."

"The suspense is killing me, LB, get on with it," she urged.

"OK, OK!" he laughed. "It all started after Joe and I won our first big case . . ." he began, filling her in on all the details, including some of the more gruesome aspects of the Executioner case.

"Jeez, I'm beginning to understand why you were so apprehensive to tell me about all this," Markita commented after hearing about the severed head. When he revealed the growing list of inconsistencies and missing evidence, she became indignant.

"Harris, this is absolutely absurd!" she exclaimed. "I can't believe what I'm hearing."

"It gets worse," he told her and went on to reveal the rest, including the attack on Judge Poe, the accusations against his grandfather, and Joe's role in the whole sordid mess.

"My goodness, Harris, you could write a suspense novel with this story," Markita said when he was done.

"It certainly has the makings of one, doesn't it?"

"Does the place where Joe went ring any bells with you?" she asked.

"Well, it seems I have heard of the town of Oakmont before, but I don't know why."

"You need to think, LB. Did a college buddy come from there? Did you read anything in the Executioner's file that maybe he was from there?"

She did not know how close her question was to the truth.

"I don't think it mentioned where he was from."

"We'll think about this together," she said confidently. "I'm sure we will get to the bottom of all this mess."

"You're right," he replied. "You know, instead of wanting to be a judge, you should be a detective. You have the curiosity for it."

"Hmmm, I would be a good one, don't you think?"

"I think you could be anything you set your mind to," he told her. "But there is one more thing I need to tell you. It's about my mother's accident." He told her about the "accident" and the threat against him and his family.

"Oh god, Harris, what are you going to do?" Markita asked, her eyes wide.

"Do you have to ask that, Chiquita? Nothing could make me dishonor the system I believe and trust in."

"I didn't mean that, LB, I meant, are you going to get a bodyguard or something?"

"I'm not sure. Hugh is trying to convince me that it's nothing, but he's been acting very strangely." He then filled her in on all the odd activity on Hugh's part surrounding his mother's accident and its subsequent investigation. "I'm convinced he's covering something up or covering for someone," Harris confided.

"Wow! You really think Hugh is corrupt? That seems pretty far-fetched, LB. He is the district attorney for God's sake."

"I don't know what to think anymore," he admitted. "My gut tells me Hugh is mixed up in this mess somehow. Uncle J says if it smells like a rat bastard, it usually is. I wish Joe would hurry up and remember."

"I'm sure he will soon, darling," Markita said, trying to offer him some comfort as well as encouragement.

"You now know as much as I do, little girl," he told her, sounding frustrated and pissed at everything he had told her; recalling all the details served to remind him of how much he still didn't know.

"The one thing I'm sure of, LB, is I'll always have your back," Markita assured him.

"Then I think it's time we had a shower, don't you, little girl? I'll definitely let you get my back," he said seductively.

"Is that an invitation, little boy?" she asked, turning to him and kissing his lips. She jumped up out of bed. "Last one in is a yellow duck."

"Baby, talking of ducks, did I ever tell you the joke about the duck that went to the pharmacy looking for lip balm?"

"No, no, no, LB, please spare me! Not your uncle J's duck joke again!" She ran naked into the bathroom to turn on the water, knowing full well she had set him up for his favorite joke. He followed her, still reciting it.

Once they had cleaned up and dressed, Harris said it was time they visited his mother, before his uncle J began calling him to give him a hard time.

"That's fine, sweetheart. I'm ready," Markita told him.

"Are you sure you are going to be OK?"

"Yes, of course," she said with a confidence she wasn't sure she felt. "I'm going to make an effort to show your mom I'm nothing like my mother."

"OK, if you're ready, let's go."

He picked up his car keys from the dressing table, turned off the boom box, and then they left for the hospital.

The two of them walked into his mother's hospital room hand in hand. The moment she laid eyes on Markita, the girl's stunning beauty and likeness to her mother instantly made the hair on the back of Mary Ellen's neck stand up.

"Hello, Mrs. Robertson," Markita greeted her. "I'm sorry to hear about your accident. I hope you are feeling better." She walked over to the bed and handed Mary Ellen a dozen roses, eleven red and one white. It was what Harris had bought for her on their first date.

"Thank you, Markita, the flowers are beautiful, just like you," Mary Ellen said graciously, although she cringed inside as she said her name.

"Thank you, Mrs. Robertson. That is so sweet of you to say."

"Please, call me Mary Ellen." She did her best to sound sincere.

Harris walked over and gave his mom her usual kiss on the cheek. "How's things, Uncle J?" he asked, glancing over at his uncle, who was, as always, sitting by his mother's side.

"Well, from the look of that beautiful diamond on Markita's finger, I would say things are fine," he replied with a knowing smile.

Harris and Markita blushed.

"Let me see please, Markita," Mary Ellen asked.

It was hard not to see the shock on her face when she looked at the ring.

"Oh my, son . . . it's almost identical to mine," she said trying not to choke on the words.

"You won't believe this, Mom, but I happened to stop and buy it from the exact same jeweler Dad bought yours from. The man remembered him, as well as the ring he chose for you. I know how much you love your ring, so I thought there would be no greater compliment than to get Markita one as beautiful as yours."

Mary Ellen loved the sentiment her son showed, but at the same time, she wanted to scream at him. How could he not think about how Markita's mother cheated with her husband, his own father? The ring would always be a reminder of that.

Harris and Markita started to feel the tension in the room. It was obvious to Markita that Mary Ellen was never going to accept her. As usual, Joshua tried to come to the rescue.

"Markita, have you been watching our courtroom star on the TV?"

"No, actually, I haven't. Is the Dixie trial being televised, LB?" she asked innocently.

Mary Ellen wanted to say, *If you loved my son, you would know it is being televised everywhere on Court TV.*

Joshua saw his wife scowling at her while Harris answered her question.

"Yes, my darling, it is. In fact, I would love it if you would come to court with me on Monday morning."

"Wild horses couldn't keep me away."

"What about elephants?" piped up Joshua. Everyone laughed at him, and at least it lessened some of the tension in the room.

"May I ask why you called Harris LB?" Mary Ellen asked Markita.

This time Harris jumped in for the save. "It's one of our pet names for each other, Mom. LB is short for 'little boy,' and I call her 'little girl.' Silly, I know, but it works for us . . ." he trailed off, not knowing what to say next.

"Hmmm, I can see why you call her little girl, but you are a man, Harris, not a little boy." Mary Ellen heard how cold her words sounded, but she could not seem to stop herself.

Oh, God, Harris thought. *This is not going well at all.* He had thought his mom was fine now, but her rudeness surprised him once more.

"Well, Mom, it's time for Markita and I to get going. She needs to unpack her things and get settled in."

"But you've just arrived, son," Mary Ellen pointed out.

"We have been here quite awhile now," he said in desperation.

Markita was so relieved that he wanted to leave; she wanted that more than anything.

"I have things to prepare for my case as well, Mom. It resumes on Monday. You know how I like to be prepared. 'No surprises' is what I always say."

He thought how corny he sounded, but his desperation to leave got the better of him. He felt like the elephant Joshua had joked about was in the room. Once again, his uncle J wanted to try to have the two of them leave on a lighter note.

"Don't forget to watch the game tomorrow, son. It's your Miami Dolphins against my Dallas Cowboys."

"Why watch the game, Uncle J? I already know the Dolphins will win it."

"Don't get so cocky there, whippersnapper. The Cowboys are 4 and 0."

"Right, it's time for them to lose this one, and we are the team to do it."

"Do you like football, Markita?" Joshua asked her, trying to draw her into the conversation.

She was afraid to answer; it seemed that whatever she said she risked Mary Ellen chastising her.

"Yes, I love it," she lied, not being a fan of sports at all. She realized she had not known Harris was so into sports, but if he loved them, then she would learn to love them too.

Harris went over and kissed his mother good-bye.

"Good-bye, Mrs. Robertson," Markita said politely. "It was nice to see you again. I hope they release you soon."

"I'll be going home on Monday, after the doctor does his rounds," Mary Ellen told her.

Markita was shocked that she was actually cordial to her.

"I'm sure you are happy about that."

"Yes, I am, Markita, and I hope you and Harris will come and visit me when I get home."

"Of course we will, Mom," Harris told her.

"How about our usual Sunday supper, son? We could make it our new family tradition, which would include Markita," Joshua suggested.

Markita smiled gratefully as she thanked him.

"You can call me Uncle J, if you like." "

"Thank you. I would like that."

"Yes, and don't forget, I'm Mary Ellen, dear." Markita wanted to leave while Harris's mother was still being courteous to her.

"Well, darling, let's get out of here and get you home," Harris said, reaching for Markita's hand.

"I like the sound of that, LB." They said their final farewells, then headed out the door, hand in hand.

As soon as they were gone, Joshua turned to his wife. "Oh boy, darling! You had me really worried there for a moment. You said you were OK with them, but again you nearly chewed the girl's head off."

"I know, Joshua, and afterwards I felt badly, but it was seeing her and how stunningly beautiful she is, and of course, the likeness to her mother. It made the hair on the back of my neck stand up."

"It was also the ring, wasn't it?"

"Yes, that too. Harris's sentiment was sweet, but he definitely is unaware of why I still wear the ring. I wear it to remind me of how bad those times were and of how lucky I am to now have you."

"Ah, my chickadee, you scored big points. Maybe I'll cook my famous spaghetti for you Monday night."

"Hmmm, darling, that sounds wonderful. You spoil me."

"Always, darling, always." He leaned over and kissed her lightly on the lips.

Meanwhile, Markita was relieved to be out of there and in the car with Harris.

"Your mother still hates me," she said sadly.

"No, I don't think so, darling. I know she was a little off at first, but I could tell she warmed up to you at the end."

"I think what my mother did with your father will always affect how she feels about me."

"I think you are wrong, little girl. Give her time. She'll come around and love you as much as I do."

"I love you too, sexy bear."

"Oh, little girl, I think that was another invitation."

"Hmmm, maybe so, my little studmuffin." He looked over at her and saw her smiling back at him as she licked her lips.

"You need to quit that until we get home, or I'll have to pull the car over right now," he warned her.

As it was, as soon as they arrived home, it was no time at all until they were upstairs, undressed, and making love.

Chapter Twenty-Four

The Kidnapping

Monday morning came around, and it was time for Harris to return to court. This time, however, he had Markita on his arm. He did his best to get through the crowds of people, especially doing his best to avoid Amber Andrews, but for him, there was no such luck.

"Good morning, Mr. Robertson," Andrews greeted him on the courthouse steps. "What is your game plan today as you resume the trial without your star witness, Joe Marble?"

"I'm happy to announce Mr. Marble is awake and expected to make a full recovery," Harris responded, expertly deflecting the question.

"That is good news, Mr. Robertson," Andrews replied, not missing a beat. "And how is your mother? I heard she was in an accident."

"She is fine and will be going home today. Thank you for asking." He continued to try to push through the crowd of cameras and reporters, but Amber Andrews wasn't done with him yet.

"May I ask who this beautiful young lady is with you?" she pried.

Amber knew her question was unwarranted, but as a woman, she was curious. She could have sworn she had seen him with her before.

"My personal life is off limits, Miss Andrews. Have a nice day." He grabbed Markita's hand and led her up the courthouse stairs and into Judge Poe's courtroom. After the bailiff made his usual announcements, the judge addressed Harris.

"Mr. Robertson, how is Mr. Marble doing?"

It was not that the judge cared; the fact was he needed to look concerned and compassionate for the television viewers. He was coming up for reelection next year.

"He is awake, Your Honor, and expected to make a full recovery."

"Ah, exceptional, Mr. Robertson. Are you going to be able to proceed without him?" Harris would have preferred to have Joe readily available to testify, but he would stall with his other witnesses for as long as possible.

"Yes, Your Honor, in fact I'm ready to call my next witness."

"Good, Mr. Robertson, then please proceed."

"The prosecution calls the medical examiner to the stand."

The bailiff swore him in. As usual, Harris had spent tedious hours laying down the foundation for his tough questions, which would follow later. There were several things he did not want to bring up until he could get Joe on the stand, including Eleanor Wordsworth's decapitated head. He had plenty of other items to question the ME on, though. Once he painted the picture for the jury, explaining that the medical examiner, along with the senator, fire chief and, last but not least, the chief of police, were all arrested naked in the pool, it would be hard for the jury to believe a word the ME or the others had to say. Despite all he did have, he still wished more than ever Joe was there to corroborate his evidence. He had his father's arrogant and egotistical smile on his face without even knowing it. The difference with him was that it was more about having confidence in himself.

He was at a good stopping point, and it was lunchtime. He asked the court if they could recess for lunch.

"That is a good suggestion, Mr. Robertson. It's been a long morning." Judge Poe gave the jury their instructions, and then they were led out. The bailiff called for the court to rise while the judge left the room.

As he tried to leave the courtroom, Amber Andrews once again stopped Harris and Markita and asked him ridiculous questions, then implied he was going easy on the medical examiner. Harris refuted her allegations, rushing away with his arm around Markita's waist. They got in the car and drove to their favorite Bistro.

"Well, if it ain't me two lil' lovies!" Brenda exclaimed when she saw them. "How have ya both bin? Its bin a long time since I have seen the likes of you two." They smiled at her, remembering how nice she had always been to them.

"Hello, Miss Brenda," Harris greeted her. "It has been too long."

"Come on then, follow me," she instructed. "I've got ya favorite spot in the corner over 'ere."

They thanked her and followed the talkative hostess to a secluded table in the back.

"So," she said to Harris as she settled them in to their booth, "I see you're on the telly again, prosecuting a prozzy, eh? Is she guilty?" She offered him a naughty wink.

"As sin," Harris replied with an equally naughty grin. "Pardon the pun."

"Not at all, you was very funny, Master 'arris." She looked back and forth between them, then asked, "I s'pose it's the usual, 'am and pepper jack cheese, aye?"

"Yes, please," they both replied. This time they did not have to hide the fact they were together by holding hands under the table. Harris stretched out his arm across the top of the table and held her hand.

"You know the last time we were here, it was a disaster," Markita said.

"Yes, but you know what? Let's never think about the negative past when we are in here. this is also the first place we ever came to together, so it holds some special memories for us."

"I agree, and I love coming here with you," Markita said. "And Miss Brenda sure is some 'fin else, Master 'arris," she gently mocked.

Harris gave a goofy smirk. "You're too funny, little girl."

His cell phone interrupted them.

"Hello, Harris, it's Robin," the young woman greeted him breathlessly. "Joe's mom and I have been watching you on TV. I hope I haven't caught you at a bad time."

"Not at all. Is everything OK?" Harris asked, concerned.

"Yes," she replied. "I wanted to let you know that Joe is remembering more and more."

"Oh, that's brilliant," Harris told her, relieved. Markita squeezed his hand. "Tell Robin I said to give Joe my best," she whispered to him. Harris did so.

"It sounds like everything is back on track for the two of you. That's great, Harris. I'm so happy for you," Robin said.

"Oh, yes, things couldn't be better, thanks. You keep working on Joe, and please let me know when there is more progress."

She promised to do so and said good-bye.

"What great news," Harris breathed as he leaned back in his seat. "If he remembers everything soon, it might not be too late to put him on the stand."

"That would be fantastic," Markita said.

"I know this sounds selfish, little girl, but I can't wait for Joe to remember everything. I get the distinct feeling he knows something, and someone found out and put a stop to him telling me."

"You could be right, LB. If you are, I hate to think what is going on around here."

"Me too, baby, me too." The two of them ate their lunch, left a large tip, and made their way back to the courtroom.

Not far away, the Executioner watched the live broadcast, his fury growing as he saw that Harris was still vigorously prosecuting the case, even after what he had done to the man's mother. He continued to watch intently for any sign that Harris was going to drop the case.

He did not, however, see it happening.

It was now time to put his next plan into action. This time, the Robertson family would not be so lucky. The Voice had laid down strict rules concerning the Robertsons; he was never to touch one single family member, or he would meet with an unpleasant ending. He'd never really needed the threat—he had always obeyed the Voice out of a sense of duty—until now. He could not simply accept what they were doing to Miss Dixie. She was the only person who had ever cared for him, and he felt it was his job to protect her. He swore he would do that, no matter what.

He turned his attention back to the television screen.

"This is Amber Andrews reporting live for Court TV. We are again seeing familiar favors being given when it comes to certain witnesses where the district attorney's office is concerned. If you tuned in this morning, you likely noticed how easily the so-called Florida Hurricane blew a suspiciously light breeze when questioning the medical examiner. I have suspected for a while that the DA's office is part of the corruption overtaking Orlando. There have been several reports of families requesting, and paying for, private autopsies after the ME's examination, only to discover that his office's findings were inaccurate. It's a devastating fact, but true. It amazes me how our great assistant DA did not bring this to light today. It seems he is more interested in the medical examiner being in the pool with a naked woman.

"My sources tell me, next Monday morning, Dixie Jackson is to take the stand. You need to stay tuned to Court TV and watch this interesting case unravel."

Smith was now ready to explode. No way was that ever going to happen. It was time to put his next plan into action. He watched the screen as Harris held Markita's arm as they made their way out of the courthouse. *Interesting*, he said to himself.

Back in his office, Hugh was paying little attention to the case before the court; rather, he was busy putting together the final arrangements for the Order's annual meeting this coming weekend. He had instructed Sassy Jo to take over Miss Dixie's operation and make preparations for the party. It would be her responsibility to make sure the members of the Order left satisfied. If anything happened to Dixie, he would sign Sassy Jo's name to the Order as the new madam. He told her it would be her responsibility to entertain the Order's members, and they were to get anything they requested. He requested at least forty of the best girls, letting Sassy Jo know that their presence would be required from early Friday morning, when the first members were to arrive, until the last member left on Saturday night. On Friday, people would be arriving and checking into hotels all day, signing in for the meeting and then enjoying the local festivities until the evening's meeting. The members would call at their own convenience as to when they would require an escort. The meeting would convene at 7:00 p.m. and would continue until midnight. Once the official meetings were over, the members were there until Saturday night solely to enjoy benefits offered by Miss Dixie's girls as a "thank you" for their services to the Order. It promised to be a most successful meeting.

Harris and Markita were on their way to a very different kind of meeting. After court, they went to visit Mary Ellen at home.

"Hi, Mom! Hi, Uncle J!" Harris shouted when he walked in the front door.

"We are in our room, son, come on in," Josh called out to them. As they made their way to Mary Ellen's room, Markita squeezed Harris's hand tightly. She was nervous about how Harris's mother would treat her today. She hoped that Mary Ellen could put aside her feelings about Markita's mother and concentrate on the two of them making a relationship, even if it was just for Harris's sake.

Harris greeted his mother warmly as he bent over to kiss her cheek, asking how she was feeling.

"I'm wonderful, son," she replied. "I'm so happy to be home, that's for sure."

"You look comfortable, Mary Ellen," Markita said, bracing herself for a scowl or sarcastic remark.

"Well, thank you, sweetie, I feel comfortable," Mary Ellen said pleasantly. Markita thought she would faint. Harris looked over and grinned at her.

"What are you grinning at, son, did I miss something?"

"Not at all, my sweet mother."

"Oh, boy, the mud is pretty thick in here tonight," Joshua quipped. "If you guys aren't careful, the three little piggies will move in, and the wolf will blow the house down." Everyone laughed.

"Oh my, Uncle J," Harris said, rolling his eyes. "As usual, you're too much."

Markita was so happy and felt more at ease around Mary Ellen than ever before.

"Did you guys see LB in court today?" she gushed. "He is so charming before he strikes."

"You're right, sweetie," Mary Ellen agreed, nodding at Markita. "He's as suave and debonair as his father was in the courtroom. It's probably what attracted your mother to my husband."

The room went silent. Markita's eyes filled with tears. Was it always going to be like this with his mother? Harris came to Markita's defense immediately.

"I'm nothing like my father!" he said heatedly. "I never cheated and never will."

Joshua came straight to Mary Ellen's defense.

"It was not your mother who cheated, son, so don't direct your anger at her. You need to apologize to her for that comment. She's not herself. She is, after all, recovering from an accident."

"I'm sorry," he said curtly, not looking at his mother. "Let's go, Markita. It's getting late, and I have to be back in court early tomorrow." He grabbed Markita's hand and turned to leave.

"Harris, please!" his mother called out, but it was too late; they had already left the room.

"Oh, boy, that went well," Joshua said, looking at his wife with a mix of empathy and frustration.

Mary Ellen started to cry. Joshua climbed onto the bed and held her in his arms.

"It's OK, baby. I know it's hard for you. I'll explain it to them for you."

"Joshua, how am I ever going to stop myself?" she sobbed. "It's not fair to the girl, but her mother and Mark betrayed me. She is a constant reminder!"

"I know, I know, baby, it's OK. Please don't cry." She laid her head on his shoulder as he held her close to him.

"I love our son so much, darling," she said softly, "but I'm going to lose him if I continue." Joshua loved it when she called him *our* son.

"It will be OK, baby. Something like this will just take time. I'll talk to Harris and explain that he needs to have patience with you. Some scars run deep. He'll understand, I'm sure of it."

"What about Markita?"

"I'll talk to her too. You know she has to be a special young lady for our son to have chosen her, even though he might be going against what we'd like for him. Look at us, for example. I'm in love with my brother's wife! I even married her." He smiled at Mary Ellen. "There are times when the heart rules over our head. That's how you became the love of my life, darling. If I had walked away, I would never have experienced what love was like. I have never been as happy as I am now . . . with you."

"Joshua Robertson, you're a wise man," Mary Ellen said through her tears.

"That's why I'm a psychologist, my darling."

She hugged him tightly. "I love you," she said.

"And I love you back."

Harris and Markita drove home in silence. They went upstairs and lay on the bed. He pulled her over to him and placed her head on his shoulder, running his fingers through her hair.

"I'm so sorry about my mother, Chiquita. Again."

"I'm so grateful to you for defending me."

"It's OK," he told her. "I'll always be there for you. I'm entrusting my life to you, remember?"

"Yes, but, LB, it hurts me to think you and your mom are fighting because of me. Not only that, but I hurt her every time she looks at me."

"Listen, little girl," Harris said, turning her face up to look into his. "My mom is a good person and will come around and love you like I do. Yes, I do think it's going to take awhile, but please give her time. It's hard on her. My dad left some mental, as well as physical, scars on her."

"You never told me that before."

"He was a bastard, Markita, the worst. I woke up one morning, and Mom was on the bathroom floor covered in blood. She tried to tell me she fell, but I knew what happened."

"Oh my gosh, LB, that's terrible," Markita whispered.

"Your mother is a stunningly beautiful woman, and I think my mom is insecure about that too," Harris added, changing the subject.

"Your mother is also a beautiful woman," Markita pointed out. "On the inside as well as out. I'm afraid I cannot say the same about mine."

"That's sweet of you to say, Chiquita. So will you please give her time and quite a few chances?" He grinned.

"For you, anything, sexy bear." She kissed him softly below his ear.

"Sexy bear! Would you like me to show you how sexy I am?"

"Are you going to get all 'grizzly' on me?" she asked, giggling.

"I'm going to do a lot more than that, little girl." He started tickling her, teasing her with his fingertips. They both reacted to the teasing, their body temperatures intensifying, their breathing becoming heavy. They quickly undressed each other and made love once again until they grew tired and fell asleep in each other's arms.

For the next two days, Markita accompanied Harris to court, but on Thursday, she decided to stay at home, telling Harris she needed to get some things taken care of. He was a little disappointed, but understood. She needed time to get herself settled, to start making his home her own.

Before court convened, he called Robin to check on Joe.

"There is nothing but good news," Robin told him. "He is remembering quite a few things now."

"That's fantastic. Does he remember why he was there or what he discovered?"

"No, sorry, Harris. It's more about his childhood and growing up, things of that nature."

"Well good," Harris told her, trying not to sound too disappointed. "Hopefully, the rest will come soon."

"I know it's frustrating," Robin told him. "He doesn't remember about us either. All he knows is he recognizes me." She didn't even try to hide her disappointment.

"Don't worry," Harris encouraged her. "Like you said, it will come. Keep working on him. Try calling him Inspector Gadget, that might work," he laughed, and she did too.

It was another long day in court, and Harris couldn't wait to get home to his beautiful Markita. He had been trying to reach her all day, but she hadn't answered the phone. He figured she must have been busy arranging to have her stuff shipped from Tallahassee to Orlando. She'd told him she needed to stop by the post office to fill out a change-of-address form as well. It sounded like she was going to have a packed day, so he couldn't fault her for not running to the phone.

Once he was home, Harris walked into the condo calling her name. When he received no answer, he headed upstairs, thinking she might be napping, or better yet, waiting for him with a sexy little surprise. Instead of Markita, however, all he found was a note on his pillow.

How sweet, he thought. He sat on the bed and eagerly started to read, thinking that she'd left him a love letter.

Dear Harris, it began. Harris thought it sounded like a "Dear John" letter and grinned; he and Markita were certainly beyond that. He started again.

> *"Dear Harris,*
> *I know you thought I was staying home today to finalize plans to move here, but the truth is, I needed to leave and couldn't bring myself to tell you in person."*

What the hell is this? he thought. *Is she joking around like when she "declined" to marry me?* It's what he was hoping, but his stomach had already anxiously turned over. He read on.

> *"I tried to tell you when you gave me the ring that I needed to decline your proposal. You were moving things along too fast for me. But I could see the hurt look on your face as well as in your eyes, so I said yes. I'm afraid your mother will never accept me. Every time she looks at me, she sees my mother. It's not going to work out for us, and I'm so sorry."*

This is so not damn funny, Harris thought. His stomach felt nauseous.

> *"I'm going home to my mom. Please do not call or contact me. This is the way it has to be. I know you're dying inside right now, but please honor my wishes."*

That was it. No signature. No "Love, Markita." He was furious.

Harris crumpled up the note in his hand. He was too angry to notice that her promise ring had slid down from the pillow, where his had lain next to the note, landing softly on the bed. Harris could not believe this was true, but then why was she not there in the condo? He checked the closet and the bathroom cabinet; all her things were gone. He fell to his knees at the side of his bed.

"Please, God," he begged. "Don't let this be true. Please let this be a nightmare and make me wake up. Please, please, God, please. I cannot lose her again, I just can't." He bent over, holding his stomach, and sobbed uncontrollably. He screamed out at God, consumed with anger and confusion.

"Please, God, please. I beg of you!" he cried out over and over. As he screamed, he hit the bed with his fist again and again. He had never hated anything or anyone like he hated God right at that moment. He screamed again, this time louder than before.

"How the hell could you send the love of my life to me and then rip her away?" he screamed at the empty room. "What kind of god are you? If you're real, then answer my prayer and make her come home right now!" He knelt there crying until he had no tears left to cry. Then he wearily dragged himself up onto the bed and lay there gasping and shaking until he had completely ran out of energy. He weakly asked God to forgive him and then fell asleep.

The sound of his cell phone ringing awakened him hours later. He jumped up and grabbed it, thinking it was Markita and this had all been a joke or a bad dream.

"Hello," he said, rushing to find out if it was her.

"Hey, whippersnapper, where are you?"

"I'm at home," he said sharply.

"Whoa, what's up there, Tiger? Court not go well today?"

"Who gives a crap?"

"Oh boy, that bad, huh?"

"I don't have time for you," Harris snapped and hung up.

Joshua was stunned as he listened to the empty sound of the dial tone.

"What is it, darling? Is he coming?" Mary Ellen asked from the bed.

"He was not in the greatest of moods," Joshua said slowly. "I think I'm going to go and see him. Is that OK with you?"

"Do you think it's because of me?"

"No, no, darling, don't worry yourself. I'm sure it was something at court today. That's what it sounded like."

"Maybe he and Markita had a fight?" Mary Ellen actually hoped they had not, especially because of the way she had been treating Markita.

"I'll call you and let you know, OK, baby?" He kissed her cheek, leaving her with her thoughts.

She knew it was wrong to blame Markita for what her husband and the girl's mother had done. She knew it was hurting Harris. She prayed to God, asking him for forgiveness. *I have been selfish and not had my heart open. Please, God, let me open my heart to Markita.* Mary Ellen felt warmth fill her. It was as if God had answered her prayer; everything was going to be OK now, she knew it.

Harris did not share that feeling. He had left the front door unlocked; Joshua let himself in when Harris did not answer his knock. Not finding his nephew downstairs, he started heading for his bedroom. From the top of the stairs, he could hear what sounded like crying. Upon opening the bedroom door, Joshua saw Harris lying on the bed, a piece of paper screwed up in his hand. Joshua went over to him, placing his hand gently on his shoulder.

"What's wrong, son?" he said softly.

"Everything, Uncle J, everything."

"OK, why don't you tell me?"

"It doesn't matter. There's nothing you can do. It's over."

"What is over, son?" Joshua was praying it was not what he was thinking.

"Why don't you go away and leave me alone?"

"Don't start that again, son. You know I'm always here for you. Come on, now, tell me what's wrong."

"Markita's gone."

"Gone where? When will she be back?" Joshua asked, not sure he wanted to hear the answer.

"She won't be back," Harris said bitterly. "That's the point. She's gone back to her mother."

"Did she tell you why?"

"No," he snapped. "She took the coward's way out and left me a note." Harris tossed the crumpled, damp paper to his uncle.

His heart broke for his nephew as he read her words. *Not again*, he said to himself. This boy went through hell as a child losing his hearing because of his father's brutality, as well as the drinking. He'd had to endure the countless nights listening to his mother crying after she had been beaten. Then the cruelty that Trudy bestowed on him and now the loss of the love of his life—again. He was not happy at reading the part about Mary Ellen; he knew it had to hurt Harris immensely.

"Go ahead, say something," Harris growled. "I'm a useless piece of shit, right?"

Joshua looked up, startled. "Don't start talking to me like that, son. I won't stand for that, even though I know you're hurting."

"I couldn't satisfy her."

"What the hell are you talking about?" Joshua demanded, confused again.

"I was probably lousy in bed. She is perfect, Uncle J. I'm not worthy of someone as beautiful as her."

"Now wait a minute, son. You stop right now. That's not true. You're handsome, intelligent, and witty, and most of all, your heart is as big as the state of Texas. I can tell love when I see it, and Markita loves you."

"Oh yeah? Really? That must be why she left, stupid."

"I'll not tell you again, Harris. You show me respect when you talk to me. I'm not the one who left you, remember that."

"Well, Mom sure as hell left me out on a limb. Why did she have to be a bitch to Markita every time she saw her?"

"OK, Harris Robertson," Joshua warned. "You're getting close to crossing the line with me. I'll not stand to hear you say things like that about your mother. I know you're upset, but think about the pain that Markita causes your mother. We have been trying to talk through things, and your mother has been trying her best. She knows that her words have hurt Markita, as well as you, but she promised me she would work harder on her feelings."

"Well, you tell her she doesn't have to work on anything now. The cause of her painful memories has left me."

"Have you tried calling her and talking?" Joshua asked, trying to steer the conversation into a more positive territory.

"You read the note. It says don't bother."

"You might want to try."

"I'll never call her again!" Harris shouted. "To hell with her and women. I'm done."

"Harris, I know this is not what you want to hear right now, but I'm telling you as a psychologist and as an uncle who loves you more than life itself: time will pass and wounds will heal. I know everyone says that, but they say it for a reason—it's because it's true."

"It doesn't matter, Uncle J. It's over, and it's done. I don't ever want to talk about her again. Tell Mom I'll be there tomorrow. Please, Uncle J. Leave me be for now. I need to be alone. I promise I'll be OK."

"Are you sure, son?"

"Yes, I'm sure. I need to be by myself and understand why the Lord sent me the love of my life and then took her away from me."

"I know this sucks, son, and it's not what you want to hear, but he has his reasons. We may not understand why, or even agree with, his decisions, but they are his, and he will reveal them when it's our time. You need to remember that, Harris."

"Whatever," Harris said wearily. "Please shut the door on your way out, Uncle J."

"Your mother and I love you, son."

"Right. Good night. Tell Mom I'll be over tomorrow."

"You need to give her some slack, son."

"It doesn't matter anymore, Uncle J. Don't you get it? She is gone. Mom can hate on her all she likes."

"I'm leaving now, Harris. I suggest you check your attitude. Your mother took a lot of hurt for you when you were younger, just remember that."

"Good night, Uncle J."

Joshua turned to go, closing the door firmly behind him.

Chapter Twenty-Five

The Annual Meeting

The alarm rang, and Harris hit the Snooze button. He felt like a Mack truck had run over him. His body felt heavy, his mind sluggish. He tried turning over, but gave up. The alarm went off again.

"Shut the hell up," he shouted at the clock. He tried opening his eyes. *Cripes, they are stuck together.* He tried rubbing them, and they slowly began to open. The alarm went off yet again.

"I said, shut the hell up!" He leaned over and thumped down on it, turning it off.

"I don't want to get up," he growled at the clock. It stared at him mutely. "Why the hell should I?" he asked it. "There is nothing to get up for." He pulled his body up, then sat there staring at the empty half of his closet.

"If I don't get my arse out of this bed, I'm going to be held in contempt of court by Judge Poe, that's for sure." He dragged his weary body out of bed and toward the shower. He caught a glimpse of himself in the mirror and saw his eyes were as puffy as the Pillsbury Doughboy. He growled again.

"Great, I'm going to look like shit on television today." He hoped that once he'd showered and properly woken up, he would look halfway human.

No such luck. He looked at himself in the mirror again after getting dressed, straightening his tie as he looked at his still-bloodshot, puffy eyes. *I'm sure Judge Poe will make some kind of snide comment when he sees me, but who cares?* he said to himself. Just then, the phone rang, and for a split second, his heart flipped. *If it's her, God, thank you for answering my prayers. She must have come to her senses and realized she'd made a mistake and wants to come back.* But what if it's not her on the phone? How would he know if he did not answer the phone?

"Hello," he answered with extreme anticipation.

"Hey, Harris. How are you today?" Robin greeted him brightly.

"Fine as I can be, I suppose," Harris responded, deeply disappointed.

Robin immediately sensed something was wrong. Along with the tone in his voice, something was definitely not sounding right. She was very intuitive when it came to people trying to hide their feelings.

"Is everything OK?" she asked.

"I don't want to get into it right now, if you don't mind."

"I thought we were friends," Robin said. "So if you need one right now, I would be more than happy to lend you my shoulder."

"Like I said, I don't want your shoulder or to talk to you."

Although shocked at his behavior, Robin gave it one more try. "Please talk to me, Harris. We have been to hell and back together." At her words, Harris felt guilty, knowing what she was going through with Joe.

"I don't want to dwell on this, but you might as well know now," he finally admitted. "Markita and I have broken up, again. She went home to Tallahassee yesterday."

"Oh my gosh! I'm so sorry, Harris. It must have been a shock."

"No shit, Sherlock . . ." He paused, trying to rein in the anger that seemed to be bubbling over without warning. "I'm sorry, Robin," he apologized quickly. "That was uncalled for. I'm not in the right frame of mind at the moment. Please excuse my rudeness." He felt bad once again for taking his bitterness out on her. This certainly was not her fault.

"I can't believe it. You sounded so happy after you picked her up."

"Like I said before, could we please drop this subject? What did you call for anyway?" he snapped at her again. He couldn't seem to stop himself. It was as if he had given up caring.

"I wanted to let you know Joe had some pretty big revelations yesterday," she told him, now relieved to change the subject.

"Good for him," he interjected. "Did he remember why he was there?"

"Not yet, but he remembers you now, which is great news, right? He also remembers the fact he works for Hugh."

"Hmmm, is that it?"

"I think it's pretty huge, don't you?" Robin asked, sounding hurt at his continued rudeness. She had thought he and Joe were close, but now Harris sounded like he couldn't care less.

"Sure, whatever, I have to get to court. Would you call me when he actually remembers something substantial?" He hung up the phone, disinterested in the fact that Joe was making progress. If he could offer no real information, what good was any of this news?

He made it to Judge Poe's courtroom with only minutes to spare. As usual, the jury entered the courtroom, followed by the judge.

The bailiff made his announcements. "Court is now in session. The Right Honorable Judge Poe presiding." He continued, giving the case number, then announced, "The *State of Florida versus Dixie Jackson*." He then instructed the room to be seated. Judge Poe glanced over at Harris to give him permission to begin and immediately noticed Harris's puffy, bloodshot eyes.

"Good morning, Mr. Robertson. Are your allergies kicking in today?" He wanted to ask if he had been out on a drunken binge, his eyes looked so bad, but just snickered inside, knowing anything more would not be appropriate with the cameras on.

"Not at all, Your Honor."

"Then please call your first witness."

Harris called Hank to the stand. Again, after hours of laying out the foundation, the two men started going at each other. Harris went round and round with Hank, asking the same question several different ways due to Nigel's continuous objections, but Hank knew the drill and managed to dodge a direct or incriminating answer every time. The man was extremely loyal to Judge Harris as well as the Order, and didn't mind bending a few rules against perjuring himself for them.

"I'll not ask you the damn question again," Harris almost screamed at him. "Answer me!"

Nigel Pope jumped to his feet. "Objection, Your Honor! He's being hostile to the witness."

"Sustained. Mr. Robertson, please tone things down. I'll not warn you again." Judge Poe could tell, along with the rest of the people in the room, Harris was not on his game today. He was agitated and close to contempt. Nigel also noticed that something had to be wrong for him to be acting like this in front of Judge Poe. He had never seen Harris act so arrogant or so reckless. He'd heard his father, Mark Robertson, could be obnoxiously conceited and arrogant in the courtroom, but still, even he would not have acted like this in front of a judge. It was totally out of character for Harris.

"I don't know how long you want to be here doing this," Harris said to Hank, "but I'm ready for a break. Answer the bloody question, so we can actually finish with your testimony and then we can all go to lunch, dammit." As soon as the words left his mouth, he knew he was in trouble. His first thought was the disrespect he'd just showed his judge, and even worse, the disrespect he indirectly had shown his uncle. *Your attitude is deplorable, son*, he heard his uncle J say inside his head.

"Objection, Your—" the judge cut Nigel off before he could say any more. He was as stunned at Harris's outbursts as Nigel was.

"Sustained and sustained again. Mr. Robertson, I warned you, and now I find you in contempt. You will pay a $5,000 fine. I think we will adjourn for today and continue this on Monday morning. Any more outbursts from you, Mr. Robertson, and you will find yourself spending some time in jail, do you understand me, young man?"

"Yes, Your Honor, my apologies to the court."

"I should hope so," Judge Poe barked. "Just remember to bring a better attitude on Monday morning."

Harris started packing up his briefcase. The courtroom was stunned into near silence by the original outburst, but people were now buzzing with conversation as they filed out.

Once outside the courtroom, Nigel stopped Harris, laying a concerned hand on his arm. "You OK, man?" he asked.

"Fine," Harris snapped. "I'm just sick of liars." Nigel's head snapped back as if from a blow; he had never seen Robertson lose his cool like this. Harris shook off Nigel's hand and stalked away from his as quickly as he could, not wanting to answer any more of his questions.

After he'd paid his fine and tried to leave, Amber Andrews shoved a microphone in his face, hoping to ask a few questions of her own.

"Mr. Robertson, that was a poor show of professionalism in there this morning, was it not?" she asked pointedly.

He rounded on her. "Listen," he snapped, pointing a finger directly in her face, "If you want to talk about professionalism, you need to start by getting a new job." He remembered his grandfather using somewhat similar words to her. He pushed past her and headed for his car.

"Well, there you have it, viewers," he heard Andrews telling the cameras as he strode away. "Yet another show of outrage by a Robertson. They think they can hail down on the courtroom and then bully the witnesses into confessions. Let's see if a $5,000 fine will calm the stormy hurricane down a bit. Stay tuned to Court TV for more exciting action concerning this case."

Watching the little drama unfold on his tiny TV screen, the Executioner was about to explode. He was glad to see Robertson losing his cool, but there was absolutely no mention of the case discontinuing or of Dixie not testifying on Monday. It was time to put his final plan into action. One thing was for sure, Harris Robertson was not going to be in Judge Poe's courtroom on Monday morning, not if the Executioner had anything to do with matters.

Across town, Harris raced home. He changed into something more comfortable, then flopped down on the bed and turned on his TV. He painfully watched himself on Court TV as he acted like a jerk in the courtroom earlier in the day. He also endured the constant interruptions as Amber Andrews took millions of viewers through his continuous outbursts. He had seen enough. He switched channels.

Shit, it was on the local channels as well. I look like a total arse, he told himself. *Damn, what a fool I am.* He knew he should never have let his emotions interfere with his career. He wouldn't score any points with his peers acting like this. If the governor gets wind of it, and with Amber Andrews around that was going to be pretty likely, it could affect his chances of becoming a judge.

Dammit, he thought. *I'll not let Markita lose me that opportunity.* He was so pissed he needed to get up and pace around the room. He needed to let off some steam. He grabbed his gym bag along with his keys from the dresser, then took off to the gym. He figured he could get rid of some frustration by going a few rotations with the weights.

Later that night, security began arriving at the courthouse. They surrounded the building, covering all the exits and entries. No one without appropriate identification was allowed in, and no one could leave until the completion of the Order's meeting at midnight. At that time, busses would be outside waiting to take them back to their hotels. In addition to the regular security already hired, Ronald Harris always had seven of his own expert marksmen situated around the perimeter of the courtroom in which they would hold their meeting. If instructed by Ronald, they would take out a member at a moment's notice.

The first person to arrive, as always, was Judge Harris. Everything needed to be in order and ready to go before anyone got there, and he liked to see that all was secure and going according to plan with his own eyes.

The judge greeted everyone as they arrived at the door, asking each member if the services provided by Sassy Jo were satisfactory. Everyone was having a great time, as usual. Once all the members on Hugh's preapproved list arrived, they entered into Judge Poe's courtroom where Ronald took the judge's chair. Hugh took his place right below the judge, in the court reporter's seat. Everyone else took a seat in the gallery. Ronald bought the meeting to order by banging down his gavel. This always pissed off Judge Poe as he had his own secret desire to take over and sit in his chair and run things himself. Of course, for now, he kept his silence.

First, the opening ceremonies took place; everyone stood up, placed their hands on their chests, and sang "The Star Spangled Banner." Following the formalities, the judge thanked the members for their contributions and favors made to the greater success of the Order for the past year. Additional required "donations" were to be given to Hugh at the end of the meeting. The members never liked this membership rule as it was they who provided the favors to the organization throughout the year to begin with. Hugh always argued that it was to cover the Order's expenses, like the "entertainment" they were enjoying, thanks to Sassy Jo, and this was usually enough to silence the complainers. The meeting was not complete without its share of awards, and this year's award for exceptional loyalty went to Hank the Tank. Judge Poe also received an award for his long-standing membership, as well as for tallying up the most child molester convictions. The senator's award was for bringing in the most new members. The judge also recognized Hugh for putting together another fabulous meeting. Ronald noted how difficult it must have been for Hugh this year with Miss Dixie being out of commission.

Hugh read the minutes of the previous meeting and then proceeded to type this year's minutes as each item was addressed. He planned to transfer the minutes of this year's meeting into the ledger later.

"The first order of business tonight, gentlemen, will be Dixie Jackson's trial."

"Ronald, I think that is a bit of a sore subject at the moment, considering your grandson is making fools of us all," said the chief of police, disgruntled.

"My grandson is not the one who ordered the raid when all our top officials were there," Ronald pointed out.

"No, Ronald, he wasn't," James admitted. "I just wanted it made quite clear that *I* was not responsible for the screwup either."

"James, I don't think you want to rehash this issue with me, do you?" Ronald retorted.

"Um, not at all, sir. I just wanted you to know it wasn't me who pushed the button on the raid," he repeated. James did not want to push the issue any further; the backs of his legs still showed bruises from Ronald's wrath, delivered by Hank the Tank.

"I don't think we should bother discussing the trial," interrupted Senator Franklyn. "What we should be discussing," he said, pointing at the judge, "is the fact that you still have not diversified our monies into different accounts, protecting the Order against your grandson inheriting it. You are getting older, and we may be running out of time if you don't get this settled soon."

"Senator Franklyn," Ronald addressed him coldly, "I'm in charge of this meeting, and, sir, you will not disrupt it. Please wait for your turn. We will get to any and all issues in good time."

"We never got to this issue at last year's meeting," Fredrick Poe said in agreement. "I'm with Senator Franklyn. Let's settle this now."

Ronald banged his gavel on the podium hard.

"I'm with Franklyn also," sputtered the mayor. "I have not been called to the stand by Harris yet, but when I am, I'll no doubt lose my position as well as my perks. I made many concessions for the Order to which I was promised compensation."

"I'll not call this meeting to order again," Ronald said, his face growing red with rage.

"I'm sorry, Ronald, but they are right. We need to have the money secured away from your grandson," Judge Poe reiterated.

"Now, now, gentlemen," Hugh said, trying to suck up to the judge. "We need to let Ronald conduct this meeting in an orderly manner." Hugh hoped this loyalty act would win him points with the judge.

"Thank you, Hugh," Ronald said graciously.

"What the hell are you licking ass for?" Poe demanded, turning on Hugh. "If it wasn't for you, we wouldn't be having Dixie Jackson's trial."

"What do you mean?" Ronald inquired.

"He's the reason this shit all went down," Poe said, pointing an accusing finger at Hugh. "Hugh came to me with some elaborate plan to get Harris to piss off the Executioner so he would go after him." Judge Poe had thrown Hugh completely under the bus, and Hugh froze like a deer in headlights.

"That's absurd," Hugh managed. "I would never put Harris at risk," he argued, trying to cover his ass. "I'm entrusted by Ronald to keep the boy safe," Hugh said, now in total fear for his life, but trying not to show it.

"Are you kidding me?" the senator interjected. "If this is the case, then I vote to have Hugh removed right now. You can put me in his place."

"What do you mean you, Franklyn? I'm the only logical option here," Judge Poe exclaimed.

"I don't think so. There is only one logical member here for that position, and that would be me," the senator reiterated.

"Listen, Franklyn, you're not even a senator anymore. What influence do you have? Better still, what are you going to be able to bring to the table now?" Judge Poe mocked him.

"First, I'll be reelected when this scandal, which Hugh caused, calms down. Furthermore, I'm loved in this state and still have a large following, not to mention the clout I possess in Washington, along with the favors I'm owed there," the senator shouted back.

"You all need to calm down," Hugh said, trying to get things under control, but not daring to look in the judge's direction.

"Hugh, I want an explanation right now," the judge demanded calmly. "Have you set up Harris to get hurt? Yes or no?"

"Of course not, Ronald. Like I said, I have been taking care of him, just as you ordered."

"I'll ask you one more time, Hugh. Yes or no?"

"Again, Ronald, no."

Poe came at Hugh again, exposing more of his plans. "Then you explain to Ronald how is it that Harris told you, and only you, that he would be in to work late the day he was taking his mother's car into the shop to get fixed. The day her brakes were mysteriously cut. You are the only one who knew that information, Hugh."

"Ronald," Hugh tried to explain. "When Harris showed me the note from the nurse, telling him it was not an accident, I'm the one who called James to get him to dispose of the evidence immediately to cover the Executioner's tracks, not to cover my own. You know very well that I have been cleaning up his messes for the past six months," Hugh said, trying to divert the issue. He was getting nervous as he desperately tried to think of how he was going to get out of this mess. He hoped his explanation covered his ass as it was definitely on the line here.

"You would not have to be cleaning up the Executioner's mess if you had not ordered these harebrained schemes of yours in the first place," Judge Poe accused, dropping him right back in the middle of the firing line. Ronald was furious, looking like he was about to come unglued.

"Harris has been telling me about some of the things going on down here," Ronald said slowly. "My suspicions are beginning to tell me that you are behind them all, Hugh."

"Ronald, you cannot believe Fredrick. I tried to protect him when he slapped around one of Dixie Jackson's girls. That's what got us in this mess with the trial in the first place. The Executioner is sweet on Dixie and went after Poe for slapping the girl because Miss Dixie asked him to." Hugh tried to throw the suspicion back at Judge Poe.

"That is a total lie!" Poe shouted. "It was Hugh who set that whole monstrosity up, and I nearly got killed because of him!"

Ronald had heard enough and knew he needed to get the meeting back under control. He gestured to Hank, who moved immediately to his side. "Hank, please have Hugh removed. Deliver him to the Executioner. You know where to go." Hank motioned to the shooter closest to Hugh. Hugh saw what was happening and was now screaming and pleading with Ronald.

"Please, Ronald, don't do this! I beg of you! I've remained loyal to you! Ronald, for God's sake, man, let me explain," Hugh screamed, begging for his life. Ronald would not even look at him as the guard dragged him, wailing, from the room

"Now," the judge asked quietly. "Is there anyone else who would like to interrupt this meeting?" The room was in silent fear.

"Let's continue on, gentlemen," Judge Harris instructed. "I do sympathize with the situation concerning my grandson and the monies belonging to the Order currently under my management. I can assure you, however, that I'm still in full control of this Order and will be for quite some time to come. I will make provisions in the diary for disbursements in the event of my death. This will so be ordered."

Ronald reverted back to the Dixie Jackson trial and instructed Judge Poe to make sure there was a mistrial next week. Poe replied he would take care of it.

"There were several other issues which needed addressing tonight, but due to the misconduct shown here this evening, we will not be able to get to everything. I'll contact all our members and see if it will be possible to hold a special meeting somewhere down the road. I will, however, end this meeting by appointing Senator Franklyn to take over for Hugh."

"Senator," Ronald warned, "do not cross me like Hugh tried to do, or you will end up meeting with the same stainless steel blade he's going to meet with tomorrow. Do you get my drift?"

"Absolutely, Ronald, and thank you for the opportunity to serve you again," the senator said. Fredrick Poe was furious, insulted, and in total disagreement with Ronald's selection, but he was not going to argue the point tonight. He would, however, be addressing the matter quite soon.

On Saturday morning, Judge Harris and his wife checked out of their hotel room, then went out to breakfast together. Afterward they proceeded over to their daughter's house. Joshua, who was not at all excited to see Ronald, met them at the door.

"Who is it?" asked Mary Ellen in the background.

"It's a surprise for you, darling," Joshua answered, trying to sound as positive and as sincere as he could. Mr. and Mrs. Harris followed Josh into the living room where Mary Ellen was sitting up for the first time since she'd arrived home from the hospital.

"Oh, Daddy, it's you!" she cried. "Mom, I can't believe it!" Mary Ellen's eyes filled with tears.

"A bit emotional, are we not, dear?" Mrs. Robertson observed, speaking in her usual high-society voice, which had no emotion to it whatsoever.

"Mary Ellen has been through quite an ordeal, Mrs. Harris. She's still recovering from her accident." Joshua glared over at Ronald. The judge went straight over to his daughter, took her in his arms and held her.

"I have missed you so much, Daddy."

"I have missed you too, baby girl." A small tear appeared in the corner of his eye. Mrs. Harris was next, and she held Mary Ellen as if she was a china doll that would break if she actually hugged her.

"Mother," exclaimed Mary Ellen, after looking into the older woman's face for a moment. "You look so much younger! And your scar! It's so faint it's barely noticeable. You look beautiful."

"Mary Ellen, you are so overdramatic. I was looking older, and your father suggested I get a face-lift. You know he does not like to discuss my scar. Would you please honor his wishes?"

"Yes, Mother," Mary Ellen said, turning to her father. "I'm sorry, Daddy."

"It's OK," he responded, patting her hand. "Your mother does look fabulous though, doesn't she?"

"Yes, she looks as beautiful as a rose in the garden next to my . . . award-winning prized rose," Joshua said as he looked over at his wife adoringly.

"Let's not get mushy please," said Mrs. Harris, followed by, "Do you have any tea I could brew?"

"Yes, Mommy. Let's go in the kitchen and make some while our men chat." Joshua gently helped Mary Ellen off the couch, and the two women headed for the kitchen.

"Mary Ellen's car accident was not an accident," Joshua told Ronald bluntly. "But you know that already, don't you?"

"I'm not sure what you are insinuating, Joshua," Ronald replied, raising an eyebrow.

"You know exactly what I'm saying. I'm sure you are quite well aware of what Harris is mixed up in."

"First of all, Joshua, I do not care for your tone. I can remember back when you yourself came to me and asked for my help."

"Yes, it was the worst mistake I ever made in my life," Joshua said, thinking about his brother.

"Hmmm, seems to have worked out well for you though, don't you think?" The judge referred to the fact that Joshua had ended up with his daughter and grandson, along with the house he was living in. The judge threw these facts at him every time they got into it. Joshua was starting to lose control.

"If one hair on my wife's head is harmed, or if any harm comes to Harris, I'll do to you what I could not do to my brother. I'll promise you that."

"My, my Joshua, when did you become so hostile? Anyway you don't have to worry about any more problems down here in Orlando. They are being dealt with—today."

"What the hell do you mean by that?" Joshua demanded, but just then the women came back with the tea. The four of them sat and chatted awhile about world events as if nothing else was wrong.

"Well, baby girl, it's time for your mother and I to leave. We are going to visit with our wonderful grandson. He's come across so charmingly on the TV, does he not, Mary Ellen?"

"Oh, Daddy, I'm so proud of him."

"You have every right in the world to think that way, baby girl. He's a good boy."

"Yes, he is, and I'll make sure he stays that way," Joshua said in an accusing tone, which of course turned his wife's head. She looked at her husband sharply.

"Daddy," she said, looking back at her father. "Before you go, there is something you should know."

"Yes, my darling, what is it?"

"Well, Harris met this girl in the office. Her name is Markita."

"Yes, dear, he told your mother and I all about her."

"Well, they broke up . . ." she started to say, but the judge interrupted her.

"Yes, baby girl, we knew about that as well."

"Well, they got back together again, but she left him again on Thursday."

"Whoa, it sounds like she must have some issues." He did not let on he knew Markita was Trudy's daughter.

"Gracious, the girl sounds like a floozy," Mrs. Robertson quipped, putting in her unwanted opinion. "He needs to stay away from her."

"She's not a floozy," Joshua said, defending Markita. "I think once they reunited, they realized they were moving a bit too fast and needed to reevaluate things, that's all."

"Yes, Joshua is right," Mary Ellen chimed in. "Harris asked her to marry him. I think maybe it scared her a little. He's not at his best right now, Daddy, so please go easy on him."

Joshua could not believe his ears. He was so extra proud of his wife for defending Markita or at least not making her look bad. His heart swelled with pride and love for her.

"Of course we will be sympathetic, Mary Ellen. I don't believe you have even asked that of us," her mother scolded her softly.

"I'm sorry, Mommy, it's just that, well, if you saw him in court yesterday . . . he was an angry young man. He was fined $5,000 in contempt. He really is not himself."

"My goodness, darling," the judge said. "That surprises me, but don't worry. I'll have a word with Judge Poe before I leave town."

"No, you won't," Joshua said, jumping up out of his chair. "You will stay out of his career," he ordered Ronald. "He deserved the fine because he disrespected the system he believes in. He did and should pay for his actions."

"Yes, yes, you're right, Joshua," Judge Harris agreed, not wanting to get into another confrontation with him, especially in front of his daughter. He took his wife's hand, and they both hugged Mary Ellen before leaving.

"What was all that about, Joshua Wayne Robertson?" Mary Ellen asked him after her parents were gone. "You almost took my father's head off."

"You're right, Mary Ellen, and I'll apologize to him later. I guess I'm concerned about Harris's display of unprofessionalism in the courtroom yesterday. Our talk last night did not exactly go pleasantly either."

"Well, OK, then. I don't like to see you and my father not getting along. You know he's my world, along with you and Harris."

"Yes, darling, I know." She reached up and squeezed his hand, a mischievous smile coming over her face.

"So, Joshua! What did you think about my mother having a face-lift after all these years?"

"Who knows, my darling? She looked twenty years younger, but still no one could ever look as beautiful as you."

"That, right there, is why I love you, Joshua Wayne Robertson."

When Judge Harris and his wife arrived at Harris's condo, they rang the doorbell several times before their grandson came down the stairs to answer it. He had totally forgotten his grandparents were going to visit him today.

"Harris, how are you, darling?" his grandmother said, her tone much more loving than the one she had recently used toward her own daughter.

"Oh, wow, I'm sorry. I forgot you were coming," Harris said, standing at the door in his pajama bottoms. "Ah, come on in please," he said embarrassed as he stood back to let them enter. His grandfather hugged him, patting him on the back, then took his hand and shook it.

"I'm so proud of you, Harris. You look great up there on the TV."

"You wouldn't be saying that if you had seen me yesterday, sir," Harris said, feeling even more embarrassed. He escorted them into his living room, where they both sat down.

"I'm going to run upstairs for a moment and put on something a little more appropriate," he told them.

"Yes, darling, that probably would be a good idea," Mrs. Robertson said in her stiff upper lip voice again. Harris quickly disappeared up the stairs.

"The place is clean, Ronald, but the boy looks deplorable, don't you think?"

"That's what a slutty woman will do to you," he replied. She didn't have time to ask what he was referring to by his comment as Harris reentered the room.

"Would you like me to have a word with Judge Poe and have him reverse your contempt charge, son?" the judge asked, completely ignoring Joshua's request that he mind his own business. "It would be my pleasure. You know Fredrick is a good friend of mine."

"No, thank you, sir. I was in the wrong."

"Such good ethics, Harris. I like that," Mrs. Robertson said.

"How long are you going to be in town, Grandfather?"

"We are leaving right after we visit with you, son. I have a game of golf with the governor tomorrow, which is going to be more important now than ever."

"What do you mean, sir?"

"I think it's time you and he met with each other as I want him to get to know you very well. It's time you started putting more time and effort toward your judgeship." Ronald felt it was time to tell the governor to replace Hugh with his grandson.

Harris loved hearing those words, especially now. It would be a good time to throw himself into his work and not have to think about Markita.

"I would appreciate that, Grandfather. I hope I can live up to your reputation and expectations."

"You will far supersede me, son."

"I don't think that is possible, sir. You are the best Supreme Court judge Florida ever appointed."

"Darling, Harris is right. This state would have fallen apart a long time ago if it hadn't been for you," his wife cooed.

"OK, enough with the compliments. My ego can't take it." The judge gave one of his deep belly laughs.

"Would you both like some lunch before you leave?" asked Harris.

"That would be nice. Why don't I go look and see what I can find in the kitchen while you men have a chat?"

"Thank you, Grandmother. There should be some ham and cheese in the fridge. I hope the bread I bought on the way home from work Thursday night is still fresh." Harris hated thinking back to last Thursday night; it made his heart ache yet again.

As his grandmother left the room, Harris leaned close to his grandfather, keeping his voice low so that only he could hear him. "Grandfather, have you found out who cut Mom's brakes?"

"I think it must have been that Executioner fellow," Ronald replied. "I believe he's trying to warn you not to put Dixie Jackson on the stand."

"Do you think I should be worried? Hugh said he probably went underground again."

"Hugh is probably right, and I have a sneaking suspicion that you won't be hearing from the Executioner for quite some time. Although, son, there is always a certain fear when we prosecute people. Who knows when they might show up again? The reason we prosecute them is because they do not use proper judgment." He chuckled at his pun.

"You know, son, things always seem to work themselves out. God always protects his children, so I wouldn't worry about Dixie Jackson too much or your mother's accident." Harris was confused by his grandfather's statement. What made him reference God protecting his children? It was as if his grandfather was talking in riddles, avoiding his question.

"You trust me, Harris, don't you?" the judge asked suddenly, seeing confusion spreading of Harris's face.

"Of course I do. You know that."

"Then leave things with me. I think the corruption here in Orlando is about to leave as we speak. Things around here will start changing now, don't worry. You continue doing the great job you are doing and start preparing for your judgeship." He put a comforting hand on Harris's shoulder. "Let me worry about the rest."

Harris was trying to read between the lines, but the things his grandfather said did not make any sense. They just sounded like more riddles.

Harris's grandmother returned with little bite-size sandwiches and some tea.

"I was quite surprised to find my favorite tea, Harris."

"I always keep some around just for your visits, Grandmother."

"That is so special of you, my darling. It's why you are my favorite grandson."

Harris cracked up. "Why, Grandmother, you told a joke! I'm your only grandchild. I never knew you had a funny side."

"I try not to show it, darling. When you are married to someone as powerful as your grandfather, you need to have a certain je ne sais quoi. I have to show the people around him I'm a strong woman and deserving of him."

"Wow, Grandmother, that sounds so cold."

"It's not cold, darling. It is what it has to be. People's lives are not always what they seem, and that goes for any class of society." He was slightly shocked; he had never heard his grandmother talk so deeply before. Her philosophy intrigued him.

"Well, Harris, we thank you for lunch, but if I don't stop your grandmother yakking, we will miss our flight."

"I'm sorry, darling. I didn't mean to ramble."

"It's OK, dear. It's time we left for the airport."

Harris could feel a little tension between his grandparents, but they all hugged before saying their good-byes. Harris waved to them as they drove away, then returned to his living room, turned on his music, and sat in his fat boy chair.

He tried going over the conversation with his grandparents, but could not make heads or tails of what either of them actually said. He was stunned and confused. He thought for a little while about his broken heart. He still could not understand what went wrong. Why didn't Markita talk to him about things? He had thought she had more compassion for people than to leave them hanging. Then he thought about Trudy; maybe Markita was more like her mother than he realized. How could he have been so wrong about her? He was starting to get angry, so he got up from his chair, looking for something to do. He picked up the plates, took them to the kitchen, and then returned for the teacups. Still frustrated, he turned off his music and went back to bed.

Someone else was even more unhappy than Harris. The Executioner was not pleased about having to leave the cabin to take care of an order from the Voice. He had things of his own to take care of, but he was curious as to why Hugh was about to lose his head. He'd received instructions to drive to an old abandoned warehouse on Forsythe Street. He parked the car and looked up the storage unit number. Again, following instructions, he found the key to the storage unit and unlocked the padlock. Inside was Hugh, tied and gagged in a chair. He looked dehydrated, but became instantly alert as soon as he saw Smith. Fear entered into his eyes, his heart beating fast. He urinated in his pants as Smith ripped the tape from his mouth.

"Please let me explain what happened," he begged.

"I'm listening," the Executioner said calmly, more out of curiosity than any sympathy any normal person might feel.

"I was ambushed by Judge Poe. He told Ronald it was you who tried to suffocate him. I told Ronald it certainly was not. I tried to cover for you, I swear I did. Judge Poe also told the Order I was trying to get Miss Dixie off. Apparently, the Order has other plans for her. It's the Order that wants to prosecute Dixie, not me. I have been pressuring Judge Poe all week to call a mistrial for you. I also figured out it was you who cut the judge's daughter's brakes, so I called the chief of police and forced him to destroy all the evidence, which could have incriminated you."

Smith may not be the smartest of men, but Hugh's ramblings sounded lame, even to him.

"Look," Hugh went on, desperate for a reprieve. "I'm about to take over the whole organization. If you let me go, I'll split the $150,000,000 with you. We can cut them all out and buy a yacht and sail to Tahiti. They will never find us."

"I guess you screwed up pretty bad, huh?"

"No, no, I didn't! That is what I'm trying to tell you! It's all Judge Poe." The Executioner was now bored. He drew his sword then swiped it across Hugh's neck without another thought. Hugh's head fell to the ground, and Smith watched for a while as it rolled across the floor. After he finished amusing himself, he left to get back to the cabin where his own plans were waiting for him.

Chapter Twenty-Six

An Uncle's Compassion

It was Sunday morning, and Harris was in a better frame of mind. Tired of staying in bed, he got up and went downstairs to brew some coffee. On Sundays, he liked to relax and read the newspaper before going over to his parents' later in the day. He thought that maybe he should get his act together and go over there for supper today. *Things need to get back to normal,* he told himself. He grabbed the cellophane bag from the doorstep and returned to the kitchen, placing the newspaper on the table. It was then that he noticed an envelope attached to the bag.

"Strange," he said out loud. "I thought I just paid the bill." He separated the envelope from the cellophane and opened it. *I warned you about hurting my family. Thought the pretty little lady went home, did ya? Guess again.* Harris threw the note on the table and just stared at it for a second.

"Oh my god, what the . . ."

He picked up the note again, this time with shaking hands. He could not read it fast enough. *Thought the pretty little lady went home. did ya? Guess again,* he read a second time. His skin tightened into gooseflesh, and his heart began to race with anxiety. His hands began shaking so badly he could hardly read the rest of what the note said. *I betcha life's been a bitch since Thursday, ain't it? No worries . . . the little lady has been entertaining me.* Harris's whole body was now shaking, the muscles in his stomach so tight he could not breathe. On top of his fear, his anger was preventing him from holding the note steady, his heart thumping against his chest so hard it felt like it was trying to escape.

Jesus Christ, Harris, control yourself. Read the damn note, you moron.

He knew now: she did not leave him. He felt like such a jerk, betraying her trust as he had done. He believed that if he had trusted in their love more, he would have seen that something was wrong. Instead, he had focused on himself, and now Markita was in danger . . . if she was even still alive. *Shut the hell up!* he ordered his fevered brain. *Read the freaking note!* He fought to get his emotions under control, forcing himself to sit before his shaking knees brought him to the floor. He began again.

> *I warned you about hurting my family. Thought the pretty little lady went home, did ya? Guess again. I betcha life's been a bitch since Thursday, ain't it? No worries . . . the little lady has been entertaining me. She did a good job of writing your Dear John letter, don't you think? She had me convinced. Of course, if she wasn't believable, I told her I would slice your head off. Aw, what a shame. Did Harris cry? I am going to give you one last chance, Mr. Assistant District Attorney. If you put Dixie on the stand in the morning, the little lady's head will roll, just like Hugh Gallagher's did yesterday. It rolled quite a long way before stopping, you know!*

The Executioner

Harris just made it to his kitchen sink in time before heaving, choking on his own vomit, vile thoughts of the Executioner and what he could be doing to his beautiful Markita running swiftly through his mind. His stomach contracted again and again until it was empty. Grabbing a towel, he wet it, then placed it on his face, willing his body back under his conscious control. This was helping no one. As he leaned on the counter, trying to take deep breaths to control his frenzied heart, the phone rang, long and loud. Harris froze for a moment, then he forced himself to walk to the phone and pick it up.

At first, all he could hear was Markita crying, then she managed to scream out, "I love you, LB!"

His barely under control emotions started to take over again as his heart began to race even faster. She sounded so afraid, and here he was puking in a sink, safe and sound in his own kitchen. He started to tell her he loved her when he heard the Executioner's voice in the background.

"Hey there, lover boy," he taunted. "The pretty lady wants a kiss, but you're not here, so I guess I'll give her one for you. Damn, she's a good bitch in bed," he added, cackling like a madman. Harris slumped back into the wall with the phone against his ear, moaning as if he were in physical pain—which it felt like he was.

"What's the matter, lover boy?" the Executioner hissed in his ear. "Not feeling well?" He let out another haunting laugh, then hung up.

Harris's legs finally gave way, and he fell to his knees, rocking back and forth, while tears of rage fell onto the cold tiled floor. His devastation left him feeling nothing. *Markita baby, I'm so, so sorry, oh god, I love you, I . . .*

The phone rang again.

"Fuck . . ." he screamed, startled. How was he going to answer it knowing it could be the Executioner wanting to taunt him again? But he had to answer it, for Markita's sake. Pulling himself up level with the counter, he pressed the Answer button.

His shaky voice answered, "OK, you bastard, what do you want?"

"Harris, it's . . ."

"Who is this?" It was definitely *not* the Executioner.

Thank God, he thought, feeling guilty for praying it would not be him, his stiff body only slightly relaxing with relief. He needed a moment to think of how to deal with the Executioner when he *did* call back—which as much as it frightened him, he prayed the man would do. He had to find out if there was chance for Markita.

"It's me Jo . . ." the familiar voice came again. "Can you hear . . . . ?"

Harris could tell it was Joe, but his cell phone seemed to be breaking up.

"Harris, go to . . ."

"Joe!" Harris was stunned. What was going on? "I can't hear you, man . . . What are you trying to say?"

"My bed . . ."

"What? Joe, you're cutting out again. Where are you? You sound like you are in an airport." Harris thought he could make out the whine of plane engines and muffled intercom announcements in the background.

"Yes, we are . . . my bed. Find the . . . I have the proof."

"Joe! Joe, I don't understand a word you are saying, man," Harris shouted, trying to figure this out.

"Get to my . . . Look on . . . bed. It covers my bed. I will . . . more proof. Our plane is . . ." Then Joe's phone completely died.

Harris felt he must be close to having a heart attack. First, the note, then the Executioner's call, and now Joe. His pulse was racing faster than he could breathe. What was Joe trying to tell him? He replayed what he remembered of their garbled communication, trying to decipher his words. Harris figured that Joe must have remembered something; maybe what he was trying to tell him could help him find Markita. He tried collecting his thoughts. "*My bed,* he kept telling me," Harris said aloud. "*Covers,* he said, *more proof.* What could he be trying to tell me?" he growled, trying to put all the pieces together.

He ran upstairs, throwing on clothes faster than he had ever done in his life. *Maybe what I am looking for is at Joe's.* He grabbed his keys and left for Joe's, forgetting to even turn off his coffeepot.

Robin had still been trying to jog Joe's memory with recent events, reminding him of when they broke into Hugh's office. Joe had begun rambling, started to have flashes, and suddenly . . . a revelation . . . all at once everything came back to him. He told Robin they needed to get to the hotel room in

Oakmont. He had hidden the proof Father Jimmy had given him, which he needed for Harris, under the mattress. He was telling Robin and his mom to start making plane reservations, while he got the hospital to release him. Getting released was going to take time, but he could not call Hugh to help speed up his release, because he knew Hugh was corrupt and would detain him longer. He also remembered that Judge Harris ran the Order, but Hugh was the one carrying out his orders. He had played him and Harris right from the beginning.

He asked his nurse to get him the hospital's chief of staff, telling her it was imperative his release was speedy; it was an official emergency. While the nurse left to see what she could do, Joe began to get dressed and ready to leave. He tried to call Harris, but his phone signal was lousy in the hospital; he would wait until he got to the airport.

Harris arrived at Joe's house and grabbed the key from under the mat. Unlocking the door, he raced down the hall into Joe's bedroom, where he started to rummage around on the bed remembering his words: "My bed . . ."

Finally, he found the binder under the covers, noting again Joe had not made his bed before leaving on his trip. Harris made a quick mental note to bust him when they next got together. Frantically, he started reading through it, but this was not fast enough for him; time was of the essence if he was to find Markita. There was no telling what the Executioner was doing to her. He forced himself to push those thoughts out of his mind; he couldn't allow anything to distract him from even the smallest clue that might help him find her.

He had only ever wanted to hurt one other person in his life, and that was Trudy, but his anger toward her was nowhere near as intense as it was for the Executioner. It was killing him inside knowing that monster could be hurting Markita in more ways than one.

As he skimmed the pages of the ledger searching for clues, his heart leapt into his throat as he realized he was entering into a world of evil and corruption. The ivory tower his grandfather had created for him was now beginning to crumble, his innocence lost. With each page, he felt a dagger thrust into his heart. Harris could not believe the words written there; he felt they had to be lies. His grandfather could not have done the heinous things he was reading, could he?

Joe said he had proof, at least I think it's what I heard him say. He read on. *Oh Jesus, holy mother of god . . . my grandmother was raped? That's how she got the scar on her face?* Back in those days, he knew women who were raped typically were looked down upon, as if it was their own fault. He could only guess how awful it had been for her.

"My god, no wonder Grandfather would not allow any of us to discuss her scar," he said aloud. He read on about the affair, about Jake Johnson, and his grandfather's role in framing him. He skimmed ahead to more recent entries, where he learned the truth about Officer Parker's death, as well as the deaths of Parker's son, Eleanor Woodsworth, even old Stewart Pope. How the hell was he supposed to face Nigel, knowing what he now knew?

His heart sank further into darkness, knowing he would have to expose his own grandfather as a murderer. He tried to read faster; it was getting late, and he could hear the thunder rolling in like it did every hot afternoon. Harris was getting frustrated as it was taking hours to read the damn book; he started flipping through the pages, skimming the contents faster and faster. How was it possible his grandfather was the head of the Klan? What was even more incomprehensible was how could he tell his own wife her child was stillborn? And worse, place the child in an orphanage?

A lightbulb suddenly went off for Harris. "The orphanage is in Oakmont," he muttered. "That must be why Joe was there. He must have been checking out a lead." He read on to find out how his grandfather turned a young boy called Philip into a murderer. Harris shook his head in disgust. *I wonder what ever happened to that child.*

It did not surprise him to find that Hugh was running the Order down here in Orlando for his grandfather; it actually made a lot of sense.

After six grueling hours, he finally finished reading the ledger. It was now dark outside, and Harris could hear the high winds; finally the storm had rolled in. There was nothing but emptiness left inside him. He felt drained, lost, and alone; the adrenaline, which once boiled inside him, turned to pure anger. Had his whole life been a lie? Did his grandfather manipulate all his cases like he did his father's? Harris could not conceive how his grandfather could hurt his own daughter by concocting an elaborate story that his father's mistress was pregnant. It floored him to read his father was willing to pay Trudy one million dollars for her silence so there would be no scandal. Was there nothing that his grandfather and father would not do to protect and further their careers? He'd always known his father was a rat bastard, but how could his grandfather, the man he'd admired and respected, be capable of the things he had read? Ultimately, he knew none of that mattered at the moment. It was time for him to snap out of the darkness and concentrate on saving Markita. He read back through the pages looking for where it said something about a cabin.

"That's it," he said. *I bet she is at the cabin off South Orange Blossom Trail.* Grabbing the binder, he tore out of the house, praying he was right and could get there in time. He tried calling his grandfather, but there was no answer, so he left a message:

"You are a rat bastard and are dead to me. You knew all along who the Executioner was. How could you betray your own wife? How could you let that animal hurt your own daughter? And now he has Markita . . . I hope you rot in hell!" Harris couldn't say any more; words seemed to fail him.

Next, he dialed his uncle J, praying he would pick up.

"Hey there, whippersnapper, how are you?"

"Uncle J! Listen to me," Harris ordered him, trying to be as clear as possible. "I don't have time to repeat myself. The Executioner has Markita. She did not leave me—he forced to write the note. He has her in a cabin in the woods off of South Orange Blossom Trail, near a corner popular with prostitutes like Dixie Jackson, when she was younger. If I don't make it, tell Mom I know everything about what my grandfather did to my father and that I love her. I love you too, Uncle J."

"Whoa, whoa, Harris," Joshua yelled, but he heard only the dial tone. The past came rushing back to him. He flashed back to the cabin where his brother and Bellamy were shot and then burned to ashes. He saw an image of Ronald Harris in his mind, and anger reared its ugly head inside him. "Please do not let history repeat itself. Please, dear God, keep Harris safe." The irony of a cabin and Ronald Harris scared Joshua to death. He knew he would need to hurry in order to help his nephew.

"I love you, Mary Ellen, pray for me and Harris please."

"Joshua, what is it?" But he was already out the door. Mary Ellen's body started to shake as she prayed. She did not know why she was praying, but she knew inside that whatever it was that was happening, it was not good. Joshua would never have left her without saying good-bye unless he had no choice.

Joe landed at Orlando International Airport, making Harris his first call as soon as the plane's wheels hit the ground.

"Hey, partner, I'm back in Orlando, about five minutes away from my house. Did you get my message to pick up the diary?"

"Yes, I did but . . ."

Joe interrupted. "Man, do I have some crazy ass shit to tell you about the diary and everything I discovered on my trip, but why don't you fill me in on what's been happening here first? Robin tells me you and the pretty lady got back together but split up again. What the hell is all that crap about?"

Harris ignored the question and instead filled Joe in on the immediate situation at hand. "I left your place a few moments ago," he said. "I'm on my way to a cabin in the woods over on Orange Blossom Trail. It is the last corner before the woods. The one where we make most arrests. It seems to be the most popular corner. It's the one Dixie Jackson used to work all the time."

"I know exactly where that is," Joe said. "What's up?"

"The Executioner has Markita."

"Son of a bitch, Harris! Are you OK?"

"Not at all. I thought she had left me, Joe. And by the way, I heard the results of our DNA test on your answering machine, so if I don't make it, I want you to know I am eternally grateful to you for the short time Markita and I had back together."

"Harris, I'm on my way. I am going by the house, and I'll pick up a weapon, then I'll meet you at the woods. Harris, listen to me," Joe said, all deadly seriousness without a trace of his usual humor. "Do *not* go in without me. I mean it, buddy. This is one mean mothering son of a bitch, do you understand me?"

"You are a good friend, Joe. I am glad you found Robin."

"Harris, don't do it, man, and do not call backup. If the Executioner hears sirens, he'll kill Markita instantly . . ." Joe heard the dial tone. "Shit, damn it!" Joe stepped on the gas.

Harris arrived at the woods. Noticing a rental car there on the corner, he parked behind it, wondering who the car could belong too. He felt the hood: it was still piping hot. Whoever it belonged to hadn't been here long.

He walked deep into the brush looking for the cabin. Suddenly he saw it. Making sure not to rustle any leaves, he quietly approached the front door, noticing it was ajar. The voice he heard inside sounded distinctly like his grandfather's. *That's impossible!* he thought. Didn't his grandfather say he was leaving for Tallahassee yesterday afternoon? He listened to the voices again, recognizing one as the Executioner's, and the other, he was now positive, was his grandfather's! He must have just gotten there as he heard the Executioner ask him who the hell he was. This confused Harris as the diary said his grandfather instructed the Executioner who to kill and when. How did he not know the man?

"I am the Voice," he heard him say.

"You are the one that sent me money? Then took me from the orphanage?"

"Yes, Philip, that was me."

It all suddenly came clear to Harris. *Philip Smith is the boy who was in the orphanage*, he realized. And on the heels of that thought, another: *He is the Executioner.*

Oh my god, that is my grandmother's son. My grandfather turned him into a killer. He is a monster, Harris thought, listening intently.

"So I owe you what?" said the Executioner.

"If it wasn't for me, your life would have been miserable."

"You think it has been a bed of roses for me?"

"It has been a hell of a lot better than people finding out you were illegitimate born from a black bastard and a white woman. You would have ended up hanging from a tree, just like your father."

"So you are the great Judge Harris?" rumbled the Executioner. "I can't say it's great to meet you after all these years. Hugh told me all about you before he became speechless." The Executioner laughed.

"Philip, I told you I would always take care of you and I have, but in return I gave you specific instructions that you could not hurt the Robertson family. Why did you go against my wishes and try to hurt my daughter, Mary Ellen?" *Huh*, thought Harris. *One count of honesty from my grandfather. He didn't know his killer went after Mom.*

"I told that stupid assistant district attorney if he hurt Miss Dixie, I would hurt one of his family. Obviously he doesn't listen too well."

Harris's thoughts raced through his mind. *He doesn't realize he tried to hurt his own sister.* He was growing more and more pissed at his grandfather, if that were possible.

"I had no idea Hugh conspired to put Dixie on trial or that you had feelings for her," Judge Harris was saying. "If you had told me you felt this way, I could have talked to him." There was a bright flash of lightning that lit up the sky. Over to his left, Ronald saw Markita lying on a table bound and gagged with a machete lying across her throat. A clap of thunder followed the lightning, making both men jump.

The Executioner took out a gun and pointed it at Ronald. The rain was starting to come down faster and harder now, and Harris couldn't hear what the two men were saying. He pushed the door open a fraction at a time, trying not to let it make a sound. He slipped in silently as another flash of lightning tore across the heavens. In the harsh light, Harris saw what his grandfather had seen moments before: Markita lying on a table with a machete poised at her throat. The two men stood to the right of her. His heart stopped beating for a moment as he assessed his surroundings. There was a wooden chair knocked to the ground on its side, and ironically, there was a hurricane lamp sitting on a shelf. It was the only source of light in the cabin except for the fierce lightning strikes, which lit up the room through the one window every few minutes. Over to his immediate right in the corner, there was a metal bed with only a mattress on top of it, no blankets or pillows from what he could see. The thunder rolled, and the lightning struck again; this time in the light he saw handcuffs attached to the bed frame. He could not bear the devastating thought which crossed his mind. The Executioner had already given him a very descriptive picture as to what he had done to his sweet Markita. There was a definite foul smell about the place. His body stiffened while he tried to get the vile images out of his mind.

He could hear the voice inside his head telling him to pull himself together. *Markita needs you to be strong . . . You can do this.*

His thoughts went back to the diary. *My grandfather may have manipulated the cases I took to trial, but it was my own expertise and quick thinking that bought the case to final justice.* He could not mess up now; he needed to be in full control. He knew this would be the stage of a lifetime, and he needed to be the star.

"Harris, what are you doing here?" Ronald asked in complete surprise as a bolt of lightning exposed his grandson crouched on the floor near the now-open doorway.

"I guess I could ask you the same question, Grandfather," Harris retorted, snapping to his feet.

"This is not what it looks like, son," Ronald said, trying to avoid his grandson's question. Harris needed to think even faster now. "Well, it looks a lot like a family reunion to me. Oh, but that's right, he's not your son, is he? He's the bastard son that you told Grandmother was stillborn, right?"

"It is not safe for you to be here, Harris," the old judge warned, not unkindly. "You need to leave, right this instant."

"Why is that, Grandfather? Is there something here you want to hide from me?"

"No one is going anywhere," said the Executioner with the haunting laugh Harris heard on the phone. "This is all starting to amuse me. Be careful though. If you start to bore me, I *will* end the show." The sound of that laugh sent chills down Harris's spine.

"I told you, Harris," the judge said again. "This is not what it looks like."

"Oh . . . pray tell, Grandfather, what is it then?"

"We can discuss this later. You need to leave."

"I am not going anywhere. I know everything."

"What do you mean?" Ronald asked, sounding concerned.

"I mean everything. From how you killed an African American for having an affair with Grandmother, to manipulating my father into having an affair with Markita's mother. You are a true rat bastard."

"Don't talk to me that way. You do not know all the facts."

"Well, Grandfather, none of us is going anywhere, so why don't you enlighten us?"

"That's a good idea. The assistant district attorney makes a good point," said Smith, still amused for the moment. To Harris's relief, he had at least lowered the gun. He chanced a glance at Markita and saw that she was staring at him mutely, silently begging him to help her. He gave her the briefest of nods, and she closed her eyes.

"I don't need to explain anything to either of you."

"Really . . . would you like me to explain to your Executioner the truth about what you did to him?"

"Harris, this is none of your business. You need to stay out of things if you know what is good for you."

"I wanna hear," said Smith, not so amused now.

"Well, it seems my grandmother had an affair with your father. You were the result of that affair, making you my uncle." Another flash of lightning struck, and a clash of thunder followed. It seemed to make all three of them nervous.

Harris continued, "My grandfather told my grandmother you were stillborn so that no one would know about you. Then, he placed you in an orphanage until it was time to train you to become a killer."

"Is that so?" Smith prided himself on being a man with no emotions, but finding out it was the Voice who had put him in the orphanage pissed him off.

"Harris, don't you understand? He's a worthless excuse for a person. Can you imagine what people would have said about that back in those days? I had already left Orlando to avoid the scandal of the affair. I could not have the disgrace of a nigger darkening my reputation, or your grandmother's, in the small town of Oakmont."

"That is enough! I will not stand here and listen to you talk like the racist rat bastard that you are," Harris yelled at him. "You disgust me. He is my uncle and a human being with feelings! How could you be so, so . . . I don't even know what words there are to describe you."

"Look at him, son," his grandfather said coldly. "There is no soul behind those eyes. He is the bastard child of your grandmother."

"He is what you made him." Harris was doing everything he could do to control his anger and needed to stall the situation until Joe got there.

"If it wasn't for me, he would have had nothing and your grandmother's reputation would have been scarred, just like her face. Is that what you would have wanted for her?"

"I would have preferred that to you framing an innocent man for what you did." Harris was starting to wonder how the hell he and Markita were going to get out of there. He could feel himself beginning to lose control, his heart beating harder against his chest. He looked over at the Executioner and could tell he was getting more and more pissed every time his grandfather called him the *N* name. Where the hell was Joe? He should have been there by now.

"So I hanged the nigger's father, Harris. He deserved to die for what he did to your grandmother."

The Executioner had finally heard enough. Emotion at last flooded him, and he was enraged. How could the Voice have been so cruel? He'd done everything he'd asked of him, but in return for what? To now find out the Voice had killed his father and kept his birth from his mother?

He cocked back the trigger on his gun and raised his hand again, firing the first bullet. There was no hesitation, no second thought, just an explosion of his rage, and a single bullet, which went between Ronald Harris's eyes.

Harris was horrified. The Executioner cocked back the trigger a second time as the judge fell limply to the ground. Harris's heart stopped, and he felt a trickle of sweat run down his back, his eyes widening, thinking how he would never forget the sound of the thump that his grandfather's body made when it hit the ground.

He needed to think fast about what he was going to do next. His thought was to try reasoning with the Executioner, so it stunned Harris when the Executioner began to speak to him.

"Well, this leaves us with an interesting predicament, don't it, nephew?" he said, eyeing Harris. "Now that Pops is dead, there is nothing stopping me from killing you. Don't worry, though. I won't take too long with the pretty lady before I kill her as well. Maybe my blood runs through your veins and you would like to watch as her head falls to the ground and rolls? I wonder whose will roll the farthest—Hugh's or hers? Just think: you could die with that image in your brain." He laughed, taunting Harris. He pointed the cocked gun right between Harris's eyes. Another bolt of lightning struck, lighting up the room. A huge clash of thunder immediately followed, shaking the ground, making the Executioner jump. He accidently pulled the trigger, and a booming explosion rang out as the bullet flew through the air.

Suddenly, Joshua was inside the cabin rushing toward Harris, and he instinctively threw himself onto his nephew. They both hit the ground hard.

The storm was directly over the cabin now; the cracks of lightning and sounds of thunder were deafening. The Executioner had not seen Joshua enter the cabin and was pleased with himself when he saw Harris's body hit the floor. The Voice and his stupid grandson were dead.

His emotions went back to being blank. *I don't need no nephew, or anyone, ever telling me again what to do,* said the Executioner to himself. Now he could concentrate on slicing the pretty lady's head off.

"Here I come, little lady," he said softly. "It'll be such a shame to slice off your head . . . You sure do have a pretty one."

Markita's eyes were open wide once again, struggling against her bonds in wild terror as the Executioner approached.

Joe Marble suddenly crashed through the cabin door, smashing it into the wall and startling the Executioner. Joe ordered him to put down his gun. The killer hesitated, his back to Joe, and then quickly spun around, pointing his own gun at Joe's head. Joe's weapon, however, was cocked and ready to fire. Another flash of lightning lit up the sky, helping Joe to focus his eyes on the Executioner, then *boom* . . . went the first shot, and then *boom, boom* . . . a second and third shot rang out. The Executioner still had not gone down, and with all the noise from the thunder, Joe was not sure what had happened.

The Executioner tried with all his might to fire back at Joe, but his muscles seemed beyond his control.

Boom . . . Joe fired again, and this time the Executioner at last began to falter. Joe was not going to let the Executioner get in one single shot. *Boom* . . . Joe hit him a fifth and final time, right in his heart, and the Executioner, Philip Smith, finally went down.

Joe let out a breath of relief, then rushed over to where Joshua and Harris were lying, flipping his cell phone open to call 911 for help.

"Harris, Harris, are you OK, buddy?" he asked desperately, shaking Harris roughly by the shoulder.

"Yes," Harris finally murmured, "but my uncle J sure is freaking heavy . . ." he finished, making a feeble attempt at a joke. Harris heard Joe explaining to the cops where the confrontation went down.

"They're on their way, buddy," Joe told him as he flipped his phone shut.

"Hey, Uncle J," Harris grunted, struggling to get up. It's OK—you can get off of me. It's over." Harris was desperate to get to Markita. He needed to know that she was OK too.

Joshua, however, made no movement. Joe knew instantly something was wrong.

"Harris," Joe said calmly. "Don't try to move your uncle. Help is on the way."

"What the hell do you mean, Joe?" Harris asked, starting to panic.

"It's going to be OK, Harris, I promise, buddy," Joe tried reassuring him, but was fearful of the outcome.

Suddenly, Harris felt a thick wetness of his uncle's blood on him, and he finally realized what was happening. "No," he said firmly. "*No!* Please, please talk to me, Uncle J, please!" Harris begged, but when he got no response, he appealed to a higher power, nearly sobbing in desperation. "Please, God, don't take my uncle, please. I beg of you." Awkwardly, he reached down until he found his uncle's hand, slick with blood, and squeezed it tightly, as if holding on for dear life.

"Harris, it's going to be OK, man. Hang in there," Joe said again.

"Joe, I can't lose him! How are Mom and I supposed to live without him? WHERE THE HELL IS THE DAMN AMBULANCE?" shouted Harris.

"It's going to be OK, Harris," Joe said, trying to calm him. "Listen, you can't move without moving your uncle, so I need to go and get Markita. You hold on. The ambulance will be here any minute."

Harris was torn. He was so afraid for his uncle, but he needed to know Markita was OK too. "Markita?" he asked. "Joe, please tell me she's OK . . ." Harris didn't think he could take another loss.

"It's OK, Harris, don't panic. I'm going to check on her right now. I hear the ambulance outside, so it won't be long now. Just hold on for a few more moments." Joe then moved away to help Markita. He prayed that the Executioner had not done her any permanent harm.

"Uncle J," Harris whispered, still squeezing Joshua's hand. "You heard Joe. The paramedics are here, it's going to be OK. You are going to be fine, I promise. Oh God, I love you, Uncle J. Please don't leave me and Mom. We need you." Tears streamed silently down his face as he prayed for his uncle's life.

As Joe approached the table Markita was tied to, he could see she was terrified, but seemed to be all in one piece. He carefully removed the wickedly sharp machete lying across her throat, reassuring her that everything was going to be OK. Once he untied her hands and feet, he gently helped her down from the table. Markita, bruised and filthy, staggered over to Harris, where she dropped down, weak-kneed, onto the floor next to him. She held his free hand and cried with him.

"Oh, LB, it's going to be OK now. Your uncle loves you. He'll fight to stay with you, I just know it. Oh, I love you so much, LB."

"I love you too, Markita," Harris said, squeezing her hand. "Please don't let me go, and please pray for my uncle J. I just can't lose him . . . He just saved my life." He gave her a sad smile, and she pressed her forehead to his.

"I know, I know, darling," she whispered. "Joshua will be fine. God will make sure of it, I know he will. And I'm not going anywhere. It's all my fault, LB. I should never have let that monster make me write that letter to you, but he told me if it wasn't convincing, he would cut your head off, slowly. I couldn't bear the thought of that, I couldn't let him hurt you," she cried. "LB, I am *so* sorry. Please forgive me."

"Of course I forgive you, my love. None of this is your fault. My grandfather made Smith into the creature he was. I only hope you can forgive me for doubting your love." Her gentle smile told him all he needed to know.

Just then the paramedics burst into the cabin and headed straight over to Joshua and Harris. After gently rolling Joshua's limp body off his nephew, they carefully placed him on a stretcher while hooking him up to all kinds of monitors. Harris sat up and held Markita tightly for a moment, before reaching out to grasp Joe in a huge bear hug.

"Thanks for everything, Inspector Gadget," Harris said. "And welcome back."

Joe clapped Harris on the back and told him to take Markita and go to the hospital with Joshua. He would stay behind to explain everything to the cops. Harris gave him a look of pure gratitude as he helped Markita into the back of the ambulance and headed for the hospital with his uncle.

"Hey, Joe, what the hell happened here?" asked an officer.

"It's a long story, Steve," Joe replied. "One that Hugh Gallagher is not going to want to hear, that's for sure."

"You're right there, Joe," Steve agreed. "I guess you haven't heard—Gallagher's head met with a sword sometime yesterday. Pretty gruesome stuff, if you ask me."

Joe spent several hours explaining everything leading up to the events which had just taken place in that cabin, being very careful not to disclose certain information. He tried processing the situation himself. *Who the hell do Harris and I report our findings to?* he wondered. It seemed that most of the state's top officials were as corrupt as Hugh. But he didn't remember seeing the present governor's name in the ledger, so maybe he could help Harris and him. If not, they were both going to be in a lot of hot water. He walked over to where the Executioner's and Judge Harris's bodies still lay. He wanted to take one last look at evil and corruption. "One injustice to an innocent child lies here today," he murmured, shaking his head sadly. "And justice was served to the other. The scales of justice have been balanced."

On the way to the hospital, Harris called his mother to tell her to meet Markita and him in the emergency room.

"How bad is it, son?" asked Mary Ellen, already racing for her car.

"Just get there as soon as you can, Mom. I love you."

At the ER, a whole team of doctors was working on Joshua when Mary Ellen arrived, but she begged them to let her see him. They were concerned it might be the last few minutes the two of them would have together, so they agreed. Harris, just coming back from checking on Markita in her own room just down the hall, joined his mother as they entered the screened space where Joshua lay. Mary Ellen bit back tears as she saw her love, still covered in blood and lying so still. She reached out and held his hand; after what seemed like forever, Joshua at last opened his eyes and gazed up at his wife.

"I love you," he whispered, and then his eyes slipped shut again. A moment later, alarms began to shrill, and Mary Ellen was pushed aside as the team of doctors and nurses once again flooded the small room.

"I don't think he's going to make it," she heard one of them say.

Mary Ellen stared for a few moments, then started to slip to the floor in a faint before Harris caught her in his arms. She came back to herself almost immediately, clinging to Harris as if her life depended on it.

"No!" she whispered sharply. "This is not right! We love each other. We were meant to be together always." Harris held his mother tightly as she sobbed into his shoulder.

"It's going to be OK, Mom, it has to be. Today Uncle J went to extreme lengths, once again, to protect me. God will protect him." And there they sat, huddled around Joshua's bed, clinging to each other in their time of darkness.

The next day, the *Orlando Sentinel* headline read:

Another Florida Hurricane Hit with Devastating Blow

Florida's Supreme Court Justice, the Right Honorable Judge Ronald Harris, was mortally wounded by a single gunshot late last night. The circumstances surrounding his death are still in question at this time.

Ronald Harris, 85, was a native Floridian who spent his entire adult life serving this great state.

He left behind his wife Barbara, to whom he was married for 64 years, his daughter Mary Ellen, and his grandson, Harris Robertson, the assistant district attorney of Orlando. Also shot was an unidentified African American male, pronounced dead at the scene. Joshua Robertson, son-in-law of Judge Harris, also suffered a gunshot wound and was in critical condition at Florida Hospital at the time of this printing. His injuries at this time are unknown.

Funeral services for Ronald Harris will be held at 1:15 p.m. on October 2, for family and friends only. The public viewing for Judge Harris will be on October 6, at 1:30 p.m. in Tallahassee, where the judge resided.

In a sidebar to the main article was another small, but interesting, piece of news:

Hugh Gallagher, Orlando's district attorney who served the city for twenty years, was found dead over the weekend. A security guard for a downtown property reported finding him late Saturday night, decapitated in an abandoned warehouse on Forsythe Street in Orlando. So far, there are no eyewitnesses. Gallagher leaves behind no known family. After an autopsy performed by the medical examiner is completed, the city will hold funeral services. Detective Joseph Marble is conducting a full investigation.

CPSIA information can be obtained at www.ICGtesting.com
Printed in the USA
LVOW040748100812

293663LV00001B/5/P

9 781469 172965